An Original Belle

E. P. Roe

Contents

AN ORIGINAL BELLE

BY

E. P. Roe

PREFACE.

No race of men, scarcely an individual, is so devoid of intelligence as not to recognize power. Few gifts are more courted. Power is almost as varied as character, and the kind of power most desired or appreciated is a good measure of character. The pre-eminence furnished by thew and muscle is most generally recognized; but, as men reach levels above the animal, other qualities take the lead. It is seen that the immaterial spirit wins the greater triumphs,--that the brainless giant, compared with the dwarf of trained intelligence, can accomplish little. The scale runs on into the moral qualities, until at last humanity has given its sanction to the Divine words, "Whosoever will be chief among you, let him be your servant." The few who have successfully grasped the lever of which Archimedes dreamed are those who have attained the highest power to serve the world.

Among the myriad phases of power, perhaps that of a gifted and beautiful woman is the most subtile and hard to define. It is not the result of mere beauty, although that may be an important element; and if wit, intelligence, learning, accomplishments, and goodness are added, all combined cannot wholly explain the power that some women possess. Deeper, perhaps more potent, than all else, is an individuality which distinguishes one woman from all others, and imparts her own peculiar fascination. Of course, such words do not apply to those who are content to be commonplace themselves, and who are satisfied with the ordinary homage of ordinary minds, or the conventional attention of men who are incited to nothing better.

One of the purposes of this story is to illustrate the power of a young girl not so beautiful or so good as many of her sisters. She was rather commonplace at first, but circumstances led her to the endeavor to be true to her own nature and conscience and to adopt a very simple scheme of life. She achieved no marvellous success, nothing beyond the ability of multitudes like herself.

I have also sought to reproduce with some color of life and reality a critical period in our civil war. The scenes and events of the story culminate practically in the summer of 1863. The novel was not written for the sake of the scenes or events. They are employed merely to illustrate character at the time and to indicate its development.

The reader in the South must be bitter and prejudiced indeed if he does not discover that I have sought to be fair to the impulses and motives of its people.

In touching upon the Battle of Gettysburg and other historical events, I will briefly say that I have carefully consulted authentic sources of information. For the graphic suggestion of certain details I am indebted to the "History of the 124th Regt. N.Y.S.V.," by Col. Charles H. Weygant, to the recollections of Capt. Thomas Taft and other veterans now living.

Lieut.-Col. H. C. Hasbrouck, commandant of Cadets at West Point, has kindly read the proof of chapters relating to the battle of Gettysburgh.

My story is also related to the New York Draft Riots of 1863, an historical record not dwelt upon before in fiction to my knowledge. It is almost impossible to impart an adequate impression of that reign of terror. I have not hoped to do this, or to give anything like a detailed and complete account of events. The scenes and incidents described, however, had their counterpart in fact. Rev. Dr. Howard Crosby of New York saw a young man face and disperse a mob of hundreds, by stepping out upon the porch of his home and shooting the leader. This event took place late at night.

I have consulted "Sketches of the Draft Riots in 1863," by Hon. J. T. Headley, the files of the Press of that time, and other records.

The Hon. Thomas C. Acton. Superintendent of the Metropolitan Police during the riot, accorded me a hearing, and very kindly followed the thread of my story through the stormy period in question.

E. P. R
CORNWALL-ON-HUDSON, N.Y., AUG. 7, 1885.

CHAPTER I.
A RUDE AWAKENING.

MARIAN VOSBURGH had been content with her recognized position as a leading belle. An evening spent in her drawing-room revealed that; but at the close of the particular evening which it was our privilege to select there occurred a trivial incident. She was led to think, and thought is the precursor of action and change in all natures too strong and positive to drift. On that night she was an ordinary belle, smiling, radiant, and happy in following the traditions of her past.

She had been admired as a child, as a school-girl, and given a place among the stars of the first magnitude since her formal debut. Admiration was as essential as sunshine; or, to change the figure, she had a large and a natural and healthful appetite for it. She was also quite as much entitled to it as the majority of her class. Thus far she had accepted life as she found it, and was in the main conventional. She was not a deliberate coquette; it was not her recognized purpose to give a heartache to as many as possible; she merely enjoyed in thoughtless exultation her power to attract young men to her side. There was keen excitement in watching them, from the moment of introduction, as they passed through the phases of formal acquaintanceship into relations that bordered on sentiment. When this point was reached experiences sometimes followed which caused not a little compunction.

She soon learned that society was full of men much like herself in some respects, ready to meet new faces, to use their old compliments and flirtation methods over and over again. They could look unutterable things at half a dozen different girls in the same season, while their hearts remained as invulnerable as old-fashioned pin-cushions, heart-shaped, that adorn country "spare rooms." But now and then a man endowed with a deep, strong nature would finally leave her side in troubled wonder or bitter cynicism. Her fair, young face, her violet eyes, so dark as to appear almost black at night, had given no token that she could amuse herself with feelings that touched the sources of life and death in such admirers.

"They should have known better, that I was not in earnest," she would say, petulantly, and more or less remorsefully.

But these sincere men, who had been so blind as to credit her with gentle truth and natural intuition, had some ideal of womanhood which had led to their blunder. Conscious of revealing so much themselves by look, tone, and touch of hand, eager to supplement one significant glance by life-long loyalty, they were slow in understanding that answering significant glances meant only, "I like you very well,--better than others, just at present; but then I may meet some one to-morrow who is a great deal more fun than you are."

Fun! With them it was a question of manhood, of life, and of that which gives the highest value and incentive to life. It was inevitable, therefore, that Marian Vosburgh should become a mirage to more than one man; and when at last the delusion vanished, there was usually a flinty desert to be crossed before the right, safe path was gained.

From year to year Mr. Vosburgh had rented for his summer residence a pretty cottage on the banks of the Hudson. The region abounded in natural beauty and stately homes. There was an infusion of Knickerbocker blood in the pre-eminently elect ones of society, and from these there was a gradual shading off in several directions, until by some unwritten law the social line was drawn. Strangers from the city might be received within the inner circle, or they might not, as some of the leaders practically decreed by their own action. Mr. Vosburgh did not care in the least for the circle or its constituents. He was a stern, quiet man; one of the strong executive hands of the government at a time when the vital questions of the day had come to the arbitrament of the sword. His calling involved danger, and required an iron will. The questions which chiefly occupied his mind were argued by the mouths of cannon.

As for Marian, she too cared little for the circle and its social dignitaries. She had no concessions to make, no court to pay. She was not a dignitary, but a sovereign, and had her own court. Gentleman friends from the city made their headquarters at a neighboring summer hotel; young men from the vicinity were attracted like moths, and the worst their aristocratic sisters could say against the girl was that she had too many male friends, and was not "of their set." Indeed, with little effort she could have won recognition from the bluest blood of the vicinage; but this was not her ambition. She cared little for the ladies of her neighborhood, and less for their ancestors, while she saw as much of the gentlemen as she desired. She had her intimates among her own sex, however, and was on the best terms with her good-natured, good-hearted, but rather superficial mother, who was a discreet, yet indulgent chaperon, proud of her daughter and of the attention she received, while scarcely able to comprehend that any serious trouble could result from it if the proprieties of life were complied with. Marian was never permitted to give that kind of encouragement which compromises a girl, and Mrs. Vosburgh felt that there her duty ceased. All that could be conveyed by the eloquent eye, the inflection of tones, and in a thousand other ways, was unnoted, and beyond her province.

The evening of our choice is an early one in June. The air is slightly chilly and damp, therefore the parlor is preferable to the vine-sheltered piazza, screened by the first tender foliage. We can thus observe Miss Vosburgh's deportment more closely, and take a brief note of her callers.

Mr. Lane is the first to arrive, perhaps for the reason that he is a downright suitor, who has left the city and business, in order to further the interests nearest his heart. He is a keen-eyed, strong-looking fellow, well equipped for success by knowledge of the world and society; resolute, also, in attaining his desired ends. His attentions to Marian have been unmistakable for some months, and he believes that he has received encouragement. In truth, he has been the recipient of the delusive regard that she is in the habit of bestowing. He is one whom she could scarcely fail to admire and like, so entertaining is he in conversation, and endowed with such vitality and feeling that his words are not airy nothings.

He greets her with a strong pressure of the hand, and his first glance reveals her power.

"Why, this is an agreeable surprise, Mr. Lane," she exclaims.

"Agreeable? I am very glad to hear that," he says, in his customary direct speech. "Yes, I ran up from the city this afternoon. On my way to lunch I became aware of the beauty of the day, and as my thoughts persisted in going up the river I was led to follow them. One's life does not consist wholly of business, you know; at least mine does not."

"Yet you have the reputation of being a busy man."

"I should hope so. What would you think of a young fellow not busy in these times?"

"I am not sure I should think at all. You give us girls too much credit for thinking."

"Oh, no; there's no occasion for the plural. I don't give 'us girls' anything. I am much too busy for that. But I know you think, Miss Marian, and have capacity for thought."

"Possibly you are right about the capacity. One likes to think one has brains, you know, whether she uses them or not. I don't think very much, however,--that is, as you use the word, for it implies the putting of one's mind on something and keeping it there. I like to let thoughts come and go as the clouds do in our June skies. I don't mean thunder-clouds and all they signify, but light vapors that have scarcely beginning or end, and no very definite being. I don't seem to have time or inclination for anything else, except when I meet you with your positive ways. I think it is very kind of you to come from New York to give me a pleasant evening."

"I'm not so very disinterested. New York has become a dull place, and if I aid you to pass a pleasant evening you insure a pleasanter one for me. What have you been doing this long June day, that you have been too busy for thought?"

"Let me see. What have I been doing? What an uncomfortable question to ask a girl! You men say we are nothing but butterflies, you know."

"I never said that of you."

"You ask a question which makes me say it virtually of myself. That is a way you keen lawyers have. Very well; I shall be an honest witness, even against myself. That I wasn't up with the lark this morning goes without saying. The larks that I know much about are on the wing after dinner in the evening. The forenoon is a variable sort of affair with many people. Literally I suppose it ends at 12 M., but with me it is rounded off by lunch, and the time of that event depends largely upon the kitchen divinity that we can lure to this remote and desolate region. 'Faix,' remarked that potentate, sniffing around disdainfully the day we arrived, 'does yez expects the loikes o' me to stop in this lonesomeness? We're jist at the ind of the wourld.' Mamma increased her wages, which were already double what she earns, and she still condescends to provide our daily food, giving me a forenoon which closes at her convenience. During this indefinite period I look after my flowers and birds, sing and play a little, read a little, entertain a little, and thus reveal to you a general littleness. In the afternoon I take a nap, so that I may be wide awake enough to talk to a bright man like you in case he should appear. Now, are you not shocked and pained at my frivolous life?"

"You have come to the country for rest and recuperation, Miss Marian?"

"Oh, what a word,--'recuperation!' It never entered my head that I had come into the country for that. Do I suggest a crying need for recuperation?"

"I wouldn't dare tell you all that you suggest to me, and I read more than you say between your lines. When I approached the house you were chatting and laughing genially with your mother."

"Oh, yes, mamma and I have as jolly times together as two girls."

"That was evident, and it made a very pleasant impression on me. One thing is not so evident, and it indicates a rather one-sided condition of affairs. I could not prevent my thoughts from visiting you often to-day before I came myself, but I fear that among your June-day occupations there has not been one thought of me."

She had only time to say, sotto voce, "Girls don't tell everything," when the maid announced, from the door, "Mr. Strahan."

This second comer was a young man precociously mature after a certain style. His home was a fine old place in the vicinity, but in his appearance there was no suggestion of the country; nor did he resemble the violet, although he was some-what redolent of the extract of that modest flower. He was dressed in the extreme of the prevailing mode, and evidently cultivated a metropolitan air, rather than the unobtrusive bearing of one who is so thoroughly a gentleman that he can afford to be himself. Mr. Strahan was quite sure of his welcome, for he felt that he brought to the little cottage a genuine Madison-avenue atmosphere. He was greeted with the cordiality which made Miss Vosburgh's drawing-room one of the pleasantest of lounging-places, whether in town or country; and under his voluble lead conversation took the character of fashionable gossip, which would have for the reader as much interest as the presentation of some of the ephemeral weeds of that period. But Mr. Strahan's blue eyes were really animated as he ventured perilously near a recent scandal in high life. His budget of news was interspersed with compliments to his hostess, which, like the extract on his handkerchief, were too pronounced. Mr. Lane regarded him with politely veiled disgust, but was too well-bred not to second Miss Vosburgh's remarks to the best of his ability.

Before long two or three more visitors dropped in. One from the hotel was a millionnaire, a widower leisurely engaged in the selection of a second wife. Another was a young artist sketching in the vicinity. A third was an officer from West Point who knew Mr. Vosburgh. There were also callers from the neighborhood during the evening. Mrs. Vosburgh made her appearance early, and was almost as skilful a hostess as her daughter. But few of the guests remained long. They had merely come to enjoy a pleasant half-hour or more under circumstances eminently agreeable, and would then drive on and pay one or two visits in the vicinity. That was the way in which nearly all Marian's "friendships" began.

The little parlor resounded with animated talk, laughter, and music, that was at the same time as refined as informal. Mrs. Vosburgh would seat herself at the piano, that a new dancing-step or a new song might be tried. The gentlemen were at liberty to light their cigars and form groups among themselves, so free from stiffness was Marian's little salon. Brief time elapsed, however, without a word to each, in her merry, girlish voice, for she had the instincts of a successful hostess, and a good-natured sense of honor, which made her feel that each guest was entitled to attention. She was not much given to satire, and the young men soon learned that she would say more briery things to their faces than behind their backs. It was also discovered that ill-natured remarks about callers who had just departed were not tolerated,--that within certain limits she was loyal to her friends, and that, she was too high-minded to speak unhandsomely of one whom she had just greeted cordially. If she did not like a man she speedily froze him out of the ranks of her acquaintance; but for such action there was not often occasion, since she and her mother had a broad, easy tolerance of those generally accepted by society. Even such as left her parlor finally with wounds for which there was no rapid healing knew that no one would resent a jest at their expense more promptly than the girl whom they might justly blame for having smiled too kindly.

Thus she remained a general favorite. It was recognized that she had a certain kind of loyalty which could be depended upon. Of course such a girl would eventually marry, and with natural hope and egotism each one felt that he might be the successful competitor. At any rate, as in war, they must take their chances, and it seems that there is never a lack of those willing to assume such risks.

Thus far, however, Marian had no inclination to give up her present life of variety and excitement. She preferred incense from many worshippers to the devotion of one. The secret of this was perhaps that her heart had remained so untouched and unconscious that she scarcely knew she had one. She understood the widower's preference, enjoyed the compliment, and should there be occasion would, in perfect good taste, beg to be excused.

Her pulse was a little quickened by Mr. Lane's downright earnestness, and when matters should come to a crisis she would say lovely things to him of her esteem, respect, regret, etc. She would wish they might remain friends--why could they not, when she liked him so much? As for love and engagement, she did not, could not, think of that yet.

She was skilful, too, in deferring such crises, and to-night, in obedience to a signal, Mrs. Vosburgh remained until even Mr. Lane despaired of another word in private, and departed, fearing to put his fate to the test.

At last the dainty apartment, the merry campaigning-ground, was darkened, and Marian, flushed, wearied, and complacent, stepped out on the piazza to breathe for a few moments the cool, fragrant air. She had dropped into a rustic seat, and was thinking over the events of the evening with an amused smile, when the following startling words arose from the adjacent shrubbery:--

"Arrah, noo, will ye niver be sinsible? Here I'm offerin' ye me heart, me loife. I'd be glad to wourk for ye, and kape ye loike a leddy. I'd be thrue to ye ivery day o' me loife,--an' ye knows it, but ye jist goes on makin' eyes at this wan an' flirtin' wid that wan an' spakin' swate to the t'other, an' kapin' all on the string till they can nayther ate nor slape nor be half the min they were till ye bewildered 'em. Ye're nothin' but a giddy, light-minded, shallow crather, a spoilin' min for your own fun. I've kep' company wid ye a year, and ye've jist blowed hot and cowld till I'm not meself any more, and have come nigh losin' me place. Noo, by St. Patrick, ye must show whether ye're a woman or a heartless jade that will sind a man to the divil for sport."

These words were poured out with the impetuosity of longsuffering endurance finally vanquished, and before the speaker had concluded Marian was on her way to the door, that she might not listen to a conversation of so delicate a nature. But she did not pass beyond hearing before part of the reply reached her.

"Faix, an' I'm no wourse than me young mistress."

It was a chance arrow, but it went straight to the mark, aad when Marian reached her room her cheeks were aflame.

CHAPTER II.
A NEW ACQUAINTANCE.

Gross matter can change form and character in a moment, when merely touched by the effective agent. It is easy to imagine, therefore, how readily a woman's quick mind might be influenced by a truth or a thought of practical and direct application. All the homilies ever written, all the counsel of matrons and sages, could not have produced on Marian so deep an impression as was made by these few chance words. They came as a commentary, not only on her past life, but on the past few hours. Was it true, then, that she was no better than the coquettish maid, the Irish servant in the family's employ? Was she, with her education and accomplishments, her social position and natural gifts, acting on no higher plane, influenced by no worthier motives and no loftier ambition? Was the ignorant girl justified in quoting her example in extenuation of a course that to a plain and equally ignorant man seemed unwomanly to the last degree?

Wherein was she better? Wherein lay the difference between her and the maid?

She covered her hot face with her hands as the question took the form: "Wherein am I worse? Is not our principle of action the same, while I have greater power and have been crippling higher types of men, and giving them, for sport, an impulse towards the devil? Fenton Lane has just gone from my side with trouble in his eyes. He will not be himself to-morrow, not half the man he might be. He left me in doubt and fear. Could I do anything oppressed with doubt and fear? He has set his heart on what can never be. Could I have prevented him from doing this? One thing at least is certain,--I have not tried to prevent it, and I fear there have been many little nameless things which he would regard as encouragement. And he is only one. With others I have gone farther and they have fared worse. It is said that

Mr. Folger, whom I refused last winter, is becoming dissipated. Mr. Arton shuns society and sneers at women. Oh, don't let me think of any more. What have I been doing that this coarse kitchen-maid can run so close a parallel between her life and mine? How unwomanly and repulsive it all seems, as that man put it! My delight and pride have been my gentleman friends, and what one of them is the better, or has a better prospect for life, because of having known me? Could there be a worse satire on all the fine things written about woman and her influence than my hitherto vain and complacent self?"

Sooner or later conscience tells the truth to all; and the sooner the better, unless the soul arraigned is utterly weak, or else belongs essentially to the criminal classes, which require almost a miracle to reverse their evil gravitation. Marian Vosburgh was neither weak nor criminal at heart. Thus far she had yielded thoughtlessly, inconsiderately, rather than deliberately, to the circumstances and traditions of her life. Her mother had been a belle and something of a coquette, and, having had her career, was in the main a good and sensible wife. She had given her husband little trouble if not much help. She had slight interest in that which made his life, and slight comprehension of it, but in affectionate indifference she let him go his way, and was content with her domestic affairs, her daughter, and her novel. Marian had unthinkingly looked forward to much the same experience as her natural lot. To-night she found herself querying: "Are there men to-day who are not half what they might have been because of mamma's delusive smiles? Have any gone down into shadows darker than those cast by misfortune and death, because she permitted herself to become the light of their lives and then turned away?"

Then came the rather painful reflection: "Mamma is not one to be troubled by such thoughts. It does not even worry her that she is so little to papa, and that he virtually carries on his life-work alone. I don't see how I can continue my old life after to-night. I had better shut myself up in a convent; yet just how I can change everything I scarcely know."

The night proved a perturbed and almost sleepless one from the chaos and bitterness of her thoughts. The old was breaking up; the new, beginning.

The morning found her listless, discontented, and unhappy. The glamour had faded out of her former life. She could not continue the tactics practised in coarse imitation by the Irish servant, who took her cue as far as possible from her mistress.

The repugnance was due as much to the innate delicacy and natural superiority of Marian's nature as to her conscience. Her clear, practical sense perceived that her course differed from the other only in being veneered by the refinements of her social position,--that the evil results were much greater. The young lady's friends were capable of receiving more harm than the maid could inflict upon her acquaintances.

There would be callers again during the day and evening, and she did not wish to see them. Their society now would be like a glass of champagne from which the life had effervesced.

At last in her restlessness and perplexity she decided to spend a day or two with her father in their city home, where he was camping out, as he termed it. She took a train to town, and sent a messenger boy to his office with a note asking him to dine with her.

Mr. Vosburgh looked at her a little inquiringly as he entered his home, which had the comfortless aspect of a city house closed for the summer.

"Am I de trop, papa? I have come to town for a little quiet, and to do some shopping."

"Come to New York for quiet?"

"Yes. The country is the gayest place now, and you know a good many are coming and going. I am tired, and thought an evening or two with you would be a pleasant change. You are not too busy?"

"It certainly will be a change for you, Marian."

"Now there's a world of satire in that remark, and deserved, too, I fear. Mayn't I stay?"

"Yes, indeed, till you are tired of me; and that won't be long in this dull place, for we are scarcely in a condition now to receive callers, you know."

"What makes you think I shall be tired of you soon, papa?"

"Oh--well--I'm not very entertaining. You appear to like variety. I suppose it is the way with girls."

"You are not consumed with admiration for girls' ways, are you, papa?"

"I confess, my dear, that I have not given the subject much research. As a naturalist would say, I have no doubt that you and your class have curious habits and interesting peculiarities. There is a great deal of life, you know, which a busy man has to accept in a general way, especially when charged with duties which are a severe and constant strain upon his mind. I try to leave you and your mother as free from care as possible. You left her well, I trust?"

"Very well, and all going on as usual. I'm dissatisfied with myself, papa, and you unconsciously make me far more so. Is a woman to be only a man's plaything, and a dangerous one at that?"

"Why, Marian, you ARE in a mood! I suppose a woman, like a man, can be very much what she pleases. You certainly have had a chance to find out what pleases most women in your circle of acquaintances, and have made it quite clear what pleases you."

"Satire again," she said, despondently. "I thought perhaps you could advise and help me."

He came and took her face between his hands, looking earnestly into her troubled blue eyes.

"Are you not content to be a conventional woman?" he asked, after a moment.

"No!" was her emphatic answer.

"Well, there are many ways of being a little outre in this age and land, especially at this stormy period. Perhaps you want a career,--something that will give you a larger place in the public eye?"

She turned away to hide the tears that would come. "O papa, you don't understand me at all, and I scarcely understand myself," she faltered. "In some respects you are as conventional as mamma, and are almost a Turk in your ideas of the seclusion of women. The idea of my wanting public notoriety! As I feel now, I'd rather go to a convent."

"We'll go to dinner first; then a short drive in the park, for you look pale, and I long for a little fresh air myself. I have been at my desk since seven this morning, and have had only a sandwich."

"Why do you have to work so hard, papa?"

"I can give you two reasons in a breath,--you mentioned 'shopping,' and my country is at war. They don't seem very near of kin, do they? Documents relating to both converge in my desk, however."

"Have I sent you more bills than usual?"

"Not more than usual."

"I believe I'm a fool."

"I know you are a very pretty little girl, who will feel better after dinner and a drive," was the laughing reply.

They were soon seated in a quiet family restaurant, but the young girl was too perturbed in mind to enjoy the few courses ordered. With self-reproach she recognized the truth that she was engaged in the rather unusual occupation of becoming acquainted with her father. He sat before her, with his face, generally stern and inscrutable, softened by a desire to be companionable and sympathetic. According to his belief she now had "a mood," and after a day or two of quiet retirement from the world she would relapse into her old enjoyment of social attention, which would be all the deeper for its brief interruption. Mr. Vosburgh was of German descent. In his daily life he had become Americanized, and was as practical in his methods as the shrewd people with whom he dealt, and whom he often outwitted. Apart from this habit of coping with life just as he found it, he had an inner nature of which few ever caught a glimpse,--a spirit and an imagination deeply tinged with German ideality and speculation. Often, when others slept, this man, who appeared so resolute, hard, and uncompromising in the performance of duties, and who was understood by but few, would read deeply in metaphysics and romantic poetry. Therefore, the men and women who dwelt in his imagination were not such as he had much to do with in real life. Indeed, he had come to regard the world of reality and that of fancy as entirely distinct, and to believe that only here and there, as a man or woman possessed something like genius, would there be a marked deviation from ordinary types. The slight differences, the little characteristic meannesses or felicities that distinguished one from another, did not count for very much in his estimation. When a knowledge of such individual traits was essential to his plans, he mastered them with singular keenness and quickness of comprehension. When such knowledge was unnecessary, or as soon as it ceased to be of service, he dismissed the extraneous personalities from his mind almost as completely as if they had had no existence. Few men were less embarrassed with acquaintances than he; yet he had an observant eye and a retentive memory. When he wanted a man he rarely failed to find the right one. In the selection and use of men he appeared to act like an intelligent and silent force, rather than as a man full of human interests and sympathies. He rarely spoke of himself, even in the most casual way. Most of those with whom he mingled knew merely that he was an agent of the government, and that he kept his own counsel. His wife was to him a type of the average American woman,--pretty, self-complacent, so nervous as to require kind, even treatment, content with feminalities, and sufficiently intelligent to talk well upon every-day affairs. In her society he smiled at her, said "Yes," good-humoredly, to almost everything, and found slight incentive to depart from his usual reticence. She had learned the limits of her range, and knew that within it there was entire liberty, beyond it a will like adamant. They got on admirably together, for she craved nothing further in the way of liberty and companionship than was accorded her, while he soon recognized that the prize carried off from other competitors could no more follow him into his realm of thought and action than she could accompany him on a campaign. At last he had concluded philosophically that it was just as well. He was engaged in matters that should not be interfered with or babbled about, and he could come and go without questioning. He had occasionally thought: "If she were such a woman as I have read of and imagined,--if she could supplement my reason with the subtilty of intuition and the reticence which some of her sex have manifested,--she would double my power and share my inner life, for there are few whom I can trust. The thing is impossible, however, and so I am glad she is content."

As for Marian, she had promised, in his view, to be but a charming repetition of her mother, with perhaps a mind of larger calibre. She had learned more and had acquired more accomplishments, but all this resulted, possibly, from her better advantages. Her drawing-room conversation seemed little more than the ordinary small talk of the day, fluent and piquant, while the girl herself was as undisturbed by the vital questions of the hour and of life, upon which he dwelt, as if she had been a child. He knew that she received much attention, but it excited little thought on his part, and no surprise. He believed that her mother was perfectly competent to look after the proprieties, and that young fellows, as had been the case with himself, would always seek pretty, well-bred girls, and take their chances as to what the women who might become their wives should prove to be.

Marian looked with awakening curiosity and interest at the face before her, yet it was the familiar visage of her father. She had seen it all her life, but now felt that she had never before seen it in its true significance--its strong lines, square jaw, and quiet gray eyes, with their direct, steady gaze. He had come and gone before her daily, petted her now and then a little, met her requests in the main good-humored-ly, paid her bills, and would protect her with his life; yet a sort of dull wonder came over her as she admitted to herself that he was a stranger to her. She knew little of his work and duty, less of his thoughts, the mental realm in which the man himself dwelt. What were its landmarks, what its characteristic features, she could not tell. One may be familiar with the outlines of a country on a map, yet be ignorant of the scenery, productions, inhabitants, governing forces, and principles. Her very father was to her but a man in outline. She knew little of the thoughts that peopled his brain, of the motives and principles that controlled his existence, giving it indi-viduality, and even less of the resulting action with which his busy life abounded. Although she had crossed the threshold of womanhood, she was still to him the self-pleasing child that he had provided for since infancy; and he was, in her view, the man to whom, according to the law of nature and the family, she was to look for the maintenance of her young life, with its almost entire separation in thoughts, pleasures, and interests. She loved him, of course. She had always loved him, from the time when she had stretched forth her baby hands to be taken and fondled for a few moments and then relinquished to others. Practically she had dwelt with others ever since. Now, as a result, she did not understand him, nor he her. She would miss him as she would oxygen from the air. Now she began to perceive that, although he was the unobtrusive source of her life, home, education, and the advantages of her lot, he was not impersonal, but a human being as truly as herself. Did he want more from her than the common and instinctive affection of a child for its parent? If to this she added intelligent love, appreciation, and sympathy, would he care? If she should be able to say, "Papa, I am kin to you, not merely in flesh and blood, but in mind, hope, and aspiration; I share with you that which makes your life, with its success and failure, not as the child who may find luxurious externals curtailed or increased, but as a sympathetic woman who understands the more vital changes in spiritual vicissitude,"--if she could truthfully say all this, would he be pleased and reveal himself to her?

Thoughts like these passed through her mind as they dined together and drove in the park. When at last they returned and sat in the dimly-lighted parlor, Mr. Vosburgh recognized that her "mood" had not passed away.

CHAPTER III.
A NEW FRIEND.

M ARIAN," asked her father, after smoking awhile in silence, "what did you mean by your emphatic negative when I asked you if you were not content to be a conventional woman? How much do you mean?"

"I wish you would help me find out, papa."

"How! don't you know?"

"I do not; I am all at sea."

"Well, my dear, to borrow your own illustration, you can't be far from shore yet. Why not return? You have seemed entirely satisfied thus far."

"Were you content with me, papa?"

"I think you have been a very good little girl, as girls go."

"'Good little girl, as girls go;' that's all."

"That's more than can be said of many."

"Papa, I'm not a little girl; I am a woman of twenty years."

"Yes, I know; and quite as sensible as many at forty."

"I am no companion for you."

"Indeed you are; I've enjoyed having you with me this evening exceedingly."

"Yes, as you would have enjoyed my society ten years ago. I've been but a little girl to you all the time. Do you know the thought that has been uppermost in my mind since you joined me?"

"How should I? How long does one thought remain uppermost in a girl's mind?"

"I don't blame you for your estimate. My thought is this,--we are not acquainted with each other."

"I think I was acquainted with you, Marian, before this mood began."

"Yes, I think you were; yet I was capable of this 'mood,' as you call it, before."

"My child," said Mr. Vosburgh, coming to her side and stroking her hair, "I have spoken more to draw you out than for anything else. Heaven forbid that you for a moment should think me indifferent to anything that relates to your welfare! You wish me to advise, to help you. Before I can do this I must have your confidence, I must know your thoughts and impulses. You can scarcely have a purpose yet. Even a quack doctor will not attempt diagnosis or prescribe his nostrum without some knowledge of the symptoms. When I last saw you in the country you certainly appeared like a conventional society girl of an attractive type, and were evidently satisfied so to remain. You see I speak frankly, and reveal to you my habit of making quick practical estimates, and of taking the world as I find it. You say you were capable of this mood--let us call it an aspiration--before. I do not deny this, yet doubt it. When people change it is because they are ripe, or ready for change, as are things in nature. One can force or retard nature; but I don't believe much in intervention. With many I doubt whether there is even much opportunity for it. They are capable of only the gradual modification of time and circumstances. Young people are apt to have spasms of enthusiasm, or of self-reproach and dissatisfaction. These are of little account in the long run, unless there is fibre enough in character to face certain questions, decide them, and then act resolutely on definite lines of conduct. I have now given you my views, not as to a little child, but as to a mature woman of twenty. Jesting apart, you ARE old enough, Marian, to think for yourself, and decide whether you will be conventional or not. The probabilities are that you will follow the traditions of your past in a very ladylike way. That is the common law. You are too well-bred and refined to do anything that society would condemn."

"You are not encouraging, papa."

"Nor am I discouraging. If you have within you the force to break from your traditions and stop drifting, you will make the fact evident. If you haven't it would be useless for me to attempt to drag, drive, or coax you out of old ways. I am too busy a man to attempt the useless. But until you tell me your present mental attitude, and what has led to it, we are talking somewhat at random. I have merely aimed to give you the benefit of some experience."

"Perhaps you are taking the right course; I rather think you are. Perhaps I prove what a child I am still, because I feel that I should like to have you treat me more as you did when I was learning to walk. Then you stretched out your hands, and sustained me, and showed me step by step. Papa, if this is a mood, and I go back to my old, shallow life, with its motives, its petty and unworthy triumphs, I shall despise myself, and ever have the humiliating consciousness that I am doing what is contemptible. No matter how one obtains the knowledge of a truth or a secret, that knowledge exists, remains, and one can't be the same afterwards. It makes my cheeks tingle that I obtained my knowledge as I did. It came like a broad glare of garish light, in which I saw myself;" and she told him the circumstances.

He burst into a hearty laugh, and remarked, "Pat did put the ethics of the thing strongly."

"He made 'the thing,' as you call it, odious then and forever. I've been writhing in self-contempt ever since. When to be conventional is to be like a kitchen-maid, and worse, do you wonder at my revolt from the past?"

"Others won't see it in that light, my dear."

"What does it matter how others see it? I have my own life to live, to make or mar. How can I go on hereafter amusing myself in what now seems a vulgar, base, unwomanly way? It was a coarse, rude hand that awakened me, papa, but I am awake. Since I have met you I have had another humiliation. As I said, I am not even acquainted with you. I have never shown any genuine interest in that which makes your life, and you have no more thought of revealing yourself and your work to me than to a child."

"Marian," said her father, slowly, "I think you are not only capable of a change, but ripe for it. You inspire hope within me, and this fact carries with it the assurance that you also inspire respect. No, my dear, you don't know much about me; very few do. No man with a nature like mine reveals himself where there is no desire for the knowledge, no understanding, no sympathy, or even where all these exist, unless prompted by his heart. You know I am the last one in the world to put myself on exhibition. But it would be a heavenly joy to me--I might add surprise--if my own daughter became like some of the women of whom I have read and dreamed; and I do read and dream of that in which you little imagine me to be interested. To the world I am a stern, reticent, practical man I must be such in my calling. In my home I have tried to be good-natured, affectionate, and philosophical. I have seen little opportunity for anything more. I do not complain, but merely state a fact which indicates the general lot. We can rarely escape the law of heredity, however. A poet and a metaphysician were among our German ancestry; therefore, leading from the business-like and matter-of-fact apartment of my mind, I have a private door by which I can slip away into the realm of speculation, romance, and ideals. You perceive that I have no unnatural or shame-faced reticence about this habit. I tell you of it the moment you show sufficient interest to warrant my speaking."

"But, papa, I cannot hope to approach or even suggest the ideals of your fancy, dressed, no doubt, in mediaeval costume, and talking in blank verse."

"That's a superficial view, Marian. Neither poetic or outlandish costume, nor the impossible language put into the mouths of their creations by the old bards, makes the unconventional woman. There is, in truth, a conventionality about these very things, only it is antiquated. It is not a woman's dress or phraseology that makes her an ideal or an inspiration, but what she is herself. No two leaves are alike on the same tree, but they are all enough alike to make but one impression. Some are more shapely than others, and flutter from their support with a fairer and more conspicuous grace to the closely observant; but there is nothing independent about them, nothing to distinguish them especially from their companions. They fulfil their general purpose, and fall away. This simile applies to the majority of people. Not only poetry and romance, but history also, gives us instances wherein men and women differ and break away from accepted types, some in absurd or grotesque ways, others through the sheer force of gifted selfishness, and others still in natural, noble development of graces of heart and mind."

"Stop generalizing, and tell me, your silly, vain, flirtatious daughter, how I can be unconventional in this prosaic midday of civilization."

"Prosaic day? You are mistaken, Marian. There never was a period like it Barbaric principles, older than Abraham, are now to triumph, or give place to a better and more enlightened human nature. We almost at this moment hear the echoes of a strife in which specimens of the best manhood of the age are arrayed against one another in a struggle such as the world has never witnessed. I have my part in the conflict, and it brings to me great responsibilities and dangers."

"Dangers! You in danger, papa?"

"Yes, certainly. Since you wish to be treated like a woman, and not a child,-- since you wish me to show my real life,--you shall know the truth. I am controlled by the government that is engaged in a life-and-death struggle to maintain its own existence and preserve for the nation its heritage of liberty. Thus far I have been able to serve the cause in quiet, unrecognized ways that I need not now explain; but I am one who must obey orders, and I wish to do so, for my heart is in the work. I am no better than other men who are risking all. Mamma knows this in a way, but she does not fully comprehend it. Fortunately she is not one of those who take very anxious thought for the morrow, and you know I am inclined to let things go on quietly as long as they will. Thus far I have merely gone to an office as I did before the war, or else have been absent on trips that were apparently civilian in character, and it has been essential that I should have as little distraction of mind as possible. I have lived long in hope that some decisive victory might occur; but the future grows darker, instead of lighter, and the struggle, instead of culminating speedily, promises to become more deadly and to be prolonged. There is but one way out of it for me, and that is through the final triumph of the old flag. Therefore, what a day will bring forth God only knows. There have been times when I wished to tell you something of this, but there seemed little opportunity. As you said, a good many were coming and going, you seemed happy and preoccupied, and I got into the habit of reasoning, 'Every day that passes without a thought of trouble is just so much gained; and it may be unnecessary to cloud her life with fear and anxiety;' yet perhaps it would be mistaken kindness to let trouble come suddenly, like an unexpected blow. I confess, however, that I have had a little natural longing to be more to my only child than I apparently was, but each day brought its increasing press of work and responsibility, its perplexing and far-reaching questions. Thus time has passed, and I said, 'Let her be a light-hearted girl as long as she can.'"

"O papa, what a blind, heartless fool I've been!"

"No, my dear, only young and thoughtless, like thousands of others. It so happened that nothing occurred to awaken you. One day of your old life begat another. That so slight a thing should make you think, and desire to be different, promises much to me, for if your nature had been shallow and commonplace, you wouldn't have been much disturbed. If you have the spirit your words indicate to-night, it will be better for you to face life in the height and depth of its reality, trusting in God and your own womanhood for strength to meet whatever comes. Those who live on this higher plane have deeper sorrows, but also far richer joys, than those

who exist from hand to mouth, as it were, in the immediate and material present. What's more, they cease to be plebeian in the meaner sense of the word, and
achieve at one step a higher caste. They have broken the conventional type, and all
the possibilities of development open at once. You are still a young, inexperienced
girl, and have done little in life except learn your lessons and amuse yourself, yet in
your dissatisfaction and aspiration you are almost infinitely removed from what you
were yesterday, for you have attained the power to grow and develop."

"You are too philosophical for me. How shall I grow or develop?"

"I scarcely know."

"What definite thing shall I do to-morrow?"

"Do what the plant does. Receive the influence that tends to quicken your best
impulses and purposes; follow your awakened conscience naturally. Do what seems
to you womanly, right, noble in little things or in great things, should there be opportunity. Did Shakespeare, as a child, propose to write the plays which have made
him chief among men? He merely yielded to the impulse when it came. The law
holds good down to you, my little girl. You have an impulse which is akin to that
of genius. Instead of continuing your old indolent, strolling gait on the dead level of
life, you have left the beaten track and faced the mountain of achievement. Every
resolute step forward takes you higher, even though it be but an inch; yet I cannot see the path by which you will climb, or tell you the height you may gain. The
main thing is the purpose to ascend. For ihose bent on noble achievement there is
always a path. God only knows to what it may bring you. One step leads to another,
and you will be guided better by the instincts and laws of your own nature than if I
tried to lead you step by step. The best I can do is to give you a little counsel, and a
helping hand now and then, as the occasion requires."

"Now in truth, papa, do not all your fine words signify about what you and
mamma used to say years ago,--'You must be a good little girl, and then you will be
happy'? It seems to me that many good people are conventionality itself."

"Many are, and if they ARE good, it is a fortunate phase of conventionality. For
instance, I know of a man who by the law of heredity and the force of circumstances
has scarcely a bad habit or trait, and has many good ones. He meets the duties of life
in an ordinary, satisfactory way, and with little effort on his part I know of another
man who externally presents nearly the same aspect to society, who is quiet and

unobtrusive in his daily life, and yet he is fighting hereditary taint and habit with a daily heroism, such as no soldier in the war can surpass. He is not conventional, although he appears to be so. He is a knight who is not afraid to face demons. Genuine strength and originality of character do not consist in saying or doing things in an unusual way. Voluntary eccentrics are even worse than the imitators of some model or the careless souls which take .their coloring from chance surroundings. Conventionality ceases when a human being begins the resolute development of his own. natural law of growth to the utmost extent. This is true because nature in her higher work is not stereotyped. I will now be as definite as you can desire. You, for instance, Marian Vosburgh, are as yet, even to yourself, an unknown quantity. You scarcely know what you are, much less what you may become. This conversation, and the feeling which led to it, prove this. There are traits and possibilities in your nature due to ancestors of whom you have not even heard. These combine with your own individual endowments by nature to make you a separate and distinct being, and you grow more separate and distinct by developing nature's gifts, traits, powers,--in brief, that which is essentially your own. Thus nature becomes your ally and sees to it with absolute certainty that you are not like other people. Following this principle of action you cannot know, nor can any one know, to just what you may attain. All true growth is from within, outward. In the tree, natural law prevents distortion or exaggeration of one part over another. In your case reason, conscience, good taste, must supervise and direct natural impulses. Thus following nature you become natural, and cease to be conventional. If you don't do this you will be either conventional or queer. Do you understand me?"

"I think I begin to. Let me see if I do. Let me apply your words to one definite problem,--How can I be more helpful and companionable to you?"

"Why, Marian, do you not see how infinitely more to me you are already, although scarcely beyond the wish to be different from what you were? I have talked to you as a man talks to a woman in the dearest and most unselfish relation of life. There is one thing, however, you never can know, and that is a father's love for a daughter: it is essentially a man's love and a man's experience. I am sure it is very different from the affection I should have for a son, did I possess one. Ever since you were a baby the phrase, 'my little girl,' has meant more than you can ever know; and now when you come voluntarily to my side in genuine sympathy, and seek to enter INTELLIGENTLY into that which makes my life, you change everything for the better, precisely as that which was in cold, gray shadow before is changed by sunlight. You add just so much by your young, fresh, womanly life to my life, and it is all the more welcome because it is womanly and different from mine. You cease to be a child, a dependant to be provided for, and become a friend, an inspiration, a confidante. These relations may count little to heavy, stolid, selfish men, to whom eating, drinking, excitement, and money-making are the chief considerations, but to men of mind and ideals, especially to a man who has devoted, his heart, brain, and life to a cause upon which the future of a nation depends, they are pre-eminent. You see I am a German at heart, and must have my world of thought and imagination, as well as the world in which men look at me with cold, hard, and even hostile eyes. Thus far this ideal world has been peopled chiefly by the shadows of those who have lived in the past or by the characters of the great creators in poetry. Now if my blue-eyed daughter can prove to me that she has too much heart and brain to be an ordinary society-girl like half a million of others, and will share my interest in the great thoughts and achievements of the past and the greater questions of to-day,-- if she can prove that when I have time I may enjoy a tryst with her in regions far remote from shallow, coarse, commonplace minds,--is not my whole life enriched? We can read some of my favorite authors together and trace their influence on the thought of the world. We can take up history and see how to-day's struggle is the result of the past. I think I could soon give you an intelligent idea of the questions of the time, for which men are hourly dying. The line of battle stretches across the continent, and so many are engaged that every few moments a man, and too often a woman from heart-break, dies that the beloved cause may triumph. Southern girls and women, as a rule, are far more awake to the events of the time than their sisters in the North. Such an influence on the struggle can scarcely be over-estimated. They create a public sentiment that drives even the cowardly into the ranks, and their words and enthusiasm incite brave young men to even chivalric courage. It is true that there are very many like them in the North, but there are also very many who restrain the men over whom they have influence,--who are indifferent, as you have been, or in sympathy with the South,--or who, as is true in most instances, do not yet see the necessity for self-sacrifice. We have not truly felt the war yet, but it will sooner or later come home to every one who has a heart. I have been in the

South, and have studied the spirit of the people. They are just as sincere and conscientious as we are, and more in earnest as yet. Christian love and faith, there, look to
Heaven for sanction with absolute sincerity, and mothers send their sons, girls their
lovers, and wives their husbands, to die if need be. For the political conspirators
who have thought first and always of their ambition I have only detestation, but
for the people of the South--for the man I may meet in the ranks and kill if I can--I
have profound respect. I should know he was wrong, I should be equally sure that
he believed himself right.

"Look at the clock, my dear, and see how long I have talked to you. Can you
now doubt that you will be companionable to me? Men down town think I am hard
as a rock, but your touch of sympathy has been as potent as the stroke of Moses'
rod. You have had an inundation of words, and the future is rosy to me with hope
because you are not asleep."

"Have I shown lack of interest, papa?"

"No, Marian, your intent eyes have been eloquent with feeling. Therefore I
have spoken so long and fully. You have, as it were, drawn the words from me. You
have made this outpouring of my heart seem as natural as breathing, for when you
look as you do to-night, I can almost think aloud to you. You have a sympathetic
face, my child, and when expressing intelligent sympathy it grows beautiful. It was
only pretty before. Prettiness is merely a thing of outline and color; beauty comes
from the soul."

She came and stood at his side, resting her arm lightly on his shoulder.

"Papa," she said, "your words are a revelation to me. Your world is indeed a
new one, and a better one than mine. But I must cease to be a girl, and become a
woman, to enter it."

"You need not be less happy; you do not loset anything. A picture is ever finer
for shadows and depth of perspective. You can't get anything very fine, in either art
or life, from mere bright surface glare."

"I can't go back to that any more; something in my very soul tells me that I
cannot; and your loneliness and danger would render even the wish to do so base.
No, I feel now that I would rather be a woman, even though it involves a crown of
thorns, than to be a shallow creature that my own heart would despise. I may never
be either wise or deep, but I shall be to you all I can."

"You do very much for me in those words alone, my darling. As I said before, no one can tell what you may become if you develop your own nature naturally."

CHAPTER IV.
WOMAN'S CHIEF RIGHT.

It was late when Marian and her father parted, and each felt that a new era had begun in their lives. To the former it was like a deep religious experience. She was awed and somewhat depressed, as well as resolute and earnest. Life was no pleasure excursion to her father. Questions involving the solemnity of danger, possibly death, occupied his mind. Yet it was not of either that he thought, but of the questions themselves. She saw that he was a large-hearted, large-brained man, who entered into the best spirit of his age, and found recreation in the best thought of the past, and she felt that she was still but a little child beside him.

"But I shall no longer be a silly child or a shallow, selfish, unfeeling girl. I know there is something better in my nature than this. Papa's words confirm what I have read but never thought of much: the chief need of men who can do much or who amount to much is the intelligent sympathy of women who understand and care for them. Why, it was the inspiration of chivalry, even in the dark ages. Well, Marian Vosburgh, if you can't excel a kitchen-maid, it would be better that you had never lived."

The sun was shining brightly when she wakened on the following morning, and when she came to breakfast their domestic handed her a note from her father, by which she was informed that he would dine with her earlier than usual, and that they would take a sail down the bay.

Brief as it was, it breathed an almost lover-like fondness and happiness. She enjoyed her first exultant thrill at her sense of power as she comprehended that he had gone to his work that day a stronger and more hopeful man.

She went out to do her shopping, and was soon in a Broadway temple of fashion, but found that she was no longer a worshipper. A week before the beautiful fabrics would have absorbed her mind and awakened intense desires, for she had a passion for dress, and few knew how to make more of it than she. But a new and stronger passion was awakening. She was made to feel at last that she had not only a woman's lovely form and features, but a woman's mind. Now she began to dream of triumphs through the latter, and her growing thought was how to achieve them. Not that she was indifferent to her costume; it should be like the soldier's accoutrements; her mind the weapon.

As is common with the young to whom any great impulse or new, deep experience comes, she was absorbed by it, and could think of little else. She went over her father's words again and again, dwelling on the last utterance, which had contained the truth uppermost in all that he had said,--"Develop the best in your own nature naturally."

What was her own nature, her starting-point? Her introspection was not very reassuring. She felt that perhaps the most hopeful indication was her strong rebound from what she at last recognized as mean and unworthy. She also had a little natural curiosity and vanity to see if her face was changing with changing motives. Was there such a difference between prettiness and beauty? She was perfectly sure she would rather be beautiful than pretty.

Her mirror revealed a perplexed young face, suggesting interrogation-points. The day was ending as it had begun, with a dissatisfaction as to the past, amounting almost to disgust, and with fears, queries, and uncertainties concerning the future. How should she take up life again? How should she go on with it?

More importunate still was the question, "What has the future in store for me and for those I love? Papa spoke of danger; and when I think of his resolute face, I know that nothing in the line of duty will daunt him. He said that it might not be kindness to leave me in my old, blind, unthinking ignorance,--that a blow, shattering everything, might come, finding us all unprepared. Oh, why don't mamma feel and see more? We have been just like comfortable passengers on a ship, while papa was facing we knew not what. I may not be of much use, but I feel now as if I wanted to be with him. To stay below with scarcely any other motive than to have a good time, and then to be paralyzed, helpless, when some shock of trouble comes, now seems silly and weak to the last degree. I am only too glad that I came to my senses in time, for if anything should happen to papa, and I had to remember all my days that I had never been much to him, and had left him to meet the stress of life and danger alone, I am sure I should be wretched from self-reproach."

When he came at six o'clock, she met him eagerly, and almost her first words were, "Papa, there hasn't been any danger to-day?"

"Oh, no; none at all; only humdrum work. You must not anticipate trouble. Soldiers, you know, jest and laugh even when going into battle, and they are all the better soldiers for the fact. No; I have given you a wrong impression. Nothing has been humdrum to-day. An acquaintance down town said: 'What's up, Vosburgh? Heard good news? Have our troops scored a point?' You see I was so brightened up that he thought nothing but a national victory could account for the improvement. Men are like armies, and are twice as effective when well supported."

"The idea of my supporting you!"

"To me it's a charming idea. Instead of coming back to a dismal, empty house, I find a blue-eyed lassie who will go with me to dinner, and add sauce piquante to every dish. Come, I am not such a dull, grave old fellow as you imagine. You shall see how gallant I can become under provocation. We must make the most of a couple of hours, for that is all that I can give you. No sail to-night, as I had planned, for a government agent is coming on from Washington to see me, and I must be absent for at least an hour or two after eight o'clock. You won't mope, will you? You have something to read? Has the day been very long and lonely? What have you been doing and thinking about?"

"When are you going to give me a chance to answer?"

"Oh, I read your answer, partly at least, in your eyes. You can amplify later. Come, get ready for the street. Put on what you please, so that you wear a smile. These are not times to worry over slight reverses as long as the vital points are safe."

The hour they passed at dinner gave Marian a new revelation of her father. The quiet man proved true the words of Emerson, "Among those who enjoy his thought, he will regain his tongue."

At first he drew her out a little, and with his keen, quick insight he understood her perplexity, her solicitude about him and herself and the future, her resolute purpose to be a woman, and the difficulties of seeing the way to the changes she desired. Instead of replying directly to her words, he skilfully led their talk to the

events of the day, and contemporaneous history became romance under his ver-
sion; the actors in the passing drama ceased to be names and officials, and were
invested with human interest. She was made to see their motives, their hopes, fears,
ambitions; she opened her eyes in surprise at his knowledge of prominent people,
their social status, relations, and family connection. A genial light of human interest played over most of his words, yet now and then they touched on the depths of
tragedy; again he seemed to be indulging in sublimated gossip, and she saw the men
and women who posed before the public in their high stations revealed in their
actual daily life.

She became so interested that at times she left her food untasted. "How can you
know all this?" she exclaimed.

"It is my business to know a great deal," he replied. "Then natural curiosity
leads me to learn more. The people of whom I have spoken are the animated pieces
on the chess-board. In the tremendous game that we are playing, success depends
largely on their strength, weakness, various traits,--in brief, their character. The
stake that I have in the game leads me to know and watch those who are exerting a
positive influence. It is interesting to study the men and women who, in any period,
made and shaped history, and to learn the secrets of their success and failure. Is it
not natural that men and women who are making history to-day--who in fact are
shaping one's own history--should be objects of stronger attention? Now, as in the
past, women exert a far greater influence on current events than you would imagine. There are but few thrones of power behind which you will not find a woman.
What I shall do or be during the coming weeks and months depends upon some of
the people I have sketched, free-handed, for you alone. You see the sphinx--for as
such I am regarded by many--opens his mouth freely to you. Can you guess some of
my motives for this kind of talk?"

"You have wanted to entertain me, papa, and you have succeeded. You should
write romances, for you but touch the names one sees in the papers and they become dramatic actors."

"I did want to entertain you and make a fair return for your society; I wish to
prove that I can be your companion as truly as you can become mine; but I have
aimed to do more. I wish you to realize how interesting the larger and higher world
of activity is. Do not imagine that in becoming a woman, earnest and thought-

ful, you are entering on an era of solemn platitudes. You are rather passing from a theatre of light comedy to a stage from which Shakespeare borrowed the whole gamut of human feeling, passion, and experience. I also wished to satisfy you that you have mind enough to become absorbed as soon as you begin to understand the significance of the play. After you have once become an intelligent spectator of real life you can no more go back to drawing-room chit-chat, gossip, and flirtation than you can lay down Shakespeare's 'Tempest' for a weak little parlor comedy. I am too shrewd a man, Marian, to try to disengage you from the past by exhortations and homilies; and now that you have become my friend, I shall be too sincere with you to disguise my purposes or methods. I propose to co-operate frankly with you in your effort, for in this way I prove my faith in you and my respect for you. Soon you will find yourself an actor in real life, as well as a spectator."

"I fear I have been one already,--a sorry one, too. It is possible to do mischief without being very intelligent or deliberate. You are making my future, so far as you are concerned, clearer than I imagined it could be. You do interest me deeply. In one evening you make it evident how much I have lost in neglecting you--for I have neglected you, though not intentionally. Hereafter I shall be only too proud if you will talk to me as you have done, giving me glimpses of your thoughts, your work, and especially your dangers, where there are any. Never deceive me in this respect, or leave me in ignorance. Whatever may be the weaknesses of my nature, now that I have waked up, I am too proud a girl to receive all that I do from your hands and then give almost my whole life and thought to others. I shall be too delighted if you are happier for my meddling and dropping down upon you. I'll keep your secrets too, you see;" and she confirmed her words by an emphatic little nod. "You can talk to me about people, big and little, with whom you have to do, just as serenely as if you were giving your confidence to an oyster.

"But, papa, I am confronted by a question of real life, just as difficult for me as any that can perplex you. I can't treat this question any more as I have done. I don't see my way at all. Now I am going to be as direct and straightforward as a man, and not beat around the bush with any womanish finesse. There is a gentleman in this city who, if he knew I was in town to-night, would call, and I might not be able to prevent him from making a formal proposal. He is a man whom I respect and like very much, and I fear I have been too encouraging,--not intentionally and deliberately you know, but thoughtlessly. He was the cleverest and the most entertaining of my friends, and always brought a breezy kind of excitement with him. Don't you see, papa? That is what I lived for, pleasure and excitement, and I don't believe that anything can be so exciting to a girl as to see a man yielding to her fascinations, whatever they may be. It gives one a delicious sense of power. I shall be frank, too. I must be, for I want your advice. You men like power. History is full of the records of those who sold their own souls for it, and walked through blood and crime to reach it. I think it is just as natural for a woman to love power also, only now I see that it is a cruel and vile thing to get it and use it merely for amusement. To me it was excitement. I don't like to think how it may all end to a man like Fenton Lane, and I am so remorseful that I am half inclined to sacrifice myself and make him as good a wife as I can."

"Do you love him?"

"No. I don't think I know what love is. When a mere girl I had a foolish little flame that went out with the first breath of ridicule. Since that time I have enjoyed gentlemen's society as naturally as any other girl of our set, perhaps more keenly. Their talk and ways are so different from those of girls! Then my love of power came in, you see. The other girls were always talking about their friends and followers, and it was my pride to surpass them all. I liked one better than another, of course, but was always as ready for a new conquest as that old fool, 'Alexander the Little,' who ran over the world and especially himself. What do you think, papa? Shall I ever see one who will make all the others appear as nothing? Or, would it be nobler to devote myself to a true, fine man, like Mr. Lane, no matter how I felt?"

"God forbid! You had better stay at your mother's side till you are as old and wrinkled as Time himself."

"I am honestly glad to hear you say so. But what am I to do? Sooner or later I shall have to refuse Mr. Lane, and others too."

"Refuse them, then. He would be less than a man who would ask a girl to sacrifice herself for him. No, my dear, the most inalienable right of your womanhood is to love freely and give yourself where you love. This right is one of the issues of this war,--that the poorest woman in this land may choose her own mate. Slavery is the corner-stone of the Confederacy, wherein millions of women can be given according to the will of masters. Should the South triumph, phases of the Old-World despotism would creep in with certainly, and in the end we should have alliances, not marriages, as is the case so generally abroad. Now if a white American girl does not make her own choice she is a weak fool. The law and public sentiment protect her. If she will not choose wisely, she must suffer the consequences, and only under the impulse of love can a true choice be made. A girl must be sadly deficient in sense if she loves a weak, bad, disreputable man, or a vulgar, ignorant one. Such mesalliances are more in seeming than in reality, for the girl herself is usually near in nature to what she chooses. There are few things that I would more earnestly guard you against than a loveless marriage. You would probably miss the sweetest happiness of life, and you would scarcely escape one of its worst miseries."

"That settles it, then. I am going to choose for myself,--to stay with you and mamma, and to continue sending you my bills indefinitely."

"They will be love letters, now."

"Very dear ones, you will think sometimes. But truly, papa, you must not let me spend more than you can afford. You should be frank on this point also, when you know I do not wish to be inconsiderate. The question still remains, What am I to do with Mr. Lane?"

"Now I shall throw you on your own resources. I believe your woman's tact can manage this question better than my reason; only, if you don't love him and do not think you can, be sure to refuse him. I have nothing against Mr. Lane, and approve of what I know about him; but I am not eager to have a rival, or to lose what I have so recently gained. Nevertheless, I know that when the true knight comes through the wood, my sleeping beauty will have another awakening, compared with which this one will seem slight indeed. Then, as a matter of course, I will quietly take my place as 'second fiddle' in the harmony of your life. But no discordant first fiddle, if you please; and love alone can attune its strings. My time is up, and, if I don't return early, go to bed, so that mamma may not say you are the worse for your days in town. This visit has made me wish for many others."

"You shall have them, for, as Shakespeare says, your wish 'jumps' with mine."

CHAPTER V.
"BE HOPEFUL, THAT I MAY HOPE."

L EFT to herself Marian soon threw down the book she tried to read, and thought grew busy with her father's later words. Was there then a knight--a man--somewhere in the world, so unknown to her that she would pass him in the street without the slightest premonition that he was the arbiter of her destiny? Was there some one, to whom imagination could scarcely give shadowy outline, so real and strong that he could look a new life into her soul, set all her nerves tingling, and her blood coursing in mad torrents through her veins? Was there a stranger, whom now she would sweep with a casual glance, who still had the power to subdue her proud maidenhood, overcome the reserve which seemed to reach as high as heaven, and lay a gentle yet resistless grasp, not only on her sacred form, but on her very soul? Even the thought made her tremble with a vague yet delicious dread. Then she sprung to her feet and threw back her head proudly as she uttered aloud the words, "If this can ever be true, my power shall be equal to his."

A moment later she was evoking half-exultant chords from the piano. These soon grew low and dreamy, and the girl said softly to herself: "I have lived more in two days than in months of the past. Truly real life is better than a sham, shallow existence."

The door-bell rang, and she started to her feet. "Who can know I am in town?" she queried.

Fenton Lane entered with extended hand and the words: "I was passing and knew I could not be mistaken in your touch. Your presence was revealed by the music as unmistakably as if I had met you on the street. Am I an intruder? Please don't order me away under an hour or two."

"Indeed, Mr. Lane, truth compels me to say that I am here in deep retirement. I have been contemplating a convent."

"May I ask your motive?"

"To repent of my sins."

"You would have to confess at a convent. Why not imagine me a venerable father, dozing after a good dinner, and make your first essay at the confessional?"

"You tax my imagination too greatly. So I should have to confess; therefore no convent for me."

"Of course not. I should protest against it at the very altar, and in the teeth of the Pope himself. Can't you repent of your sins in some other way?"

"I suppose I shall have to."

"They would be a queer lot of little peccadilloes. I should like to set them all under a microscope."

"I would rather that your glass should be a goblet brimmed from Lethe."

"There is no Lethe for me, Miss Marian, so far as you are concerned."

"Come, tell me the news from the seat of war," she said, abruptly.

"This luxurious arm-chair is not a seat of war."

"Papa has been telling me how Southern girls make all the men enlist."

"I'll enlist to-morrow, if you ask me to."

"Oh, no. You might be shot, and then you would haunt me all my life."

"May I not haunt you anyway?" said Lane, resolutely, for he had determined not to let this opportunity pass. She was alone, and he would confirm the hope which her manner for months had inspired. "Come, Miss Marian," he continued, springing to his feet and approaching her side, his dark eyes full of fire and entreaty; "you cannot have misunderstood me. You know that while not a soldier I am also not a carpet-knight and have not idled in ladies' bowers. I have worked hard and dreamed of you. I am willing to do all that a man can to win you. Cowardice has not kept me from the war, but you. If it would please you I would put on the blue and shoulder a musket to-morrow. If you will permit more discretion and time, I can soon obtain a commission as an officer. But before I fight other battles, I wish to win the supreme victory of my life. Whatever orders I may take from others, you shall ever be my superior officer. You have seen this a long time; a woman of your mind could not help it. I have tried to hope with all a lover's fondness that you gave me glimpses of your heart also, but of this nothing would satisfy a man of my nature but absolute assurance."

He stood proudly yet humbly before her, speaking with strong, impassioned, fluent utterance, for he was a man who had both the power and the habit of expression.

She listened with something like dismay. Her heart, instead of kindling, grew only more heavy and remorseful. Her whole nature shrunk, while pity and compunction wrung tears from her eyes. This was real life in very truth. Here was a man ready to give up safe, luxurious existence, a career already successful, and face death for her. She knew him well enough to be sure that if he could wear her colors he would march away with the first regiment that would receive him. He was not a man to be influenced by little things, but yielded absolutely to the supreme impulses of his life. If she said the word, he would make good his promise with chivalrous, straightforward promptness, facing death, and all that death could then mean to him, with a light, half-jaunty courage characteristic of the ideal soldier. She had a secret wonder at herself that she could know all this and yet be so vividly conscious that what he asked could never be. Her womanly pity said yes; her woman's heart said no. He was eager to take her in his arms, to place the kiss of life-long loyalty on her lips; but in her very soul she felt that it would be almost sacrilege for him to touch her; since the divine impulse to yield, without which there can be no divine sanction, was absent.

She listened, not as a confused, frightened girl, while he spoke that which she had guessed before. Other men had sued, although none had spoken so eloquently or backed their words by such weight of character. Her trouble, her deep perplexity, was not due to a mere declaration, but was caused by her inability to answer him. The conventional words which she would have spoken a few days before died on her lips. They would be an insult to this earnest man, who had the right to hope for something better. What was scarcely worse--for there are few emergencies in which egotism is wholly lost--she would appear at once to him and to herself in an odious light. Her course would be well characterized by the Irish servant's lover, for here was a man who from the very fineness of his nature, if wronged, might easily go to the devil.

His words echoed her thought, for her hesitation and the visible distress on her face led him to exclaim, in a voice tense with something like agony: "O Marian, since you hesitate, hesitate longer. Think well before you mar--nay, spoil--my life. For God's sake don't put me off with some of the sham conventionalities current with society girls. I could stand anything better than that. I am in earnest; I have always been in earnest; and I saw from the first, through all your light, graceful disguises, that you were not a shallow, brainless, heartless creature,--that a noble woman was waiting to be wakened in your nature. Give me time; give yourself time. This is not a little affair that can be rounded off according to the present code of etiquette; it is a matter of life or death to me. Be more merciful than a rebel bullet."

She buried her face in her hands and sobbed helplessly.

He was capable of feeling unknown depths of tenderness, but there was little softness in his nature. As he looked down upon her, his face grew rigid and stern. In her sobs he read his answer,--the unwillingness, probably the inability, of her heart to respond to his,--and he grew bitter as he thought of the past.

With the cold, quiet tones of one too strong, controlled, and well-bred to give way violently to his intense anger, he said: "This is a different result from what you led me to expect. All your smiles end in these unavailing tears. Why did you smile so sweetly after you understood me, since you had nothing better in store? I was giving you the homage, the choice of my whole manhood, and you knew it. What were you giving me? Why did your eyes draw out my heart and soul? Do you think that such a man as I can exist without heart and soul? Did you class me with Strahan, who can take a refusal as he would lose a game of whist? No, you did not. I saw in your very eyes a true estimate of Strahan and all his kind. Was it your purpose to win a genuine triumph over a man who cared nothing for other women? Why then don't you enjoy it? You could not ask for anything more complete."

"Trample on me--I deserve it," she faltered.

After a moment's pause, he resumed: "I have no wish to trample on you. I came here with as much loyalty and homage as ever a man brought to a woman in any age. I have offered you any test of my love and truth that you might ask. What more could a man do? As soon as I knew what you were to me, I sought your father's permission to win you, and I told you my secret in every tone and glance. If your whole nature shrunk from me, as I see it does, you could have told me the truth months since, and I should have gone away honoring you as a true-hearted, honest girl, who would scorn the thought of deceiving and misleading an earnest man. You knew I did not belong to the male-flirt genus. When a man from some sacred impulse of his nature would give his very life to make a woman happy, is it too much to ask that she should not deliberately, and for mere amusement, wreck his life? If she does not want his priceless gift, a woman with your tact could have revealed the truth by one glance, by one inflection of a tone. Not that I should have been discouraged so easily, but I should have accepted an unspoken negative long since with absolute respect. But now--" and he made a gesture eloquent with protest and despair.

"But now," she said, wearily, "I see it all in the light in which you put it. Be content; you have spoiled my life as truly as I have yours."

"Yes, for this evening. There will be only one less in your drawing-room when you return."

"Very well," she replied, quietly. Her eyes were dry and hot now, and he could almost see the dark lines deepening under them, and the increasing pallor of her face. "I have only this to say. I now feel that your words are like blows, and they are given to one who is not resisting, who is prostrate;" and she rose as if to indicate that their interview should end.

He looked at her uneasily as she stood before him, with her pallid face averted, and every line of her drooping form suggesting defeat rather than triumph; yes, far more than defeat--the apathetic hopelessness of one who feels himself mortally wounded.

"Will you please tell me just what you mean when you say I have spoiled your life?" he asked.

"How should I know? How should anyone know till he has lived out its bitterness? What do you mean by the words? Perhaps you will remember hereafter that your language has been inconsistent as well as merciless. You said I was neither brainless nor heartless; then added that you had spoiled my life merely for one evening. But there is no use in trying to defend myself: I should have little to urge except thoughtlessness, custom, the absence of evil intention,--other words should prove myself a fool, to avoid being a criminal. Go on and spoil your life; you seem to be wholly bent upon it. Face rebel bullets or do some other reckless thing. I only wish to give you the solace of knowing that you have made me as miserable as a girl can be, and that too at a moment when I was awakening to better things. But I am wasting your valuable time. You believe in your heart that Mr. Strahan can console me with his gossip to-morrow evening, whatever happens."

"Great God! what am I to believe?"

She turned slowly towards him and said, gravely: "Do not use that name, Mr. Lane. He recognizes the possibility of good in the weakest and most unworthy of His creatures. He never denounces those who admit their sin and would turn from it."

He sprung to her side and took her hand. "Look at me," he pleaded.

His face was so lined and eloquent with suffering that her own lip quivered.

"Mr. Lane," she said, "I have wronged you. I am very sorry now. I've been sorry ever since I began to think--since you last called. I wish you could forgive me. I think it would be better for us both if you could forgive me."

He sunk into a chair and burying his face in his hands groaned aloud; then, in bitter soliloquy, said: "O God! I was right--I knew I was not deceived. She is just the woman I believed her to be. Oh, this is worse than death!"

No tears came into his eyes, but a convulsive shudder ran through his frame like that of a man who recoils from the worst blow of fate.

"Reproach--strike me, even," she cried. "Anything is better than this. Oh, that I could--but how can I? Oh, what an unutterable fool I have been! If your love is so strong, it should also be a little generous. As a woman I appeal to you."

He rose at once and said: "Forgive me; I fear that I have been almost insane,-- that I have much to atone for."

"O Mr. Lane, I entreat you to forgive me. I did admire you; I was proud of your preference,--proud that one so highly thought of and coveted by others should single me out. I never dreamt that my vanity and thoughtlessness could lead to this. If you had been ill or in trouble, you would have had my honest sympathy, and few could have sacrificed more to aid you. I never harbored one thought of cold-blooded malice. Why must I be punished as if I had committed a deliberate crime? If I am the girl you believe me to be, what greater punishment could I have than to know that I had harmed a man like you? It seems to me that if I loved any one I could suffer for him and help him, without asking anything in return. I could give you honest friendship, and take heart-felt delight in every manly success that you achieved. As a weak, faulty girl, who yet wishes to be a true woman, I appeal to you. Be strong, that I may be strong; be hopeful, that I may hope; be all that you can be, that I may not be disheartened on the very threshold of the better life I had chosen."

He took her hand, and said: "I am not unresponsive to your words. I feel their full force, and hope to prove that I do; but there is a tenacity in my nature that I cannot overcome. You said, 'if you loved'--do you not love any one?"

"No. You are more to me--twice more--than any man except my father."

"Then, think well. Do not answer me now, unless you must. Is there not a chance for me? I am not a shadow of a man, Marian. I fear I have proved too well how strong and concentrated my nature is. There is nothing I would not do or dare--"

"No, Mr. Lane; no," she interrupted, shaking her head sadly, "I will never consciously mislead a man again a single moment. I scarcely know what love is; I may never know; but until my heart prompts me, I shall never give the faintest hope or encouragement of this nature. I have been taught the evil of it too bitterly."

"And I have been your remorseless teacher, and thus perhaps have destroyed my one chance."

"You are wrong. I now see that your words were natural to one like you, and they were unjust only because I was not deliberate. Mr. Lane, let me be your friend. I could give you almost a sister's love; I could be so proud of you!"

"There," he said. "You have triumphed after all. I pledge you my word--all the manhood I possess--I will do whatever you ask."

She took his hand in both her own with a look of gratitude he never forgot, and spoke gladly: "Now you change everything. Oh, I am so glad you did not go away before! What a sad, sleepless night I should have had, and sad to-morrows stretching on indefinitely! I ask very much, very much indeed,--that you make the most and best of yourself. Then I can try to do the same. It will be harder for you than for me. You bring me more hope than sadness; I have given you more sadness than hope. Yet I have absolute faith in you because of what papa said to me last night. I had asked him how I could cease to be what I was, be different, you know, and he said, 'Develop the best in your own nature naturally.' If you will do this I shall have no fears."

"Yet I have been positively brutal to you to-night."

"No man can be so strong as you are and be trifled with. I understand that now, Mr. Lane. You had no sentimentality to be touched, and my tears did not move you in the least until you believed in my honest contrition."

"I have revealed to you one of my weaknesses. I am rarely angry, but when I am, my passion, after it is over, frightens me. Marian, you do forgive me in the very depths of your heart?"

"I do indeed,--that is, if I have anything to forgive under the circumstances."

"Poor little girl! how pale you are! I fear you are ill."

"I shall soon be better,--better all my life for your forgiveness and promise."

"Thank God that we are parting in this manner," he said. "I don't like to think of what might have happened, for I was in the devil's own mood. Marian, if you make good the words you have spoken to-night, if you become the woman you can be, you will have a power possessed by few. It was not your beauty merely that fascinated me, but a certain individuality,--something all your own, which gives you an influence apparently absolute. But I shall speak no more in this strain. I shall try to be as true a friend as I am capable of becoming, although an absent one. I must prove myself by deeds, not words, however. May I write to you sometimes? I will direct my letters under the care of your father, and you may show them to him or your mother, as you wish."

"Certainly you may, and you will be my first and only gentleman correspondent. After what has passed between us, it would be prudery to refuse. Moreover, I wish to hear often of your welfare. Never for a moment will my warm interest cease, and you can see me whenever you wish. I have one more thing to ask,--please take up your old life to-morrow, just where you left off. Do nothing hastily, or from impulse. Remember you have promised to make the most and best of yourself, and that requires you to give conscience and reason fair hearing. Will you also promise this?"

"Anything you asked, I said."

"Then good-by. Never doubt my friendship, as I shall not doubt yours."

Her hand ached from the pressure of his, but the pain was thus drawn from her heart.

CHAPTER VI.
A SCHEME OF LIFE.

MARIAN waited for her father's return, having been much too deeply excited for the speedy advent of quiet sleep. When at last he came she told him everything. As she described the first part of the interview his brow darkened, but his face softened as she drew toward the close. When she ceased he said:--

"Don't you see I was right in saying that your own tact would guide you better than my reason? If I, instead of your own nature, had directed you, we should have made an awful mess of it. Now let me think a moment. This young fellow has suggested an idea to me,--a general line of action which I think you can carry out. There is nothing like a good definite plan,--not cast-iron, you know, but flexible and modified by circumstances as you go along, yet so clear and defined as to give you something to aim at. Confound it, that's what's the matter with our military authorities. If McClellan is a ditch-digger let them put a general in command; or, if he is a general, give him what he wants and let him alone. There is no head, no plan. I confess, however, that just now I am chiefly interested in your campaigns, which, after all, stand the best chance of bringing about union, in spite of your negative mood manifested to-night. Nature will prove too strong for you, and some day--soon probably--you will conquer, only to surrender yourself. Be that as it may, the plan I suggest need not be interfered with. Be patient. I'm only following the tactics in vogue,--taking the longest way around to the point to be attacked. Lane said that if you carried out your present principle of action you would have a power possessed by few. I think he is right. I'm not flattering you. Little power of any kind can co-exist with vanity. The secret of your fascination is chiefly in your individuality. There are other girls more beautiful and accomplished who have not a tithe of it. Now and then a woman is peculiarly gifted with the power to influence men,--strong men, too. You had this potency in no slight degree when neither your heart nor your brain was very active. You will find that it will increase with time, and if you are wise it will be greater when you are sixty than at present. If you avoid the Scylla of vanity on the one hand, and the Charybdis of selfishness on the other, and if the sympathies of your heart keep pace with a cultivated mind, you will steadily grow in social influence. I believe it for this reason: A weak girl would have been sentimental with Lane, would have yielded temporarily, either to his entreaty or to his anger, only to disappoint him in the end, or else would have been conventional in her refusal and so sent him to the bad, probably. You recognized just what you could be to him, and had the skill--nature, rather, for all was unpremeditated--to obtain an influence by which you can incite him to a better manhood and a greater success, perhaps, than if he were your accepted lover. Forgive this long preamble: I am thinking aloud and feeling my way, as it were. What did you ask him to promise? Why, to make the most and best of himself. Why not let this sentence suggest the social scheme of your life? Drop fellows who have neither brains nor heart,--no good mettle in them,--and so far as you have influence strive to inspire the others to make the most and best of themselves. You would not find the kitchen-maid a rival on this plan of life; nor indeed, I regret to say, many of your natural associates. Outwardly your life will appear much the same, but your motive will change everything, and flow through all your action like a mountain spring, rendering it impossible for you to poison any life."

"O papa, the very possibility of what you suggest makes life appear beautiful. The idea of a convent!"

"Convents are the final triumph of idiocy. If bad women could be shut up and made to say prayers most of the time, no harm at least would be done,--the good, problematical; but to immure a woman of sweet, natural, God-bestowed impulses is the devil's worst practical joke in this world. Come, little girl, it's late. Think over the scheme; try it as you have a chance; use your power to incite men to make the most and best of themselves. This is better than levying your little tribute of flattery and attention, like other belles,--a phase of life as common as cobble-stones and as old as vanity. For instance, you have an artist among your friends. Possibly you can make him a better artist and a better fellow in every way. Drop all muffs and sticks; don't waste yourself on them. Have considerable charity for some of the wild fellows, none for their folly, and from the start tolerate no tendencies toward sentimentality. You will find that the men who admire girls bent on making eyes rather than making men will soon disappear. Sensible fellows won't misunderstand you, even though prompted to more than friendship; and you will have a circle of friends of which any woman might be proud. Of course you will find at times that unspoken negatives will not satisfy; but if a woman has tact, good sense, and sincerity, her position is impregnable. As long as she is not inclined to love a man herself, she can, by a mere glance, not only define her position, but defend it. By simple dignity and reserve she can say to all, 'Thus far and no farther.' If, without encouragement, any one seeks to break through this barrier he meets a quiet negative which he must respect, and in his heart does respect. Now, little girl, to sum up your visit, with its long talks and their dramatic and unexpected illustration, I see nothing to prevent you from going forward and making the best and most of your life according to nature and truth. You have a good start, and a rather better chance than falls to the lot of the majority."

"Truly," said Marian, thoughtfully, "we don't appear to grow old and change by time so much as by what happens,--by what we think and feel. Everything appears changed, including you and myself."

"It's more in appearance than in reality. You will find the impetus of your old life so strong that it will be hard even to change the direction of the current. You will be much the same outwardly, as I said before. The stream will flow through the same channel of characteristic traits and habits. The vital change must be in the stream itself,--the motive from which life springs."

How true her father's words seemed on the following evening after her return! Her mother, as she sat down, to their dainty little dinner, looked as if her serenity had been undisturbed by a single perplexing thought during the past few days. There was the same elegant, yet rather youthful costume for a lady of her years; the same smiling face, not yet so full in its outline as to have lost all its girlish beauty. It was marred by few evidences of care and trouble, nor was it spiritualized by thought or deep experience.

Marian observed her closely, not with any disposition towards cold or conscious criticism, but in order that she might better understand the conditions of her own life. She also had a wakening curiosity to know just what her mother was to her father and he to her. The hope was forming that she could make them more to each other. She had too much tact to believe that this could be done by general exhortations. If anything was to be accomplished it must be by methods so fine and unobtrusive as to be scarcely recognized.

Her father's inner life had been a revelation to her, and she was led to query: "Why does not mamma understand it? CAN she understand it?" Therefore she listened attentively to the details of what had happened in her absence. She waited in vain for any searching and intelligent questions concerning the absent husband. Beyond that he was well, and that everything about the house was just as she had left it, Mrs. Vosburgh appeared to have no interest. She was voluble over little household affairs, the novel that just then absorbed her, and especially the callers and their chagrin at finding the young girl absent.

"Only the millionnaire widower remained any length of time when learning that you were away," said the lady, "and he spent most of the evening with me. I assure you he is a very nice, entertaining old fellow."

"How did he entertain you? What did he talk about?"

"Let me remember. Now I think of it, what didn't he talk about? He is one of the most agreeable gossips I ever met,--knows everybody and everything. He has at his finger-ends the history of all who were belles in my time, and" (complacently) "I find that few have done better than I, while some, with all their opportunities, chose very crooked sticks."

"You are right, mamma. It seems to me that neither of us half appreciates papa. He works right on so quietly and steadily, and yet he is not a machine, but a man."

"Oh, I appreciate him. Nine out of ten that he might have married would have made him no end of trouble. I don't make him any. Well, after talking about the people we used to know, Mr. Lanniere began a tirade against the times and the war, which he says have cost him a hundred thousand dollars; but he took care in a quiet way to let me know that he has a good many hundred thousands left. I declare, Marian, you might do a great deal worse."

"Do you not think I might do a great deal better?" the young girl asked, with a frown.

"I have no doubt you think so. Girls will be romantic. I was, myself; but as one goes on in life one finds that a million, more or less, is a very comfortable fact. Mr. Lanniere has a fine house in town, but he's a great traveller, and an habitue of the best hotels of this country and Europe. You could see the world with him on its golden side."

"Well, mamma, I want a man,--not an habitue. What's more, I must be in love with the man, or he won't stand the ghost of a chance. So you see the prospects are that you will have me on your hands indefinitely. Mr. Lanniere, indeed! What should I be but a part of his possessions,--another expensive luxury in his luxurious life? I want a man like papa,--earnest, large-brained, and large-hearted,--who, instead of inveighing against the times, is absorbed in the vital questions of the day, and is doing his part to solve them rightly. I would like to take Mr. Lanniere into a military hospital or cemetery, and show him what the war has cost other men."

"Why, Marian, how you talk!"

"I wish I could make you know how I feel. It seems to me that one has only to think a little and look around in order to feel deeply. I read of an awful battle while coming up in the cars. We have been promised, all the spring, that Richmond would be taken, the war ended, and all go on serenely again; but it doesn't look like it."

"What's the use of women distressing themselves with such things?" said Mrs. Vosburgh, irritably. "I can't bear to think of war and its horrors, except as they give spice to a story. Our whole trouble is a big political squabble, and you know I detest politics. It is just as Mr. Lanniere says,--if our people had only let slavery alone all would have gone on veil. The leaders on both sides will find out before the summer is over that they have gone too far and fast, and they had better settle their differences with words rather than blows. We shall all be shaking hands ana making up before Christmas."

"Papa doesn't think so."

"Your father is a German at heart. He has the sense to be practical about every-day affairs and enjoy a good dinner, but he amuses himself with cloudy speculations and ideals and vast questions about the welfare of the world, or the 'trend of the centuries,' as he said one day to me. I always try to laugh him out of such vague nonsense. Has he been talking to you about the 'trend of the centuries'?"

"No, mamma, he has not," replied Marian, gravely; "but if he does I shall try to understand what he means and be interested. I know that papa feels deeply about the war, and means to take the most effective part in it that he can, and that he does not think it will end so easily as you believe. These facts make me feel anxious, for I know how resolute papa is."

"He has no right to take any risks," said the lady, emphatically.

"He surely has the same right that other men have."

"Oh, well," concluded Mrs. Vosburgh, with a shrug, "there is no use in borrowing trouble. When it comes to acting, instead of dreaming and speculating on vast, misty questions, I can always talk your father into good sense. That is the best thing about him,--he is well-balanced, in spite of his tendency to theories. When I show him that a thing is quixotic he laughs, shrugs his shoulders, and good-naturedly goes on in the even tenor of his way. It was the luckiest thing in the world for him when he married me, for I soon learned his weak points, and have ever guarded him against them. As a result he has had a quiet, prosperous career. If he wishes to serve the government in some civilian capacity, and is well paid for it, why shouldn't he? But I would never hear of his going to the front, fighting, and marching in Virginia mud and swamps. If he ever breathes such a thought to you, I hope you will aid me in showing him how cruel and preposterous it is."

Marian sighed, as she thought: "I now begin to see how well papa understands mamma, but has she any gauge by which to measure him? I fear he has found his home lonely, in spite of good dinners."

"Come, my dear," resumed Mrs. Vosburgh, "we are lingering too long. Some of your friends may be calling soon, although I said I did not know whether you would be at home to-night or not. Mr. Lanniere will be very likely to come, for I am satisfied that he has serious intentions. What's more, you might do worse,--a great deal worse."

"Three times you have said that, mamma, and I don't like it," said Marian, a little indignantly. "Of course I might do worse; I might kill him, and I should be tempted to if I married him. You know that I do not care for him, and he knows it, too. Indeed, I scarcely respect him. You don't realize what you are saying, for you would not have me act from purely mercenary motives?"

"Oh, certainly not; but Mr. Lanniere is not a monster or a decrepit centenarian. He is still in his prime, and is a very agreeable and accomplished man of the world. He is well-connected, moves in the best society, and could give his wife everything."

"He couldn't give me happiness, and he would spoil my life."

"Oh well, if you feel so, there is nothing more to be said. I can tell you, though, that multitudes of girls would be glad of your chance; but, like so many young people, you have romantic ideas, and do not appreciate the fact that happiness results chiefly from the conditions of our lot, and that we soon learn to have plenty of affection for those who make them all we could desire;" and she touched a bell for the waitress, who had been temporarily dismissed.

The girl came in with a faint smile on her face. "Has she been listening?" thought Marian. "That creature, then, with her vain, pretty, yet vulgar face, is the type of what I was. She has been lighting the drawing-room for me to do what she proposes to do later in the evening. She looks just the same. Mamma is just the same. Callers will come just the same. How unchanged all is, as papa said it would be! I fear much may be unchangeable."

She soon left the dining-room for the parlor, her dainty, merry little campaigning-ground. What should be its future record? Could she carry out the scheme of life which her father had suggested? "Well," she concluded, with an ominous flash in her eyes at her fair reflection in the mirror, "whether I can incite any one to better things or not, I can at least do some freezing out. That gossipy, selfish old Mr. Lanniere must take his million to some other market. I have no room in my life for him. Neither do I dote on the future acquaintance of Mr. Strahan. I shall put him on probation. If men don't want my society and regard on the new conditions, they can stay away; if they persist in coming, they must do something finer and be something finer than in the past. The friendship of one man like Fenton Lane is worth more than the attention of a wilderness of muffs and sticks, as papa calls them. What I fear is that I shall appear goody-goody, and that would disgust every one, including myself."

CHAPTER VII.
SURPRISES.

MR. Lanniere evidently had serious intentions, for he came unfashionably early. He fairly beamed on the young girl when he found her at home. Indeed, as she stood before him in her radiant youth, which her evening costume enhanced with a fine taste quickly recognized by his practised eyes, he very justly regarded her as better than anything which his million had purchased hitherto. It might easily be imagined that he had added a little to the couleur de rose of the future by an extra glass of Burgundy, for he positively appeared to exude an atmosphere of affluence, complacency, and gracious intention. The quick-witted girl detected at once his King-Cophetua air, and she was more amused than embarrassed. Then the eager face of Fenton Lane arose in her fancy, and she heard his words, "I would shoulder a musket and march away to-morrow if you bade me!" How insignificant was all that this man could offer, as compared with the boundless, self-sacrificing love of the other, before whom her heart bowed in sincere homage if nothing more! What was this man's offer but an expression of selfishness? And what could she ever be but an accessory of his Burgundy? Indeed, as his eyes, humid from wine, gloated upon her, and he was phrasing his well-bred social platitudes and compliments, quite oblivious of the fact that HER eyes were taking on the blue of a winter sky, her cheeks began to grow a little hot with indignation and shame. He knew that she did not love him, that naturally she could not, and that there had been nothing in their past relations to inspire even gratitude and respect towards him. In truth, his only effort had been to show his preference and to indicate his wishes. What then could his offer mean but the expectation that she would take him as a good bargain, and, like any well-bred woman of the world, comply with all its conditions? Had she given him the impression that she could do this? While the possibility made her self-reproachful, she was conscious of rising resentment towards him who was so complacently assuming that she was for sale.

"Indeed, Miss Vosburgh," was the conclusion of his rather long preliminaries, "you must not run away soon again. June days may be charming under any circumstances, but your absence certainly insures dull June evenings."

"You are burdening your conscience without deceiving me," the young girl replied, demurely, "and should not so wrong yourself. Mamma said that you were very entertaining, and that last evening was a delightful one. It could scarcely be otherwise. It is natural that people of the same age should be congenial. I will call mamma at once."

"I beg you will not,--at least not just yet. I have something to say to which I trust you will listen kindly and favorably. Do you think me so very old?"

"No older than you have a perfect right to be, Mr. Lanniere," said the girl, laughing. "I can think of no reason for your reproachful tone."

"Let me give you one then. Your opinions are of immense importance to me."

"Truly, Mr. Lanniere, this is strange beyond measure, especially as I am too young to have formed many opinions."

"That fact only increases my admiration and regard One must reach my years in order to appreciate truly the dewy freshness of youth. The world is a terra incognita to you yet, and your opinions of life are still to be formed. Let me give you a chance to see the world from lofty, sunny elevations."

"I am too recently from my geography not to remember that while elevations may be sunny they are very cold," was the reply, with a charming little shiver. "Mont Blanc has too much perspective."

"Do not jest with me or misunderstand me, Miss Vosburgh," he said, impressively. "There is a happy mean in all things."

"Yes, Mr. Lanniere, and the girl who means to be happy should take care to discover it."

"May it not be discovered for her by one who is better acquainted with life? In woman's experience is not happiness more often thrust upon her than achieved? I, who know the world and the rich pleasures and triumphs it affords to one who, in the military phrase of the day, is well supported, can offer you a great deal,--more than most men, I assure you."

"Why, Mr. Lanniere," said the young girl, looking at him with demure surprise, "I am perfectly contented and happy. No ambition for triumphs is consuming me. What triumphs? As for pleasure, each day brings all and more than I deserve. Young as one may be, one can scarcely act without a motive."

"Then I am personally nothing to you?" he said stiffly, and rising.

"Pardon me, Mr. Lanniere. I hope my simple directness may not appear childish, but it seems to me that I have met your suggestions with natural answers; What should you be to me but an agreeable friend of mamma's?"

He understood her fence perfectly, and was aware that the absence of a mercenary spirit on her part made his suit appear almost ridiculous. If her clear young eyes would not see him through a golden halo, but only as a man and a possible mate, what could he be to her? Even gold-fed egotism could not blind him to the truth that she was looking at HIM, and that the thought of bartering herself for a little more of what she had to her heart's content already was not even considered. There was distressing keenness in the suggestion that, not wanting the extraneous things he offered, no motive was left. He was scarcely capable of suspecting her indignation that he should deem her capable of sacrificing her fair young girlhood for greater wealth and luxury, even had she coveted them,--an indignation enhanced by her new impulses. The triumphs, happiness, and power which she now was bent on achieving could never be won under the dense shade of his opulent selfishness. He embodied all that was inimical to her hopes and plans, all that was opposed to the motives and inspiration received from her father, and she looked at him with unamiable eyes.

While he saw this to some extent, he was unaccustomed to denial by others or by himself. She was alluringly beautiful, as she stood before him,--all the more valued because she valued herself so highly, all the more coveted because superior to the sordid motives upon which even he had counted as the chief allies in his suit. In the intense longing of a self-indulgent nature he broke out, seizing her hand as he spoke: "O Miss Marian, do not deny me. I know I could make you happy. I would give you everything. Your slightest wish should be law. I would be your slave."

"I do not wish a slave," she replied, freezingly, withdrawing her hand. "I am content, as I told you; but were I compelled to make a choice it should be in favor of a man to whom I could look up, and whom I could aid in manly work. I shall not make a choice until compelled to by my heart."

"If your heart is still your own, give me a chance to win it," resumed the suitor, seeking vainly to take her hand again. "I am in my prime, and can do more than most men. I will put my wealth at your disposal, engage in noble charities, patriotic--"

This interview had been so absorbing as to make them oblivious of the fact that another visitor had been admitted to the hall. Hearing voices in the drawing-room, Mr. Strahan entered, and now stood just behind Mr. Lanniere, with an expression in which dismay, amusement, and embarrassment were so comically blended that Marian, who first saw him, had to cover her face with her handkerchief to hide her sense of the ludicrous.

"Pardon me," said the inopportune new-comer, "I--I--"

"Maledictions on you!" exclaimed the goaded millionnaire, now enraged beyond self-control, and confronting the young fellow with glaring, bloodshot eyes.

This greeting put Strahan entirely at his ease, and a glimpse of Marian's mirth had its influence also. She had turned instantly away, and gone to the farther side of the apartment.

"Come now, Mr. Lanniere," he said, with an assumption of much dignity; "there is scant courtesy in your greeting, and without reason. I have the honor of Miss Vosburgh's acquaintance as truly as yourself. This is her parlor, and she alone has the right to indicate that I am unwelcome. I shall demand no apologies here and now, but I shall demand them. I may appear very young--"

"Yes, you do; very young. I should think that ears like yours might have--" And then the older man paused, conscious that the violence of his anger was carrying him too far.

Strahan struck a nonchalant attitude, as he coolly remarked: "My venerable friend, your passion is unbecoming to your years. Miss Vosburgh, I humbly ask your pardon that my ears were not long enough to catch the purport of this interview. I am not in the habit of listening at a lady's door before I enter. My arrival at a moment so awkward for me was my misfortune. I discovered nothing to your discredit, Mr. Lanniere. Indeed, your appreciation of Miss Vosburgh is the most creditable thing I know about you,--far more so than your insults because I merely entered the door to which I was shown by the maid who admitted me. Miss Vosburgh, with your permission I will now depart, in the hope that you will forgive the annoyance--"

"I cannot give you my permission under the circumstances, Mr. Strahan. You have committed no offence against me, or Mr. Lanniere, either, as he will admit after a little thought. Let us regard the whole matter as one of those awkward little affairs over which good breeding can speedily triumph. Sit down, and I will call mamma."

"Pardon me, Miss Vosburgh," said Mr. Lanniere, in a choking voice, for he could not fail to note the merriment which the mercurial Strahan strove in vain to suppress; "I will leave you to more congenial society. I have paid you the highest compliment in my power, and have been ill-requited."

As if stung, the young girl took a step towards him, and said, indignantly: "What was the nature of your compliment? What have you asked but that I should sell myself for money? I may have appeared to you a mere society girl, but I was never capable of that. Good-evening, sir."

Mr. Lanniere departed with tingling ears, and a dawning consciousness that he had over-rated his million, and that he had made a fool of himself generally.

All trace of mirth passed from Strahan's expression, as he looked at the young girl's stern, flushed face and the angry sheen of her eyes.

"By Jove!" he exclaimed, "that's magnificent. I've seen a girl now to whom I can take off my hat, not as a mere form. Half the girls in our set would have given their eyes for the chance of capturing such a man. Think what a vista of new bonnets he suggests!"

"You are probably mistaken. One girl has proved how she regarded the vista, and I don't believe you had any better opinion of me than of the others. Come now, own up. Be honest. Didn't you regard me as one of the girls 'in our set' as you phrase it, that would jump at the chance?"

"Oh, nonsense, Miss Marian. The idea--"

She checked him by a gesture. "I wish downright sincerity, and I shall detect the least false note in your words."

Strahan looked into her resolute, earnest eyes a moment, and then revealed a new trait. He discarded the slight affectation that characterized his manner, stood erect, and returned her gaze steadily. "You ask for downright sincerity?" he said.

"Yes; I will take nothing less."

"You have no right to ask it unless you will be equally sincere with me."

"Oh, indeed; you are in a mood for bargains, as well as Mr. Lanniere."

"Not at all. You have stepped out of the role of the mere society girl. In that guise I shall be all deference and compliments. On the basis of downright sincerity I have my rights, and you have no right to compel me to give an honest opinion so personal in its nature without giving one in return."

"I agree," she said, after a moment's thought.

"Well, then, while I was by no means sure, I thought it was possible, even probable, that you would accept a man like Lanniere. I have known society girls to do such things, haven't you?"

"And I tell you, Mr. Strahan, that you misjudge a great many society girls."

"Oh, you must tell me a great deal more than that. Have I not just discovered that I misjudged one? Now pitch into Arthur Strahan."

"I am inclined to think that I have misjudged you, also; but I will keep my compact, and give you the impression you made, and you won't like it."

"I don't expect to; but I shall expect downright sincerity."

"Very well. I'll test you. You are not simple and manly, even in your dress and manner; you are an anomaly in the country; you are inclined to gossip; and it's my belief that a young man should do more in life than amuse himself."

Strahan flushed, but burst out laughing as he exclaimed, "My photograph, by Jupiter!"

"Photographs give mere surface. Come, what's beneath it?"

"In one respect, at least, I think I am on a par with yourself. I have enough honest good-nature to listen to the truth with thanks."

"Is that all?"

"Come, Miss Marian, what is the use of words when I have had such an example of deeds? I have caught you, red-handed, in the act of giving a millionnaire his conge. In the face of this stern fact do you suppose I am going to try to fish up some germs of manhood for your inspection? As you have suggested, I must do something, or I'm out of the race with you. I honestly believe, though, I am not such a fool as I have seemed. I shall always be something of a rattle-brain, I suppose, and if I were dying I could not help seeing the comical side of things." He hesitated a moment, and then asked, abruptly, "Miss Marian, have you read to-day's paper?"

"Yes, I have," with a tinge of sadness in her tone.

"Well, so have I. Think of thousands of fine young fellows lying stiff and stark in those accursed swamps!"

"Yes," she cried, with a rush of tears, "I WILL think of them. I will try to see them, horrible as the sight is, even in fancy. When they died so heroically, shame on me if I turn away in weak, dainty disgust! Oh, the burning shame that Northern girls don't think more of such men and their self-sacrifice!"

"You're a trump, Miss Marian; that's evident. Well, one little bit of gossip about myself, and then I must go. I have another engagement this evening. Old Lanniere was right. I'm young, and I've been very young. Of late I've made deliberate effort to remain a fool; but a man has got to be a fool or a coward down to the very hard-pan of his soul if the logic of recent events has no effect on him. I don't think I am exactly a coward, but the restraint of army-life, and especially roughing it, is very distasteful. I kept thinking it would all soon be over, that more men were in now than were needed, and that it was a confounded disagreeable business, and all that. But my mind wasn't at rest; I wasn't satisfied with the ambitions of my callow youth; and, as usual when one is in trouble and in doubt about a step, I exaggerated my old folly to disguise my feelings. But this Richmond campaign, and the way Stonewall Jackson has been whacking our fellows in the Shenandoah, made me feel that I was standing back too long, and the battle described in to-day's paper brought me to a decision. I'm in for it, Miss Marian. You may think I'm not worth the powder required to blow me up, but I'm going to Virginia as soon as I can learn enough not to be more dangerous to those around me than to the enemy."

She darted to his side, and took his hand, exclaiming, "Mr. Strahan! forgive me; I've done you a hundred-fold more injustice than you have me!"

He was visibly embarrassed, a thing unusual with him, and he said, brusquely: "Oh, come now, don't let us have any pro patria exaltation. I don't resemble a hero any more than I do a doctor of divinity. I'm just like lots of other young fellows who have gone, only I have been slower in going, and my ardor won't set the river on fire. But the times are waking up all who have any wake-up in them, and the exhibition of the latest English cut in coats and trousers is taking on a rather inglorious aspect. How ridiculous it all seems in the light of the last battle! Jove! but I HAVE been young!"

He did look young indeed, with his blond mustache and flushed face, that was almost as fair as a girl's. She regarded him wonderingly, thinking how strangely events were applying the touchstone to one and another. But the purpose of this boyish-appearing exquisite was the most unexpected thing in the era of change that had begun. She could scarcely believe it, and exclaimed, "You face a cannon?"

"I don't look like it, do I? I fancy I would. I should be too big a coward to run away, for then I should have to come back to face you, which would be worse, you know. I'm not going to do any bragging, however. Deeds, deeds. Not till I have laid out a Johnny, or he has laid me out, can I take rank with you after your rout of the man of millions. I don't ask you to believe in me yet."

"Well, I do believe in you. You are making an odd yet vivid impression on me. I believe you will face danger just as you did Mr. Lanniere, in a half-nonchalant and a half-satirical mood, while all the time there will be an undercurrent of downright earnestness and heroism in you, which you will hide as if you were ashamed of it."

He flushed with pleasure, but only laughed, "We'll see." Then after a moment he added, "Since we are down to the bed-rock in our talk I'll say out the rest of my say, then follow Lanniere, and give him something more to digest before he sleeps."

"Halt, sir--military jargon already--how can you continue your quarrel with Mr. Lanniere without involving my name?"

Strahan looked blank for a second, then exclaimed: "Another evidence, of extreme youth! Lanniere may go to thunder before I risk annoying you."

"Yes, thank you; please let him go to thunder. He won't talk of the affair, and so can do you no harm."

"Supposing he could, that would be no excuse for annoying you."

"I think you punished him sufficiently before he went, and without ceasing to be a gentleman, too. If you carry out your brave purpose you need not fear for your reputation."

"Well, Miss Marian, I shall carry it out. Society girl as I believed you to be, I like you better than the others. Don't imagine I'm going to be sentimental. I should stand as good a chance of winning a major-general's stars as you. I've seen better fellows raising the siege and disappearing, you know. Well, the story I thought would be short is becoming long. I wanted to tell you first what I proposed; for, hang it all! I've read it in your eyes that you thought I was little better than a popinjay, and I wished to prove to you that I could be a man after my fashion."

"I like your fashion, and am grateful for your confidence. What's more, you won't be able to deceive me a bit hereafter. I shall persist in admiring you as a brave man, and shall stand up for you through thick and thin."

"You always had a kind of loyalty to us fellows that we recognized and appreciated."

"I feel now as if I had not been very loyal to any one, not even myself. As with you, however, I must let the future tell a different story."

"If I make good my words, will you be my friend?"

"Yes, yes indeed, and a proud one. But oh!"--she clasped her hand over her eyes,--"what is all this tending to? When I think of the danger and suffering to which you may--"

"Oh, come now," he interrupted, laughing, but with a little suspicious moisture in eyes as blue as her own; "it will be harder for you to stay and think of absent friends than for them to go. I foresee how it will turn out. You will be imagining high tragedy on stormy nights when we shall be having a jolly game of poker. Good-night. I shall be absent for a time,--going to West Point to be coached a little by my friend Captain Varrum."

He drew himself up, saluted her a la militaire, right-about-faced with the stiffness of a ramrod, and was departing, when a light hand touched his arm, and Marian said, with a look so kind and sympathetic that his eyes fell before it: "Report to me occasionally, Captain Strahan. There are my colors;" and she gave him a white rose from her belt.

His mouth quivered slightly, but with a rather faltering laugh he replied, as he put the rose to his lips, "Never let the color suggest that I will show the white feather;" and then he began his military career with a precipitate retreat.

CHAPTER VIII.
CHARMED BY A CRITIC.

WHAT next?" was Marian's wondering query after Mr. Strahan's departure. The change of motive which already had had no slight influence on her own action and feeling had apparently ushered in a new era in her experience; but the sense of novelty in personal affairs was quite lost as she contemplated the transformation in the mercurial Strahan, who had apparently been an irredeemable fop. That the fastidious exquisite should tramp through Virginia mud, and face a battery of hostile cannon, appeared to her the most marvellous of human paradoxes. An hour before she would have declared the idea preposterous. Now she was certain he would do all that he had said, and would do it in the manner satirical and deprecatory towards himself which she had suggested.

Radical as the change seemed, she saw that it was a natural one as he had explained it. If there was any manhood in him the times would evoke it. After all, his chief faults had been youth and a nature keenly sensitive to certain social influences. Belonging to a wealthy and fashionable clique in the city, he had early been impressed by the estimated importance of dress and gossip. To excel in these, therefore, was to become pre-eminent. As time passed, however, the truth, never learned by some, that his clique was not the world, began to dawn on him. He was foolish, but not a fool; and when he saw young fellows no older than himself going to the front, when he read of their achievements and sufferings, he drew comparisons. The result was that he became more and more dissatisfied. He felt that he was anomalous, in respect not only to the rural scenery of his summer home, but to the times, and the conviction was growing that the only way to right himself was to follow the host of American youth who had gone southward. It was a conviction to which he could not readily yield, and which he sought to disguise by exaggerating his well-known characteristics. People of his temperament often shrink from revealing their deeper feelings, believing that these would seem to others so incongruous as to call forth incredulous smiles. Strahan was not a coward, except in the presence of ridicule. This had more terrors for him than all the guns of the Confederacy; and he knew that every one, from his own family down, would laugh at the thought of his going to the war. In a way that puzzled him a little he felt that he would not care so much if Marian Vosburgh did not laugh. The battle of which he had read to-day had at last decided him; he must go; but if Marian would give him credit for a brave, manly impulse, and not think of him as a ludicrous spectacle when he donned the uniform, he would march away with a light heart. He did not analyze her influence over him, but only knew that she had a peculiar fascination which it was not in his impressionable nature to resist.

Thus it may be seen that he only gave an example of the truth that great apparent changes are the result of causes that have long been secretly active.

Marian, like many others, did not sufficiently take this fact into account, and was on the qui vive for other remarkable manifestations. They did not occur. As her father had predicted, life, in its outward conditions, resumed its normal aspects. Her mother laughed a little, sighed a little, when she heard the story of Mr. Lanniere's final exit; the coquettish kitchen-maid continued her career with undisturbed complacency; and Marian to her own surprise found that, after the first days of her enthusiasm had passed, it required the exertion of no little will-power to refrain from her old motives and tactics. But she was loyal to herself and to her implied promise to her father. She knew that he was watching her,--that he had set his heart on the development, in a natural way, of her best traits. She also knew that if she faltered she must face his disappointment and her own contempt.

She had a horror, however, of putting on what she called "goody-goody airs," and under the influence of this feeling acted much like her old self. Not one of her callers could have charged her with manifesting a certain kind of misleading favor, but her little salon appeared as free from restraint as ever, and her manner as genial and lively. It began to be observed by some, however, that while she participated unhesitatingly in the light talk of others, she herself would occasionally broach topics of more weight, especially such as related to the progress of the war; and more than once she gave such direction to her conversation with the artist as made his eyes kindle.

Her father was satisfied. He usually came home late on Saturday, and some of her gentleman friends who were in the habit of dropping in of a Sunday evening, were soon taught that these hours were engaged.

"You need not excuse yourself on my account," her father had said to her.

"But I shall," was her prompt response. "After all you have done and are doing for me, it's a pity if I can't give you one evening in the week. You are looking after other people in New York; I'm going to look after you; and you shall find that I am a sharp inquisitor. You must reveal enough of the secrets of that mysterious office of yours to satisfy me that you are not in danger."

He soon began to look forward with glad anticipation to his ramble by her side in the summer twilight. He saw that what he had done and what he had thought during the week interested her deeply, and to a girl of her intelligence he had plenty to tell that was far from commonplace. She saw the great drama of her country's history unfolding, and not only witnessed the events that were presented to the world, but was taken behind the scenes and shown many of the strange and secret causes that were producing them. Moreover expectation of something larger and greater was constantly raised. After their walk they would return to the house, and she would sing or read to him until she saw his eyes heavy with the sleep that steals gradually and refreshingly into a weary man's brain.

Mrs. Vosburgh observed this new companionship with but little surprise and no jealousy. "It was time," she said, "that Marian should begin to do something for her father, and not leave everything to me."

One thing puzzled Marian: weeks were passing and she neither saw nor heard anything of Lane or Strahan. This fact, in view of what had been said at parting, troubled her. She was not on calling terms with the latter's family, and therefore was unable to learn anything from them. Even his male friends in the neighborhood did not know where he was or what he was doing. Her father had taken the pains to inform himself that Lane was apparently at work in his law-office as usual. These two incipient subjects of the power she hoped to wield seemed to have dropped her utterly, and she was discouraged.

On the last day of June she was taking a ramble in a somewhat wild and secluded place not far from her home, and thinking rather disconsolately that her father had overrated her influence,--that after all she was but a pretty and ordinary girl, like millions of others,--a fact that Lane and Strahan had at last discovered. Suddenly she came upon the artist, sketching at a short distance from her. As she turned to retreat a twig snapped under her foot, revealing her presence. He immediately arose and exclaimed, "Miss Vosburgh, is it I that you fear, or a glimpse of my picture?"

"Neither, of course. I feared I might dispel an inspired mood. Why should I intrude, when you have nature before you and the muse looking over your shoulder?"

"Over my left shoulder, then, with a mocking smile. You are mistaken if you fancy you can harm any of my moods. Won't you stay and criticise my picture for me?"

"Why, Mr. Blauvelt, I'm not an art critic."

"Yes, you are,--one of the class I paint for. Our best critics are our patrons, cultivated people."

"I should never think of patronizing you."

"Perhaps you might entertain the thought of encouraging me a little, if you felt that I was worth it."

"Now, Mr. Blauvelt, notwithstanding the rural surroundings, you must remember that I was bred in the city. I know the sovereign contempt that you artists have for the opinions of the people. When it comes to art, I'm only people."

"No such generalization will answer in your case. You have as distinct an individuality as any flower blooming on this hillside."

"There are flowers and flowers. Some are quite common."

"None are commonplace to me, for there is a genuine bit of nature in every one. Still you are right: I was conscious of the fragrance from this eglantine-bush here, until you came."

"Oh, then let me go at once."

"I beg that you will not. You are the eglantine in human form, and often quite as briery."

"Then you should prefer the bush there, which gives you its beauty and fragrance without a scratch. But truly your comparison is too far-fetched, even for an artist or a poet, for I suppose they are near of kin. To sensible, matter-of-fact girls, nothing is more absurd than your idealization of us. See how quickly and honestly I can disenchant you. In the presence of both nature and art I am conscious that it is nearly lunch-time. You are far from your boarding-place, so come and take your luck with us. Mamma will be glad to see you, and after lunch I may be a more amiable critic."

"As a critic, I do not wish you to be amiable, but honest severity itself. That you stumbled upon me accidentally in your present mood is my good fortune. Tell me the faults in my picture in the plainest English, and I will gratefully accept your invitation; for the hospitality at your cottage is so genial that bread and cheese would be a banquet. I have a strong fancy for seeing my work through your eyes, and so much faith in you that I know you will tell me what you think, since I ask you to do so."

"Why have you faith in me?" she asked, with a quick, searching glance.

"I belong somewhat to the impressionist school, and my impression of you leads to my words."

"If you compel me to be honest, I must say I'm not capable of criticising your picture. I know little of art, and nothing of its TECHNIQUE."

"Eyes like yours should be able to see a great deal, and, as I said, I am possessed by the wish to know just what they do see. There is the scene I was sketching, and here the canvas. Please, Miss Marian."

"It will be your own fault, now, if you don't like what I say," laughed the young girl, with ready tact, for a quick glance or two had already satisfied her that the picture was not to her taste. "My only remark is this, Mr. Blauvelt,--Nature does not make the same impression on me that it does on you. There is the scene, as you say. How can I make you understand what I feel? Nature always looks so natural to me! It awakens within me various emotions, but never surprise,--I mean that kind of surprise one has when seeing a lady dressed in colors that do not harmonize. To my eye, even in gaudy October, Nature appears to blend her effects so that there is nothing startling or incongruous."

"Is there anything startling and incongruous in my picture?"

"I have not said that. You see you have brought me into perplexity, you have taken me beyond my depth, by insisting on having my opinion. I have read a good many art criticisms first and last. Art is gabbled about a good deal in society, you know, and we have to keep a set of phrases on hand, whether we understand them or not. But since you believe in impressions, and will have mine, it is this as nearly as I can express it. You are under the influence of a school or a fashion in art, and perhaps unconsciously you are controlled by this when looking at the scene there. It seems to me that if I were an artist I should try to get on my canvas the same effects that nature produces, and I would do it after my own fashion and not after some received method just then prevailing. Let me illustrate what I mean by a phase of life that I know more about. There are some girls in society whose ambition it is to dress in the latest style. They are so devoted to fashion that they appear to forget themselves, and are happy if their costume reflects the mode of the hour, even though it makes them look hideous. My aim would be to suggest the style rather unobtrusively, and clothe myself becomingly. I'm too egotistical to be ultra-fashionable. Since I, who am in love chiefly with myself, can so modify style, much more should you, who are devoted to nature, make fashion in art subservient to nature."

"You are right. I have worked too much in studios and not enough out of doors. Ever since I have been sketching this summer, I have had a growing dissatisfaction, and a sense of being trammelled. I do believe, as you say, that a certain received method or fashion of treatment has been uppermost in my mind, and I have been trying to torture--nature into conformity. I'll paint this thing all out and begin again."

"No, don't do that. Are not pictures like people a little? If I wanted to improve in some things, it wouldn't do for me to be painted all out. Cannot changes for the better come by softening features here and bringing out others there, by colorings a little more like those before us, and--pardon me--by not leaving so much to the imagination? You artists can see more between the lines than we people can."

"Let me try;" and with eager eyes he sat down before his easel again. "Now see if I succeed a little," he added, after a moment.

His whole nature appeared kindled and animated by hope. He worked rapidly and boldly. His drawing had been good before, and, as time passed, nature's sweet, true face began to smile upon him from his canvas. Marian grew almost as absorbed as himself, learning by actual vision how quick, light strokes can reproduce and preserve on a few square inches the transitory beauty of the hour and the season.

At times she would stimulate his effort by half-spoken sentences of satisfaction, and at last he turned and looked up suddenly at her flushed, interested face.

"You are the muse," he exclaimed, impetuously, "who, by looking over my shoulder, can make an artist of me."

She instinctively stepped farther away, saying, decisively, "Be careful then to regard me as a muse."

She had replied to his ardent glance and tone, even more than to his words. There was not a trace of sentiment in her clear, direct gaze. The quiet dignity and reserve of her manner sobered him instantly. Her presence, her words, the unexpected success in the new departure which she had suggested, had excited him deeply; yet a moment's thought made it clear that there had been nothing on her part to warrant the hope of more than friendly interest. This interest might easily be lost by a few rash words, while there was slight reason that he should ever hope for anything more. Then also came the consciousness of his straitened circumstances and the absurdity of incurring obligations which he might never be able to meet. He had assured himself a thousand times that art should be his mistress, yet here he was on the eve of acting like a fool by making love to one who never disguised her expensive tastes. He was not an artist of the olden school,--all romance and passion,--and the modishly dressed, reserved maiden before him did not, in the remotest degree, suggest a languishing heroine in days of yore, certain to love against sense and reason. The wild, sylvan shade, the June atmosphere, the fragrance of the eglantine, even the presence of art, in whose potent traditions mood is the highest law, could not dispel the nineteenth century or make this independent, clear-headed American girl forget for a moment what was sensible and right. She stood there alone under the shadow of the chestnuts, and by a glance defined her rights, her position towards her companion, and made him respect them. Nor was he headlong, passionate, absurd. He was a part of his age, and was familiar with New York society. The primal instincts of his nature had obtained ascendency for a mordent. Ardent words to the beautiful girl who looked over his shoulder and inspired his touch seemed as natural as breath. She had made herself for the moment a part of his enthusiasm. But what could be the sequel of ardent words, even if successful, but prosaic explanations and the facing of the inexorable problem of supporting two on an income that scarcely sufficed for the Bohemian life of one?

He had sufficient self-control, and was mentally agile enough to come down upon his feet. Rising, he said, quietly: "If you will be my muse, as far as many other claims upon your time and thoughts permit, I shall be very grateful. I have observed that you have a good eye for harmony in color, and, what is best of all, I have induced you to be very frank. See how much you have helped me. In brief--Bless me! how long have you been here?"

He pulled out his watch in comic dismay, and held it towards her. "No lunch for us to-day," he concluded, ruefully.

"Well," exclaimed Marian, laughing, "this is the first symptom I have ever had of being an artist. It was quite natural that you should forget the needs of sublunary mortals, but that I should do so must prove the existence of an undeveloped trait. I could become quite absorbed in art if I could look on and see its wonders like a child. You must come home with me and take your chance. If lunch is over, we'll forage."

He laughingly shouldered his apparatus, and walked by her side through the June sunshine and shade, she in the main keeping up the conversation. At last he said, rather abruptly: "Miss Vosburgh, you do not look on like a child,--rather, with more intelligence than very many society girls possess; and--will you forgive me?--you defend yourself like a genuine American woman. I have lived abroad, you know, and have learned how to value such women. I wish you to know how much I respect you, how truly I appreciate you, and how grateful and honored I shall feel if you will be simply a frank, kind friend. You made use of the expression 'How shall I make you understand?' So I now use it, and suggest what I mean by a question,--Is there not something in a man's nature which enables him to do better if some woman, in whom he believes, shows that she cares?"

"I should be glad if this were true of some men," she said, gently, "because I do care. I'll be frank, too. Nothing would give me a more delicious sense of power than to feel that in ways I scarcely understood I was inciting my friends to make more of themselves than they would if they did not know me. If I cannot do a little of what you suggest, of what account am I to my friends?"

"Your friends can serve a useful purpose by amusing you."

"Then the reverse is true, and I am merely amusing to my friends. Is that the gist of your fine words, after all?" and her face flushed as she asked the question.

"No, it is not true, Miss Vosburgh. You have the power of entertaining your friends abundantly, but you could make me a better artist, and that with me would mean a better man, if you took a genuine interest in my efforts."

"I shall test the truth of your words," was her smiling response. "Meanwhile you can teach me to understand art better, so that I shall know what I am talking about." Then she changed the subject.

CHAPTER IX.
A GIRL'S LIGHT HAND.

ON the evening of the 3d of July Marian drove down in her phaeton to the station for her father, and was not a little surprised to see him advancing towards her with Mr. Lane. The young man shook hands with her cordially, yet quietly, and there was something in his expression that assured her of the groundlessness of all the fears she had entertained.

"I have asked Mr. Lane to dine with us," said her father. "He will walk over from the hotel in the course of half an hour."

While the gentlemen had greeted her smilingly, there had been an expression on their faces which suggested that their minds were not engrossed by anticipation of a holiday outing. Marian knew well what it meant. The papers had brought to every home in the land the tidings of the awful seven days' fighting before Richmond. So far from taking the city, McClellan had barely saved his army. Thousands of men were dead in the swamps of the Chickahominy; thousands were dying in the sultry heat of the South and on the malarial banks of the James.

Mr. Vosburgh's face was sad and stern in its expression, and when Marian asked, "Papa, is it so bad as the papers say?" he replied: "God only knows how bad it is. For a large part of our army it is as bad as it can be. The most terrible feature of it all to me is that thick-headed, blundering men are holding in their irresolute hands the destinies of just such brave young fellows as Mr. Lane here. It is not so dreadful for a man to die if his death furthers a cause which he believes to be sacred, but to die from the sheer stupidity and weakness of his leaders is a bitter thing. Instead of brave action, there is fatal blundering all along the line. For a long time the President, sincere and true-hearted as he is, could not learn that he is not a military man, and he has permitted a large part of our armies to be scattered all over Virginia. They have accomplished next to nothing. McClellan long since proved that he would not advance without men enough to walk over everything. He is as heavy as one of his own siege guns. He may be sure, if he has all he wants, but is mortally slow, and hadn't brains enough to realize that the Chickahominy swamps thinned his army faster than brave fighting. He should have been given the idle, useless men under McDowell and others, and then ordered to take Richmond. If he wouldn't move, then they should have put a man in his place who would, and not one who would sit down and dig. At last he has received an impetus from Richmond, instead of Washington, and he has moved at a lively pace, but to the rear. His men were as brave as men could be; and if the courage shown on the retreat, or change of base, as some call it, had been manifested in an advance, weeks ago, Richmond would have been ours. The 'change of base' has carried us well away from the point attacked, brave men have suffered and died in vain, and the future is so clouded that only one thing is certain."

"What is that, papa?" was the anxious query.

"We must never give up. We must realize that we are confronting some of the best soldiers and generals the world has known. The North is only half awake to its danger and the magnitude of its task. We have sent out comparatively few of our men to do a disagreeable duty for us, while we take life comfortably and luxuriously as before. The truth will come home to us soon, that we are engaged in a life-and-death struggle."

"Papa, these events will bring no changes to you? In your work, I mean?"

"Not at present. I truly believe, Marian, that I can serve my country more effectively in the performance of the duties with which I am now charged. But who can tell what a day will bring forth? Lane is going to the front. He will tell you all about it. He is a manly fellow, and no doubt will explain why you have not heard from him."

"Real life has come in very truth," thought Marian, as she went to her room to prepare for dinner; "but on every side it also brings the thought of death."

Her face was pale, and clouded with apprehension, when she joined the gentlemen; but Lane was so genial and entertaining at dinner as to make it difficult for her to believe that he had resolved on a step so fraught with risk. When at last they were alone in the drawing-room she said, "Is it true that you intend to enter the army?"

"Yes, and it is time that it was true," was his smiling reply.

"I don't feel like laughing, Mr. Lane. Going to Virginia does not strike me as a pleasure excursion. I have thought a great deal since I saw you last. You certainly have kept your promise to be a distant and absent friend."

He looked at her eagerly, as he said, "You have thought a great deal--have you thought about me?"

"Certainly," she replied, with a slight flush; "I meant all that I said that evening."

That little emphasized word dispelled the hope that had for a moment asserted itself. Time and a better acquaintance with her own heart had not brought any change of feeling to her, and after a moment he said, quietly: "I think I can prove that I have been a sincere and loyal friend as well as an absent one. Having never felt--well, you cannot know--it takes a little time for a fellow to--pardon me; let all that go. I have tried to gain self-control, and I have obeyed your request, to do nothing rash, literally. I remained steadily at work in my office a certain number of hours every day. If the general hope that Richmond would be taken, and the war practically ended, had proved well founded, for the sake of others I should have resisted my inclination to take part in the struggle. I soon concluded, however, that it would be just as well to prepare for what has taken place, and so gave part of my afternoons and evenings to a little useful training. I am naturally very fond of a horse, and resolved that if I went at all it should be as a cavalry-man, so I have been giving not a little of my time to horseback exercise, sabre, pistol, and carbine practice, and shall not be quite so awkward as some of the other raw recruits. I construed McClellan's retreat into an order for me to advance, and have come to you as soon as I could to report progress."

"Why could you not have come before?--why could you not have told me?" she asked, a little reproachfully.

"Some day perhaps you will know," he replied, turning away for a moment.

"I feared that maturer thought had convinced you that I could not be much of a friend,--that I was only a gay young girl who wouldn't appreciate an earnest man's purposes."

"Miss Marian, you wrong me in thinking that I could so wrong you. Never for a moment have I entertained such a thought. I can't explain to you all my experience. I wished to be more sure of myself, to have something definite to tell you, that would prove me more worthy of your friendship."

"My faith in you has never faltered a moment, Mr. Lane. While your words make me proud indeed, they also make me very sad. I don't wonder that you feel as you do about going, and were I a man I should probably take the same course. But I am learning at last what this war means. I can't with a light heart see my friends go."

"Let it be with a brave heart, then. There are tears in your eyes, Miss Marian."

"Why should there not be? O Mr. Lane, I am not coldhearted and callous. I am not so silly and shallow as I seemed."

"I never thought you so--"

By a gesture she stopped him, as she continued: "I recognized the expression on papa's face and yours the moment I saw you, and I know what it means."

"Yes, Miss Marian; and I recognize the expression on your face. Were you a man you would have gone before this."

"I think it would be easier to go than to stay and think of all one's friends must face."

"Of course it would be for one like you. You must not look on the dark side, however. You will scarcely find a jollier set of men than our soldiers."

"I fear too many are reckless. This you have promised me not to be."

"I shall keep my promise; but a soldier must obey orders, you know. O Miss Marian, it makes such a difference with me to know that you care so much! Knowing you as I do now, it would seem like black treason to do or be anything unmanly."

Callers were now announced, and before an hour had passed there were half a dozen or more young men in the drawing-room. Some were staying at the hotel, but the majority were from the villas in the neighborhood, the holiday season permitting the return of those in business. However dark and crimson might be the tide of thought that flowed through the minds of those present, in memory of what had occurred during the last few days, the light of mirth played on the surface. The times afforded themes for jest, rather than doleful predictions. Indeed, in accordance with a principle in human nature, there was a tendency to disguise feelings and anxiety by words so light as to border on recklessness. Questions as to future action were coming home to all the young men, but not for the world would they permit one another, or especially a spirited young girl, to suspect that they were awed, or made more serious even, by the thought that the battle was drawing nearer to them. Lane was a leader in the gayety. His presence was regarded by some with both surprise and surmise. It had been thought that he had disappeared finally below Miss Vosburgh's horizon, but his animated face and manner gave no indication of a rejected and despondent suitor.

The mirth was at its height when Strahan entered, dressed plainly in the uniform of a second lieutenant. He was greeted with a shout of laughter by the young men, who knew him well, and by a cordial pressure from Marian's hand. This made the gauntlet which he knew he must run of little consequence to him. All except Lane drew up and gave him a military salute.

"Pretty fair for the awkward squad," he remarked, coolly.

"Come, report, report," cried several voices; "where have you been?"

"In Virginia."

"Why, of course, fellows, he's been arranging the change of base with McClellan, only the army went south and he came north."

"I've been farther south than any of you."

"See here, Strahan, this uniform is rather new for a veteran's."

"Yes; never dealt in old clothes."

"Where's your command?"

"Here, if you'll all enlist. I think I could make soldiers of some of you."

"Why, fellows, what a chance for us! If Strahan can't teach us the etiquette of war, who can?"

"Yes, gentlemen; and I will give you the first rule in advance. Always face the music."

"Dance music, you mean. Strahan has been at West Point and knows that a fellow in civilian togs stands no chance. How he eclipses us all to-night with the insignia of rank on his shoulders! Where will you make headquarters?"

"At home, for the present."

"That's right. We knew you would hit upon the true theory of campaigning. Never was there a better strategic point for your operations, Strahan, than the banks of the Hudson."

"I shall try to prove you right. A recruiting sergeant will join me in a day or two, and then I can accommodate you all with muskets."

"All? Not Miss Marian?"

"Those possessing her rank and influence do not carry muskets."

"Come, fellows, let us celebrate the 4th by enlisting under Strahan," cried the chief spokesman, who was not a very friendly neighbor of the young officer. "It won't be long before we shall know all the gossip of the Confederacy."

"You will certainly have to approach near enough to receive some very direct news."

"Gentlemen," cried Marian, "a truce! Mr. Strahan has proved that he can face a hot fire, and send back good shots, even when greatly outnumbered. I have such faith in him that I have already given him my colors. You may take my word for it that he will render a good account of himself. I am now eager to hear of his adventures."

"I haven't had any, Miss Marian. What I said about Virginia was mere bluff,-- merely made an excursion or two on the Virginia side of the Potomac, out of curiosity."

"But what does this uniform mean?"

"Merely what it suggests. I went to Washington, which is a great camp, you know. Through relatives I had some influence there, and at last obtained a commission at the bottom of the ladder in a new regiment that is to be recruited. Meanwhile I was put through the manual of arms, with a lot of other awkward fellows, by a drill officer. I kept shady and told my people to be mum until something came out of it all. Come, fellows, thirteen dollars a month, hard tack, and glory! Don't all speak at once!"

"I'm with you as far as going is concerned," said Lane, shaking Strahan's hand warmly, "only I've decided on the cavalry."

"Were I a man, you should have one recruit for your regiment to-night," said Marian. "You have gone to work in a way that inspires confidence."

"I foresee, fellows, that we shall all have to go, or else Miss Marian will cross us out of her books," remarked one of the young men.

"No, indeed," she replied. "I would not dare urge any one to go. But those who, like Mr. Lane and Mr. Strahan, decide the question for themselves, cannot fail to carry my admiration with them."

"That's the loudest bugle call I expect to hear," remarked Mr. Blauvelt, who entered at that moment.

"Here's the place to open your recruiting-office," added another, laughing. "If Miss Marian would be free with her colors, she could raise a brigade."

"I can assure you beforehand that I shall not be free with them; much less will I hold them out as an inducement. Slight as may be their value, they must be earned."

"What chivalrous deed has Strahan performed?" was asked, in chorus.

"One that I appreciate, and I don't give my faith lightly,"

"Mr. Strahan, I congratulate you," said Lane, with a swift and somewhat reproachful glance at Marian; "you have already achieved your best laurels."

"I've received them, but not earned them yet. Miss Marian gives a fellow a good send-off, however, and time will tell the story with us all. I must now bid you good-evening," he said to the young girl. "I merely stopped for a few moments on my way from the train."

She followed him to the door, and said, sotto voce: "You held your own splendidly. Your first report is more than satisfactory;" and he departed happier than any major-general in the service.

When the rest had gone, Lane, who had persistently lingered, began: "No doubt it will appear absurd to you that a friend should be jealous. But Strahan seems to have won the chief honors."

"Perhaps he has deserved them, Mr. Lane. I know what your opinion of him was, and I think you guessed mine. He has won the chief battle of life,--victory over himself. Ever since I have known you, you have inspired my respect as a strong, resolute man. In resolving upon what you would do instinctively Mr. Strahan has had such a struggle that he has touched my sympathies. One cannot help feeling differently toward different friends, you know. Were I in trouble, I should feel that I could lean upon you. To encourage and sustain would always be my first impulse with Mr. Strahan. Are you content?"

"I should try to be, had I your colors also."

"Oh, I only gave him a rose. Do you want one?"

"Certainly."

"Well, now you are even," she said, laughing, and handing him one of those she wore.

He looked at it thoughtfully for a moment, and then said, quietly: "Some would despise this kind of thing as the merest sentiment. With others it would influence the sternest action and the supreme moments of life."

CHAPTER X.
WILLARD MERWYN.

URING her drives Marian had often passed the entrance to one of the finest old places in the vicinity, and, although aware that the family was absent in Europe, she had observed that the fact made no difference in the scrupulous care of that portion of the grounds which was visible. The vista from the road, however, was soon lost among the boles and branches of immense overshadowing oaks. Even to the passer-by an impression of seclusion and exclusion was given, and Marian at last noted that no reference was made to the family in the social exchanges of her little drawing-room. The dwelling to which the rather stiff and stately entrance led was not visible from the car-windows as she passed to and from the city, so abrupt was the intervening bluff, but upon one occasion from the deck of a steamboat she had caught glimpses through the trees of a large and substantial brick edifice.

Before Strahan had disappeared for a time, as we have related, her slight curiosity had so far asserted itself that she had asked for information concerning the people who left their beautiful home untenanted in June.

"I fancy I can tell you more about them than most people in this vicinity, but that is not so very much. The place adjoins ours, and as a boy I fished and hunted with Willard Merwyn a good deal. Mrs. Merwyn is a widow and a Southern-bred woman. A Northern man of large wealth married her, and then she took her revenge on the rest of the North by having as little to do with it as possible. She was said to own a large property in the South,--plantation, negroes, and all that. The place on the Hudson belonged to the Merwyn side of the house, and the family have only spent a few summers here and have been exclusive and unpopular. My mother made their acquaintance abroad, and they knew it would be absurd to put on airs with us; so the ladies of the two families have exchanged more or less formal visits, but in the main they have little to do with the society of this region. As boys Willard and myself did not care a fig for these things, and became very good friends. I have not seen him for several years; they have all been abroad; and I hear that he has become an awful swell."

"Why then, if he ever returns, you and he will be good friends again," Marian had laughingly replied and had at once dismissed the exclusive Merwyns from her mind.

On the morning of the 4th of July Strahan had come over to have a quiet talk with Marian, and had found Mr. Lane there before him. By feminine tactics peculiarly her own, Marian had given them to understand that both were on much the same footing, and that their united presence did not form "a crowd;" and the young men, having a common ground of purpose and motive, were soon at ease together, and talked over personal and military matters with entire freedom, amusing the young girl with accounts of their awkwardness in drill and of the scenes they had witnessed. She was proud indeed of her two knights, as she mentally character-ized them,--so different, yet both now inspiring a genuine liking and respect. She saw that her honest goodwill and admiration were evoking their best manhood and giving them as much happiness as she would ever have the power to bestow, and she felt that her scheme of life was not a false one. They understood her fully, and knew that the time had passed forever when she would amuse herself at their expense. She had become an inspiration of manly endeavor, and had ceased to be the object of a lover's pursuit. If half-recognized hopes lurked in their hearts, the fulfilment of these must be left to time.

"By the way," remarked Strahan, as he was taking his leave, "I hear that these long-absent Merwyns have deigned to return to their native land,--for their own rather than their country's good though, I fancy. I suppose Mrs. Merwyn feels that it is time she looked after her property and maintained at least the semblance of loyalty. I also hear that they have been hob-nobbing with the English aristocracy, who look upon us Yankees as a 'blasted lot of cads, you know.' Shall I bring young Merwyn over to see you after he arrives?"

"As you please," she replied, with an indifferent shrug.

Strahan had a half-formed scheme in his mind, but when he called upon young

Merwyn he was at first inclined to hesitate. Great as was his confidence in Marian, he had some vaguely jealous fears, more for the young girl than for himself, in subjecting her to the influence of the man that his boyhood's friend had become.

Willard Merwyn was a "swell" in Strahan's vernacular, but even in the early part of their interview he gave the impression of being something more, or rather such a superior type of the "swell" genus, that Marian's friend was conscious of a fear that the young girl might be dazzled and interested, perhaps to her sorrow.

Merwyn had developed into a broad-shouldered man, nearly six feet in height. His quiet, courteous elegance did not disguise from one who had known him so well in boyhood an imperious, self-pleasing nature, and a tenacity of purpose in carrying out his own desires. He accepted of his quondam friend's uniform without remark. That was Strahan's affair and not his, and by a polite reserve, he made the mercurial fellow feel that his affairs were his own. Strahan chafed under this polished reticence, this absence of all curiosity.

"Blast him!" thought the young officer, "he acts like a superior being, who has deigned to visit America to look after his rents, and intimates that the country has no further concern with him or he with it. Jove! I'd give all the pay I ever expect to get to see him a rejected suitor of my plucky little American girl;" and he regarded his host with an ill-disposed eye. At last he resolved to take the initiative boldly.

"How long do you expect to remain here, Merwyn?"

"I scarcely know. It depends somewhat on my mother's plans."

"Thunder! It's time you had plans of your own, especially when a man has your length of limb and breadth of chest."

"I have not denied the possession of plans," Merwyn quietly remarked, his dark eye following the curling, upward flight of smoke from his cigar.

"You certainly used to be decided enough sometimes, when I wanted you to pull an oar."

"And you so good-naturedly let me off," was the reply, with a slight laugh.

"I didn't let you off good-naturedly, nor do I intend to now. Good heavens, Merwyn! don't you read the papers? There's a chance now to take an oar to some purpose. You were brave enough as a boy."

Merwyn's eyes came down from the curling smoke to Strahan's face with a flash, and he rose and paced the room for a moment, then said, in his old quiet tones, "They say the child is father of the man."

"Oh well, Merwyn," was the slightly irritable rejoinder, "I have and ever had, you remember, a way of expressing my thoughts. If, while abroad, you have become intolerant of that trait, why, the sooner we understand each other the better. I don't profess to be anything more than an American, and I called to-day with no other motive than the obvious and natural one."

A shade of annoyance passed over Merwyn's face, but as Strahan ceased he came forward and held out his hand, saying: "I like you all the better for speaking your thoughts,--for doing just as you please. You must be equally fair and yield to me the privilege of keeping my thoughts, and doing as I please."

Strahan felt that there was nothing to do but to take the proffered hand, so irresistible was the constraint of his host's courtesy, although felt to be without warmth or cordiality. Disguising his inward protest by a light laugh he said: "I could shake hands with almost any one on such a mutual understanding. Well, since we have begun on the basis of such absolute frankness on my part, my next thought is, What shall be our relations while you are here? I am a busier fellow than I was at one time, and my stay is also uncertain, and sure to be brief. I do not wish to be unneighborly in remembrance of old times, nor do I wish to be obtrusive. In the natural order of things, I should show you, a comparative stranger, some attention, inform you about the natives and transient residents, help you amuse yourself, and all that. But I have not the slightest desire to make unwelcome advances. I have plenty of such in prospect south of Mason and Dixon's line."

Merwyn laughed with some heartiness as he said: "You have attained one attribute of a soldier assuredly,--bluntness. Positively, Strahan, you have developed amazingly. Why, only the other day we were boys squabbling to determine who should have the first shot at an owl we saw in the mountains. The result was, the owl took flight. You never gave in an inch to me then, and I liked you all the better for it. Come now, be reasonable. I yield to you your full right to be yourself; yield as much to me and let us begin where we left off, with only the differences that years have made, and we shall get on as well as ever."

"Agreed," said Strahan, promptly. "Now what can I do for you? I have only certain hours at my disposal."

"Well," replied Merwyn, languidly, "come and see me when you can, and I'll walk over to your quarters--I suppose I should so call them--and have a smoke with you occasionally. I expect to be awfully dull here, but between the river and the mountains I shall have resources."

"You propose to ignore society then?"

"Why say 'ignore'? That implies a conscious act. Let us suppose that society is as indifferent to me as I to it."

"There's a little stutterer down at the hotel who claims to be an English lord."

"Bah, Strahan! I hope your sword is sharper than your satire. I've had enough of English lords for the present."

"Yes, Merwyn, you appear to have had enough of most things,--perhaps too much. If your countrymen are uninteresting, you may possibly wish to meet some of your countrywomen. I've been abroad enough to know that you have never found their superiors."

"Well, that depends upon who my countrywoman is. I should prefer to see her before I intrude--"

"Risk being bored, you mean."

"As you please. Fie, Strahan! you are not cultivating a soldier's penchant for women?"

"It hasn't needed any cultivating. I have my opinion of a man who does not admire a fine woman."

"So have I, only each and all must define the adjective for themselves."

"It has been defined for me. Well, my time is up. We'll be two friendly neutral powers, and, having marked out our positions, can maintain our frontiers with diplomatic ease. Good-morning."

Merwyn laughingly accompanied his guest to the door, but on the piazza, they met Mrs. Merwyn, who involuntarily frowned as she saw Strahan's uniform, then with quiet elegance she greeted the young man. But he had seen her expression, and was somewhat formal.

"We shall hope to see your mother and sisters before long," the lady remarked.

Strahan bowed, and walked with military erectness down the avenue, his host looking after him with cynical and slightly contemptuous good-nature; but Mrs. Merwyn followed the receding figure with an expression of great bitterness.

Her appearance was that of a remarkable woman. She was tall, and slight; every motion was marked by grace, but it was the grace of a person accustomed to command. One would never dream of woman's ministry when looking at her. Far more than would ever be true of Marian she suggested power, but she would govern through her will, her pride and prejudices. The impress of early influences had sunk deep into her character. The only child of a doting father, she had ruled him, and, of course, the helpless slaves who had watched her moods and trembled at her passion. There were scars on human backs to-day, which were the results of orders from her girlish lips. She was not greatly to blame. Born of a proud and imperious ancestry, she had needed the lessons of self-restraint and gentleness from infancy. Instead, she had been absolute, even in the nursery; and as her horizon had widened it had revealed greater numbers to whom her will was law. From childhood she had passed into maidenhood with a dower of wealth and beauty, learning early, like Marian, that many of her own race were willing to become her slaves.

In the South there is a chivalric deference to women far exceeding that usually paid to the sex at the North, and her appearance, temperament, and position evoked that element to the utmost. He knows little of human nature who cannot guess the result. Yet, by a common contradiction, the one among her many suitors who won such love as she could give was a Northern man as proud as herself. He stood alone in his manner of approach, made himself the object of her thoughts by piquing her pride, and met her varying moods by a quiet, unvarying dignity that compelled her respect. The result was that she yielded to the first man who would not yield undue deference to her.

Mr. Merwyn employed his power charily, however, or rather with principle. He quietly insisted on his rights; but as he granted hers without a word, and never irritated her by small, fussy exactions, good-breeding prevented any serious clashing of wills, and their married life had passed in comparative serenity. As time elapsed her will began, in many ways, to defer to his quieter and stronger will, and then, as if life must teach her that there is no true control except self-control, Mr. Merwyn died, and left her mistress of almost everything except herself.

It must not be supposed, however, that her self-will was a passionate, moody absolutism. She had outgrown that, and was too well-bred ever to show much temper. The tendency of her mature purposes and prejudices was to crystallize into a

few distinct forms. With the feminine logic of a narrow mind, she made her husband an exception to the people among whom he had been born and bred. Wid-
owed, she gave her whole heart to the South. Its institutions, habits, and social code
were sacred, and all opponents thereof sacrilegious enemies. To that degree that
they were hostile, or even unbelieving, she hated them.

During the years immediately preceding the war she had been abroad superin-
tending the education of Willard and two younger daughters, and when hostilities
began she was led to believe that she could serve the cause better in England than
on her remote plantation. In her fierce partisanship, or rather perverted patriotism,-
-for in justice it must be said that she knew no other country than the South,--she
was willing to send her son to Richmond. He thwarted this purpose by quietly
manifesting one of his father's traits.

"No," he said, "I will not fight against the section to which my father belonged.
To my mind it's a wretched political squabble at best, and the politicians will settle
it before long. I have my life before me, and don't propose to be knocked on the
head for the sake of a lot of political John Smiths, North or South."

In vain she tried to fire his heart with dreams of Southern empire. He had made
up that part of himself derived from Northern birth--his mind--and would not yield.
Meantime his Southern, indolent, pleasure-loving side was appealed to powerfully
by aristocratic life abroad, and he felt it would be the sheerest folly to abandon his
favorite pursuits. He was little more then than a graceful animal, shrewd enough
to know that his property was chiefly at the North, and that it would be unwise to
endanger it.

Mrs. Merwyn's self-interest and natural affection led her to yield to necessity
with fairly good grace. The course resolved upon by Willard preserved her son and
the property. When the South had accomplished its ambitious dreams she believed
she would have skill enough to place him high among its magnates, while, if he
were killed in one of the intervening battles,--well, she was loyal enough to incur
the risk, but at heart she did not deeply regret that she had escaped the probable
sacrifice.

Thus time passed on, and she used her social influence in behalf of her section,
but guardedly, lest she should jeopardize the interests of her children. In May of
the year in which our story opened, the twenty-first birthday of Willard occurred,

and was celebrated with befitting circumstance. He took all this quietly, but on the morning of the day following he said to his mother:--

"You remember the provisions of my father's will. My share of the property was to be transferred to me when I should become of age. We ought to return to New York at once and have the necessary papers made out."

In vain she protested that the property was well managed, that the income was received regularly, that he could have this, and that it would be intensely disagreeable for her to visit New York. He, who had yielded indifferently to all her little exactions, was inexorable, and the proud, self-willed woman found that he had so much law and reason on his side that she was compelled to submit.

Indeed, she at last felt that she had been unduly governed by her prejudices, and that it might be wise to go and see for themselves that their affairs were managed to the best advantage. Deep in her heart was also the consciousness that it was her husband's indomitable will that she was carrying out, and that she could never escape from that will in any exigency where it could justly make itself felt. She therefore required of her son the promise that their visit should be as unobtrusive as possible, and that he would return with her as soon as he had arranged matters to his mind. To this he had readily agreed, and they were now in the land for which the mother had only hate and the son indifference.

CHAPTER XI.
AN OATH AND A GLANCE.

As Strahan disappeared in the winding of the avenue a sudden and terrible thought occurred to Mrs. Merwyn. She glanced at her son, who had walked to the farther end of the piazza, and stood for a moment with his back towards her. His manly proportions made her realize, as she had never done before, that he had attained his majority,--that he was his own master. He had said he would not fight against the North, but, as far as the South was concerned, he had never committed himself. And then his terrible will!

She went to her room and thought. He was in a land seething with excitement and patriotic fervor. She knew not what influences a day might bring to bear upon him. Above all else she feared taunts for lack of courage. She knew that her own passionate pride slept in his breast and on a few occasions she had seen its manifestations. As a rule he was too healthful, too well organized and indolent, to be easily irritated, while in serious matters he had not been crossed. She knew enough of life to be aware that his manhood had never been awakened or even deeply moved, and she was eager indeed to accomplish their mission in the States and return to conditions of life not so electrical.

In the mean time she felt that she must use every precaution. She summoned a maid and asked that her son should be sent to her.

The young man soon lounged in, and threw himself into an easy chair.

His mother looked at him fixedly for a moment, and then asked, "Why is young Strahan in THAT uniform?"

"I didn't ask him," was the careless reply. "Obviously, however, because he has entered the service in some capacity."

"Did he not suggest that it would be a very proper thing for you to do, also?"

"Oh, of course. He wouldn't be Strahan if he hadn't. He has a high appreciation of a 'little brief authority,' especially if vested in himself. Believing himself to be so heroic he is inclined to call others to account."

"I trust you have rated such vaporings at their worth."

"I have not rated them at all. What do I care for little Strahan or his opinions? Nil."

"Shall you see much of him while we are compelled to remain in this detestable land?"

"More of him than of any one else, probably. We were boys together, and he amuses me. What is more to the point, if I make a Union officer my associate I disarm hostile criticism and throw an additional safeguard around my property. There is no telling to what desperate straits the Northern authorities may be reduced, and I don't propose to give them any grounds for confiscation."

"You are remarkably prudent, Willard, for a young man of Southern descent."

"I am of Northern descent also," he replied, with a light laugh. "Father was as strong a Northern man--so I imagine--as you are a Southern woman, and so, by a natural law, I am neutral, brought to a standstill by two equal and opposite forces."

The intense partisan looked at him with perplexity, and for a moment felt a strange and almost superstitious belief in his words. Was there a reciprocal relation of forces which would render her schemes futile? She shared in the secret hopes and ambitions of the Southern leaders. Had Northern and Southern blood so neutralized the heart of this youth that he was indifferent to both sections? and had she, by long residence abroad, and indulgence, made him so cosmopolitan that he merely looked upon the world as "his oyster"? She was not the first parent who, having failed to instil noble, natural principles in childhood, is surprised and troubled at the outcome of a mind developing under influences unknown or unheeded. That the South would be triumphant she never doubted a moment. It would not merely achieve independence, but also a power that would grow like the vegetation of its genial climate, and extend until the tapering Isthmus of Panama became the national boundary of the empire. But what part would be taken by this strange son who seemed equally endowed with graceful indolence and indomitable will? Were his tireless strength and energy to accomplish nothing better than the climbing of distant mountains? and would he maintain indifference towards a struggle for a dominion beyond Oriental dreams? Physically and mentally he seemed capable of doing what he chose; practically he chose to do what he pleased from hour to hour. Amusing himself with a languid, good-natured disregard of what he looked upon as trivial affairs, he was like adamant the moment a supreme and just advantage was his. He was her husband over agaim, with strange differences. What could she do at the present moment but the thing she proposed to do?

"Willard," she said, slowly, and in a voice that pierced his indifference, "have you any regard for me?"

"Certainly. Have I shown any want of respect?"

"That is not the question at all. You are young, Willard, and you live in the future. I live much in the past. My early home was in the South, where my family, for generations, has been eminent. Is it strange, then, that I should love that sunny land?"

"No, mamma."

"Well, all I ask at present is that you will promise me never, under any motive, to take up arms against that land of my ancestors."

"I have not the slightest disposition to do so."

"Willard, what to-day is, is. Neither you nor I know what shall be on the morrow. I never expected to marry a Northern man, yet I did so; nor should I regret it if I consulted my heart only. He was different from all his race. I did not foresee what was coming, or I could have torn my heart out before involving myself in these Northern complications. I cannot change the past, but I must provide for the future. O Willard, to your eyes your Northern fortune seems large. But a few years will pass before you will be shown what a trifle it is compared with the prizes of power and wealth that will be bestowed upon loyal Southerners. You have an ancestry, an ability, that would naturally place you among the foremost. Terrible as would be the sacrifice on my part, I could still give you my blessing if you imitated young Strahan in one respect, and devoted yourself heart, soul, and sword to our cause."

"The probable result would be that you and my sisters would be penniless, I sleeping in mud, and living on junk and hoe-cake. Another result, probable, only a little more remote, is that the buzzards would pick my bones. Faugh! Oh, no. I've settled that question, and it's a bore to think a question over twice. There are thousands of Americans in Europe. Their wisdom suits me until this tea-pot tempest is over. If any one doubts my courage I'll prove it fast enough, but, if I had my way, the politicians, North and South, should do their own fighting and starving."

"But, Willard, our leaders are not mere politicians. They are men of grand, far-reaching schemes, and when their plans are accomplished, they will attain regal power and wealth."

"Visions, mamma, visions. I have enough of my father's blood in my veins to be able to look at both sides of a question. Strahan asked me severely if I did not read the papers;" and he laughed lightly. "Well, I do read them, at least enough of them to pick out a few grains of truth from all the chaff. The North and South have begun fighting like two bull-dogs, and it's just a question which has the longer wind and the more endurance. The chances are all in favor of the North. I shall not throw myself and property away for the sake of a bare possibility. That's settled."

"Have you ice-water in your veins?" his mother asked, passionately.

"I have your blood, madam, and my father's, hence I am what I am."

"Well, then you must be a man of honor, of your word. Will you promise never to take arms against the South?"

"I have told you I have no disposition to do so."

"The promise, then, can cost you little, and it will be a relief to my mind."

"Oh, well, mamma, if it will make you feel any easier, I promise with one exception. Both South and North must keep their hands off the property my father gave me."

"If Southern leaders were dictating terms in New York City, as they will, ere long, they would never touch your property."

"They had better not."

"You know what I mean, Willard. I ask you never to assume this hated Northern uniform, or put your foot on Southern soil with a hostile purpose."

"Yes, I can promise that."

"Swear it to me then, by your mother's honor and your father's memory."

"Is not my word sufficient?"

"These things are sacred to me, and I wish them treated in a sacred manner. If you will do this my mind will be at rest and I may be able to do more for you in the future."

"To satisfy you, I swear never to put on the Northern uniform or to enter the South with a hostile purpose."

She stepped forward and touched his forehead with her lips, as she said: "The compact is sealed. Your oath is registered on earth and in heaven. Your simple word as a man of honor will satisfy me as to one other request. I wish you never to speak to any one of this solemn covenant between us."

"I'm not in the habit of gossiping over family affairs," he replied, haughtily.

"I know that, and also that your delicacy of feeling would keep you from speaking of a matter so sacred to me. But I am older and more experienced than you, and I shall feel safer if you promise. You would not gossip about it, of course. You might refer to it to some friend or to the woman who became your wife. I can foresee complications which might make it better that it should be utterly unknown. You little know how I dream and plan for you, and I only ask you never to speak of this interview and its character to a living soul."

"Certainly, mother, I can promise this. I should feel it small business to babble about anything which you take so to heart. These visions of empire occupy your mind and do no harm. I only hope you will meet your disappointment philosophically. Good-by now till lunch."

"Poor mamma!" thought the young man, as he started out for a walk; "she rails against Northern fanatics, forgetting tnat it is just possible to be a little fanatical on the Southern side of the line."

As he strode along in the sunshine his oath weighed upon him no more than if he had promised not to go out in his sail-boat that day.

At last, after surmounting a rather steep hill, he threw himself on the grass under the shade of a tree. "It's going to be awfully slow and stupid here," he muttered, "and it will be a month or two before we can return. I hoped to be back in time to join the Montagues in climbing Mont Blanc, and here I am tied up between these mole-hill mountains and city law-offices. How shall I ever get through with the time?"

A pony-phaeton, containing two ladies, appeared at the foot of the hill and slowly approached. His eyes rested on it in languid indifference, but, as it drew nearer, the younger of the two ladies fixed his attention. Her charming summer costume at first satisfied his taste, and, as her features became distinct, he was surprised at their beauty, as he thought at first; but he soon felt that animation redeemed the face from mere prettiness. The young girl was talking earnestly, but a sudden movement of the horse caused her to glance toward the road-side, and she encountered the dark eyes of a stranger. Her words ceased instantly. A slight frown contracted her brow, and, touching her horse with her whip, she passed on rapidly.

"By Jove! Strahan is right. If I have many such countrywomen in the neighborhood, I ought to find amusement."

He rose and sauntered after the phaeton, and saw that it turned in at a pretty little cottage, embowered in vines and trees. Making a mental note of the locality, he bent his steps in another direction, laughing as he thought: "From that one glance I am sure that those blue eyes will kindle more than one fellow before they are quenched. I wonder if Strahan knows her. Well, here, perhaps, is a chance for a summer lark. If Strahan is enamored I'd like to cut him out, for by all the fiends of dulness I must find something to do."

Strahan had accepted an invitation to lunch at the Vosburghs' that day, and arrived, hot and flushed, from his second morning's drill.

"Well!" he exclaimed, "I've seen the great Mogul."

"I believe I have also," replied Marian. "Has he not short and slightly curly hair, dark eyes, and an impudent stare?"

"I don't recognize the 'stare' exactly. Merwyn is polite enough in his way, and confound his way! But the rest of your description tallies. Where did you see him?"

She explained. "That was he, accomplishing his usual day's work. O ye dogs of war! how I would like to have him in my squad one of these July days! Miss Marian, I'd wear your shoe-tie in my cap the rest of my life, if you would humble that fellow and make him feel that he never spoke to a titled lady abroad who had not her equal in some American girl. It just enrages me to see a New-York man, no better born than myself, putting on such superior and indifferent airs. If he'd come to me and say, 'Strahan, I'm a rebel, I'm going to fight and kill you if I can,' I'd shake hands with him as I did not to-day. I'd treat him like a jolly, square fellow, until we came face to face in a fair fight, and then--the fortune of war. As it was, I felt like taking him by the collar and shaking him out of his languid grace. He told me to mind my own business so politely that I couldn't take offence, although he gave scarcely any other reason than that he proposed to mind his. When I met his Southern mother on the piazza, she looked at me in my uniform at first as if I had been a toad. They are rebels at heart, and yet they stand aloof and sneer at the North, from which they derive protection and revenue. I made his eyes flash once though," chuckled the young fellow in conclusion.

Marian laughed heartily as she said: "Mr. Strahan, if you fight as well as you talk, I foresee Southern reverses. You have no idea how your indignation becomes you. 'As well-born,' did you say? Why, my good friend, you are worth a wilderness of such lackadaisical fellows. Ciphers don't count unless they stand after a significant figure; neither do such men, unless stronger men use them."

"Your arithmetic is at fault, Miss Marian. Ciphers do have the power of pushing a significant figure way back to the right of the decimal point, and, as a practical fact, these elegant human ciphers usually stand before good men and true in society. I don't believe it would be so with you, but few of us would stand a chance with most girls should this rich American, with his foreign airs and graces, enter the lists against us."

In her sincerity and earnestness, she took his hand and said: "I thank you for your tribute. You are right. Though this person had the wealth of the Indies, and every external grace, he could not be my friend unless he were a MAN. I've talked with papa a good deal, and believe there are men in the Southern army just as honest and patriotic as you are; but no cold-blooded, selfish betwixt-and-betweens shall ever take my hand."

"Make me a promise," cried Strahan, giving the hand he held a hearty and an approving shake.

"Well?"

"If opportunity offers, make this fellow bite the dust."

"We'll see about that. I may not think it worth the while, and I certainly shall not compromise myself in the slightest degree."

"But if I bring him here you will be polite to him?"

"Just about as polite as he was to you, I imagine."

"Miss Marian, I wouldn't have any harm come to you for the wide world. If--if anything should turn out amiss I'd shoot him, I certainly would."

The girl's only answer was a merry peal of laughter.

CHAPTER XII.
"A VOW."

BENT, as was Strahan, upon his scheme of disturbing Merwyn's pride and indifference, he resolved to permit several days to pass before repeating his call. He also, as well as Marian, was unwilling to compromise himself beyond a certain point, and it was his hope that he might receive a speedy visit. He was not disappointed, for on the ensuing day Merwyn sauntered up the Strahan avenue, and, learning that the young officer had gone to camp, followed him thither. The cold glance from the fair stranger in the phaeton dwelt in his memory, and he was pleased to find that it formed sufficient incentive to action.

Strahan saw him coming with a grim smile, but greeted him with off-hand cordiality. "Sorry, Merwyn," he said, "I can give you only a few moments before I go on duty."

"You are not on duty evenings?"

"Yes, every other evening."

"How about to-night?"

"At your service."

"Are you acquainted with the people who reside at a cottage--" and he described Marian's abode.

"Yes."

"Who are they?"

"Mr. Vosburgh has rented the place as a summer residence for his family. His wife and daughter are there usually, and he comes when he can.

"And the daughter's name?"

"Miss Marian Vosburgh."

"Will you introduce me to her?"

"Certainly."

"I sha'n't be poaching on your grounds, shall I?"

"Miss Vosburgh honors me with her friendship,--nothing more."

"Is it so great an honor?"

"I esteem it as such."

"Who are they, anyway?"

"Well, as a family I regard them as my equals, and Miss Marian as my superior."

"Oh come, Strahan, gossip about them a little."

The officer burst out laughing. "Well," he said, "for a man of your phenomenal reticence you are asking a good many questions."

Merwyn colored slightly and blundered: "You know my motive, Strahan; one does not care to make acquaintances that are not quite--" and then the expression of his host's eyes checked him.

"I assure you the Vosburghs are 'QUITE,'" Strahan said, coldly. "Did I not say they were my equals? You may esteem yourself fortunate if Miss Vosburgh ever permits you to feel yourself to be her equal."

"Why, how so?" a little irritably.

"Because if a man has brains and discernment the more he sees of her the more will he be inclined to doubt his equality."

Merwyn smiled in a rather superior way, and, with a light laugh, said: "I understand, Strahan. A man in your plight ought to feel in that way; at least, it is natural that he should. Now see here, old fellow, I'll keep aloof if you say so."

"Why should you? You have seen few society queens abroad who received so much and so varied homage as Miss Vosburgh. There are half a dozen fellows there, more or less, every evening, and you can take your chances among them."

"Oh, she's a bit of a coquette, then?"

"You must discover for yourself what she is," said the young man, buckling on his sword. "She has my entire respect."

"You quite pique my curiosity. I'll drive in for you this evening."

At the hour appointed, Strahan, in civilian's dress, stepped into Merwyn's carriage and was driven rapidly to the cottage. Throwing the reins to a footman, the young fellow followed the officer with a confidence not altogether well founded, as he soon learned. Many guests were present, and Lane was among them. When Merwyn was presented Marian was observed to bow merely and not give her hand, as was her custom when a friend of hers introduced a friend. Some of the residents in the vicinity exchanged significant smiles when they saw that the fastidious and exclusive Willard Merwyn had joined their circle. Mrs. Vosburgh, who was helping to entertain the guests, recognized nothing in his presence beyond a new social triumph for her daughter, and was very gracious. To her offices, as hostess, he found himself chiefly relegated for a time.

This suited him exactly, since it gave him a chance for observation; and certainly the little drawing-room, with its refined freedom, was a revelation to him. Conversation, repartee, and jest were unrestrained. While Lane was as gay as any present, Merwyn was made to feel that he was no ordinary man, and it soon came out in the natural flow of talk that he, too, was in the service. Merwyn was introduced also to a captain of the regular army, and, whatever be might think of these people, he instinctively felt that they would no more permit themselves to be patronized than would the sons of noble houses abroad. Indeed, he was much too adroit to attempt anything of the kind, and, with well-bred ease, made himself at home among them in general conversation.

Meanwhile, he watched Marian with increasing curiosity. To him she was a new and very interesting type. He had seen no such vivacity and freedom abroad, and his experience led him to misunderstand her. "She is of the genus American girl, middle class," he thought, "who, by her beauty and the unconventionality of her drawing-room, has become a quasi-belle. None of these men would think of marrying her, unless it is little Strahan, and he wouldn't five years hence. Yet she is piquant and fascinating after her style, a word and a jest for each and all, and spoken with a sort of good-comradeship, rather than with an if-you-please-sir air. I must admit, however, that there is nothing loud in tone, word, or manner. She is as delicate and refined as her own beauty, and, although this rather florid mamma is present as chaperon, the scene and the actors are peculiarly American. Well, I owe Strahan a good turn. I can amuse myself with this girl without scruple."

At last he found an opportunity to say, "We have met once before, I believe, Miss Vosburgh."

"Met? Where?"

"Where I was inclined to go to sleep, and you gave me such a charming frown that I awakened immediately and took a long ramble."

"I saw a person stretched at lazy length under the trees yesterday. You know the horror ladies have of intoxicated men on the road-side."

"Was that the impression I made? Thanks."

"The impression made was that we had better pass as quickly as possible."

"You made a very different impression. Thanks to Strahan I am here this evening in consequence, and am delighted that I came."

"'Delighted' is a strong word, Mr. Merwyn. Now that we are speaking of impressions, mine is that years have elapsed since you were greatly delighted at anything."

"What gives you such an impression?"

"Women can never account for their intuitions."

"Women? Do not use such an elderly word in regard to one appearing as if just entering girlhood."

"O Mr. Merwyn! have you not learned abroad that girls of my age are elderly indeed compared with men of yours?"

He bit his lip. "English girls are not so--"

"Fast?"

"I didn't say that. They certainly have not the vivacity and fascination that I am discovering in your drawing-room."

"Why, Mr. Merwyn! one would think you had come to America on a voyage of discovery, and were surprised at the first thing you saw."

"I think I could show you things abroad that would interest you."

"All Europe could not tempt me to go abroad at this time. In your estimation I am not even a woman,--only a girl, and yet I have enough girlhood to wish to take my little part in the events of the day."

He colored, but asked, quietly, "What part are you taking?"

"Such questions," she replied, with a merry, half-mocking flash of her eyes, "I answer by deeds. There are those who know;" and then, being addressed by Mr. Lane, she turned away, leaving him with confused, but more decided sensations than he had known for a long time.

His first impulse was to leave the house, but this course would only subject him to ridicule on the part of those who remained. After a moment or two of reflection he remembered that she had not invited him, and that she had said nothing essentially rude. He had merely chosen to occupy a position in regard to his country that differed radically from hers, and she had done little more than define her position.

"She is a Northern, as mamma is a Southern fanatic, with the difference that she is a young, effervescing creature, bubbling over with the excitement of the times," he thought. "That fellow in uniform, and the society of men like Strahan and Lane, have turned her head, and she has not seen enough of life to comprehend a man of the world. What do I care for her, or any here? Her briery talk should only amuse me. When she learns more about who I am and what I possess she will be inclined to imitate her discreet mamma and think of the main chance; meanwhile I escape a summer's dulness and ennui;" and so he philosophically continued his observations and chatted with Mrs. Vosburgh and others until, with Strahan, he took his departure, receiving from Marian a bow merely, while to Strahan she gave her hand cordially.

"You seem to be decidedly in Miss Vosburgh's good graces," said Merwyn, as they drove away.

"I told you she was my friend."

"Is it very difficult to become her friend?"

"Well, that depends. You should not find it difficult, since you are so greatly my superior."

"Oh, come, Strahan."

"Pardon me, I forgot I was to express only my own thoughts, not yours."

"You don't know my thoughts or circumstances. Come now, let us be good comrades. I will begin by thanking you cordially for introducing me to a charming young girl. I am sure I put on no airs this evening."

"They would not have been politic, Merwyn, and, for the life of me, I can see no reason for them."

"Very well. Therefore you didn't see any. How like old times we are! We were always together, yet always sparring a little."

"You must take us as we are in these times," said Strahan, with a light laugh, for he felt it would jeopardize his scheme, or hope rather, if he were too brusque with his companion. "You see it is hard for us to understand your cosmopolitan indifference. American feeling just now is rather tense on both sides of the line, and if you will recognize the fact you will understand us better."

"I think I am already aware of the fact. If Miss Vosburgh were of our sex you would soon have another recruit."

"I'd soon have a superior officer, you mean."

"I fancy you are rather under her thumb already."

"It's a difficult position to attain, I assure you."

"How so?"

"I have observed that, towards a good many, Miss Vosburgh is quite your equal in indifference."

"I like her all the better for that fact."

"So do I."

"How is it that you are so favored?"

"No doubt it seems strange to you. Mere caprice on her part, probably."

"You misunderstand me. I would like to learn your tactics."

"Jove! I'd like to teach you. Come down to-morrow and I'll give you a musket."

"You are incorrigible, Strahan. Do you mean that her good-will can be won only at the point of the bayonet?"

"No one coached me. Surely you have not so neglected your education abroad that you do not know how to win a lady's favor."

"You are a neutral, indeed."

"I wouldn't aid my own brother in a case of this kind."

"You are right; in matters of this kind it is every one for himself. You offered to show me, a stranger, some attention, you know."

"Yes, Merwyn, and I'll keep my word. I will give you just as good courtesy as I receive. The formalities have been complied with and you are acquainted with Miss Vosburgh. You have exactly the same vantage that I had at the start, and you certainly cannot wish for more. If you wish for further introductions, count on me."

Merwyn parted from his plain-spoken companion, well content. Strahan's promise to return all the courtesy he received left a variable standard in Merwyn's hands that he could employ according to circumstances or inclination. He was satisfied that his neighbor, in accordance with a trait very common to young men, cherished for Miss Vosburgh a chivalric and sentimental regard at which he would smile when he became older. Merwyn, however, had a certain sense of honor, and would not have attempted deliberately to supplant one to whom he felt that he owed loyalty. His mind having been relieved of all scruples of this character, he looked forward complacently to the prospect of winning--what? He did not trouble himself to define the kind of regard he hoped to inspire. The immediate purpose to kill time, that must intervene before he could return to England, was sufficient. There was promise of occupation, mild excitement, and an amusing triumph, in becoming the foremost figure in Marian's drawing-room.

There is scarcely need to dwell upon the events of a few subsequent weeks and the gradual changes that were taking place. Life with its small vicissitudes rarely results from deliberate action. Circumstances, from day to day, color and shape it; yet beneath the rippling, changing surface a great tide may be rising. Strahan was succeeding fairly well in his recruiting service, and, making allowances for his previous history, was proving an efficient officer. Marian was a loyal, steadfast friend, reprimanding with mirthful seriousness at times, and speaking earnest and encouraging words at others. After all, the mercurial young fellow daily won her increased respect and esteem. He had been promoted to a captaincy, and such was the response of the loyal North, during that dreary summer of disaster and confused counsels, that his company was nearly full, and he was daily expecting orders for departure. His drill ground had become the occasional morning resort of his friends, and each day gave evidence of improved soldierly bearing in his men.

Merwyn thus far had characteristically carried out his plans to "kill time." Thoroughly convinced of his comparative superiority, he had been good-naturedly tolerant of the slow recognition accorded to it by Marian. Yet he believed he was making progress, and the fact that her favor was hard to win was only the more incitement. If she had shown early and decided preference his occupation would have been gone; for what could he have done in those initiatory weeks of their acquaintance if her eyes and tones had said, "I am ready to take you and your wealth"? The attitude she maintained, although little understood, awakened a kind of respect, while the barriers she quietly interposed aroused a keener desire to surmount them. By hauteur and reserve at times he had made those with whom he associated feel that his position in regard to the civil conflict was his own affair. Even Marian avoided the subject when talking with him, and her mother never thought of mentioning it. Indeed, that thrifty lady would have been rather too encouraging had not her daughter taken pains to check such a spirit. At the same time the young girl made it emphatically understood that discussion of the events of the war should be just as free when he was present as when he was absent.

Yet in a certain sense he was making progress, in that he awakened anger on her part, rather than indifference. If she was a new type to him so was he to her, and she found her thoughts reverting to him in hostile analysis of his motives and character. She had received too much sincere homage and devotion not to detect something cynical and hollow in his earlier attentions. She had seen glances toward her mother, and had caught in his tones an estimate which, however true, incensed her greatly. Her old traits began to assert themselves, and gradually her will accorded with Strahan's hope. If, without compromising herself, she could humble this man, bringing him to her feet and dismissing him with a rather scornful refusal, such an exertion of power would give her much satisfaction. Yet her pride, as well as her principle, led her to determine that he should sue without having received any misleading favor on her part.

Merwyn had never proposed to sue at all, except in the way of conventional gallantry. For his own amusement he had resolved to become her most intimate and familiar friend, and then it would be time to go abroad. If false hopes were raised it would not much matter; Strahan or some one else would console her. He admitted that his progress was slow, and her reserve hard to combat. She would neither drive nor sail with him unless she formed one of a party. Still in this respect he was on the same footing with her best friends. One thing did trouble him, however; she had never given him her hand, either in greeting or in parting.

At last he brought about an explanation that disturbed his equanimity not a little. He had called in the morning, and she had chatted charmingly with him on impersonal matters, pleasing him by her intelligent and gracefully spoken ideas on the topics broached. As a society girl she met him on this neutral ground without the slightest restraint or embarrassment. As he also talked well she had no scruple in enjoying a pleasure unsought by herself, especially as it might lead to the punishment which she felt that he deserved. Smilingly she had assured herself, when he was announced, "If he's a rebel at heart, as I've been told, I've met the enemy before either Mr. Lane or Mr. Strahan."

When Merwyn rose to take his leave he held out his hand and said: "I shall be absent two or three days. In saying good-by won't you shake hands?"

She laughingly put her hands behind her back and said, "I can't."

"Will not, you mean?"

"No, I cannot. I've made a vow to give my hand only to my own friends and those of my country."

"Do you look upon me as an enemy?"

"Oh, no, indeed."

"Then not as a friend?"

"Why, certainly not, Mr. Merwyn. You know that you are not my friend. What does the word mean?"

"Well," said he, flushing, "what does it mean?"

"Nothing more to me than to any other sincere person. One uses downright sincerity with a friend, and would rather harm himself than that friend."

"Why is not this my attitude towards you?"

"You, naturally, should know better than I."

"Indeed, Miss Vosburgh, you little know the admiration you have excited," he said, gallantly.

An inscrutable smile was her only response.

"That, however, has become like the air you breathe, no doubt."

"Not at all. I prize admiration. What woman does not? But there are as many kinds of admiration as there are donors."

"Am I to infer that mine is of a valueless nature?"

"Ask yourself, Mr. Merwyn, just what it is worth."

"It is greater than I have ever bestowed upon any one else," he said, hastily; for this tilt was disturbing his self-possession.

Again she smiled, and her thought was, "Except yourself."

He, thinking her smile incredulous, resumed: "You doubt this?"

"I cannot help thinking that you are mistaken."

"How can I assure you that I am not?"

"I do not know. Why is it essential that I should be so assured?"

He felt that he was being worsted, and feared that she had detected the absence of unselfish good-will and honest purpose toward her. He was angry with himself and her because of the dilemma in which he was placed. Yet what could he say to the serene, smiling girl before him, whose unflinching blue eyes looked into his with a keenness of insight that troubled him? His one thought now was to achieve a retreat in which he could maintain the semblance of dignity and good breeding.

With a light and deferential laugh he said: "I am taught, unmistakably, Miss Vosburgh, that my regard, whatever it may be, is of little consequence to you, and that it would be folly for me to try to prove a thing that would not interest you if demonstrated. I feel, however, that one question is due to us both,--Is my society a disagreeable intrusion?"

"If it had been, Mr. Merwyn, you would have been aware of the fact before this. I have enjoyed your conversation this morning."

"I hope, then, that in the future I can make a more favorable impression, and that in time you will give me your hand."

Her blue eyes never left his face as he spoke, and they grew dark with a meaning that perplexed and troubled him. She merely bowed gravely and turned away.

Never had his complacency been so disturbed. He walked homeward with steps that grew more and more rapid, keeping pace with his swift, perturbed thoughts. As he approached his residence he yielded to an impulse; leaped a wall, and struck out for the mountains.

CHAPTER XIII.
A SIEGE BEGUN.

EITHER she is seeking to enhance her value, or else she is not the girl I imagined her to be at all," was Willard Merwyn's conclusion as he sat on a crag high upon the mountain's side. "Whichever supposition is true, I might as well admit at once that she is the most fascinating woman I ever met. She IS a woman, as she claims to be. I've seen too many mere girls not to detect their transparent deceits and motives at once. I don't understand Marian Vosburgh; I only half believe in her, but I intend to learn whether there is a girl in her station who would unhesitatingly decline the wealth and position that I can offer. Not that I have decided to offer these as yet, by any means, for I am in a position to marry wealth and rank abroad; but this girl piques my curiosity, stirs my blood, and is giving wings to time. At this rate the hour of our departure may come before I am ready for it. I was mistaken in one respect the first evening I met her. Lane, as well as Strahan and others, would marry her if they could. She might make her choice from almost any of those who seek her society, and she is not the pretty little Bohemian that I imagined. Either none of them has ever touched her heart, or else she knows her value and vantage, and she means to make the most of them. If she knew the wealth and position I could give her immediately, would not these certainties bring a different expression into her eyes? I am not an ogre, that she should shrink from me as the only incumbrance."

Could he have seen the girl's passion after he left her he would have understood her dark look at their parting. Hastily seeking her own room she locked the door to hide the tears of anger and humiliation that would come.

"Well," she cried, "I AM punished for trifling with others. Here is a man who seeks me in my home for no other purpose than his own amusement and the gratification of his curiosity. He could not deny it when brought squarely to the issue. He could not look me in the eyes and say that he was my honest friend. He would flirt with me, if he could, to beguile his burdensome leisure; but when I defined what some are to me, and more would be, if permitted, he found no better refuge than gallantry and evasion. What can he mean? what can he hope except to see me in his power, and ready to accept any terms he may choose to offer? O Arthur Strahan! your wish now is wholly mine. May I have the chance of rejecting this man as I never dismissed one before!"

It must not be supposed that Willard's frequent visits to the Vosburgh cottage had escaped Mrs. Merwyn's vigilant solicitude, but her son spoke of them in such a way that she obtained the correct impression that he was only amusing himself. Her chief hope was that her son would remain free until the South had obtained the power it sought. Then an alliance with one of the leading families in the Confederacy would accomplish as much as might have resulted from active service during the struggle. She had not hesitated to express this hope to him.

He had smiled, and said: "One of the leading theories of the day is the survival of the fittest. I am content to limit my theory to a survival. If I am alive and well when your great Southern empire takes the lead among nations there will be a chance for the fulfilment of your dream. If I have disappeared beneath Southern mud there won't be any chance. In my opinion, however, I should have tenfold greater power with our Southern friends if I introduced to them an English heiress."

His mother had sighed and thought: "It is strange that this calculating boy should be my son. His father was self-controlled and resolute, but he never manifested such cold-blooded thought of self, first and always."

She did not remember that the one lesson taught him from his very cradle had been that of self-pleasing. She had carried out her imperious will where it had clashed with his, and had weakly compensated him by indulgence in the trifles that make up a child's life. SHE had never been controlled or made to yield to others in thoughtful consideration of their rights and feelings, and did not know how to instil the lesson; therefore--so inconsistent is human nature--when she saw him developing her own traits, she was troubled because his ambitions differed from her own. Had his hopes and desires coincided with hers he would have been a model youth in her eyes, although never entertaining a thought beyond personal and family advantage. Apparently there was a wider distinction between them, for she was capable of suffering and sacrifice for the South. The possibilities of his nature were as yet unrevealed.

His course and spirit, however, set her at rest in regard to his visits to Marian Vosburgh, and she felt that there was scarcely the slightest danger that he would compromise himself by serious attentions to the daughter of an obscure American official.

Willard returned from his brief absence, and was surprised at his eager anticipation of another interview with Marian. He called the morning after his arrival, and learning that she had just gone to witness a drill of Strahan's company, he followed, and arrived almost as soon as she did at the ground set apart for military evolutions.

He was greeted by Marian in her old manner, and by Strahan in his off-hand way. The young officer was at her side, and a number of ladies and gentlemen were present as spectators. Merwyn took a camp-stool, sat a little apart, and nonchalantly lighted a cigar.

Suddenly there was a loud commotion in the guard-house, accompanied by oaths and the sound of a struggle. Then a wild figure, armed with a knife, rushed toward Strahan, followed by a sergeant and two or three privates. At a glance it was seen to be the form of a tall, powerful soldier, half-crazed with liquor.

"--you!" exclaimed the man; "you ordered me to be tied up. I'll larn you that we ain't down in Virginny yet!" and there was reckless murder in his bloodshot eyes.

Although at that moment unarmed, Strahan, without a second's hesitation, sprung at the man's throat and sought to catch his uplifted hand, but could not reach it. The probabilities are that the young officer's military career would have been ended in another second, had not Merwyn, without removing his cigar from his mouth, caught the uplifted arm and held it as in a vise.

"Stand back, Strahan," he said, quietly; but the young fellow would not loosen his hold. Therefore Merwyn, with his left hand upon the collar of the soldier, jerked him a yard away, and tripped him up so that he fell upon his face. Twisting the fellow's hands across his back, Merwyn said to the sergeant, "Now tie him at your leisure."

This was done almost instantly, and the foul mouth was also stopped by a gag.

Merwyn returned to his camp-stool, and coolly removed the cigar from his mouth as he glanced towards Marian. Although white and agitated, she was speaking eager, complimentary, and at the same time soothing words to Strahan, who, in accordance with his excitable nature, was in a violent passion. She did not once glance towards the man who had probably saved her friend's life, but Strahan came and shook hands with him cordially, saying: "It was handsomely and bravely done, Merwyn. I appreciate the service. You ought to be an officer, for you could make a good one,--a better one than I am, for you are as cool as a cucumber."

Others, also, would have congratulated Merwyn had not his manner repelled them, and in a few moments the drill began. Long before it was over Marian rose and went towards her phaeton. In a moment Merwyn was by her side.

"You are not very well, Miss Vosburgh," he said. "Let me drive you home."

She bowed her acquiescence, and he saw that she was pale and a little faint; but by a visible effort she soon rallied, and talked on indifferent subjects.

At last she said, abruptly: "I am learning what war means. It would seem that there is almost as much danger in enforcing discipline on such horrible men as in facing the enemy."

"Of course," said Merwyn, carelessly. "That is part of the risk."

"Well," she continued, emphatically, "I never saw a braver act than that of Mr. Strahan. He was unarmed."

"I was also!" was the somewhat bitter reply, "and you did not even thank me by a look for saving your friend from a bad wound to say the least."

"I beg your pardon, Mr. Merwyn, you were armed with a strength which made your act perfectly safe. Mr. Strahan risked everything."

"How could he help risking everything? The infuriated beast was coming towards you as well as him. Could he have run away? You are not just to me, or at least you are very partial"

"One can scarcely help being partial towards one's friends. I agree with you, however; Mr. Strahan could not have taken any other course. Could you, with a friend in such peril?"

"Certainly not, with any one in such peril. Let us say no more about the trifle."

She was silent a moment, and then said, impetuously: "You shall not misunderstand me. I don't know whether I am unjust or not. I do know that I was angered, and cannot help it. You may as well know my thoughts. Why should Mr. Strahan and others expose themselves to such risks and hardships while you look idly on, when you so easily prove yourself able to take a man's part in the struggle? You may think, if you do not say it, that it is no affair of mine; but with my father, whom I love better than life, ready at any moment to give his life for a cause, I cannot patiently see utter indifference to that cause in one who seeks my society."

"I think your feelings are very natural, Miss Vosburgh, nor do I resent your censure. You are surrounded by influences that lead you to think as you do. You can scarcely judge for me, however. Be fair and just. I yield to you fully--I may add, patiently--the right to think, feel, and act as you think best. Grant equal rights to me."

"Oh, certainly," she said, a little coldly; "each one must choose his own course for life."

"That must ever be true," he replied, "and it is well to remember that it is for life. The present condition of affairs is temporary. It is the hour of excited impulses rather than of cool judgment. Ambitious men on both sides are furthering their own purposes at the cost of others."

"Is that your idea of the war, Mr. Merwyn?" she asked, looking searchingly into his face.

"It is indeed, and time will prove me right, you will discover."

"Since this is your view, I can scarcely wonder at your course," she said, so quietly that he misunderstood her, and felt that she half conceded its reasonableness. Then she changed the subject, nor did she revert to it in his society.

As August drew to its close, Marian's circle shared the feverish solicitude felt in General Pope's Virginia campaign. Throughout the North there was a loyal response to the appeal for men, and Strahan's company was nearly full. He expected at any hour the orders which would unite the regiment at Washington.

One morning Mr. Lane came to say good-by. It was an impressive hour which he spent with Marian when bidding her perhaps a final farewell. She was pale, and her attempts at mirthfulness were forced and feeble. When he rose to take his leave she suddenly covered her face with her hand, and burst into tears.

"Marian!" he exclaimed, eagerly, for the deep affection in his heart would assert itself at times, and now her emotion seemed to warrant hope.

"Wait," she faltered. "Do not go just yet."

He took her unresisting hand and kissed it, while she stifled her sobs.

"Miss Marian," he began, "you know how wholly I am yours--"

"Please do not misunderstand me," she interrupted. "I scarcely know how I could feel differently if I were parting with my twin brother. You have been such a true, generous friend! Oh, I am all unstrung. Papa has been sent for from Washington, and we don't know when he'll return or what service may be required of him. I only know that he is like you, and will take any risk that duty seems to demand. I have so learned to lean upon you and trust you that if anything happened--well, I felt that I could go to you as a brother. You are too generous to blame me that I cannot feel in any other way. See, I am frank with you. Why should I not be when the future is so uncertain? Is it a little thing that I should think of you first and feel that I shall miss you most when I am so distraught with anxiety?"

"No, Miss Marian. To me it is a sacred thing. I want you to know that you have a brother's hand and heart at your disposal."

"I believe you. Come," she added, rising and dashing away her tears, "I must be brave, as you are. Promise me that you will take no risks beyond those required by duty, and that you will write to me."

"Marian," he said, in a low, deep voice, "I shall ever try to do what, in your heart, you would wish. You must also promise that if you are ever in trouble you will let me know."

"I promise."

He again kissed her hand, like a knight of the olden time.

At the last turn of the road from which he was visible she waved her handkerchief, then sought her room and burst into a passion of tears.

"Oh," she sobbed, "as I now feel I could not refuse him anything. I may never see him again, and he has been so kind and generous!"

The poor girl was indeed morbid from excitement and anxiety. Her pale face began to give evidence of the strain which the times imposed on her in common with all those whose hearts had much at stake in the conflict.

In vain her mother remonstrated with her, and told her that she was "meeting trouble half-way." Once the sagacious lady had ventured to suggest that much uncertainty might be taken out of the future by giving more encouragement to Mr. Merwyn. "I am told that he is almost a millionnaire in his own right," she said.

"What is he in his own heart and soul?" had been the girl's indignant answer. "Don't speak to me in that way again, mamma."

Meanwhile Merwyn was a close observer of all that was taking place, and was coming to what he regarded as an heroic resolution. Except as circumstances evoked an outburst of passion, he yielded to habit, and coolly kept his eye on the main chances of his life, and these meant what he craved most.

Two influences had been at work upon his mind during the summer. One resulted from his independent possession of large property. He had readily comprehended the hints thrown out by his lawyer that, if he remained in New York, the times gave opportunity for a rapid increase in his property, and the thought of achieving large wealth for himself, as his father had done before him, was growing in attractiveness. His indolent nature began to respond to vital American life, and he asked himself whether fortune-making in his own land did not promise more than fortune-seeking among English heiresses; moreover, he saw that his mother's devotion to the South increased daily, and that feeling at the North was running higher and becoming more and more sharply defined. As a business man in New York his property would be safe beyond a doubt, but if he were absent and affiliating with those known to be hostile to the North, dangerous complications might arise.

Almost unconsciously to himself at first the second influence was gaining daily in power. As he became convinced that Marian was not an ordinary girl, ready for a summer flirtation with a wealthy stranger, he began to give her more serious thought, to study her character, and acknowledge to himself her superiority. With every interview the spell of her fascination grew stronger, until at last he reached the conclusion which he regarded as magnanimous indeed. Waiving all questions of rank and wealth on his part he would become a downright suitor to this fair countrywoman. It did not occur to him that he had arrived at his benign mood by asking himself the question, "Why should I not please myself?" and by the oft-recurring thought: "If I marry rank and wealth abroad the lady may eventually remind me of her condescension. If I win great wealth here and lift this girl to my position she will ever be devoted and subservient and I be my own master. I prefer to marry a girl that pleases me in her own personality, one who has brains as well as beauty. When these military enthusiasts have disappeared below the Southern horizon, and time hangs more heavily on her hands, she will find leisure and thought for me. What is more, the very uncertainties of her position, with the advice of her prudent mamma, will incline her to the ample provision for the future which I can furnish."

Thus did Willard Merwyn misunderstand the girl he sought, so strong are inherited and perverted traits and lifelong mental habits. He knew how easily, with his birth and wealth, he could arrange a match abroad with the high contracting powers. Mrs. Vosburgh had impressed him as the chief potentate of her family, and not at all averse to his purpose. He had seen Mr. Vosburgh but once, and the quiet, reticent man had appeared to be a second-rate power. He had also learned that the property of the family was chiefly vested in the wife. Of course, if Mr. Vosburgh had been in the city, Merwyn would have addressed him first, but he was absent and the time of his return unknown.

The son knew his mother would be furious, but he had already discounted that opposition. He regarded this Southern-born lady as a very unsafe guide in these troublous times. Indeed, he cherished a practical kind of loyalty to her and his sisters.

"Only as I keep my head level," he said to himself, "are they safe. Mamma would identify herself with the South to-day if she could, and with a woman's lack of foresight be helpless on the morrow. Let her dream her dreams and nurse her prejudices. I am my father's son, and the responsible head of the family; and I part with no solid advantage until I receive a better one. I shall establish mamma and the girls comfortably in England, and then return to a city where I can soon double my wealth and live a life independent of every one."

This prospect grew to be so attractive that he indulged, like Mr. Lanniere, in King Cophetua's mood, and felt that one American girl was about to become distinguished indeed.

Watching his opportunity he called upon Mrs. Vosburgh while Marian was out of the way, formally asking her, in her husband's absence, for permission to pay his addresses; and he made known his financial resources and prospects with not a little complacent detail.

Mrs. Vosburgh was dignified and gracious, enlarged on her daughter's worth, hinted that she might be a little difficult to win by reason of the attentions she had received and her peculiar views, yet left, finally, the impression that so flattering proposals could not be slighted.

Merwyn went home with a sigh of relief. He would no longer approach Marian with doubtful and ill-defined intentions, which he believed chiefly accounted for the clever girl's coldness towards him.

CHAPTER XIV.
OMINOUS.

SUBORDINATE only to her father and two chief friends, in Marian's thoughts, was her enemy, for as such she now regarded Willard Merwyn. She had felt his attentions to be humiliating from the first. They had presented her former life, in which her own amusement and pleasure had been her chief thought, in another and a very disagreeable light. These facts alone would have been sufficient to awaken a vindictive feeling, for she was no saint. In addition, she bitterly resented his indifference to a cause made so dear by her father's devotion and her friends' brave self-sacrifice. Whatever his motive might be, she felt that he was cold-blooded, cowardly, or disloyal, and such courtesy as she showed him was due to little else than the hope of inflicting upon him some degree of humiliation. She had seen too many manifestations of honest interest and ardent love to credit him with any such emotion, and she had no scruples in wounding his pride to the utmost.

Meanwhile events in the bloody drama of the war were culminating. The Union officers were thought to have neither the wisdom to fight at the right time nor the discretion to retreat when fighting was worse than useless. In consequence thousands of brave men were believed by many to have died in vain once more on the ill-fated field of Bull Run.

One morning, the last of August, Strahan galloped to the Vosburgh cottage and said to Marian, who met him at the door: "Orders have come. I have but a few minutes in which to say good-by. Things have gone wrong in Virginia, and every available man is wanted in Washington."

His flushed face was almost as fair as her own, and gave him a boyish aspect in spite of his military dress, but unhesitating resolution and courage beamed from his eyes.

"Oh, that I were a man!" Marian cried, "and you would have company. All those who are most to me will soon be perilling their lives."

"Guess who has decided to go with me almost at the last moment."

"Mr. Blauvelt?"

"Yes; I told him that he was too high-toned to carry a musket, but he said he would rather go as a private than as an officer. He wishes no responsibility, he says, and, beyond mere routine duty, intends to give all his time and thoughts to art. I am satisfied that I have you to thank for this recruit."

"Indeed, I have never asked him to take part in the war."

"No need of your asking any one in set terms. A man would have to be either a coward, or else a rebel at heart, like Merwyn, to resist your influence. Indeed, I think it is all the stronger because you do not use it openly and carelessly. Every one who comes here knows that your heart is in the cause, and that you would have been almost a veteran by this time were you of our sex. Others, besides Blauvelt, obtained the impulse in your presence which decided them. Indeed, your drawing-room has been greatly thinned, and it almost looks as if few would be left to haunt it except Merwyn."

"I do not think he will haunt it much longer, and I should prefer solitude to his society."

"Well," laughed Strahan, "I think you will have a chance to put one rebel to rout before I do. I don't blame you, remembering your feeling, but Merwyn probably saved my life, and I gave him my hand in a final truce. Friends we cannot be while he maintains his present cold reserve. As you told me, he said he would have done as much for any one, and his manner since has chilled any grateful regard on my part. Yet I am under deep obligations, and hereafter will never do or say anything to his injury."

"Don't trouble yourself about Mr. Merwyn, Arthur. I have my own personal score to settle with him. He has made a good foil for you and my other friends, and I have learned to appreciate you the more. YOU have won my entire esteem and respect, and have taught me how quickly a noble, self-sacrificing purpose can develop manhood. O Arthur, Heaven grant that we may all meet again! How proud I shall then be of my veteran friends! and of you most of all. You are triumphing over yourself, and you have won the respect of every one in this community."

"If I ever become anything, or do anything, just enter half the credit in your little note-book," he said, flushing with pleasure.

"I shall not need a note-book to keep in mind anything that relates to you. Your courage has made me a braver, truer girl. Arthur, please, you won't get reckless in camp? I want to think of you always as I think of you now. When time hangs heavy on your hands, would it give you any satisfaction to write to me?"

"Indeed it will," cried the young officer. "Let me make a suggestion. I will keep a rough journal of what occurs and of the scenes we pass through, and Blauvelt will illustrate it. How should you like that? It will do us both good, and will be the next best thing to running in of an evening as we have done here."

Marian was more than pleased with the idea. When at last Strahan said farewell, he went away with every manly impulse strengthened, and his heart warmed by the evidences of her genuine regard.

In the afternoon Blauvelt called, and, with Marian and her mother, drove to the station to take part in an ovation to Captain Strahan and his company. The artist had affairs to arrange in the city before enlisting, and proposed to enter the service at Washington.

The young officer bore up bravely, but when he left his mother and sisters in tears, his face was stern with effort. Marian observed, however, that his last glance from the platform of the cars rested upon herself. She returned home depressed and nervously excited, and there found additional cause for solicitude in a letter from her father informing her of the great disaster to Union arms which poor generalship had invited. This, as she then felt, would have been bad enough, but in a few tender, closing words, he told her that they might not hear from him in some time, as he had been ordered on a service that required secrecy and involved some danger. Mrs. Vosburgh was profuse in her lamentations and protests against her husband's course, but Marian went to her room and sobbed until almost exhausted.

Her nature, however, was too strong, positive, and unchastened to find relief in tears, or to submit resignedly. Her heart was full of bitterness and revolt, and her partisanship was becoming almost as intense as that of Mrs. Merwyn.

The afternoon closed with a dismal rain-storm, which added to her depression, while relieving her from the fear of callers. "O dear!" she exclaimed, as she rose from the mere form of supper, "I have both head-ache and heart-ache. I am going to try to get through the rest of this dismal day in sleep."

"Marian, do, at least, sit an hour or two with me. Some one may come and divert your thoughts."

"No one can divert me to-night. It seems as if an age had passed since we came here in June."

"Your father knows how alone we are in the world, with no near relatives to call upon. I think he owes his first duty to us."

"The men of the North, who are right, should be as ready to sacrifice everything as the men of the South, who are wrong; and so also should Northern women. I am proud of the fact that my father is employed and trusted by his government. The wrong rests with those who caused the war."

"Every man can't go and should not go. The business of the country must be carried on just the same, and rich business men are as important as soldiers. I only wish that, in our loneliness and with the future so full of uncertainty, you would give sensible encouragement to one abundantly able to give you wealth and the highest position."

"Mr. Merwyn?"

"Yes, Mr. Merwyn," continued her mother, with an emphasis somewhat irritable. "He is not an old, worn-out millionnaire, like Mr. Lanniere. He is young, exceedingly handsome, so high-born that he is received as an equal in the houses of the titled abroad. He has come to me like an honorable man, and asked for the privilege of paying his addresses. He would have asked your father had he been in town. He was frank about his affairs, and has just received, in his own name, a very large property, which he proposes to double by entering upon business in New York."

"What does his mother think of his intentions toward me?" the young girl asked, so quietly, that Mrs. Vosburgh was really encouraged.

"He says that he and his mother differ on many points, and will differ on this one, and that is all he seemed inclined to say, except to remark significantly that he had attained his majority."

"It was he whom you meant, when you said that some one might come who would divert my thoughts?"

"I think he would have come, had it not been for the storm."

"Mamma, you have not given him any encouragement? You have not compromised yourself, or me?"

Mrs. Vosburgh bridled with the beginnings of resentment, and said, "Marian, you should know me too well--"

"There, there, mamma, I was wrong to think of such a thing; I ask your pardon."

"I may have my sensible wishes and preferences," resumed the lady, complacently, "but I have never yet acted the role of the anxious, angling mamma. I cannot help wishing, however, that you would consider favorably an offer like this one, and I certainly could not treat Mr. Merwyn otherwise than with courtesy."

"That was right and natural of you, mamma. You have no controversy with Mr. Merwyn; I have. I hate and detest him. Well, since he may come, I shall dress and be prepared."

"O Marian! you are so quixotic!"

"Dear mamma, you are mistaken. Do not think me inconsiderate of you. Some day I will prove I am not by my marriage, if I marry;" and she went to her mother and kissed her tenderly.

Then by a sudden transition she drew herself up with the dark, inscrutable expression that was becoming characteristic since deeper experiences had entered into her life, and said, firmly:--

"Should I do as you suggest, I should be false to those true friends who have gone to fight, perhaps to die; false to my father; false to all that's good and true in my own soul. As to my heart," she concluded, with a contemptuous shrug, "that has nothing to do with the affair. Mamma, you must promise me one thing. I do not wish you to meet Mr. Merwyn to-night. Please excuse yourself if he asks for you. I will see him."

"Mark my words, Marian, you will marry a poor man."

"Oh, I have no objection to millionnaires," replied the girl, with a short, un-mirthful laugh, "but they must begin their suit in a manner differing from that of two who have favored me;" and she went to her room.

As Merwyn resembled his deceased parent, so Marian had inherited not a little of her father's spirit and character. Until within the last few months her mother's influence had been predominant, and the young girl had reflected the social conventionalities to which she was accustomed. No new traits had since been created. Her increasing maturity had rendered her capable of revealing qualities inherent in her nature, should circumstances evoke them. The flower, as it expands, the plant as it grows, is apparently very different, yet the same. The stern, beautiful woman who is arraying herself before her mirror, as a soldier assumes his arms and equipments, is the same with the thoughtless, pleasure-loving girl whom we first met in her drawing-room in June; but months of deep and almost tragic experience have called into activity latent forces received from her father's soul,--his power of sustained action, of resolute purpose, of cherishing high ideals, and of white, quiet anger.

Her toilet was scarcely completed when Willard Merwyn was announced.

CHAPTER XV.
SCORN.

I
T is essential that we should go back several hours in our story. On the morning of the day that witnessed the departure of Strahan and his company Merwyn's legal adviser had arrived and had been closeted for several hours with his client. Mr. Bodoin was extremely conservative. Even in youth he had scarcely known any leanings toward passion of any kind or what the world regards as folly. His training had developed and intensified natural characteristics, and now to preserve in security the property intrusted to his care through a stormy, unsettled period had become his controlling motive. He looked upon the ups and downs of political men and measures with what seemed to him a superior and philosophical indifference, and he was more than pleased to find in Merwyn, the son of his old client, a spirit so in accord with his own ideas.

They had not been very long together on this fateful day before he remarked: "My dear young friend, it is exceedingly gratifying to find that you are level-headed, like your father. He was a man, Willard, whom you do well to imitate. He secured what he wanted and had his own way, yet there was no nonsense about him. I was his intimate friend as well as legal adviser, and I know, perhaps, more of his life than any one else. Your mother, to-day, is the handsomest woman of her years I ever saw, but when she was of your age her beauty was startling, and she had almost as many slaves among the first young men of the South as there were darkies on the plantation, yet your father quietly bore her away from them all. What is more, he so managed as to retain her respect and affection to the last, at the same time never yielding an inch in his just rights or dignity, and he ever made Mrs. Merwyn feel that her just rights and dignity were equally sacred. Proud as your mother was, she had the sense to see that his course was the only proper one. Their marriage, my boy, always reminded me of an alliance between two sovereign and alien powers. It was like a court love-match abroad. Your father, a Northern man, saw the beautiful Southern heiress, and he sued as if he were a potentate from a foreign realm. Well-born and accustomed to wealth all his life, he matched her pride with a pride as great, and made his offer on his feet as if he were conferring as much as he should receive. That, in fact, was the only way to win a woman who had been bowed down to all her life. After marriage they lived together like two independent sovereigns, sometimes here, then in the city house, and, when Mrs. Merwyn so desired it, on the Southern plantation, or abroad. He always treated her as if she were a countess or a queen in her own right and paid the utmost deference to her Southern ideas, but never for a moment permitted her to forget that he was her equal and had the same right to his Northern views. In regard to financial matters he looked after her interests as if he were her prime minister, instead of a husband wishing to avail himself of anything. In his own affairs he consulted me constantly and together we planted his investments on the bed-rock. These reminiscences will enable you to understand the pleasure with which I recognize in you the same traits. Of course you know that the law gives you great power over your property. If you were inclined to dissipation, or, what would be little better in these times, were hot-headed and bent on taking part in this losing fight of the South, I should have no end of trouble."

"You, also, are satisfied, then, that it will be a losing fight?" Merwyn had remarked.

"Yes, even though the South achieves its independence. I am off at one side of all the turmoil, and my only aim is to keep my trusts safe, no matter who wins. I see things as they are up to date and not as I might wish them to be if under the influence of passion or prejudice. The South may be recognized by foreign powers and become a separate state, although I regard this as very doubtful. In any event the great North and West, with the immense tides of immigration pouring in, will so preponderate as to be overshadowing. The Southern empire, of which Mrs. Merwyn dreams, would dwindle rather than grow. Human slavery, right or wrong, is contrary to the spirit of the age. But enough of this political discussion. I only touch upon it to influence your action. By the course you are pursuing you not only preserve all your Northern property, but you will also enable me to retain for your mother and sisters the Southern plantation. This would be impossible if you were seeking 'the bubble, reputation, at the cannon's mouth' on either side. Whatever happens, there must still be law and government. Both sides will soon get tired of this exhausting struggle, and then those who survive and have been wise will reap the advantage. Now, as to your own affairs, the legal formalities are nearly completed. If you return and spend the winter in New York I can put you in the way of vastly increasing your property, and by such presence and business activity you will disarm all criticism which your mother's Southern relations may occasion."

"Mamma will bitterly oppose my return."

"I can only say that what I advise will greatly tend to conserve Mrs. Merwyn's interests. If you prefer, we can manage it in this way: after you have safely established your mother and sisters abroad I can write you a letter saying that your interests require your presence."

And so it had been arranged, and the old lawyer sat down to dinner with Mrs. Merwyn, paying her the courtly deference which, while it gratified her pride, was accepted as a matter of course--as a part of her husband's legacy. He had soon afterwards taken his departure, leaving his young client in a most complacent and satisfactory mood.

It may thus be seen that Merwyn was not an unnatural product of the influences which had until now guided his life and formed his character. The reminiscences of his father's friend had greatly increased his sense of magnanimity in his intentions towards Marian. In the overweening pride of youth he felt as if he were almost regally born and royally endowed, and that a career was opening before him in which he should prove his lofty superiority to those whose heads were turned by the hurly-burly of the hour. Young as he was, he had the sense to be in accord with wise old age, that looked beyond the clouds and storm in which so many would be wrecked. Nay, even more, from those very wrecks he would gather wealth.

"The time and opportunity for cool heads," he smilingly assured himself, "is when men are parting with judgment and reason."

Such was his spirit when he sought the presence of the girl whose soul was keyed up to almost a passion of self-sacrifice. His mind belittled the cause for which her idolized father was, at that moment, perilling his life, and to which her dearest friends had consecrated themselves. He was serene in congratulating himself that "little Strahan" had gone, and that the storm would prevent the presence of other interlopers.

Although the room was lighted as usual, he had not waited many moments before a slight chill fell upon his sanguine mood. The house was so still, and the rain dripped and the wind sighed so dismally without, that a vague presentiment of evil began to assert itself. Heretofore he had found the apartment full of life and mirth, and he could not help remembering that some who had been its guests might now be out in the storm. Would she think of this also?

The parlor was scarcely in its usual pretty order, and no flowers graced the table. Evidently no one was expected. "All the better," he assured himself; "and her desolation will probably incline her the more to listen to one who can bring golden gleams on such a dreary night."

A daily paper, with heavy headlines, lay on a chair near him. The burden of these lines was DEFEAT, CARNAGE, DEATH.

They increased the slight chill that was growing upon him, and made him feel that possibly the story of his birth and greatness which he had hoped to tell might be swallowed up by this other story which fascinated him with its horror.

A slight rustle caused him to look up, and Marian stood before him. Throwing aside the paper as if it were an evil spell, he rose, would have offered his hand had there been encouragement, but the girl merely bowed and seated herself as she said: "Good-evening, Mr. Merwyn. You are brave to venture out in such a storm."

Was there irony in the slight accent on the word "brave"? How singularly severe was her costume, also!--simple black, without an ornament. Yet he admitted that he had never seen her in so effective a dress, revealing, as it did, the ivory whiteness of her arms and neck.

"There is only one reason why I should not come this evening,--you may have hoped to escape all callers."

"It matters little what one hopes in these times," she said, "for events are taking place which set aside all hopes and expectations."

In her bitter mood she was impatient to have the interview over, so that she accomplished her purpose. Therefore she proposed, contrary to her custom with him, to employ the national tragedy, to which he was so indifferent, as one of her keenest weapons.

"It is quite natural that you should feel so, Miss Vosburgh, in regard to such hopes as you have thus far entertained--"

"Since they are the only hopes I know anything about, Mr. Merwyn, I am not indifferent to them. I suppose you were at the depot to see your friend, Mr. Strahan, depart?" and the question was asked with a steady, searching scrutiny that was a little embarrassing.

Indeed, her whole aspect produced a perplexed, wondering admiration, for she seemed breathing marble in her cold self-possession. He felt, however, that the explanation which he must give of his absence when so many were evincing patriotic good-will would enable him to impress her with the fact that he had superior interests at stake in which she might have a share.

Therefore he said, gravely, as if the reason were ample: "I should have been at the depot, of course, had not my legal adviser come up from town to-day and occupied me with very important business. Mr. Bodoin's time is valuable to him, and he presented, for my consideration, questions of vital interest. I have reached that age now when I must not only act for myself, but I also have very delicate duties to perform towards my mother and sisters."

"Mr. Strahan had a sad duty to perform towards his mother and sisters,--he said good-by to them."

"A duty which I shall soon have to perform, also," Merwyn said.

She looked at him inquiringly. Had he at last found his manhood, and did he intend to assert it? Had he abandoned his calculating policy, and was he cherishing some loyal purpose? If this were true and she had any part in his decision, it would be a triumph indeed; and, while she felt that she could never respond to any such proposition as he had made through her mother, she could forget the past and give him her hand in friendly encouragement towards such a career as Lane and Strahan had chosen. She felt that it would be well not to be over-hasty in showing resentment, but if possible to let him reveal his plans and character fully. She listened quietly, therefore, without show of approval or disapproval, as he began in reply to her questioning glance.

"I am going to be frank with you this evening, Miss Vosburgh. The time has come when I should be so. Has not Mrs. Vosburgh told you something of the nature of my interview with her?"

The young girl merely bowed.

"Then you know how sincere and earnest I am in what--in what I shall have to say."

To his surprise he felt a nervous trepidation that he would not have imagined possible in making his magnanimous offer. He found this humble American girl more difficult to approach than any other woman he had ever met.

"Miss Vosburgh," he continued, hesitatingly, "when I first entered this room I did not understand your true worth and superiority, but a sense of these has been growing on me from that hour to this. Perhaps I was not as sincere as I--I--should have been, and you were too clever not to know it. Will you listen to me patiently?"

Again she bowed, and lower this time to conceal a slight smile of triumph.

Encouraged, he proceeded: "Now that I have learned to know you well, I wish you to know me better,--to know all about me. My father was a Northern man with strong Northern traits; my mother, a Southern woman with equally strong Southern traits. I have been educated chiefly abroad. Is it strange, then, that I cannot feel exactly as you do, or as some of your friends do?"

"As we once agreed, Mr. Merwyn, each must choose his own course for life."

"I am glad you have reminded me of that, for I am choosing for life and not for the next ten months or ten years. As I said, then, all this present hurly-burly will soon pass away." Her face darkened, but in his embarrassment and preoccupation he did not perceive it. "I have inherited a very large property, and my mother's affairs are such that I must act wisely, if not always as she would wish."

"May I ask what Mrs. Merwyn would prefer?"

"I am prepared to be perfectly frank about myself," he replied, hesitatingly, "but--"

"Pardon me. It is immaterial."

"I have a perfect right to judge and act for myself," resumed Merwyn, with some emphasis.

"Thank you. I should remember that."

The words were spoken in a low tone and almost as if in soliloquy, and her face seemed to grow colder and more impassive if possible.

With something approaching dismay Merwyn had observed that the announcement of his large fortune had had no softening influence on the girl's manner, and he thought, "Truly, this is the most dreary and business-like wooing that I ever imagined!"

But he had gone too far to recede, and his embarrassment was beginning to pass into something like indignation that he and all he could offer were so little appreciated.

Restraining this feeling, he went on, gravely and gently: "You once intimated that I was young, Miss Vosburgh, yet the circumstances and responsibilities of my lot have led me to think more, perhaps, than others of my age, and to look beyond the present hour. I regard the property left me by my father as a trust, and I have learned to-day that I can greatly increase and probably double it. It is my intention, after taking my mother and sisters abroad, to return to New York and to enter cautiously into business under the guidance of my legal adviser, who is a man of great sagacity. Now, as you know, I have said from the first that it is natural for you to feel deeply in regard to the events of the day; but I look beyond all this turmoil, distraction, and passion, which will be as temporary as it is violent. I am thinking for you as truly as for myself. Pardon me for saying it; I am sure I am in a better condition of mind to think for you than you are to judge for yourself. I can give you the highest social position, and make your future a certainty. From causes I can well understand the passion of the hour has been swaying you--"

She rose, and by an emphatic gesture stopped him, and there was a fire in the blue eyes that had been so cold before. She appeared to have grown inches as she stood before him and said, in tones of concentrated scorn: "You are indeed young, yet you speak the calculating words of one so old as to have lost every impulse of youth. Do you know where my father is at this moment?"

"No," he faltered.

"He is taking part, at the risk of his life, in this temporary hurly-burly, as you caricature it. It is he who is swaying me, and the memory of the brave men whom you have met here and to whom you fancied yourself superior. Did not that honored father exist, or those brave friends, I feel within my soul that I have womanhood enough to recognize and feel my country's need in this supreme hour of her peril. You thoughtful beyond your years?--you think for me? What did you think of me the first evening you spent here? What were your thoughts as you came again and again? To what am I indebted for this honor, but the fact that you could only beguile a summer's ennui by a passing flirtation which would leave me you little cared where, after you had joined your aristocratic friends abroad? Now your plans have changed, and, after much deliberation, you have come to lift me to the highest position! Never dream that I can descend to your position!"

He was fairly trembling with anger and mortification, and she was about to leave the apartment.

"Stay!" he said, passing his hand across his brow as if to brush away confusion of mind; "I have not given you reason for such contempt, and it is most unreasonable."

"Why is it unreasonable?" she asked, her scornful self-control passing into something like passion. "I will speak no more of the insult of your earlier motives towards me, now that you think you can afford to marry me. In your young egotism you may think a girl forgets and forgives such a thing easily if bribed by a fortune. I will let all that be as if it were not, and meet you on the ground of what is, at this present hour. I despise you because you have no more mind or manhood--take it as you will--than to think that this struggle for national life and liberty is a mere passing fracas of politicians. Do you think I will tamely permit you to call my noble father little better than a fool? He has explained to me what this war means--he, of twice your age, and with a mind as large as his manhood and courage. You have assumed to be his superior, also, as well as that of Mr. Lane and Mr. Strahan, who are about to peril life in the 'hurly-burly.' What are your paltry thousands to me? Should I ever love, I will love a MAN; and had I your sex and half your inches, I should this hour be in Virginia, instead of defending those I love and honor against your implied aspersions. Had you your mother's sentiments I should at least respect you, although she has no right to be here enjoying the protection of a government that she would destroy."

He was as pale as she had become flushed, and again he passed his hand over his brow confusedly and almost helplessly. "It is all like a horrid dream," he muttered.

"Mr. Merwyn, you have brought this on yourself," she said, more calmly. "You have sought to wrong me in my own home. Your words and manner have ever been an insult to the cause for which my father may die--O God!" she exclaimed, with a cry of agony--"for which he may now be dead! Go, go," she added, with a strong repellent gesture. "We have nothing in common: you measure everything with the inch-rule of self."

As if pierced to the very soul he sprung forward and seized her hand with almost crushing force, as he cried: "No, I measure everything hereafter by the breadth of your woman's soul. You shall not cast me off in contempt. If you do you are not a woman,--you are a fanatic, worse than my mother;" and he rushed from the house like one distraught.

Panting, trembling, frightened by a volcanic outburst such as she had never dreamed of, Marian sunk on a lounge, sobbing like a child.

CHAPTER XVI.
AWAKENED AT LAST.

IT may well be imagined that Mrs. Vosburgh was not far distant during the momentous interview described in the last chapter, and, as Merwyn rushed from the house as if pursued by the furies, she appeared at once on the scene, full of curiosity and dismay.

Exclamations, questionings, elicited little from Marian. The strain of the long, eventful day had been too great, and the young girl, who might have been taken as a type of incensed womanhood a few moments before, now had scarcely better resources than such remedies as Mrs. Vosburgh's matronly experience knew how to apply. Few remain long on mountain-tops, physical or metaphorical, and deep valleys lie all around them. Little else could be done for the poor girl than to bring the oblivion of sleep, and let kindly Nature nurse her child back to a more healthful condition of body and mind.

But it would be long before Willard Merwyn would be amenable to the gentle offices of nature. Simpson, the footman, flirting desperately with the pretty waitress in the kitchen below, heard his master's swift, heavy step on the veranda, and hastened out only in time to clamber into his seat as Merwyn drove furiously away in the rain and darkness. Every moment the trembling lackey expected they would all go to-wreck and ruin, but the sagacious animals were given their heads, and speedily made their way home.

The man took the reeking steeds to the stable, and Merwyn disappeared. He did not enter the house, for he felt that he would stifle there, and the thought of meeting his mother was intolerable. Therefore, he stole away to a secluded avenue, and strode back and forth under the dripping trees, oblivious, in his fierce perturbation, of outward discomfort.

Mrs. Merwyn waited in vain for him to enter, then questioned the attendant.

"Faix, mum, I know nothin' at all. Mr. Willard druv home loike one possessed, and got out at the door, and that's the last oi've seen uv 'im."

The lady received the significant tidings with mingled anxiety and satisfaction. Two things were evident. He had become more interested in Miss Vosburgh than he had admitted, and she, by strange good fortune, had refused him.

"It was a piece of folly that had to come in some form, I suppose," she soliloquized, "although I did not think Willard anything like so sure to perpetrate it as most young men. Well, the girl has saved me not a little trouble, for, of course, I should have been compelled to break the thing up;" and she sat down to watch and wait. She waited so long that anxiety decidedly got the better of her satisfaction.

Meanwhile the object of her thoughts was passing through an experience of which he had never dreamed. In one brief hour his complacency, pride, and philosophy of life had been torn to tatters. He saw himself as Marian saw him, and he groaned aloud in his loathing and humiliation. He looked back upon his superior airs as ridiculous, and now felt that he would rather be a private in Strahan's company than the scorned and rejected wretch that he was. The passionate nature inherited from his mother was stirred to its depths. Even the traits which he believed to be derived from his father, and which the calculating lawyer had commended, had secured the young girl's most withering contempt; and he saw how she contrasted him with her father and Mr. Lane,--yes, even with little Strahan. In her bitter words he heard the verdict of the young men with whom he had associated, and of the community. Throughout the summer he had dwelt apart, wrapped in his own self-sufficiency and fancied superiority. His views had been of gradual growth, and he had come to regard them as infallible, especially when stamped with the approval of his father's old friend; but the scathing words, yet ringing in his ears, showed him that brave, conscientious manhood was infinitely more than his wealth and birth. As if by a revelation from heaven he saw that he had been measuring everything with the little rule of self, and in consequence he had become so mean and small that a generous-hearted girl had shrunk from him in loathing.

Then in bitter anger and resentment he remembered how he was trammelled by his oath to his mother. It seemed to him that his life was blighted by this pledge and a false education. There was no path to her side who would love and honor only a MAN.

At last the mere physical manifestations of passion and excitement began to pass away, and he felt that he was acting almost like one insane as he entered the house.

Mrs. Merwyn met him, but he said, hoarsely, "I cannot talk with you to-night."

"Willard, be rational. You are wet through. You will catch your death in these clothes."

"Nothing would suit me better, as I feel now;" and he broke away.

He was so haggard when he came down late the next morning that his mother could not have believed such a change possible in so short a time. "It is going to be more serious than I thought," was her mental comment as she poured him out a cup of coffee.

It was indeed; for after drinking the coffee in silence, he looked frowningly out of the window for a time; then said abruptly to the waiter, "Leave the room."

The tone was so stern that the man stole out with a scared look.

"Willard," began Mrs. Merwyn, with great dignity, "you are acting in a manner unbecoming your birth and breeding."

Turning from the window, he fixed his eyes on his mother with a look that made her shiver.

At last he asked, in a low, stern voice, "Why did you bind me with that oath?"

"Because I foresaw some unutterable folly such as you are now manifesting."

"No," he said, in the same cold, hard tone. "It was because your cursed Confederacy was more to you than my freedom, than my manhood,--more to you than I am myself."

"O Willard! What ravings!"

"Was my father insane when he quietly insisted on his rights, yielding you yours? What right had you to cripple my life?"

"I took the only effective means to prevent you from doing just that for yourself."

"How have you succeeded?"

"I have prevented you, as a man of honor, from doing, under a gust of passion, what would spoil all my plans and hopes."

"I am not a man. You have done your best to prevent me from being one. You have bound me with a chain, and made me like one of the slaves on your plantation. Your plans and hopes? Have I no right to plans and hopes?"

"You know my first thought has been of you and for you."

"No, I do not know this. I now remember that, when you bound me, a thoughtless, selfish, indolent boy, you said that you would have torn your heart out rather than marry my father had you foreseen what was coming. This miserable egotist, Jeff Davis, and his scheme of empire, cost what it may, are more to you than husband or child. A mother would have said: 'You have reached manhood and have the rights of a man. I will advise you and seek to guide you. You know my feelings and views, and in their behalf I will even entreat you; but you have reached that age when the law makes you free, and holds you accountable to your own conscience.' Of what value is my life if it is not mine? I should have the right to make my own life, like others."

"You have the right to make it, but not to mar it."

"In other words, your prejudices, your fanaticism, are to take the place of my conscience and reason. You expect me to carry a sham of manhood out into the world. I wish you to release me from my oath."

"Never," cried Mrs. Merwyn, with a passion now equal to his own. "You have fallen into the hands of a Delilah, and she has shorn you of your manhood. Infatuated with a nameless Northern girl, you would blight your life and mine. When you come to your senses you will thank me on your knees that I interposed an oath that cannot be broken between you and suicidal folly;" and she was about to leave the room.

"Stop," he said, huskily. "When I bound myself I did so without realizing what I did. I was but a boy, knowing not the future. I did it out of mere good-will to you, little dreaming of the fetters you were forging. Since you will not release me and treat me as a man I shall keep the oath. I swore never to put on the uniform of a Union soldier, or to step on Southern soil with a hostile purpose, but you have taught me to detest your Confederacy with implacable hate; and I shall use my means, my influence, all that I am, to aid others to destroy it."

"What! are you not going back to England with us?"

"Yes."

"Before you have been there a week this insane mood will pass away."

"Did my father's moods pass away?"

"Your father--" began the lady, impetuously, and then hesitated.

"My father always yielded you your just rights and maintained his own. I shall imitate his example as far as I now may. The oath is a thing that stands by itself. It will probably spoil my life, but I cannot release myself from it."

"You leave me only one course, Willard,--to bear with you as if you were a passionate child. You never need hope for my consent to an alliance with the under-bred creature who has been the cause of this folly."

"Thank you. You now give me your complete idea of my manhood. I request that these subjects be dismissed finally between us. I make another pledge,--I shall be silent whenever you broach them;" and with a bow he left the apartment.

Half an hour later he was climbing the nearest mountain, resolved on a few hours of solitude. From a lofty height he could see the little Vosburgh cottage, and, by the aid of a powerful glass, observed that the pony phaeton did not go out as usual, although the day was warm and beautiful after the storm.

The mists of passion were passing from his mind, and in strong reaction from his violent excitement he sunk, at first, into deep depression. So morbid was he that he cried aloud: "O my father! Would to God that you had lived! Where are you that you can give no counsel, no help?"

But he was too young to give way to utter despondency, and at last his mind rallied around the words he had spoken to Marian. "I shall, hereafter, measure everything by the breadth of your woman's soul."

As he reviewed the events of the summer in the light of recent experience, he saw how strong, unique, and noble her character was. Faults she might have in plenty, but she was above meannesses and mercenary calculation. The men who had sought her society had been incited to manly action, and beneath all the light talk and badinage earnest and heroic purposes had been formed; he meanwhile, poor fool! had been too blinded by conceited arrogance to understand what was taking place. He had so misunderstood her as to imagine that after she had spent a summer in giving heroic impulses she would be ready to form an alliance that would stultify all her action, and lose her the esteem of men who were proving their regard in the most costly way. He wondered at himself, but thought:--

"I had heard so much about financial marriages abroad that I had gained the impression that no girl in these days would slight an offer like mine. Even her own mother was ready enough to meet my views. I wonder if she will ever forgive me, ever receive me again as a guest, so that I can make a different impression. I fear she will always think me a coward, hampered as I am by a restraint that I cannot break. Well, my only chance is to take up life from her point of view, and to do the best I can. There is something in my nature which forbids my ever yielding or giving up. So far as it is now possible I shall keep my word to her, and if she has a woman's heart she may, in time, so far relent as to give me a place among her friends. This is now my ambition, for, if I achieve this, I shall know I am winning such manhood as I can attain."

When Merwyn appeared at dinner he was as quiet and courteous as if nothing had happened; but his mother was compelled to note that the boyishness had departed out of his face, and in its strong lines she recognized his growing resemblance to his father.

Two weeks later he accompanied his mother and sisters to England. Before his departure he learned that Marian had been seriously ill, but was convalescent, and that her father had returned.

Meantime and during the voyage, with the differences natural to the relation of mother and son, his manner was so like that of his father towards her that she was continually reminded of the past, and was almost led to fear that she had made a grave error in the act she had deemed so essential. But her pride and her hopes for the future prevented all concession.

"When he is once more in society abroad this freak will pass away," she thought, "and some English beauty will console him."

But after they were well established in a pretty villa near congenial acquaintances, Merwyn said one morning, "I shall return to New York next week."

"Willard! how can you think of such a thing? I was planning to spend the latter part of the winter in Rome."

"That you may easily do with your knowledge of the city and your wide circle of friends."

"But we need you. We want you to be with us, and I think it most unnatural in you to leave us alone."

"I have taken no oath to dawdle around Europe indefinitely. I propose to return to New York and go into business."

"You have enough and more than enough already."

"I certainly have had enough of idleness."

"But I protest against it. I cannot consent."

"Mamma," he said, in the tone she so well remembered, "is not my life even partially my own? What is your idea of a man whom both law and custom make his own master? Even as a woman you chose for yourself at the proper age. What strange infatuation do you cherish that you can imagine that a son of Willard Merwyn has no life of his own to live? It is now just as impossible for me to idle away my best years in a foreign land as it would be for me to return to my cradle. I shall look after your interests and comfort to the best of my ability, and, if you decide to return to New York, you shall be received with every courtesy."

"I shall never return to New York. I would much prefer to go to my plantation and share the fortunes of my own people."

"I supposed you would feel in that way, and I will do all in my power to further your wishes, whatever they may be. My wishes, in personal matters, are now equally entitled to respect. I shall carry them out;" and with a bow that precluded all further remonstrance he left the room.

A day or two later she asked, abruptly, "Will you use your means and influence against the South?"

"Yes."

Mrs. Merwyn's face became rigid, but nothing more was said. When he bade her good-by there was an evident struggle in her heart, but she repressed all manifestations of feeling, and mother and son parted.

CHAPTER XVII.
COMING TO THE POINT.

WHEN the tide has long been rising the time comes for it to recede. From the moment of Marian's awakening to a desire for a better womanhood, she had been under a certain degree of mental excitement and exaltation. This condition had culminated with the events that wrought up the loyal North into suspense, anguish, and stern, relentless purpose.

While these events had a national and world-wide significance, they also pressed closely, in their consequences, on individual life. It has been shown how true this was in the experience of Marian. Her own personal struggle alone, in which she was combating the habits and weakness of the past, would not have been a trivial matter,--it never is when there is earnest endeavor,--but, in addition to this, her whole soul had been kindling in sympathy with the patriotic fire that was impelling her dearest friends towards danger and possible death. Lane's, Strahan's, and Blauvelt's departure, and her father's peril, had brought her to a point that almost touched the limit of endurance. Then had come the man whose attentions had been so humiliating to her personally, and who represented to her the genius of the Rebellion that was bringing her such cruel experience. She saw his spirit of condescension even in his offer of marriage; worse still, she saw that he belittled the conflict in which even her father was risking his life; and her indignation and resentment had burst forth upon him with a power that she could not restrain.

The result had been most unexpected. Instead of slinking away overwhelmed with shame and confusion, or departing in haughty anger, Merwyn had revealed to her that which is rarely witnessed by any one,--the awakening of a strong, passionate nature. In the cynical, polished, self-pleasing youth was something of which she had not dreamed,--of which he was equally unaware. Her bitter words pierced through the strata of self-sufficiency and pride that had been accumulating for years. She stabbed with truth the outer man and slew it, but the inner and possible manhood felt the sharp thrust and sprung up wounded, bleeding, and half desperate with pain. That which wise and kindly education might have developed was evoked in sudden agony, strong yet helpless, overwhelmed with the humiliating conscious-ness of what had been, and seeing not the way to what she would honor. Yet in that supreme moment the instinct asserted itself that she, who had slain his meaner self, had alone the power to impart the impulse toward true manhood and to give the true measure of it. Hence a declaration so passionate, and an appeal so full of his immense desire and need, that she was frightened, and faltered helplessly.

In the following weary days of suffering and weakness, she realized that she was very human, and not at all the exalted heroine that she had unconsciously come to regard herself. The suitor whom she had thought to dismiss in contempt and anger, and to have done with, could not be banished from her mind. The fact that he had proved himself to be all that she had thought him did not satisfy her, for the reason that he had apparently shown himself to be so much more. She had judged him superficially, and punished him accordingly. She had condemned him unsparingly for traits which, except for a few short months, had been her own char-acteristics. While it was true that they seemed more unworthy in a man, still they were essentially the same.

"But he was not a man," she sighed. "He was scarcely more than the selfish boy that wealth, indulgence, and fashionable life had made him. Why was I so blind to this? Why could I not have seen that nothing had ever touched him deeply enough to show what he was, or, at least, of what he was capable? What was Strahan before his manhood was awakened? A little gossiping exquisite. Even Mr. Lane, who was always better than any of us, has changed wonderfully since he has had exceptional motives for noble action. What was I, myself, last June, when I was amusing myself at the expense of a man whom I knew to be so good and true? In view of all this, instead of having a little charity for Mr. Merwyn, who, no doubt, is only the natu-ral product of the influences of his life, I only tolerated him in the vindictive hope of giving the worst blow that a woman can inflict. I might have seen that he had a deeper nature; at least, I might have hoped that he had, and given him a chance to reveal it. Perhaps there has never been one who tried to help him toward true manhood. He virtually said that his mother was a Southern fanatic, and his associations have been with those abroad who sympathized with her. Is it strange that a mere boy of twenty-one should be greatly influenced by his mother and her aristocratic friends? He said his father was a Northern man, and he may have imbibed the notion that he could not fight on either side. Well, if he will give up such a false idea, if he will show that he is not cold-blooded and calculating, as his last outbreak seemed to prove, and can become as brave and true a soldier as Strahan, I will make amends by treating him as I do Strahan, and will try to feel as friendly towards him. He shall not have the right to say I'm 'not a woman but a fanatic.'"

She proved herself a woman by the effort to make excuses for one towards whom she had been severe, by her tendency to relent after she had punished to her heart's content.

"But," added the girl aloud, in the solitude of her room, "while I may give him my hand in some degree of kindliness and friendship, if he shows a different spirit, he shall never have my colors, never my loyal and almost sisterly love, until he has shown the courage and manhood of Mr. Lane and Mr. Strahan. They shall have the first place until a better knight appears."

When, one September evening, her father quietly entered his home he gave her an impulse towards convalescence beyond the power of all remedies. There were in time mutual confidences, though his were but partial, because relating to affairs foreign to her life, and tending to create useless anxieties in respect to the future. He was one of those sagacious, fearless agents whom the government, at that period, employed in many and secret ways. For obvious reasons the nature and value of their services will never be fully known.

Marian was unreserved in her relation of what had occurred, and her father smiled and reassured her.

"In one sense you are right," he said. "We should have a broader, kindlier charity for all sorts of people, and remember that, since we do not know their antecedents and the influences leading to their actions, we should not be hasty to judge. Your course might have been more Christian-like towards young Merwyn, it is true. Coming from you, however, in your present state of development, it was very natural, and I'm not sure but he richly deserved your words. If he has good mettle he will be all the better for them. If he spoke from mere impulse and goes back to his old life and associations, I'm glad my little girl was loyal and brave enough to lodge in his memory truths that he won't forget. Take the good old doctrine to your relenting heart and don't forgive him until he 'brings forth fruits meet for repentance.' I'm proud of you that you gave the young aristocrat such a wholesome lesson in regard to genuine American manhood and womanhood."

Mrs. Vosburgh's reception of her husband was a blending of welcome and reproaches. What right had he to overwhelm them with anxiety, etc., etc.?

"The right of about a million men who are taking part in the struggle," he replied, laughing at her good-naturedly.

"But I can't permit or endure it any longer," said his wife, and there was irritation in her protest.

"Well, my dear," he replied, with a shrug, "I must remain among the eccentric millions who continue to act according to their own judgment."

"Mamma!" cried Marian, who proved that she was getting well by a tendency to speak sharply, "do you wish papa to be poorer-spirited than any of the million? What kind of a man would he be should he reply, 'Just as you say, my dear; I've no conscience, or will of my own'? I do not believe that any girl in the land will suffer more than I when those I love are in danger, but I'd rather die than blockade the path of duty with my love."

"Yes, and some day when you are fatherless you may repent those words," sobbed Mrs. Vosburgh.

"This will not answer," said Mr. Vosburgh, in a tone that quieted both mother and daughter, who at this stage were inclined to be a little hysterical. "A moment's rational thought will convince you that words cannot influence me. I know exactly what I owe to you and to my country, and no earthly power can change my course a hair's breadth. If I should be brought home dead to-morrow, Marian would not have the shadow of a reason for self-reproach. She would have no more to do with it than with the sunrise. Your feelings, in both instances, are natural enough, and no doubt similar scenes are taking place all over the land; but men go just the same, as they should do and always have done in like emergencies. So wipe away your tears, little women. You have nothing to cry about yet, while many have."

The master mind controlled and quieted them. Mrs. Vosburgh looked at her husband a little curiously, and it dawned upon her more clearly than ever before that the man whom she managed, as she fancied, was taking his quiet, resolute way through life with his own will at the helm.

Marian thought, "Ah, why does not mamma idolize such a man and find her best life in making the most of his life?"

She had, as yet, scarcely grasped the truth that, as disease enfeebles the body, so selfishness disables the mind, robbing it of the power to care for others, or to understand them. In a sense Mr. Vosburgh would always be a stranger to his wife. He had philosophically and patiently accepted the fact, and was making the best of the relation as it existed.

It was now decided that the family should return at once to their city home. Mr. Vosburgh had a few days of leisure to superintend the removal, and then his duties would become engrossing.

The evening before their departure was one of mild, charming beauty, and as the dining-room was partially dismantled, it was Mr. Vosburgh's fancy to have the supper-table spread on the veranda. The meal was scarcely finished when a tall, broad-shouldered man appeared at the foot of the steps, and Sally, the pretty waitress, manifested a blushing consciousness of his presence.

"Wud Mr. Vosburgh let me spake to him a moment?" began the stranger.

Marian recognized the voice that, from the shrubbery, had given utterance to the indignant protest against traits which had once characterized her own life and motives. Thinking it possible that her memory was at fault, she glanced at Sally's face and the impression was confirmed. "What ages have passed since that June evening!" she thought.

"Is it anything private, my man?" asked Mr. Vosburgh, pushing back his chair and lighting a cigar.

"Faix, zur, it's nothin' oi'm ashamed on. I wish to lave the country and get a place on the perlace force," repeated the man, with an alacrity which showed that he wished Sally to hear his request.

"You look big and strong enough to handle most men."

"Ye may well say that, zur; oi've not sane the man yit that oi was afeared on."

Sally chuckled over her knowledge that this was not true in respect to women, while Marian whispered to her father: "Secure him the place if you can, papa. You owe a great deal to him and so do I, although he does not know it. This is the man whose words, spoken to Sally, disgusted me with my old life. Don't you remember?"

Mr. Vosburgh's eyes twinkled, as he shot a swift glance at Sally, whose face was redder than the sunset. The man's chief attraction to the city was apparent.

"What's your name?" the gentleman asked.

"Barney Ghegan, zur."

"Are you perfectly loyal to the North? Will you help carry out the laws, even against your own flesh and blood, if necessary?"

"Oi'll 'bey orders, zur," replied the man, emphatically. "Oi've come to Amarekay to stay, and oi'll stan' by the goovernment."

"Can you bring me a certificate of your character?"

"Oi can, zur, for foive years aback."

"Bring it then, Barney, and you shall go on the force; for you're a fine, stronglooking man,--the kind needed in these days," said Mr. Vosburgh, glad to do a good turn for one who unwittingly had rendered him so great a service, and also amused at this later aspect of the affair.

This amusement was greatly enhanced by observing Barney's proud, triumphant glance at Sally. Turning quickly to note its effect on the girl, Mr. Vosburgh caught the coquettish maid in the act of making a grimace at her much-tormented suitor.

Sally's face again became scarlet, and in embarrassed haste she began to clear the table.

Barney was retiring slowly, evidently wishing for an interview with his elusive charmer before he should return to his present employers, and Mr. Vosburgh goodnaturedly put in a word in his favor.

"Stay, Barney, and have some supper before you go home. In behalf of Mrs. Vosburgh I give you a cordial invitation."

"Yes," added the lady, who had been quietly laughing. "Now that you are to be so greatly promoted we shall be proud to have you stay."

Barney doffed his hat and exclaimed, "Long loife to yez all, espacially to the swate-faced young leddy that first spoke a good wourd for me, oi'm a-thinkin';" and he stepped lightly around to the rear of the house.

"Sally," said Mr. Vosburgh, with preternatural gravity.

The girl courtesied and nearly dropped a dish.

"Mr. Barney Ghegan will soon be receiving a large salary."

Sally courtesied again, but her black eyes sparkled as she whisked the rest of the things from the table and disappeared. She maintained her old tactics during supper and before the other servants, exulting in the fact that the big, strong man was on pins and needles, devoid of appetite and peace.

"'Afeared o' no mon,' he says," she thought, smilingly. "He's so afeared o' me that he's jist a tremblin'."

After her duties were over, Barney said, mopping his brow: "Faix, but the noight is warm. A stroll in the air wudn't be bad, oi'm a-thinkin'."

"Oi'm cool as a cowcumber," remarked Sally. "We'll wait for ye till ye goes out and gits cooled off;" and she sat down complacently, while the cook and the laundress tittered.

An angry sparkle began to assert itself in Barney's blue eyes, and he remarked drily, as he took his hat, "Yez moight wait longer than yez bargained for."

The shrewd girl saw that she was at the length of her chain, and sprung up, saying: "Oh, well, since the mistress invited ye so politely, ye's company, and it's me duty to thry to entertain ye. Where shall we go?" she added, as she passed out with him.

"To the rustic sate, sure. Where else shud we go?"

"A rustic sate is a quare place for a stroll."

"Oi shall have so much walkin' on me bate in New York, that it's well to begin settin' down aready, oi'm a-thinkin'."

"Why, Barney, ye're going to be a reg'lar tramp. Who'd 'a thought that ye'd come down to that."

"Ah! arrah, wid ye nonsense! Sit ye down here, for oi'm a-goin' to spake plain the noight. Noo, by the Holy Vargin, oi'm in arenest. Are ye goin' to blow hot, or are ye goin' to blow could?"

"Considerin' the hot night, Barney, wouldn't it be better for me to blow could?"

Barney scratched his head in perplexity. "Ye know what I mane," he ejaculated.

"Where will ye foind the girl that tells all she knows?"

"O Sally, me darlint, what's the use of batin' around the bush? Ye know that a cat niver looked at crame as oi look on ye," said Barney, in a wheedling tone, and trying the tactics of coaxing once more.

He sat down beside her and essayed with his insinuating arm to further his cause as his words had not done.

"Arrah, noo, Barney Ghegan, what liberties wud ye be takin' wid a respectable girl?" and she drew away decidedly.

He sprung to his feet and exploded in the words: "Sally Maguire, will ye be me woife? By the holy poker! Answer, yis or no."

Sally rose, also, and in equally pronounced tones replied: "Yes, Barney Ghegan, I will, and I'll be a good and faithful one, too. It's yeself that's been batin' round the bush. Did ye think a woman was a-goin' to chase ye over hill and down dale and catch ye by the scruff of the neck? What do ye take me for?"

"Oi takes ye for better, Sally, me darlint;" and then followed sounds suggesting the popping of a dozen champagne corks.

Mr. Vosburgh, his wife, and Marian had been chatting quietly on the piazza, unaware of the scene taking place in the screening shrubbery until Barney's final question had startled the night like a command to "stand and deliver."

Repressing laughter with difficulty they tiptoed into the house and closed the door.

CHAPTER XVIII.
A GIRL'S STANDARD.

THE month of September, 1862, was a period of strong excitement and profound anxiety on both sides of the vague and shifting line which divided the loyal North from the misguided but courageous South. During the latter part of August Gen. Pope had been overwhelmed with disaster, and what was left of his heroic army was driven within the fortifications erected for the defence of Washington. Apparently the South had unbounded cause for exultation. But a few weeks before their capital had been besieged by an immense army, while a little to the north, upon the Rappahannock, rested another Union army which, under a leader like Stonewall Jackson, would have been formidable enough in itself to tax Lee's skill and strength to the utmost. Except in the immediate vicinity of the capital and Fortress Monroe scarcely a National soldier had been left in Virginia. The Confederates might proudly claim that the generalship of Lee and the audacity of Jackson had swept the Northern invaders from the State.

Even more important than the prestige and glory won was the fact that the Virginian farmers were permitted to gather their crops unmolested. The rich harvests of the Shenandoah Valley and other regions, that had been and should have been occupied by National troops, were allowed to replenish the Confederate granaries. There were rejoicings and renewed confidence in Southern homes, and smiles of triumph on the faces of sympathizers abroad and throughout the North.

But the astute leaders of the Rebellion were well aware that the end had not yet come, and that, unless some bold, paralyzing blow was struck, the struggle was but fairly begun. In response to the request for more men new armies were springing up at the North. The continent shook under the tread of hosts mustering with the stern purpose that the old flag should cover every inch of the heritage left by our fathers.

Therefore, Lee was not permitted to remain on the defensive a moment, but was ordered to cross the Potomac in the rear of Washington, threatening that city and Baltimore. It was supposed that the advent of a Southern army into Maryland would create such an enthusiastic uprising that thinned ranks would be recruited, and the State brought into close relation with the Confederate Government. These expectations were not realized. The majority sympathized with Barbara Frietchie,

"Bravest of all in Frederick town,"

rather than with their self-styled deliverers; and Lee lost more by desertion from his own ranks than he gained in volunteers. In this same town of Frederick, by strange carelessness on the part of the rebels, was left an order which revealed to McClellan Lee's plans and the positions which his divided army were to occupy during the next few days. Rarely has history recorded such opportunities as were thus accidentally given to the Union commander.

The ensuing events proved that McClellan's great need was not the reinforcements for which he so constantly clamored, but decision and energy of character. Had he possessed these qualities he could have won for himself, from the fortuitous order which fell into his hands, a wreath of unfading laurel, and perhaps have saved almost countless lives of his fellow-countrymen. As it was, if he had only advanced his army a little faster, the twelve thousand Union soldiers, surrendered by the incompetent and pusillanimous Gen. Miles, would have been saved from the horrors of captivity and secured as a valuable reinforcement. To the very last, fortune appeared bent on giving him opportunity. The partial success won on the 17th of September, at the battle of Antietam, might easily have been made a glorious victory if McClellan had had the vigor to put in enough troops, especially including Burnside's corps, earlier in the day. Again, on the morning of the 18th, he had only to take the initiative, as did Grant after the first day's fighting at Shiloh, and Lee could scarcely have crossed the Potomac with a corporal's guard. But, as usual, he hesitated, and the enemy that robbed him of one of the highest places in history was not the Confederate general or his army, but a personal trait,--indecision. In the dawn of the 19th he sent out his cavalry to reconnoitre, and learned that his antagonist was safe in Virginia. Fortune, wearied at last, finally turned her back upon her favorite. The desperate and bloody battle resulted in little else than the ebb of the tide of war southward. Northern people, it is true, breathed more freely. Philadelphia, Baltimore, and Washington were safe for the present, but this seemed a meagre reward for millions of treasure and tens of thousands of lives, especially when the capture of Richmond and the end of the Rebellion had been so confidently promised.

If every village and hamlet in the land was profoundly stirred by these events, it can well be understood that the commercial centre of New York throbbed like an irritated nerve under the telegraph wires concentring there from the scenes of action. Every possible interest, every variety of feeling, was touched in its vast and heterogeneous population, and the social atmosphere was electrical with excitement.

From her very constitution, now that she had begun to comprehend the nature of the times, Marian Vosburgh could not breathe this air in tranquillity. She was, by birthright, a spirited, warm-hearted girl, possessing all a woman's disposition towards partisanship. Everything during the past few months had tended to awaken a deep interest in the struggle, and passing events intensified it. Not only in the daily press did she eagerly follow the campaign, but from her father she learned much that was unknown to the general public. To a girl of mind the great drama in itself could not fail to become absorbing, but when it is remembered that those who had the strongest hold upon her heart were imperilled actors in the tragedy, the feeling with which she watched the shifting scenes may in some degree be appreciated. She often saw her father's brow clouded with deep anxiety, and dreaded that each new day might bring orders which would again take him into danger.

While the letters of her loyal friend, Lane, veiled all that was hard and repulsive in his service, she knew that the days of drill and equipment would soon be over, and that the new regiment must participate in the dangers of active duty. This was equally true of Strahan and Blauvelt. She laughed heartily over their illustrated journal, which, in the main, gave the comic side of their life. But she never laid it aside without a sigh, for she read much between the lines, and knew that the hour of battle was rapidly approaching. Thus far they had been within the fortifications at Washington, for the authorities had learned the folly of sending undisciplined recruits to the front.

At last, when the beautiful month of October was ended, and Lee's shat-

tered army was rested and reorganized, McClellan once more crossed the Potomac. Among the reinforcements sent to him were the regiments of which Lane and
Strahan were members. The letters of her friends proved that they welcomed the
change and with all the ardor of brave, loyal men looked forward to meeting the
enemy. In heart and thought she went with them, but a sense of their danger fell,
like a shadow, across her spirit. She appeared years older than the thoughtless girl
for whom passing pleasure and excitement had been the chief motives of life; but in
the strengthening lines of her face a womanly beauty was developing which caused
even strangers to turn and glance after her.

If Merwyn still retained some hold upon her thoughts and curiosity, so much
could scarcely be said of her sympathy. He had disappeared from the moment when
she had harshly dismissed him, and she was beginning to feel that she had been
none too severe, and to believe that his final words had been spoken merely from
impulse. If he were amusing himself abroad, Marian, in her intense loyalty, would
despise him; if he were permitting himself to be identified with his mother's circle
of Southern sympathizers, the young girl's contempt would be tinged with detestation. He had approached her too nearly, and humiliated her too deeply, to be readily forgotten or forgiven. His passionate outbreak at last had been so intense as to
awaken strong echoes in her woman's soul. If return to a commonplace fashionable
life was to be the only result of the past, she would scarcely ever think of him without an angry sparkle in her eyes.

After she had learned that her friends were in the field and therefore exposed
to the dangers of battle at any time, she had soliloquized, bitterly: "He promised
to 'measure everything by the breadth of my woman's soul.' What does he know
about a true woman's soul? He has undoubtedly found his selfish nature and his
purse more convenient gauges of the world. Well, he knows of one girl who cannot
be bought."

Her unfavorable impression was confirmed one cold November morning. Passing down Madison Avenue, her casual attention was attracted by the opening of a
door on the opposite side of the street. She only permitted her swift glance to take
in the fact that it was Merwyn who descended the steps and entered an elegant
coupe driven by a man in a plain livery. After the vehicle had been whirled away,
curiosity prompted her to retrace her steps that she might look more closely at the

residence of the man who had asked her to be his wife. It was evidently one of the finest and most substantial houses on the avenue.

A frown contracted. the young girl's brow as she muttered: "He aspired to my hand,--he, who fares sumptuously in that brown-stone palace while such men as Mr. Lane are fortunate to have a canvas roof over their heads. He had the narrowness of mind to half-despise Arthur Strahan, who left equal luxury to face every danger and hardship. Thank Heaven I planted some memories in his snobbish soul!"

Thereafter she avoided that locality.

In the evening, with words scarcely less bitter, she mentioned to her father the fact that she had seen Merwyn and his home.

Mr. Vosburgh smiled and said, "You have evidently lost all compunctions in regard to your treatment of the young fellow."

"I have, indeed. The battle of Antietam alone would place a Red Sea between me and any young American who can now live a life of selfish luxury. Think how thousands of our brave men will sleep this stormy night on the cold, rain-soaked ground, and then think of his cold-blooded indifference to it all!"

"Why think of him at all, Marian?" her father asked, with a quizzical smile.

The color deepened slightly in her face as she replied: "Why shouldn't I think of him to some extent? He has crossed my path in no ordinary way. His attentions at first were humiliating, and he awakened an antipathy such as I never felt towards any one before. He tried to belittle you, my friends, and the cause to which you are devoted. Then, when I told him the truth about himself, he appeared to have manhood enough to comprehend it. His words made me think of a man desperately wounded, and my sympathies were touched, and I felt that I had been unduly severe and all that. In fact, I was overwrought, ill, morbid, conscience-stricken as I remembered my own past life, and he appeared to feel what I said so awfully that I couldn't forget it. I had silly dreams and hopes that he would assert his manhood and take a loyal part in the struggle. But what has been his course? So far as I can judge, it has been in keeping with his past. Settling down to a life of ease and money-making here would be little better, in my estimation, than amusing himself abroad. It would be simply another phase of following his own mood and inclinations; and I shall look upon his outburst and appeal as hysterical rather than passionate and sincere."

Mr. Vosburgh listened, with a half-amused expression, to his daughter's indignant and impetuous words, but only remarked, quietly, "Suppose you find that you have judged Mr. Merwyn unjustly?"

"I don't think I have done so. At any rate, one can only judge from what one knows."

"Stick to that. Your present impressions and feelings do you credit, and I am glad that your friends' loyal devotion counts for more in your esteem than Merwyn's wealth. Still, in view of your scheme of life to make the most and best of men of brains and force, I do not think you have given the young nabob time and opportunity to reveal himself fully. He may have recently returned from England, and, since his mother was determined to reside abroad, it was his duty to establish her well before returning. You evidently have not dismissed him from your thoughts. Since that is true, do not condemn him utterly until you see what he does. What if he again seeks your society?"

"Well, I don't know, papa. As I feel to-night I never wish to see him again."

"I'm not sure of that, little girl. You are angry and vindictive. If he were a nonentity you would be indifferent."

"Astute papa! That very fact perplexes me. But haven't I explained why I cannot help thinking of him to some extent?"

"No, not even to yourself."

Marian bit her lip with something like vexation, then said, reproachfully, "Papa, you can't think that I care for him?"

"Oh, no,--not in the sense indicated by your tone. But your silly dreams and hopes, as you characterize them, have taken a stronger hold upon you than you realize. You are disappointed as well as angry. You have entertained the thought that he might do something, or become more in harmony with the last words he spoke to you."

"Well, he hasn't."

"You have not yet given him sufficient time, perhaps. I shall not seek to influence you in the matter, but the question still presents itself: What if he again seeks your society and shows a disposition to make good his words?"

"I shall not show him," replied Marian, proudly, "greater favor than such friends as Mr. Lane and Mr. Strahan required. Without being influenced by me, they decided to take part in the war. After they had taken the step which did so much credit to their manly courage and loyalty, they came and told me of it. If Mr. Merwyn should show equal spirit and patriotism and be very humble in view of the past, I should, of course, feel differently towards him. If he don't--"and the girl shook her head ominously.

Her father laughed heartily. "Why!" he exclaimed; "I doubt whether in all the sunny South there is such a little fire-eater as we have here."

"No, papa, no," cried Marian, with suddenly moistening eyes. "I regret the war beyond all power of expression. I could not ask, much less urge, any one to go, and my heart trembles and shrinks when I think of danger threatening those I love. But I honor--I almost worship--courage, loyalty, patriotism. Do you think I can ever love any one as I do you? Yet I believe you would go to Richmond to-morrow if you were so ordered. I ask nothing of this Merwyn, or of any one; but he who asks my friendship must at least be brave and loyal enough to go where my father would lead. Even if I loved a man, even if I were married, I would rather that the one *I* loved did all a man's duty, though my heart was broken and my life blighted in consequence, than to have him seeking safety and comfort in some eminently prudent, temporizing course."

Mr. Vosburgh put his arm around his daughter, as he looked, for a moment, into her tear-dimmed eyes, then kissed her good-night, and said, quietly, "I understand you, Marian."

"But, papa!" she exclaimed, in sudden remorsefulness, "you won't take any risks that you can honorably escape?"

"I promise you I won't go out to-night in search of the nearest recruiting sergeant," replied her father, with a reassuring laugh.

CHAPTER XIX.
PROBATION PROMISED.

MERWYN had been in the city some little time when Marian, unknown to him, learned of his presence. He, also, had seen her more than once, and while her aspect had increased his admiration and a feeling akin to reverence, it had also disheartened him. To a degree unrecognized by the girl herself, her present motives and stronger character had changed the expression of her face. He had seen her when unconscious of observation and preoccupied by thoughts which made her appear grave and almost stern, and he was again assured that the advantages on which he had once prided himself were as nothing to her compared with the loyalty of friends now in Virginia. He could not go there, nor could he explain why he must apparently shun danger and hardship. He felt that his oath to his mother would be, in her eyes, no extenuation of his conduct. Indeed, he believed that she would regard the fact that he could give such a pledge as another proof of his unworthiness to be called an American. How could it be otherwise when he himself could not look back upon the event without a sense of deep personal humiliation?

"I was an idiotic fool when I gave away manhood and its rights," he groaned. "My mother took advantage of me."

In addition to the personal motive to conceal the fact of his oath, he had even a stronger one. The revelation of his pledge would be proof positive of his mother's disloyalty, and might jeopardize the property on which she and his sisters depended for support. Moreover, while he bitterly resented Mrs. Merwyn's course towards him he felt that honor and family loyalty required that he should never speak a word to her discredit. The reflection implied in his final words to Marian had been wrung from him in the agony of a wounded spirit, and he now regretted them.

Henceforth he would hide the fetters which in restraining him from taking the part in the war now prompted by his feelings also kept him from the side of the girl who had won the entire allegiance of his awakened heart. He did not know how to approach her, and feared lest a false step should render the gulf between them impassable. He saw that her pride, while of a different character, was greater than his own had ever been, and that the consideration of his birth and wealth, which he had once dreamed must outweigh all things else, would not influence her in the slightest degree. Men whom she regarded as his equals in these respects were not only at her feet but also facing the enemy as her loyal knights. How pitiable a figure in her eyes he must ever make compared with them!

But there is no gravitation like that of the heart. He felt that he must see her again, and was ready to sue for even the privilege of being tolerated in her drawing-room on terms little better than those formerly accorded him.

When he arrived in New York he had hesitated as to his course. His first impulse had been to adopt a life of severe and inexpensive simplicity. But he soon came to look upon this plan as an affectation. There was his city home, and he had a perfect right to occupy it, and abundant means to maintain it. After seeing Marian's resolute, earnest face as she passed in the street unconscious of his scrutiny, and after having learned more about her father from his legal adviser, the impression grew upon him that he had lost his chance, and he was inclined to take refuge in a cold, proud reticence and a line of conduct that would cause no surmises and questionings on the part of the world. He would take his natural position, and live in such a way as to render curiosity impertinent.

He had inherited too much of his father's temperament to sit down in morbid brooding, and even were he disposed toward such weakness he felt that his words to Marian required that he should do all that he was now free to perform in the advancement of the cause to which she was devoted. She might look with something like contempt on a phase of loyalty which gave only money when others were giving themselves, but it was the best he could do. Whether she would ever recognize the truth or not, his own self-respect required that he should keep his word and try to look at things from her point of view, and, as far as possible, act accordingly. For a time he was fully occupied with Mr. Bodoin in obtaining a fuller knowledge of his property and the nature of its investment. Having learned more definitely about his resources he next followed the impulse to aid the cause for which he could not fight.

A few mornings after the interview between Marian and her father described in the previous chapter, Mr. Vosburgh, looking over his paper at the breakfast-table, laughed and said: "What do you think of this, Marian? Here is Merwyn's name down for a large donation to the Sanitary and Christian Commissions."

His daughter smiled satirically as she remarked, "Such heroism takes away my breath."

"You are losing the power, Marian," said her mother, irritably, "of taking moderate, common-sense views of anything relating to the war. If the cause is first in your thoughts why not recognize the fact that Mr. Merwyn can do tenfold more with his money than if he went to the front and 'stopped a bullet,' as your officer friends express themselves? You are unfair, also. Instead of giving Mr. Merwyn credit for a generous act you sneer at him."

The girl bit her lip, and looked perplexed for a moment. "Well, then," she said, "I will give him credit. He has put himself to the inconvenience of writing two checks for amounts that he will miss no more than I would five cents."

"Ask your father," resumed Mrs. Vosburgh, indignantly, "if the men who sustain these great charities and the government are not just as useful as soldiers in the field. What would become of the soldiers if business in the city should cease? Your ideas, carried out fully, would lead your father to start to the front with a musket, instead of remaining where he can accomplish the most good."

"You are mistaken, mamma. My only fear is that he will incur too many risks as it is. I have never asked any one to go to the front, and I certainly would not ask Mr. Merwyn. Indeed, when I think of the cause, I would rather he should do as you suggest. I should be glad to have him give thousands and increase the volume of business by millions; but if he gave all he has, he could not stand in my estimation with men who offer their lives and risk mutilation and untold suffering from wounds. I know nothing of Mr. Merwyn's present motives, and they may be anything but patriotic. He may think it to his advantage to win some reputation for loyalty, when it is well known that his mother has none at all. Those two gifts, paltry for one of his means, count very little in these days of immense self-sacrifice. I value, in times of danger, especially when great principles are at stake, self-sacrifice and uncalculating heroism above all things, and I prefer to choose my friends from among those who voluntarily exhibit these qualities. No man living could win my favor who took risks merely to please me. Mr. Merwyn is nothing to me, and if I should ever meet him again socially, which is not probable, I should be the last one to suggest that he should go to the war; but if he, or any one, wishes my regard, there must be a compliance with the conditions on which I give it. I am content with the friends I have."

Mr. Vosburgh looked at his daughter for a moment as if she were fulfilling his ideal, and soon after departed for his office. A few days after, when the early shadows of the late autumn were gathering, he was interrupted in his preparations to return up town by the entrance of the subject of the recent discussion.

Merwyn was pale and evidently embarrassed as he asked, "Mr. Vosburgh, have you a few moments of leisure?"

"Yes," replied the gentleman, briefly.

He led the way to a private office and gave his caller a chair.

The young man was at a loss to begin a conversation necessarily of so delicate a nature, and hesitated.

Mr. Vosburgh offered no aid or encouragement, for his thought was, "This young fellow must show his hand fully before I commit myself or Marian in the slightest degree."

"Miss Vosburgh, no doubt, has told you of the character of our last interview," Merwyn began at last, plunging in medias res.

"My daughter is in the habit of giving me her confidence," was the quiet reply.

"Then, sir, you know how unworthy I am to make the request to which I am nevertheless impelled. In justice I can hope for nothing. I have forfeited the privilege of meeting Miss Vosburgh again, and I do not feel that it would be right for me to see her without your permission. The motives which first led me into her society were utterly unworthy of a true man, and had she been the ordinary society girl that I supposed she was, the results might have been equally deserving of condemnation. I will not plead in extenuation that I had been unfortunate in my previous associations, and in the influences that had developed such character as I had. Can you listen to me patiently?"

The gentleman bowed.

"I eventually learned to comprehend Miss Vosburgh's superiority in some degree, and was so fascinated by her that I offered marriage in perfect good faith; but the proposal was made in a complacent and condescending spirit that was so perfectly absurd that now I wonder at my folly. Her reply was severe, but not so severe as I deserved, and she led me to see myself at last in a true light. It is little I can now ask or hope. My questions narrow down to these: Is Miss Vosburgh disposed to give me only justice? Have I offended her so deeply that she cannot meet me again? Had my final words no weight with her? She has inspired in me the earnest wish to achieve such character as I am capable of,--such as circumstances permit. During the summer I saw her influence over others. She was the first one in the world who awakened in my own breast the desire to be different. I cannot hope that she will soon, if ever, look upon me as a friend; but if she can even tolerate me with some degree of kindliness and good-will, I feel that I should be the better and happier for meeting her occasionally. If this is impossible, please say to her that the pledge implied among the last words uttered on that evening, which I shall never forget, shall be kept. I shall try to look at right and duty as she would."

As he concluded, Mr. Vosburgh's face softened somewhat. For a while the young man's sentences had been a little formal and studied, evidently the result of much consideration; they had nevertheless the impress of truth. The gentleman's thought was: "If Mr. Merwyn makes good his words by deeds this affair has not yet ended. My little girl has been much too angry and severe not to be in danger of a reaction."

After a moment of silence he said: "Mr. Merwyn, I can only speak for myself in this matter. Of course, I naturally felt all a father's resentment at your earlier attentions to my daughter. Since you have condemned them unsparingly I need not refer to them again. I respect your disposition to atone for the past and to enter on a life of manly duty. You have my hearty sympathy, whatever may be the result. I also thank you for your frank words to me. Nevertheless, Miss Vosburgh must answer the questions you have asked. She is supreme in her drawing-room, and alone can decide whom she will receive there. I know she will not welcome any one whom she believes to be unworthy to enter. I will tell her all that you have said."

"I do not hope to be welcomed, sir. I only ask to be received with some degree of charity. May I call on you to-morrow and learn Miss Vosburgh's decision?"

"Certainly, at any hour convenient to you."

Merwyn bowed and retired. When alone he said, with a deep sigh of relief: "Well, I have done all in my power at present. If she has a woman's heart she won't be implacable."

"What kept you so late?" Mrs. Vosburgh asked, as her husband came down to dinner.

"A gentleman called and detained me."

"Give him my compliments when you see him again," said Marian, "and tell him that I don't thank him for his unreasonable hours. You need more recreation, papa. Come, take us out to hear some music to-night."

A few hours later they were at the Academy, occupying balcony seats. Marian was glancing over the house, between the acts, with her glass, when she suddenly arrested its motion, and fixed it on a lonely occupant of an expensive box. After a moment she handed the lorgnette to her father, and directed him whither to look. He smiled and said, "He appears rather pensive and preoccupied, doesn't he?"

"I don't fancy pensive, preoccupied men in these times. Why didn't he fill his box, instead of selfishly keeping it all to himself?"

"Perhaps he could not secure the company he wished."

"Who is it?" Mrs. Vosburgh asked.

She was told, and gave Merwyn a longer scrutiny than the others.

"Shall I go and give him your compliments and the message you spoke of at dinner?" resumed Mr. Vosburgh, in a low tone.

"Was it Mr. Merwyn that called so late?" she asked, with a sudden intelligence in her eyes.

Her father nodded, while the suggestion of a smile hovered about his mouth.

"Just think of it, Marian!" said Mrs. Vosburgh. "We all might now be in that box if you had been like other girls."

"I am well content where I am."

During the remainder of the evening Mr. Vosburgh observed some evidences of suppressed excitement in Marian, and saw that she managed to get a glimpse of that box more than once. Long before the opera ended it was empty. He pointed out the fact, and said, humorously, "Mr. Merwyn evidently has something on his mind."

"I should hope so; and so have you, papa. Has he formally demanded my hand with the condition that you stop the war, and inform the politicians that this is their quarrel, and that they must fight it out with toothpicks?"

"No; his request was more modest than that."

"You think I am dying with curiosity, but I can wait until we get home."

When they returned, Mr. Vosburgh went to his library, for he was somewhat owlish in his habits.

Marian soon joined him, and said: "You must retire as soon as you have finished that cigar. Even the momentous Mr. Merwyn shall not keep us up a second longer. Indeed, I am so sleepy already that I may ask you to begin your tale to-night, and end with 'to be continued.'"

He looked at her so keenly that her color rose a little, then said, "I think, my dear, you will listen till I say 'concluded;'" and he repeated the substance of Merwyn's words.

She heard him with a perplexed little frown. "What do you think I ought to do, papa?"

"Do you remember the conversation we had here last June?"

"Yes; when shall I forget it?"

"Well, since you wish my opinion I will give it frankly. It then became your ambition to make the most and best of men over whom you had influence, if they were worth the effort. Merwyn has been faulty and unmanly, as he fully admits himself, but he has proved apparently that he is not commonplace. You must take your choice, either to resent the past, or to help him carry out his better purposes. He does not ask much, although no doubt he hopes for far more. In granting his request you do not commit yourself to his hopes in the least."

"Well, papa, he said that I couldn't possess a woman's heart and cast him off in utter contempt, so I think I shall have to put him on probation. But he must be careful not to presume again. I can be friendly to many, but a friend to very few. Before he suggests that relation he must prove himself the peer of other friends."

CHAPTER XX.
"YOU THINK ME A COWARD."

MERWYN had not been long in the city before he was waited upon and asked to do his share towards sustaining the opera, and he had carelessly taken a box which had seldom been occupied. On the evening after his interview with Mr. Vosburgh, his feeling of suspense was so great that he thought he could beguile a few hours with music. He found, however, that the light throng, and even the harmonious sounds, irritated, rather than diverted, his perturbed mind, and he returned to his lonely home, and restlessly paced apartments rendered all the more dreary by their magnificence.

He proved his solicitude in a way that led Mr. Vosburgh to smile slightly, for when that gentleman entered his office, Merwyn was awaiting him.

"I have only to tell you," he said, in response to the young man's questioning eyes, "that Miss Vosburgh accedes to your request as you presented it to me;" and in parting he gave his hand with some semblance of friendliness.

Merwyn went away elated, feeling that he had gained all for which he had a right to hope. Eager as he was for the coming interview with Marian, he dreaded it and feared that he might be painfully embarrassed. In this eagerness he started early for an evening call; but when he reached his destination, he hesitated, passing and repassing the dwelling before he could gather courage to enter. The young girl would have smiled, could she have seen her former suitor, once so complacent and condescending. She certainly could not complain of lack of humility now.

At last he perceived that two other callers had passed in, and he followed them, feeling that their presence would enable both him and the object of his thoughts to take refuge in conventionalities.

He was right in this view, for with a scarcely perceptible increase of color, and a polite bow, Marian received him as she would any other mere calling acquaintance, introduced him to the two gentlemen present, and conversation at once became general. Merwyn did not remain long under constraint. Even Marian had to admit to herself that he acquitted himself well and promised better for the future. When topics relating to the war were broached, he not only talked as loyally as the others, but also proved himself well informed. Mrs. Vosburgh soon appeared and greeted him cordially, for the lady was ready enough to entertain the hopes which his presence again inspired. He felt that his first call, to be in good taste, should be rather brief, and he took his departure before the others, Marian bowing with the same distant politeness that had characterized her greeting. She made it evident that she had granted just what he had asked and nothing more. Whether he could ever inspire anything like friendliness the future only would reveal. He had serious doubts, knowing that he suffered in contrast with even the guests of the present evening. One was an officer home on sick-leave; the other exempted from military duty by reason of lameness, which did not extend to his wit and conversational powers. Merwyn also knew that he would ever be compared with those near friends now in Virginia.

What did he hope? What could he hope? He scarcely knew, and would not even entertain the questions. He was only too glad that the door was not closed to him, and, with the innate hopefulness of youth, he would leave the future to reveal its possibilities. He was so thoroughly his father's son that he would not be disheartened, and so thoroughly himself that the course he preferred would be the one followed, so far as was now possible.

"Well?" said Mr. Vosburgh, when Marian came to the library to kiss him goodnight.

"What a big, long question that little word contains!" she cried, laughing, and there was a little exhilaration in her manner which did not escape him.

"You may tell me much, little, or nothing."

"I will tell you nothing, then, for there is nothing to tell. I received and parted with Mr. Merwyn on his terms, and those you know all about. Mamma was quite gracious, and my guests were polite to him."

"Are you willing to tell me what impression he made in respect to his loyalty?"

"Shrewd papa! You think this the key to the problem. Perhaps it is, if there is any problem. Well, so far as WORDS went he proved his loyalty in an incidental way, and is evidently informing himself concerning events. If he has no better proof to offer than words, his probation will end unfavorably, even though he may not be immediately aware of the fact. Of course, now that I have granted his request, I must be polite to him so long as he chooses to come."

"Was he as complacent and superior as ever?"

"Whither is your subtlety tending? Are you, as well as mamma, an ally of Mr. Merwyn? You know he was not. Indeed, I must admit that, in manner, he carried out the spirit of his request."

"Then, to use your own words, he was 'befittingly humble'? No, I am not his ally. I am disposed to observe the results of your experiment."

"There shall be no experimenting, papa. Circumstances have enabled him to understand me as well as he ever can, and he must act in view of what he knows me to be. I shall not seek to influence him, except by being myself, nor shall I lower my standard in his favor."

"Very well, I shall note his course with some interest. It is evident, however, that the uncertainties of his future action will not keep either of us awake."

When she left him, he fell into a long revery, and his concluding thoughts were: "I doubt whether Marian understands herself in respect to this young fellow. She is too resentful. She does not feel the indifference which she seeks to maintain. The subtle, and, as yet, unrecognized instinct of her womanhood leads her to stand aloof. This would be the natural course of a girl like Marian towards a man who, for any cause, had gained an unusual hold upon her thoughts. I must inform myself thoroughly in regard to this Mr. Merwyn. Thus far her friends have given me little solicitude; but here is one, towards whom she is inclined to be hostile, that it may be well to know all about. Even before she is aware of it herself, she is on the defensive against him, and this, to a student of human nature, is significant. She virtually said to-night that he must win his way and make his own unaided advances toward manhood. Ah, my little girl! if it was not in him ever to have greater power over you than Mr. Strahan, you would take a kindlier interest in his efforts."

If Marian idolized her father as she had said, it can readily be guessed how much she was to him, and that he was not forgetful of his purpose to learn more about one who manifested so deep an interest in his daughter, and who possibly had the power to create a responsive interest. It so happened that he was acquainted with Mr. Bodoin, and had employed the shrewd lawyer in some government affairs. Another case had arisen in which legal counsel was required, and on the following day advice was sought.

When this part of the interview was over, Mr. Vosburgh remarked, casually, "By the way, I believe you are acquainted with Mr. Willard Merwyn and his affairs."

"Yes," replied the lawyer, at once on the alert.

"Do your relations to Mr. Merwyn permit you to give me some information concerning him?"

The attorney thought rapidly. His client had recently been inquiring about Mr. Vosburgh, and, therefore, the interest was mutual. On general principles it was important that the latter should be friendly, for he was a secret and trusted agent of the government, and Mrs. Merwyn's course might render a friend at court essential. Although the son had not mentioned Marian's name, Mr. Bodoin shrewdly guessed that she was exerting the influence that had so greatly changed the young man's views and plans. The calculating lawyer had never imagined that he would play the role of match-maker, but he was at once convinced that, in the stormy and uncertain times, Merwyn could scarcely make a better alliance than the one he meditated. Therefore with much apparent frankness the astute lawyer told Mr. Vosburgh all that was favorable to the young man.

"I think he will prove an unusual character," concluded the lawyer, "for he is manifesting some of his father's most characteristic traits," and these were mentioned. "When, after attaining his majority, the son returned from England, he was in many respects little better than a shrewd, self-indulgent boy, indifferent to everything but his own pleasure, but, for some reason, he has greatly changed. Responsibility has apparently sobered him and made him thoughtful. I have also told him much about my old friend and client, his father, and the young fellow is bent on imitating him. While he is very considerate of his mother and sisters, he has identified himself with his father's views, and has become a Northern man to the backbone. Even to a degree contrary to my advice, he insists on investing his means in government bonds."

This information was eminently satisfactory, and even sagacious Mr. Vosburgh did not suspect the motives of the lawyer, whom he knew to be eager to retain his good-will, since it was in his power to give much business to those he trusted.

"I may become Merwyn's ally after all, if he makes good his own and Mr. Bodoin's words," was his smiling thought, as he returned to his office.

He was too wise, however, to use open influence with his daughter, or to refer to the secret interview. Matters should take their own course for the present, while he remained a vigilant observer, for Marian's interest and happiness were dearer to him than his own life.

Merwyn sought to use his privilege judiciously, and concentrated all his faculties on the question of his standing in Marian's estimation. During the first few weeks, it was evident that his progress in her favor was slow, if any were made at all. She was polite, she conversed with him naturally and vivaciously on topics of general interest, but there appeared to be viewless and impassable barriers between them. Not by word or sign did she seek to influence his action.

She was extremely reticent about herself, and took pains to seem indifferent in regard to his life and plans, but she was beginning to chafe under what she characterized as his "inaction." Giving to hospitals and military charities and buying United-States bonds counted for little in her eyes.

"He parades his loyalty, and would have me think that he looks upon the right to call on me as a great privilege, but he does not care enough about either me or the country to incur any risk or hardship."

Thoughts like these were beginning not only to rekindle her old resentment, but also to cause a vague sense of disappointment. Merwyn had at least accomplished one thing,--he confirmed her father's opinion that he was not commonplace. Travel, residence abroad, association with well-bred people, and a taste for reading, had given him a finish which a girl of Marian's culture could not fail to appreciate. Because he satisfied her taste and eye, she was only the more irritated by his failure in what she deemed the essential elements of manhood. In spite of the passionate words he had once spoken, she was beginning to believe that a cold, calculating persistency was the corner-stone of his character, that even if he were brave enough to fight, he had deliberately decided to take no risks and enjoy his fortune. If this were true, she assured herself, he might shoulder the national debt if he chose, but he could never become her friend.

Then came the terrible and useless slaughter of Fredericksburg. With the fatuity that characterized the earlier years of the war, the heroic army of the Potomac, which might have annihilated Lee on previous occasions, was hurled against heights and fortifications that, from the beginning, rendered the attack hopeless.

Marian's friends were exposed to fearful perils, but passed through the conflict unscathed. Her heart went out to them in a deeper and stronger sympathy than ever, and Merwyn in contrast lost correspondingly.

During the remaining weeks of December, she saw that her father was almost haggard from care and anxiety, and he was compelled to make trips to Washington and even to the front.

"The end has not come yet," he had said to her, after one of these flying visits. "Burnside has made an awful blunder, but he is eager to retrieve himself, and now has plans on foot that promise better. The disaffection among his commanding officers and troops is what I am most afraid of--more, indeed, than of the rebel army. Unlike his predecessor, he is determined to move, to act, and I think we may soon hear of another great battle."

Letters from her friends confirmed this view, especially a brief note from Lane, in which the writer, fearing that it might be his last, had not wholly veiled his deep affection. "I am on the eve of participating in an immense cavalry movement," it began, "and it may be some time before I can write to you again, if ever."

The anxiety caused by this missive was somewhat relieved by a humorous account of the recall of the cavalry force. She then learned, through her father, that the entire army was again on the move, and that another terrific battle would be fought in a day or two.

"Burnside should cross the Rappahannock to-day or to-morrow, at the latest," Mr. Vosburgh had remarked at breakfast, to which he had come from the Washington owl-train.

It was the 20th of December, and when the shadows of the early twilight were gathering, Burnside had, in fact, massed his army at the fords of the river, and his troops, "little Strahan" among them, were awaiting orders to enter the icy tide in the stealthy effort to gain Lee's left flank. There are many veterans now living who remember the terrific "storm of wind, rain, sleet, and snow" that assailed the unsheltered army. It checked further advance more effectually than if all the rebel forces had been drawn up on the farther shore. After a frightful night, the Union army was discovered in the dawn by Lee.

Even then Burnside would have crossed, and, in spite of his opponent's preparations and every other obstacle, would have fought a battle, had he not been paralyzed by a foe with which no general could cope,--Virginia mud. The army mired helplessly, supply trains could not reach it. With difficulty the troops were led back to their old quarters, and so ended the disastrous campaigns of the year, so far as the army of the Potomac was concerned.

The storm that drenched and benumbed the soldiers on the Rappahannock was equally furious in the city of New York, and Mr. Vosburgh sat down to dinner frowning and depressed. "It seems as if fate is against us," he said. "This storm is general, I fear, and may prove more of a defence to Lee than his fortifications at Fredericksburg. It's bad enough to have to cope with treachery and disaffection."

"Treachery, papa?"

"Yes, treachery," replied her father, sternly. "Scoundrels in our own army informed Washington disunionists of the cavalry movement of which Captain Lane wrote you, and these unmolested enemies at the capital are in constant communication with Lee. When will our authorities and the North awake to the truth that this is a life-and-death struggle, and that there must be no more nonsense?"

"Would to Heaven I were a man!" said the young girl. "At this very moment, no doubt, Mr. Merwyn is enjoying his sumptuous dinner, while my friends may be fording a dark, cold river to meet their death. Oh! I can't eat anything to-night."

"Nonsense!" cried her mother, irritably.

"Come, little girl, you are taking things too much to heart. I am very glad you are not a man. In justice, I must also add that Mr. Merwyn is doing more for the cause than any of your friends. It so happens that I have learned that he is doing a great deal of which little is known."

"Pardon me," cried the girl, almost passionately. "Any man who voluntarily faces this storm, and crosses that river to-night or to-morrow, does infinitely more in my estimation."

Her father smiled, but evidently his appetite was flagging also, and he soon went out to send and receive some cipher despatches.

Merwyn was growing hungry for some evidence of greater friendliness than he had yet received. Hitherto, he had never seen Marian alone when calling, and the thought had occurred that if he braved the storm in paying her a visit, the effort might be appreciated. One part of his hope was fulfilled, for he found her drawing-room empty. While he waited, that other stormy and memorable evening when he had sought to find her alone flashed on his memory, and he feared that he had made a false step in coming.

This impression was confirmed by her pale face and distant greeting. In vain he put forth his best efforts to interest her. She remained coldly polite, took but a languid part in the conversation, and at times even permitted him to see that her thoughts were preoccupied. He had been humble and patient a long time, and now, in spite of himself, his anger began to rise.

Feeling that he had better take his leave while still under self-control, and proposing also to hint that she had failed somewhat in courtesy, he arose abruptly and said: "You are not well this evening, Miss Vosburgh? I should have perceived the fact earlier. I wish you good-night."

She felt the slight sting of his words, and was in no mood to endure it. Moreover, if she had failed in such courtesy as he had a right to expect, he should know the reason, and she felt at the moment willing that he should receive the implied reproach.

Therefore she said: "Pardon me, I am quite well. It is natural that I should be a little distraite, for I have learned that my friends are exposed to this storm, and will probably engage in another terrible battle to-morrow, or soon."

Again the old desperate expression, that she remembered so well, came into his eyes as he exclaimed, bitterly: "You think me a coward because I remain in the city? What is this storm, or that battle, compared with what I am facing! Good-night;" and, giving her no chance for further words, he hastened away.

CHAPTER XXI.
FEARS AND PERPLEXITIES.

MERWYN found the storm so congenial to his mood that he breasted it for hours before returning to his home. There, in weariness and reaction, he sank into deep dejection.

"What is the use of anger?" he asked himself, as he renewed the dying fire in his room. "In view of all the past, she has more cause for resentment than I, while it is a matter of indifference to her whether I am angry or not. I might as well be incensed at ice because it is cold, and she is ice to me. She has her standard and a circle of friends who come up to it. This I never have done and never can do. Therefore she only tolerates me and is more than willing that I should disappear below her horizon finally. I was a fool to speak the words I did to-night. What can they mean to her when nothing is left for me, apparently, but a safe, luxurious life? Such outbreaks can only seem hysterical or mere affectations, and there shall be no more of them, let the provocation be what it may. Indeed, why should I inflict myself on her any more? I cannot say that she has not a woman's heart, but I wronged and chilled it from the first, and cannot now retrieve myself. If I should go to her to-morrow, even in a private's uniform, she would give me her hand cordially, but she compares me with hundreds of thousands who seem braver men than I. It is useless for me to suggest that I am doing more than those who go to fight. Her thought would be: 'I have all the friends I need among more knightly spirits who are not afraid to look brave enemies in the face, and without whom the North would be disgraced. Let graybeards furnish the sinews of war; let young men give their blood if need be. It is indeed strange that a man's arm should be paralyzed, and his best hope in life blighted, by a mother!'"

If he could have known Marian's thoughts and heard the conversation that ensued with her father, he would not have been so despondent.

When he left her so abruptly she again experienced the compunctions she had felt before. Whether he deserved it or not she could not shut her eyes to the severity of the wound inflicted, or to his suffering. In vain she tried to assure herself that he did deserve it. Granting this, the thoughts asserted themselves: "Why am I called upon to resent his course? Having granted his request to visit me, I might, at least, be polite and affable on his own terms. Because he wishes more, and perhaps hopes for more, this does not, as papa says, commit me in the least. He may have some scruple in fighting openly against the land of his mother's ancestry. If that scruple has more weight with him than my friendly regard, that is his affair. His words to-night indicated that he must be under some strong restraint. O dear! I wish I had never known him; he perplexes and worries me. The course of my other friends is simple and straightforward as the light. Why do I say other friends? He's not a friend at all, yet my thoughts return to him in a way that is annoying."

When her father came home she told him what had occurred, and unconsciously permitted him to see that her mind was disturbed. He did not smile quizzically, as some sagacious people would have done, thus touching the young girl's pride and arraying it against her own best interests, it might be. With the thought of her happiness ever uppermost, he would discover the secret causes of her unwonted perturbation. Not only Merwyn--about whom he had satisfied himself--should have his chance, but also the girl herself. Mrs. Vosburgh's conventional match-making would leave no chance for either. The profounder man believed that nature, unless interfered with by heavy, unskilful hands, would settle the question rightly.

He therefore listened without comment, and at first only remarked, "Evidently, Marian, you are not trying to make the most and best of this young fellow."

"But, papa, am I bound to do this for people who are disagreeable to me and who don't meet my views at all?"

"Certainly not. Indeed, you may have frozen Merwyn out of the list of your acquaintances already."

"Well," replied the girl, almost petulantly, "that, perhaps, will be the best ending of the whole affair."

"That's for you to decide, my dear."

"But, papa, I FEEL that you don't approve of my course."

"Neither do I disapprove of it. I only say, according to our bond to be frank, that you are unfair to Merwyn. Of course, if he is essentially disagreeable to you, there is no occasion for you to make a martyr of yourself."

"That's what irritates me so," said the girl, impetuously. "He might have made himself very agreeable. But he undervalued and misunderstood me so greatly from the first that it was hard to forgive him."

"If he hadn't shown deep contrition and regret for that course I shouldn't wish you to forgive him, even though his antecedents had made anything better scarcely possible."

"Come down to the present hour, then. What he asked of you is one thing. I see what he wishes. He desires, at least, the friendship that I give to those who fulfil my ideal of manhood in these times. He has no right to seek this without meeting the conditions which remove all hesitation in regard to others. It angers me that he does so. I feel as if he were seeking to buy my good-will by donations to this, that, and the other thing. He still misunderstands me. Why can't he realize that, to one of my nature, fording the icy Rappahannock to-night would count for more than his writing checks for millions?"

"Probably he does understand it, and that is what he meant by his words to-night, when he said, 'What is this storm, or what a battle?'"

She was overwrought, excited, and off her guard, and spoke from a deep impulse. "A woman, in giving herself, gives everything. If he can't give up a scruple--I mean if his loyalty is so slight that his mother's wishes and dead ancestors--"

"My dear little girl, you are not under the slightest obligation to give anything," resumed her father, discreetly oblivious to the significance of her words. "If you care to give a little good-will and kindness to one whom you have granted the right to visit you, they will tend to confirm and develop the better and manly qualities he is now manifesting. You know I have peculiar faculties of finding out about people, and, incidentally and casually, I have informed myself about this Mr. Merwyn. I think I can truly say that he is doing all and more than could be expected of a young fellow in his circumstances, with the one exception that he does not put on our uniform and go to the front. He may have reasons--very possibly, as you think, mistaken and inadequate ones--which, nevertheless, are binding on his conscience. What else could his words mean to-night? He is not living a life of pleasure-seeking and dissipation, like so many other young nabobs in the city. Apparently he has not sought much other society than yours. Pardon me for saying it, but you have not given him much encouragement to avoid the temptations that are likely to assail a lonely, irresponsible young fellow. In one sense you are under no obligation to do this; in another, perhaps you are, for you must face the fact that you have great influence over him. This influence you must either use or throw away, as you decide. You are not responsible for this influence; neither are your friends responsible for the war. When it came, however, they faced the disagreeable and dangerous duties that it brought."

"O papa! I have been a stupid, resentful fool."

"No, my dear; at the worst you have been misled by generous and loyal impulses. Your deep sympathy with recent events has made you morbid, and therefore unfair. To your mind Mr. Merwyn represented the half-hearted element that shuns meeting what must be met at every cost. If this were true of him I should share in your spirit, but he appears to be trying to be loyal and to do what he can in the face of obstacles greater than many overcome."

"I don't believe he will ever come near me again!" she exclaimed.

"Then you are absolved in the future. Of course we can make no advances towards a man who has been your suitor."

Merwyn's course promised to fulfil her fear,--she now acknowledged to herself that it was a fear,--for his visits ceased. She tried to dismiss him from her thoughts, but a sense of her unfairness and harshness haunted her. She did not see why she had not taken her father's view, or why she had thrown away her influence that accorded with the scheme of life to which she had pledged herself. The very restraint indicated by his words was a mystery, and mysteries are fascinating. She remembered, with compunction, that not even his own mother had sought to develop a true, manly spirit in him. "Now he is saying," she thought, bitterly, "that I, too, am a fanatic,--worse than his mother."

Weeks passed and she heard nothing from him, nor did her father mention his name. While her regret was distinct and positive, it must not be supposed that it gave her serious trouble. Indeed, the letters of Mr. Lane, and the semi-humorous journal of Strahan and Blauvelt, together with the general claims of society and her interest in her father's deep anxieties, were fast banishing it from her mind, when, to her surprise, his card was handed to her one stormy afternoon, late in January.

"I am sorry to intrude upon you, Miss Vosburgh," he began, as she appeared, "but--"

"Why should you regard it as an intrusion, Mr. Merwyn?"

"I think a lady has a right to regard any unwelcome society as an intrusion."

"Admitting even so much, it does not follow that this is an intrusion," she said, laughing. Then she added, with slightly heightened color: "Mr. Merwyn, I must at least keep my own self-respect, and this requires an acknowledgment. I was rude to you when you last called. But I was morbid from anxiety and worry over what was happening. I had no right to grant your request to call upon me and then fail in courtesy."

"Will you, then, permit me to renew my old request?" he asked, with an eagerness that he could not disguise.

"Certainly not. That would imply such utter failure on my part! You should be able to forgive me one slip, remembering the circumstances."

"You have the most to forgive," he replied, humbly. "I asked for little more than toleration, but I felt that I had not the right to force even this upon you."

"I am glad you are inclined to be magnanimous," she replied, laughing. "Women usually take advantage of that trait in men--when they manifest it. We'll draw a line through the evening of the 20th of December, and, as Jefferson says, in his superb impersonation of poor old Rip, 'It don't count.' By the way, have you seen him?" she asked, determined that the conversation should take a different channel.

"No; I have been busy of late. But pardon me, Miss Vosburgh, I'm forgetting my errand shamefully. Do not take the matter too seriously. I think you have no reason to do so. Mr. Strahan is in the city and is ill. I have just come from him."

Her face paled instantly, and she sank into a chair.

"I beg of you not to be so alarmed," he added, hastily. "I shall not conceal anything from you. By the merest chance I saw him coming up Broadway in a carriage, and, observing that he looked ill, jumped into a hack and followed him to his residence. You had reason for your anxiety on December 20th, for he took a severe cold from exposure that night. For a time he made light of it, but at last obtained sick-leave. He asked me to tell you--"

"He has scarcely mentioned the fact that he was not well;" and there was an accent of reproach in the young girl's tones.

"I understand Strahan better than I once did, perhaps because better able to understand him," was Merwyn's quiet reply. "He is a brave, generous fellow, and, no doubt, wished to save you from anxiety. There has been no chance for him to say very much to me."

"Was he expected by his family?"

"They were merely informed, by a telegram, that he was on his way. He is not so well as when he started. Naturally he is worse for the journey. Moreover, he used these words, 'I felt that I was going to be ill and wished to get home.'"

"Has a physician seen him yet?"

"Yes, I brought their family physician in the hack, which I had kept waiting. He fears that it will be some time before his patient is out again. I have never been seriously ill myself, but I am sure--I mean, I have heard--that a few words often have great influence in aiding one in Strahan's condition to triumph over disease. It is often a question of will and courage, you know. I will take a note to him if you wish. Poor fellow! he may have his biggest fight on hand while the others are resting in winter quarters."

"I shall be only too glad to avail myself of your offer. Please excuse me a moment."

When she returned he saw traces of tears in her eyes. She asked, eagerly, "Will you see him often?"

"I shall call daily."

"Would it be too much trouble for you to let me know how he is, should he be very seriously ill?" Then, remembering that this might lead to calls more frequent than she was ready to receive, or than he would find it convenient to make, she added: "I suppose you are often down town and might leave word with papa at his office. I have merely a formal acquaintance with Mrs. Strahan and her daughters, and, if Mr. Strahan should be very ill, I should have to rely upon you for information."

"I shall make sure that you learn of his welfare daily until he is able to write to you, and I esteem it a privilege to render you this service."

He then bowed and turned away, and she did not detain him. Indeed, her mind was so absorbed by her friend's danger that she could not think of much else.

The next day a note, addressed to Mr. Vosburgh, was left at his office, giving fuller particulars of Strahan's illness, which threatened to be very serious indeed. High fever had been developed, and the young soldier had lost all intelligent consciousness. Days followed in which this fever was running its course, and Merwyn's reports, ominous in spite of all effort to disguise the deep anxiety felt by Strahan's friends, were made only through Mr. Vosburgh. Marian began to regret her suggestion that the information should come in this way, for she now felt that Merwyn had received the impression that his presence would not be agreeable. She was eager for more details and oppressed with the foreboding that she would never see her light-hearted friend again. She was almost tempted to ask Merwyn to call, but felt a strange reluctance to do so.

"I gave him sufficient encouragement to continue his visits," she thought, "and he should distinguish between the necessity of coming every day and the privilege of coming occasionally."

One evening her father looked very grave as he handed Marian the note addressed to him.

"O papa!" exclaimed the girl, "he's worse!"

"Yes, I fear Strahan is in a very critical condition. I happened to meet Merwyn when he left the note to-day, and the young fellow himself looked haggard and ill. But he carelessly assured me that he was perfectly well. He said that the crisis of Strahan's fever was approaching, and that the indications were bad."

"Papa!" cried the girl, tearfully, "I can't endure this suspense and inaction. Why would it be bad taste for us to call on Mrs. Strahan this evening? She must know how dear a friend Arthur is to me. I don't care for conventionality in a case like this. It seems cold-blooded to show no apparent interest, and it might do Arthur good if he should learn that we had been there because of our anxiety and sympathy."

"Well, my dear, what you suggest is the natural and loyal course, and therefore outweighs all conventionality in my mind. We'll go after dinner."

Marian's doubt as to her reception by Mrs. Strahan was speedily dispelled, for the sorrow-stricken mother was almost affectionate in her welcome.

"Arthur, in his delirium, often mentions your name," she said, "and then he is in camp or battle again, or else writing his journal. I have thought of sending for you, but he wouldn't have known you. He does not even recognize me, and has not for days. Our physician commands absolute quiet and as little change in those about him as possible. What we should have done without Mr. Merwyn I scarcely know. He is with him now, and has watched every night since Arthur's return. I never saw any one so changed, or else we didn't understand him. He is tireless in his strength, and womanly in his patience. His vigils are beginning to tell on him sadly, but he says that he will not give up till the crisis is past. If Arthur lives he will owe his life largely to one who, last summer, appeared too indolent to think of anything but his own pleasure. How we often misjudge people! They were boys and playmates together, and are both greatly changed. O Miss Vosburgh, my heart just stands still with dread when I think of what may soon happen. Arthur had become so manly, and we were so proud of him! He has written me more than once of your influence, and I had hoped that the way might open for our better acquaintance."

"Do you think the crisis may come to-night?" Marian asked, with quivering lips.

"Yes, it may come now at any hour. The physician will remain all night."

"Oh, I wish I might know early in the morning. Believe me, I shall not sleep."

"You shall know, Miss Vosburgh, and I hope you will come and see me, whatever happens. You will please excuse me now, for I cannot be away from Arthur at this time. I would not have seen any one but you."

At one o'clock in the morning there was a ring at Mr. Vosburgh's door. He opened it, and Merwyn stood there wrapped in his fur cloak. "Will you please give this note to Miss Vosburgh?" he said. "I think it contains words that will bring welcome relief and hope. I would not have disturbed you at this hour had I not seen your light burning;" and, before Mr. Vosburgh could reply, he lifted his hat and strode away.

The note ran as follows:

"MY DEAR MISS VOSBURGH:--Arthur became conscious a little before twelve. He was fearfully weak, and for a time his life appeared to flicker. I alone was permitted to be with him. After a while I whispered that you had been here. He smiled and soon fell into a quiet sleep. Our physician now gives us strong hopes.

"Sincerely and gratefully yours,

"CHARLOTTE STRAHAN."

Marian, who had been sleepless from thoughts more evenly divided between her friend and Merwyn than she would have admitted even to herself, handed the note to her father. Her face indicated both gladness and perplexity. He read and returned it with a smile.

"Papa," she said, "you have a man's straightforward common-sense. I am only a little half-girl and half-woman. Do you know, I almost fear that both Mrs. Strahan and Mr. Merwyn believe I am virtually engaged to Arthur."

"Their belief can't engage you," said her father, laughing. "Young Strahan will get well, thanks to you and Merwyn. Mrs. Strahan said that both were greatly changed. Merwyn certainly must have a hardy nature, for he improves under a steady frost."

"Papa!" cried Marian, with a vivid blush, "you are a deeper and more dangerous ally of Mr. Menvyn than mamma. I am on my guard against you both, and I shall retire at once before you begin a panegyric that will cease only when you find I am asleep."

"Yes, my dear, go and sleep the sleep of the unjust!"

CHAPTER XXII.
A GIRL'S THOUGHTS AND IMPULSES.

SLEEP, which Marian said would cut short her father's threatened panegyrics of Merwyn, did not come speedily. The young girl had too much food for thought.

She knew that Mrs. Strahan had not, during the past summer, misunderstood her son's faithful nurse. In spite of all prejudice and resentment, in spite of the annoying fact that he would intrude so often upon her thoughts, she had to admit the truth that he was greatly changed, and that, while she might be the cause, she could take to herself no credit for the transformation. To others she had given sincere and cordial encouragement. Towards him she had been harsh and frigid. He must indeed possess a hardy nature, or else a cold persistence that almost made her shiver, it was so indomitable.

She felt that she did not understand him; and she both shrunk from his character and was fascinated by it. She could not now charge him with disregard of her feelings and lack of delicacy. His visits had ceased when he believed them to be utterly repugnant; he had not availed himself of the opportunity to see her often afforded by Strahan's illness, and had been quick to take the hint that he could send his reports to her father. There had been no effort to make her aware of his self-sacrificing devotion to her friend. The thing that was irritating her was that he could approach so nearly to her standard and yet fail in a point that to her was vital. His course indicated unknown characteristics or circumstances, and she felt that she could never give him her confidence and unreserved regard while he fell short of the test of manhood which she believed that the times demanded. If underneath all his apparent changes for the better there was an innate lack of courage to meet danger and hardship, or else a cold, calculating purpose not to take these risks, she would shrink from him in strong repulsion. She knew that the war had developed not a few constitutional cowards,--men to be pitied, it is true, but with a commiseration that, in her case, would be mingled with contempt. On the other hand, if he reasoned, "I will win her if I can; I will do all and more than she can ask, but I will not risk the loss of a lifetime's enjoyment of my wealth," she would quietly say to him by her manner: "Enjoy your wealth. I can have no part in such a scheme of existence; I will not give my hand, even in friendship, to a man who would do less than I would, were I in his place."

If her father was right, and he had scruples of conscience, or some other unknown restraint, she felt that she must know all before she would give her trust and more. If he could not satisfy her on these points, as others had done so freely and spontaneously, he had no right to ask or expect more from her than ordinary courtesy.

Having thus resolutely considered antidotes for a tendency towards relentings not at all to her mind, and met, as she believed, her father's charge of unfairness, her thoughts, full of sympathy and hope, dwelt upon the condition of her friend. Recalling the past and the present, her heart grew very tender, and she found that he occupied in it a foremost place. Indeed, it seemed to her a species of disloyalty to permit any one to approach his place and that of Mr. Lane, for both formed an inseparable part of her new and more earnest life.

She, too, had changed, and was changing. As her nature deepened and grew stronger it was susceptible of deeper and stronger influences. Under the old regime pleasure, excitement, triumphs of power that ministered to vanity, had been her superficial motives. To the degree that she had now attained true womanhood, the influences that act upon and control a woman were in the ascendant. Love ceased to dwell in her mind as a mere fastidious preference, nor could marriage ever be a calculating choice, made with the view of securing the greatest advantages. She knew that earnest men loved her without a thought of calculation,--loved her for herself alone. She called them friends now, and to her they were no more as yet. But their downright sincerity made her sincere and thoughtful. Her esteem and affection for them were so great that she was not at all certain that circumstances and fuller acquaintance might not develop her regard towards one or the other of them into a far deeper feeling. In their absence, their manly qualities appealed to her imagination. She had reached a stage in spiritual development where her woman's nature was ready for its supreme requirement. She could be more than friend, and was conscious of the truth; and she believed that her heart would make a positive and final choice in accord with her intense and loyal sympathies. In the great drama of the war centred all that ideal and knightly action that has ever been so fascinating to her sex, and daily conversation with her father had enabled her to understand what lofty principles and great destinies were involved. She had been shown how President Lincoln's proclamation, freeing the slaves, had aimed a fatal blow at the chief enemies of liberty, not only in this land, but in all lands. Mr. Vosburgh was a philosophical student of history, and, now that she had become his companion, he made it clear to her how the present was linked to the past. Instead of being imbued with vindictiveness towards the South, she was made to see a brave, self-sacrificing, but misled people, seeking to rivet their own chains and blight the future of their fair land. Therefore, a man like Lane, capable of appreciating and acting upon these truths, took heroic proportions in her fancy, while Strahan, almost as delicate as a girl, yet brave as the best, won, in his straightforward simplicity, her deepest sympathy. The fact that the latter was near, that his heart had turned to her even from under the shadow of death, gave him an ascendency for the time.

"To some such man I shall eventually yield," she assured herself, "and not to one who brings a chill of doubt, not to one unmastered by loyal impulses to face every danger which our enemies dare meet."

Then she slept, and dreamt that she saw Strahan reaching out his hands to her for help from dark, unknown depths.

She awoke sobbing, and, under the confused impulse of the moment, exclaimed: "He shall have all the help I can give; he shall live. While he is weaker, he is braver than Mr. Lane. He triumphed over himself and everything. He most needs me. Mr. Lane is strong in himself. Why should I be raising such lofty standards of self-sacrifice when I cannot give love to one who most needs it, most deserves it?"

CHAPTER XXIII.
"MY FRIENDSHIP IS MINE TO GIVE."

STRAHAN'S convalescence need not be dwelt upon, nor the subtle aid given by Marian through flowers, fruit, and occasional calls upon his mother. These little kindnesses were tonics beyond the physician's skill, and he grew stronger daily. Mrs. Strahan believed that things were taking their natural course, and, with the delicacy of a lady, was content to welcome the young girl in a quiet, cordial manner. Merwyn tacitly accepted the mother's view, which she had not wholly concealed in the sick-room, and which he thought had been confirmed by Marian's manner and interest. With returning health Strahan's old sense of humor revived, and he often smiled and sighed over the misapprehension. Had he been fully aware of Marian's mood, he might have given his physician cause to look grave over an apparent return of fever.

In the reticence and delicacy natural to all the actors in this little drama, thoughts were unspoken, and events drifted on in accordance with the old relations. Merwyn's self-imposed duties of nurse became lighter, and he took much-needed rest. Strahan felt for him the strongest good-will and gratitude, but grew more and more puzzled about him. Apparently the convalescent was absolutely frank concerning himself. He spoke of his esteem and regard for Marian as he always had done; his deeper affection he never breathed to any one, although he believed the young girl was aware of it, and he did not in the least blame her that she had no power to give him more than friendship. Of his military plans and hopes he spoke without reserve to Merwyn, but in return received little confidence. He could not doubt the faithful attendant who had virtually twice saved his life, but he soon found a barrier of impenetrable reserve, which did not yield to any manifestations of friendliness. Strahan at last came to believe that it veiled a deep, yet hopeless regard for Marian.

This view, however, scarcely explained the situation, for he found his friend even more reticent in respect to the motives which kept him a civilian.

"I'd give six months' pay," said the young officer, on one occasion, "if we had you in our regiment, and I am satisfied that I could obtain a commission for you. You would be sure of rapid promotion. Indeed, with your wealth and influence you could secure a lieutenant-colonelcy in a new regiment by spring. Believe me, Merwyn, the place for us young fellows is at the front in these times. My blood's up,--what little I have left,--and I'm bound to see the scrimmage out. You have just the qualities to make a good officer. You could control and discipline men without bluster or undue harshness. We need such officers, for an awful lot of cads have obtained commissions."

Merwyn had walked to a window so that his friend could not see his face, and at last he replied, quietly and almost coldly: "There are some things, Strahan, in respect to which one cannot judge for another. I am as loyal as you are now, but I must aid the cause in my own way. I would prefer that you should not say anything more on this subject, for it is of no use. I have taken my course, and shall reveal it only by my action. There is one thing that I can do, and shall be very glad to do. I trust we are such good friends that you can accept of my offer. Your regiment has been depleted. New men would render it more effective and add to your chances of promotion. It will be some time before you are fit for active service. I can put you in the way of doing more than your brother-officers in the regiment, even though you are as pale as a ghost. Open a recruiting office near your country home again,--you can act at present through a sergeant,--and I will give you a check which will enable you to add to the government bounty so largely that you can soon get a lot of hardy country fellows. No one need know where the money comes from except ourselves."

Strahan laughed, and said: "It is useless for me to affect squeamishness in accepting favors from you at this late day. I believed you saved my life last summer, and now you are almost as haggard as I am from watching over me. I'll take your offer in good faith, as I believe you mean it. I won't pose as a self-sacrificing patriot only. I confess that I am ambitious. You fellows used to call me 'little Strahan.' YOU are all right now, but there are some who smile yet when my name is mentioned, and who regard my shoulder-straps as a joke. I've no doubt they are already laughing at the inglorious end of my military career. I propose to prove that I can be a soldier as well as some bigger and more bewhiskered men. I have other motives also;" and his thought was, "Marian may feel differently if I can win a colonel's eagles."

Merwyn surmised as much, but he only said, quietly: "Your motives are as good as most men's, and you have proved yourself a brave, efficient officer. That would be enough for me, had I not other motives also."

"Hang it all! I would tell you my motives if you would be equally frank."

"Since I cannot be, you must permit me to give other proofs of friendship. Nor do I expect, indeed I should be embarrassed by receiving, what I cannot return."

"You're an odd fish, Merwyn. Well, I have ample reason to give you my faith and loyalty, as I do. Your proposition has put new life into me already. I needn't spend idle weeks--"

"Hold on. One stipulation. Your physician must regulate all your actions. Remember that here, as at the front, the physician is, at times, autocrat."

Mervvyn called twice on Marian during his friend's convalescence, and could no longer complain of any lack of politeness. Indeed, her courtesy was slightly tinged with cordiality, and she took occasion to speak of her appreciation of his vigils at Strahan's side. Beyond this she showed no disposition towards friendliness. At the same, time, she could not even pretend to herself that she was indifferent. He piqued both her pride and her curiosity, for he made no further effort to reveal himself or to secure greater favor than she voluntarily bestowed. She believed that her father looked upon her course as an instance of feminine prejudice, of resentment prolonged unnaturally and capriciously,--that he was saying to himself, "A man would quarrel and have done with it after amends were made, but a woman--"

"He regards this as my flaw, my weakness, wherein I differ from him and his kind," she thought. "I can't help it. Circumstances have rendered it impossible for me to feel toward Mr. Merwyn as toward other men. I have thought the matter out and have taken my stand. If he wishes more than I now give he must come up to my ground, for I shall not go down to his."

She misunderstood her father. That sagacious gentleman said nothing, and quietly awaited developments.

It was a glad day for Arthur Strahan when, wrapped and muffled beyond all danger, he was driven, in a close carriage, to make an afternoon visit to Marian. She greeted him with a kindness that warmed his very soul, and even inspired hopes which he had, as yet, scarcely dared to entertain. Time sped by with all the old easy interchange of half-earnest nonsense. A deep chord of truth and affection vibrated through even jest and merry repartee. Yet, so profound are woman's intuitions in respect to some things, that, now she was face to face with him again, she feared, before an hour passed, that he could never be more to her than when she had given him loyal friendship in the vine-covered cottage in the country.

"By the way," he remarked, abruptly, "I suppose you never punished Merwyn as we both, at one time, felt that he deserved? He admits that he calls upon you quite frequently, and speaks of you in terms of strongest respect. You know I am his sincere, grateful friend henceforth. I don't pretend to understand him, but I trust him, and wish him well from the depths of my heart."

"I also wish him well," Marian remarked, quietly.

He looked at her doubtfully for a moment, then said, "Well, I suppose you have reasons for resentment, but I assure you he has changed very greatly."

"How do you know that, when you don't understand him?"

"I do know it," said the young fellow, earnestly. "Merwyn never was like other people. He is marked by ancestry; strong-willed, reticent on one side, proud and passionate on the other. My own mother was not more untiring and gentle with me than he, yet if I try to penetrate his reserve he becomes at once distant, and almost cold. When I thought he was seeking to amuse himself with you I felt like strangling him; now that I know he has a sincere respect for you, if not more, I have nothing against him. I wish he would join us in the field, and have said as much to him more than once. He has the means to raise a regiment himself, and there are few possessing more natural ability to transform raw recruits into soldiers."

"Why does he not join you in the field?" she asked, quickly, and there was a trace of indignation in her tones.

"I do not think he will ever speak of his reasons to any one. At least, he will not to me."

"Very well," she said; and there was significance in her cold, quiet tones.

"They result from no lack of loyalty," earnestly resumed Strahan, who felt that for some reason he was not succeeding as his friend's advocate. "He has generously increased my chances of promotion by giving me a large sum towards recruiting my regiment."

"After your hard experience, are you fully determined to go back?" she asked, with a brilliant smile. "Surely you have proved your courage, and, with your impaired health, you have a good reason not for leaving the task to stronger men."

"And take my place contentedly among the weaker ones in your estimation?" he added, flushing. "How could you suggest or think such a thing? Certainly I shall go back as soon as my physician permits, and I shall go to stay till the end, unless I am knocked over or disabled."

Her eyes flashed exultantly as she came swiftly to him. "Now you can understand me," she said, giving him her hand. "My friendship and honor are for men like you and Mr. Lane and Mr. Blauvelt, who offer all, and not for those who offer--MONEY."

"By Jove, Miss Marian, you make me feel as if I could storm Richmond single-handed."

"Don't think I say this in any callous disregard of what may happen. God knows I do not; but in times like these my heart chooses friends among knightly men who voluntarily go to meet other men as brave. Don't let us talk any more about Mr. Merwyn. I shall always treat him politely, and I have gratefully acknowledged my indebtedness for his care of you. He understands me, and will give me no opportunity to do as you suggested, were I so inclined. His conversation is that of a cultivated man, and as such I enjoy it; but there it all ends."

"But I don't feel that I have helped my friend in your good graces at all," protested Strahan, ruefully.

"Has he commissioned you to help him?" she asked, quickly.

"No, no, indeed. You don't know Merwyn, or you never would have asked that question."

"Well, I prefer as friends those whom I do know, who are not inshrouded in mystery or incased in reticence. No, Arthur Strahan, my friendship is mine to give, be it worth much or little. If he does not care enough for it to take the necessary risks, when the bare thought of shunning them makes you flush hotly, he cannot have it. All his wealth could not buy one smile from me. Now let all this end. I respect your loyalty to him, but I have my own standard, and shall abide by it;" and she introduced another topic.

CHAPTER XXIV.
A FATHER'S FORETHOUGHT.

STRAHAN improved rapidly in health, and was soon able to divide his time between his city and his country home. The recruiting station near the latter place was successful in securing stalwart men, who were tempted by the unusually large bounties offered through Merwyn's gift. The young officer lost no opportunities of visiting Marian's drawing-room, and, while his welcome continued as cordial as ever, she, nevertheless, indicated by a frank and almost sisterly manner the true state of her feelings toward him. The impulse arising at the critical hour of his illness speedily died away. His renewed society confirmed friendship, but awakened nothing more, and quieter thoughts convinced her that the future must reveal what her relations should be to him and to others.

As he recovered health her stronger sympathy went out to Mr. Lane, who had not asked for leave of absence.

"I am rampantly well," he wrote, "and while my heart often travels northward, I can find no plausible pretext to follow. I may receive a wound before long which will give me a good excuse, since, for our regiment, there is prospect of much active service while the infantry remain in winter quarters. It is a sad truth that the army is discouraged and depleted to a degree never known before. Homesickness is epidemic. A man shot himself the other day because refused a furlough. Desertions have been fearfully numerous among enlisted men, and officers have urged every possible excuse for leaves of absence. A man with my appetite stands no chance whatever, and our regimental surgeon laughs when I assure him that I am suffering from acute heart-disease. Therefore, my only hope is a wound, and I welcome our prospective raid in exchange for dreary picket duty."

Marian knew what picket duty and raiding meant in February weather, and wrote words of kindly warmth that sustained her friend through hard, prosaic service.

She also saw that her father was burdened with heavy cares and responsibilities. Disloyal forces and counsels were increasing in the great centres at the North, and especially in New York City. Therefore he was intrusted with duties of the most delicate and difficult nature. It was her constant effort to lead him to forget his anxieties during such evenings as he spent at home, and when she had congenial callers she sometimes prevailed upon him to take part in the general conversation. It so happened, one evening, that Strahan and Merwyn were both present. Seeing that the latter felt a little de trop, Mr. Vosburgh invited him to light a cigar in the dining-room, and the two men were soon engaged in animated talk, the younger being able to speak intelligently of the feeling in England at the time. By thoughtful questions he also drew out his host in regard to affairs at home.

The two guests departed together, and Marian, observing the pleased expression on her father's face, remarked, "You have evidently found a congenial spirit."

"I found a young fellow who had ideas and who was not averse to receiving more."

"You can relieve my conscience wholly, papa," said the young girl, laughing. "When Mr. Merwyn comes hereafter I shall turn him over to you. He will then receive ideas and good influence at their fountain-head. You and mamma are inclined to give him so much encouragement that I must be more on the defensive than ever."

"That policy would suit me exactly," replied her father, with a significant little nod. "I don't wish to lose you, and I'm more afraid of Merwyn than of all the rest together."

"More afraid of HIM!" exclaimed the girl, with widening eyes.

"Of him."

"Why?"

"Because you don't understand him."

"That's an excellent reason for keeping him at a distance."

"Reason, reason. What has reason to do with affairs of this kind?"

"Much, in my case, I assure you. Thank you for forewarning me so plainly."

"I've no dark designs against your peace."

Nevertheless, these half-jesting words foreshadowed the future, so far as Mr. Vosburgh and Mr. Merwyn were concerned. Others were usually present when the latter called, and he always seemed to enjoy a quiet talk with the elder man. Mrs. Vosburgh never failed in her cordiality, or lost hope that his visits might yet lead to a result in accordance with her wishes. Marian made much sport of their protege, as she called him, and, since she now treated him with the same courtesy that other mere calling acquaintances received, the habit of often spending part of the evening at the modest home grew upon him. Mr. Vosburgh soon discovered that the young man was a student of American affairs and history. This fact led to occasional visits by the young man to the host's library, which was rich in literature on these subjects.

On one stormy evening, which gave immunity from other callers, Marian joined them, and was soon deeply interested herself. Suddenly becoming conscious of the fact, she bade them an abrupt good-night and went to her room with a little frown on her brow.

"It's simply exasperating," she exclaimed, "to see a young fellow of his inches absorbed in American antiquities when the honor and liberty of America are at stake. Then, at times, he permits such an expression of sadness to come into his big black eyes! He is distant enough, but I can read his very thoughts, and he thinks me obduracy itself. He will soon return to his elegant home and proceed to be miserable in the most luxurious fashion. If he were riding with Mr. Lane, to-night, on a raid, he would soon distinguish between his cherished woe and a soldier's hardships."

Nevertheless, she could do little more than maintain a mental protest at his course, in which he persevered unobtrusively, yet unfalteringly. There was no trace of sentiment in his manner toward her, nor the slightest conscious appeal for sympathy. His conversation was so intelligent, and at times even brilliant, that she could not help being interested, and she observed that he resolutely chose subjects of an impersonal character, shunning everything relating to himself. She could not maintain any feeling approaching contempt, and the best intrenchment she could find was an irritated perplexity. She could not deny that his face was growing strong in its manly beauty. Although far paler and thinner than when she had first seen it, a heavy mustache and large, dark, thoughtful eyes relieved it from the charge of effeminacy. Every act, and even his tones, indicated high breeding, and she keenly appreciated such things. His reserve was a stimulus to thought, and his isolated life was unique for one in his position, while the fact that he sought her home and society with so little to encourage him was strong and subtle homage. More than all, she thought she recognized a trait in him which rarely fails to win respect,--an unfaltering will. Whatever his plans or purposes were, the impression grew stronger in her mind that he would not change them.

"But I have a pride and a will equal to his," she assured herself. "He can come thus far and no farther. Papa thinks I will yield eventually to his persistence and many fascinations. Were this possible, no one should know it until he had proved himself the peer of the bravest and best of my time."

Winter had passed, and spring brought not hope and gladness, but deepening dread as the hour approached when the bloody struggle would be renewed. Mr. Lane had participated in more than one cavalry expedition, but had received no wounds. Strahan was almost ready to return, and had sent much good material to the thinned ranks of his regiment. His reward came promptly, for at that late day men were most needed, and he who furnished them secured a leverage beyond all political influence. The major in his regiment resigned from ill-health, and Strahan was promoted to the vacancy at once. He received his commission before he started for the front, and he brought it to Marian with almost boyish pride and exultation. He had called for Merwyn on his way, and insisted on having his company. He found the young fellow nothing loath.

Merwyn scarcely entertained the shadow of a hope of anything more than that time would soften Marian's feelings toward him. The war could not last forever. Unexpected circumstances might arise, and a steadfast course must win a certain kind of respect. At any rate it was not in his nature to falter, especially when her tolerance was parting with much of its old positiveness. His presence undoubtedly had the sanction of her father and mother, and for the former he was gaining an esteem and liking independent of his fortunes with the daughter. Love is a hardy plant, and thrives on meagre sustenance. It was evident that the relations between Marian and Strahan were not such as he had supposed during the latter's illness. Her respect and friendship he would have, if it took a lifetime to acquire them. He would not be balked in the chief purpose of his life, or retreat from the pledge, although it was given in the agony of humiliation and defeat. As long as he had reason to believe that her hand and heart were free, it was not in human nature to abandon all hope.

On this particular evening Mr. Vosburgh admitted the young men, and Marian, hearing Strahan's voice, called laughingly from the parlor: "You are just in time for the wedding. I should have been engaged to any one except you."

"Engaged to any one except me? How cruel is my fate!"

"Pardon me," began Merwyn quickly, and taking his hat again; "I shall repeat my call at a time more opportune."

Marian, who had now appeared, said, in polite tones: "Mr. Merwyn, stay by all means. I could not think of separating two such friends. Our waitress has no relatives to whom she can go, therefore we are giving her a wedding from our house."

"Then I am sure there is greater reason for my leave-taking at present. I am an utter stranger to the bride, and feel that my presence would seem an intrusion to her, at least. Nothing at this time should detract from her happiness. Good-evening."

Marian felt the force of his words, and was also compelled to recognize his delicate regard for the feelings of one in humble station. She would have permitted him to depart, but Mr. Vosburgh interposed quickly: "Wait a moment, Mr. Merwyn; I picked up a rare book, down town, relating to the topic we were discussing the other evening. Suppose you go up to my library. I'll join you there, for the ceremony will soon be over. Indeed, we are now expecting the groom, his best man, and the minister. It so happens that the happy pair are Protestants, and so we can have an informal wedding."

"Oh, stay, Merwyn," said Strahan. "It was I who brought you here, and I shouldn't feel that the evening was complete without you."

The former looked doubtfully at Marian, who added, quickly: "You cannot refuse papa's invitation, Mr. Merwyn, since it removes the only scruple you can have. It is, perhaps, natural that the bride should wish to see only familiar faces at this time, and it was thoughtful of you to remember this, but, as papa says, the affair will soon be over."

"And then," resumed Strahan, "I have a little pie to show you, Miss Marian, in which Merwyn had a big finger."

"I thought that was an affair between ourselves," said Merwyn, throwing off his overcoat.

"Oh, do not for the world reveal any of Mr. Merwyn's secrets!" cried the girl.

"It is no secret at all to you, Miss Marian, nor did I ever intend that it should be one," Strahan explained.

"Mr. Merwyn, you labor under a disadvantage in your relations with Mr. Strahan. He has friends, and friendship is not based on reticence."

"Therefore I can have no friends, is the inference, I suppose."

"That cannot be said while I live," began the young officer, warmly; but here a ring at the door produced instant dispersion. "I suppose I can be present," Strahan whispered to Marian. "Barney Ghegan is an older acquaintance of mine than of yours, and your pretty waitress has condescended to smile graciously on me more than once, although my frequent presence at your door must have taxed her patience."

"You have crossed her palm with too much silver, I fear, to make frowns possible. Silver, indeed! when has any been seen? But money in any form is said to buy woman's smiles."

"Thank Heaven it doesn't buy yours."

"Hush! Your gravity must now be portentous."

The aggressive Barney, now a burly policeman, had again brought pretty Sally Maguire to terms, and on this evening received the reward of his persistent wooing. After the ceremony and a substantial supper, which Mrs. Vosburgh graced with her silver, the couple took their brief wedding journey to their rooms, and Barney went on duty in the morning, looking as if all the world were to his mind.

When Mr. Vosburgh went up to his library his step was at first unnoted, and he saw his guest sitting before the fire, lost in a gloomy revery. When observed, he asked, a little abruptly: "Is the matter to which Mr. Strahan referred a secret which you wish kept?"

"Oh, no! Not as far as I am concerned. What I have done is a bagatelle. I merely furnished a little money for recruiting purposes."

"It is not a little thing to send a good man to the front, Mr. Merwyn."

"Nor is it a little thing not to go one's self," was the bitter reply. Then he added, hastily, "I am eager to see the book to which you refer."

"Pardon me, Mr. Merwyn, your words plainly reveal your inclination. Would you not be happier if you followed it?"

"I cannot, Mr. Vosburgh, nor can I explain further. Therefore, I must patiently submit to all adverse judgment." The words were spoken quietly and almost wearily.

"I suppose that your reasons are good and satisfactory."

"They are neither good nor satisfactory," burst out the young man with sudden and vindictive impetuosity. "They are the curse of my life. Pardon me. I am forgetting myself. I believe you are friendly at least. Please let all this be as if it were not." Then, as if the possible import of his utterance had flashed upon him, he drew himself up and said, coldly, "If, under the circumstances, you feel I am unworthy of trust--"

"Mr. Merwyn," interrupted his host, "I am accustomed to deal with men and to be vigilantly on my guard. My words led to what has passed between us, and it ends here and now. I would not give you my hand did I not trust you. Come, here is the book;" and he led the way to a conversation relating to it.

Merwyn did his best to show a natural interest in the subject, but it was evident that a tumult had been raised in his mind difficult to control. At last he said: "May I take the book home? I will return it after careful reading."

Mr. Vosburgh accompanied him to the drawing-room, and Marian sportively introduced him to Major Strahan.

For a few minutes he was the gayest and most brilliant member of the party, and then he took his leave, the young girl remarking, "Since you have a book under your arm we cannot hope to detain you, for I have observed that, with your true antiquarian, the longer people have been dead the more interesting they become."

"That is perfectly natural," he replied, "for we can form all sorts of opinions about them, and they can never prove that we are wrong."

"More's the pity, if we are wrong. Good-night."

"Order an extra chop, Merwyn, and I'll breakfast with you," cried Strahan. "I've only two days more, you know."

"Well, papa," said Marian, joining him later in the library, "did you and Mr. Merwyn settle the precise date when the Dutch took Holland?"

"'More's the pity, if we ARE wrong!' I have been applying your words to the living rather than to the dead."

"To Mr. Merwyn, you mean."

"Yes."

"Has he been unbosoming himself to you?"

"Oh, no, indeed!"

"Why then has he so awakened your sympathy?"

"I fear he is facing more than any of your friends."

"And, possibly, fear is the reason."

"I do not think so."

"It appears strange to me, papa, that you are more ready to trust than I am. If there is nothing which will not bear the light, why is he so reticent even to his friend?"

"I do not know the reasons for his course, nor am I sure that they would seem good ones to me, but my knowledge of human nature is at fault if he is not trustworthy. I wish we did know what burdens his mind and trammels his action. Since we do not I will admit, to-night, that I am glad you feel toward him just as you do."

"Papa, you entertain doubts at last."

"No, I admit that something of importance is unknown and bids fair to remain so, but I cannot help feeling that it is something for which he is not to blame. Nevertheless, I would have you take no steps in the dark, were the whole city his."

"O papa! you regard this matter much too seriously. What steps had I proposed taking? How much would it cost me to dispense with his society altogether?"

"I do not know how much it might cost you in the end."

"Well, you can easily put the question to the test."

"That I do not propose to do. I shall not act as if what may be a great misfortune was a fault. Events will make everything clear some day, and if they clear him he will prove a friend whom I, at least, shall value highly. He is an unusual character, one that interests me greatly, whatever future developments may reveal. It would be easy for me to be careless or arbitrary, as I fear many fathers are in these matters. I take you into my confidence and reveal to you my thoughts. You say that your reason has much to do with this matter. I take you at your word. Suspend judgment in regard to Merwyn. Let him come and go as he has done. He will not presume on such courtesy, nor do you in any wise commit yourself, even to the friendly regard that you have for others. For your sake, Marian, for the chances which the future may bring, I should be glad if your heart and hand were free when I learn the whole truth about this young fellow. I am no match-maker in the vulgar acceptation of the word, but I, as well as you, have a deep interest at stake. I have informed myself in regard to Mr. Merwyn, senior. The son appears to have many of the former's traits. If he can never meet your standard or win your love that ends the matter. But, in spite of everything, he interests you deeply, as well as myself; and were he taking the same course as your friend who has just left, he would stand a better chance than that friend. You see how frank I am, and how true to my promise to help you."

Marian came and leaned her arm on his shoulder as she looked thoughtfully into the glowing grate.

At last she said: "I am grateful for your frankness, papa, and understand your motives. Many girls would not make the sad blunders they do had they such a counsellor as you, one who can be frank without being blunt and unskilful. In respect to these subjects, even with a daughter, there must be delicacy as well as precision of touch."

"There should also be downright common-sense, Marian, a recognition of tacts and tendencies, of what is and what may be. On one side a false delicacy often seals the lips of those most interested, until it is too late to speak; on the other, rank, wealth, and like advantages are urged without any delicacy at all. These have their important place, but the qualities which would make your happiness sure are intrinsic to the man. You know it is in my line to disentangle many a snarl in human conduct. Look back on the past without prejudice, if you can. Merwyn virtually said that he would make your standard of right and wrong his,--that he would measure things as you estimate them, with that difference, of course, inherent in sex. Is he not trying to do so? Is he not acting, with one exception, as you would wish? Here comes in the one thing we don't understand. As you suggest, it may be a fatal flaw in the marble, but we don't know this. The weight of evidence, in my mind, is against it. His course toward Strahan--one whom he might easily regard as a rival--is significant. He gave him far more than money; he drained his own vitality in seeking to restore his friend to health. A coarse, selfish man always cuts a sorry figure in a sick-room, and shuns its trying duties even in spite of the strongest obligations. You remember Mrs. Strahan's tribute to Merwyn. Yet there was no parade of his vigils, nor did he seek to make capital out of them with you. Now I can view all these things dispassionately, as a man, and, as I said before, they give evidence of an unusual character. Apparently he has chosen a certain course, and he has the will-power to carry it out. Your heart, your life, are still your own. All I wish is that you should not bestow them so hastily as not to secure the best possible guaranties of happiness. This young man has crossed your path in a peculiar way. You have immense influence over him. So far as he appears free to act you influence his action. Wait and see what it all means before you come to any decision about him. Now," he concluded, smiling, "is my common-sense applied to these affairs unnatural or unreasonable?"

"I certainly can wait with great equanimity," she replied, laughing, "and I admit the reasonableness of what you say as you put it. Nor can I any longer affect any disguises with you. Mr. Merwyn DOES interest me, and has retained a hold upon my thoughts which has annoyed me. He has angered and perplexed me. It has seemed as if he said, 'I will give you so much for your regard; I will not give, however, what you ask.' As you put it to-night, it is the same as if he said, 'I cannot.' Why can he not? The question opens unpleasant vistas to my mind. It will cost me little, however, to do as you wish, and my curiosity will be on the qui vive, if nothing more."

CHAPTER XXV.
A CHAINED WILL.

IN due time Strahan departed, hopeful and eager to enter on the duties pertaining to his higher rank. He felt that Marian's farewell had been more than she had ever given him any right to expect. Her manner had ever been too frank and friendly to awaken delusive hopes, and, after all, his regard for her was characterized more by boyish adoration than by the deep passion of manhood. To his sanguine spirit the excitement of camp and the responsibilities of his new position formed attractions which took all poignant regret from his leave-taking, and she was glad to recognize this truth. She had failed signally to carry out her self-sacrificing impulse, when he was so ill, to reward his heroism and supplement his life with her own; and she was much relieved to find that he appeared satisfied with the friendship she gave, and that there was no need of giving more. Indeed, he made it very clear that he was not a patriotic martyr in returning to the front, and his accounts of army life had shown that the semi-humorous journal, kept by himself and Blauvelt, was not altogether a generous effort to conceal from her a condition of dreary duty, hardship, and danger. Life in the field has ever had its fascinations to the masculine nature, and her friends were apparently finding an average enjoyment equal to her own. She liked them all the better for this, since, to her mind, it proved that that the knightly impulses of the past were unspent,--that, latent in the breasts of those who had seemed mere society fellows, dwelt the old virile forces.

"I shall prove," she assured herself, proudly, "that since true men are the same now as when they almost lived in armor, so ladies in their bowers have favors only for those to whom heroic action is second nature."

Blauvelt had maintained the journal during Strahan's absence, doing more with pencil than pen, and she had rewarded him abundantly by spicy little notes, full of cheer and appreciation. She had no scruples in maintaining this correspondence, for in it she had her father's sanction, and the letters were open to her parents' inspection when they cared to see them. Indeed, Mr. and Mrs. Vosburgh enjoyed the journal almost as much as Marian herself.

After Strahan's departure, life was unusually quiet in the young girl's home. Her father was busy, as usual, and at times anxious, for he was surrounded by elements hostile to the government. Aware, however, that the army of the Potomac was being largely reinforced, that General Hooker was reorganizing it with great success, and that he was infusing into it his own sanguine spirit, Mr. Vosburgh grew hopeful that, with more genial skies and firmer roads, a blow would be struck which would intimidate disloyalty at the North as well as in the South.

Marian shared in this hopefulness, although she dreaded to think how much this blow might cost her, as well as tens of thousands of other anxious hearts.

At present her mind was at rest in regard to Mr. Lane, for he had written that his regiment had returned from an expedition on which they had encountered little else than mud, sleet, and rain. The prospects now were that some monotonous picket-duty in a region little exposed to danger would be their chief service, and that they would be given time to rest and recruit.

This lull in the storm of war was Merwyn's opportunity. The inclement evenings often left Marian unoccupied, and she divided her time between her mother's sitting-room and her father's library, where she often found her quondam suitor, and not infrequently he spent an hour or two with her in the parlor. In a certain sense she had accepted her father's suggestions. She was studying the enigma with a lively curiosity, as she believed, and had to admit to herself that the puzzle daily became more interesting. Merwyn pleased her fastidious taste and interested her mind, and the possibilities suggested by her own and her father's words made him an object of peculiar and personal interest. The very uniqueness of their relations increased her disposition to think about him. It might be impossible that he should ever become even her friend; he might become her husband. Her father's remark, "I don't know how much it might cost you to dismiss him finally," had led to many questionings. Other young men she substantially understood. She could gauge their value, influence, and attractiveness almost at once; but what possibilities lurked in this reticent man who came so near her ideal, yet failed at a vital point? The wish, the effort to understand him, gave an increasing zest to their interviews. He had asked her to be his wife. She had understood him then, and had replied as she would again if he should approach her in a similar spirit. Again, at any hour he would ask her hand if she gave him sufficient encouragement, and she knew it. He would be humility itself in suing for the boon, and she knew this also, yet she did not understand him at all. His secret fascinated her, yet she feared it. It must be either some fatal flaw in his character, or else a powerful restraint imposed from without. If it was the former she would shrink from him at once; if the latter, it would indeed be a triumph, a proof of her power, to so influence him that he would make her the first consideration in the world.

Every day, however, increased her determination to exert this influence only by firmly maintaining her position. If he wished her friendship and an equal chance with others for more, he must prove himself the equal of others in all respects. By no words would she ever now hint that he should take their course; but she allowed herself to enhance his motives by permitting him to see her often, and by an alluring yet elusive courtesy, of which she was a perfect mistress.

This period was one of mingled pain and pleasure to Merwyn. Remembering his interview with Mr. Vosburgh, he felt that he had been treated with a degree of confidence that was even generous. But he knew that from Mr. Vosburgh he did not receive full trust,--that there were certain topics which each touched upon with restraint. Even with the father he was made to feel that he had reached the limit of their friendly relations. They could advance no farther unless the barrier of his reserve was broken down.

He believed that he was dissipating the prejudices of the daughter; that she was ceasing to dislike him personally. He exerted every faculty of his mind to interest her; he studied her tastes and views with careful analysis, that he might speak to her intelligently and acceptably. The kindling light in her eyes, and her animated tones, often proved that he succeeded. Was it the theme wholly that interested her? or was the speaker also gaining some place in her thoughts? He never could be quite certain as to these points, and yet the impression was growing stronger that if he came some day and said, quietly, "Good-by, Miss Vosburgh, I am going to face every danger which any man dare meet," she would give him both hands in friendly warmth, and that there would be an expression on her face which had never been turned towards him.

A stormy day, not far from the middle of April, ended in a stormier evening. Marian had not been able to go out, and had suffered a little from ennui. Her mother had a headache, Mr. Vosburgh had gone to keep an appointment, and the evening promised to be an interminable one to the young girl. She unconsciously wished that Merwyn would come, and half-smilingly wondered whether he would brave the storm to see her.

She was not kept long in suspense, for he soon appeared with a book which he wished to return, he said.

"Papa is out," Marian began, affably, "and you will have to be content with seeing me. You have a morbidly acute conscience, Mr. Merwyn, to return a book on a night like this."

"My conscience certainly is very troublesome."

Almost before she was aware of it the trite saying slipped out, "Honest confession is good for the soul."

"To some souls it is denied, Miss Vosburgh;" and there was a trace of bitterness in his tones. Then, with resolute promptness, he resumed their usual impersonal conversation.

While they talked, the desire to penetrate his secret grew strong upon the young girl. It was almost certain that they would not be interrupted, and this knowledge led her to yield to her mood. She felt a strange relenting towards him. A woman to her finger-tips, she could not constantly face this embodied mystery without an increasing desire to solve it. Cold curiosity, however, was not the chief inspiration of her impulse. The youth who sat on the opposite side of the glowing grate had grown old by months as if they were years. His secret was evidently not only a restraint, but a wearing burden. By leading her companion to reveal so much of his trouble as would give opportunity for her womanly ministry, might she not, in a degree yet unequalled, carry out her scheme of life to make the "most and best of those over whom she had influence"?

"Many brood over an infirmity, a fault, or an obligation till they grow morbid," she thought. "I might not be able to show him what was best and right, but papa could if we only knew."

Therefore her words and tones were kinder than usual, and she made slight and delicate references to herself, that he might be led to speak of himself. At last she hit upon domestic affairs as a safe, natural ground of approach, and gave a humorous account of some of her recent efforts to learn the mysteries of housekeeping, and she did not fail to observe his wistful and deeply-interested expression.

Suddenly, as if it were the most natural thing in the world, she remarked: "I do not see how you manage to keep house in that great, empty mansion of yours."

"You know, then, where I live?"

"Oh, yes. I saw you descend the steps of a house on Madison Avenue one morning last fall, and supposed it was your home."

"You were undoubtedly right. I can tell you just how I manage, or rather, how everything IS managed, for I have little to do with the matter. An old family servant looks after everything and provides me with my meals. She makes out my daily menu according to her 'own will,' which is 'sweet' if not crossed."

"Indeed! Are you so indifferent? I thought men gave much attention to their dinners."

"I do to mine, after it is provided. Were I fastidious, old Cynthy would give me no cause for complaint. Then I have a man who looks after the fires and the horses, etc. I am too good a republican to keep a valet. So you see that my domestic arrangements are simple in the extreme."

"And do those two people constitute your whole household?" she asked, wondering at a frankness which seemed complete.

"Yes. The ghosts and I have the house practically to ourselves most of the time."

"Are there ghosts?" she asked, laughing, but with cheeks that began to burn in her kindling interest.

"There are ghosts in every house where people have lived and died; that is, if you knew and cared for the people. My father is with me very often!"

"Mr. Merwyn, I don't understand you!" she exclaimed, without trying to disguise her astonishment. The conversation was so utterly unlike anything that had occurred between them before that she wondered whither it was leading. "I fear you are growing morbid," she added.

"I hope not. Nor will you think so when I explain. Of course nothing like gross superstition is in my mind. I remember my father very well, and have heard much about him since he died. Therefore he has become to me a distinct presence which I can summon at will. The same is true of others with whom the apartments are associated. If I wish I can summon them."

"I am at a loss to know which is the greater, your will or your imagination."

"My imagination is the greater."

"It must be great, indeed," she said, smiling alluringly, "for I never knew of one who seemed more untrammelled in circumstances than you are, or more under the dominion of his own will."

"Untrammelled!" he repeated, in a low, almost desperate tone.

"Yes," she replied, warmly,--"free to carry out every generous and noble impulse of manhood. I tell you frankly that you have led me to believe that you have such impulses."

His face became ashen in its hue, and he trembled visibly. He seemed about to speak some words as if they were wrung from him, then he became almost rigid in his self-control as he said, "There are limitations of which you cannot dream;" and he introduced a topic wholly remote from himself.

A chill benumbed her very heart, and she scarcely sought to prevent it from tingeing her words and manner. A few moments later the postman left a letter. She saw Lane's handwriting and said, "Will you pardon me a moment, that I may learn that my FRIEND is well?"

Glancing at the opening words, her eyes flashed with excitement as she exclaimed: "The campaign has opened! They are on the march this stormy night."

"May I ask if your letter is from Strahan?" Merwyn faltered.

"It is not from Mr. Strahan," she replied, quietly.

He arose and stood before her as erect and cold as herself. "Will you kindly give Mr. Vosburgh that book?" he said.

"Certainly."

"Will you also please say that I shall probably go to my country place in a day or two, and therefore may not see him again very soon."

She was both disappointed and angry, for she had meant kindly by him. The very consciousness that she had unbent so greatly, and had made what appeared to her pride an unwonted advance, incensed her, and she replied, in cold irony: "I will give papa your message. It will seem most natural to him, now that spring has come, that you should vary your mercantile with agricultural pursuits."

He appeared stung to the very soul by her words, and his hands clinched in his desperate effort to restrain himself. His white lips moved as he looked at her from eyes full of the agony of a wounded spirit. Suddenly his tense form became limp, and, with a slight despairing gesture, he said, wearily: "It is of no use. Good-by."

CHAPTER XXVI.
MARIAN'S INTERPRETATION OF MERWYN.

Shallow natures, like shallow waters, are easily agitated, and outward manifestations are in proportion to the shallowness. Superficial observers are
chiefly impressed by visible emotion and tumult.

With all her faults, Marian had inherited from her father a strong nature.
Her intuitions had become womanly and keen, and Merwyn's dumb agony affected
her more deeply than a torrent of impetuous words or any outward evidence of distress. She went back to her chair and shed bitter tears; she scarcely knew why, until
her father's voice aroused her by saying, "Why, Marian dear, what IS the matter?"

"Oh, I am glad you have come," she said. "I have caused so much suffering that
I feel as if I had committed a crime;" and she gave an account of the recent interview.

"Let me reassure you," said her father, gravely. "You did mean kindly by Merwyn, and you gave him, without being unwomanly, the best chance he could possibly have to throw off the incubus that is burdening his life. If, with the opportunity
he had to-night, and under the influence of his love, he did not speak, his secret is
one of which he cannot speak. At least, I fear it is one of which he dares not speak
to you, lest it should be fatal to him and all his hopes. I cannot even guess what it
is, but at all events it is of a serious nature, too grave to be regarded any longer as
secondary in our estimate of Mr. Merwyn's character. The shadow of this mystery
must not fall on you, and I am glad he is going away. I hoped that your greater
kindness and mine might lead him to reveal his trouble, that we could help him,
and that a character in many respects so unique and strong might be cleared of
its shadows. In this case we might not only have rendered a fellow-being a great
service, but also have secured a friend capable of adding much to our happiness.

This mystery, however, proves so deep-rooted and inscrutable that I shall be glad to withdraw you from his influence until time and circumstance make all plain, if they ever can. These old families often have dark secrets, and this young man, in attaining his majority and property, has evidently become the possessor of one of them. In spite of all his efforts to do well it is having a sinister influence over his life, and this influence must not extend to yours. The mere fact that he does not take an active part in the war is very subordinate in itself. Thousands who might do this as well as he are very well content to stay at home. The true aspect of the affair is this: A chain of circumstances, unforeseen, and uncaused by any premeditated effort on our part, has presented to his mind the most powerful motives to take a natural part in the conflict. It has gradually become evident that the secret of his restraint is a mystery that affects his whole being. Therefore, whether it be infirmity, fault, or misfortune, he has no right to impose it on others, since it seems to be beyond remedy. Do you not agree with me?"

"I could not do otherwise, papa. Yet, remembering how he looked to-night, I cannot help being sorry for him, even though my mind inclines to the belief that constitutional timidity restrains him. I never saw a man tremble so, and he turned white to his very lips. Papa, have you read 'The Fair Maid of Perth'?"

"Yes."

"Don't you remember MacIan, the young chief of Clan Quhele? This character always made a deep impression on me, awakening at the same time pity and the strongest repulsion. I could never understand him. He was high-born, and lived at an age when courage was the commonest of traits, while its absence was worse than crime. For the times he was endowed with every good quality except the power to face danger. This from the very constitution of his being he could not do, and he, beyond all others, understood his infirmity, suffering often almost mortal agony in view of it. For some reason I have been led to reread this story, and, in spite of myself, that wretched young Scottish chieftain has become associated in my mind with Willard Merwyn. He said to-night that his imagination was stronger than his will. I can believe it from his words. His dead father and others have become distinct presences to him. In the same way he calls up before his fancy the horrors of a battle-field, and he finds that he has not the power to face them, that he cannot do it, no matter what the motives may be. He feels that he would be simply overwhelmed with horror and faint-heartedness, and he is too prudent to risk the shame of exposure."

"Well," said her father, sighing, as if he were giving up a pleasing dream, "you have thought out an ingenious theory which, if true, explains Merwyn's course, perhaps. A woman's intuitions are subtle, and often true, but somehow it does not satisfy me, even though I can recall some things which give color to your view. Still, whatever be the explanation, all MUST be explained before we can give him more than ordinary courtesy."

It soon became evident that Merwyn had gone to his country place, for his visits ceased. The more Marian thought about him,--and she did think a great deal,--the more she was inclined to believe that her theory explained everything. His very words, "You think me a coward," became a proof, in her mind, that he was morbidly sensitive on this point, and ever conscious of his infirmity. He was too ready to resent a fancied imputation on his courage.

She strove to dismiss him from her thoughts, but with only partial success. He gave her the sense of being baffled, defeated. What could be more natural than that a high-spirited young man should enter the army of his own free will? He had not entered it even with her favor, possibly her love, as a motive. Yet he sought her favor as if it were the chief consideration of existence. With her theory, and her ideal of manhood, he was but the mocking shadow of a man, but so real, so nearly perfect, that she constantly chafed at the defect. Even her father had been deeply impressed by the rare promise of his young life,--a promise which she now believed could never be kept, although few might ever know it.

"I must be right in my view," she said. "He proves his loyalty by an unflagging interest in our arms, by the gift of thousands. He is here, his own master. He would not shun danger for the sake of his cold-hearted mother, from whom he seems almost estranged. His sisters are well provided for, and do not need his care. He does not live for the sake of pleasure, like many other young men. Merciful Heaven! I blush even to think the words, much more to speak them. Why does he not go, unless his fear is greater than his love for me? why is he not with Lane and Strahan, unless he has a constitutional dread that paralyzes him? He is the Scottish chieftain, MacIan, over again. All I can do now is to pity him as one to whom Nature has been exceedingly cruel, for every fibre in my being shrinks from such a man."

And so he came to dwell in her mind as one crippled, from birth, in his very soul.

Meanwhile events took place which soon absorbed her attention. Lane's letter announcing the opening of the campaign proved a false alarm, although, from a subsequent letter, she learned that he had had experiences not trifling in their nature. On the rainy night, early in April, that would ever be memorable to her, she had said to Merwyn, "The army is on the march."

This was true of the cavalry corps, and part of it even crossed the upper waters of the Rappahannock; but the same storm which dashed the thick drops against her windows also filled the river to overflowing, and the brave troopers, recalled, had to swim their horses in returning. Lane was among these, and his humorous account of the affair was signed, "Your loyal amphibian!"

A young girl of Marian's temperament is a natural hero-worshipper, and he was becoming her hero. Circumstances soon occurred which gave him a sure place in this character.

By the last of April, not only the cavalry, but the whole army, moved, the infantry taking position on the fatal field of Chancellorsville. Then came the bloody battle, with its unspeakable horrors and defeat. The icy Rappahannock proved the river of death to thousands and thousands of brave men.

Early in May the Union army, baffled, depleted, and discouraged, was again in its old quarters where it had spent the winter. Apparently the great forward movement had been a failure, but it was the cause of a loss to the Confederate cause from which it never recovered,--that of "Stonewall" Jackson. So transcendent were this man's boldness and ability in leading men that his death was almost equivalent to the annihilation of a rebel army. He was a typical character, the embodiment of the genius, the dash, the earnest, pure, but mistaken patriotism of the South. No man at the North more surely believed he was right than General Jackson, no man more reverently asked God's blessing on efforts heroic in the highest degree. He represented the sincere but misguided spirit which made every sacrifice possible to a brave people, and his class should ever be distinguished from the early conspirators who were actuated chiefly by ambition and selfishness.

His death also was typical, for he was wounded by a volley fired, through misapprehension, by his own men. The time will come when North and South will honor the memory of Thomas J. Jackson, while, at the same time, recognizing that his stout heart, active brain, and fiery zeal were among the chief obstructions to the united and sublime destiny of America. The man's errors were due to causes over which he had little control; his noble character was due to himself and his faith in God.

Many days passed before Marian heard from Lane, and she then learned that the raid in which he had participated had brought him within two miles of Richmond, and that he had passed safely through great dangers and hardships, but that the worst which he could say of himself was that he was "prone to go to sleep, even while writing to her."

The tidings from her other friends were equally reassuring. Their regiment had lost heavily, and Blauvelt had been made a captain almost in spite of himself, while Strahan was acting as lieutenant-colonel, since the officer holding that rank had been wounded. There was a dash of sadness and tragedy in the journal which the two young men forwarded to her after they had been a few days in their old camp at Falmouth, but Strahan's indomitable humor triumphed, and their crude record ended in a droll sketch of a plucked cock trying to crow. She wrote letters so full of sympathy and admiration of their spirit that three soldiers of the army of the Potomac soon recovered their morale.

The month of May was passing in mocking beauty to those whose hopes and happiness were bound up in the success of the Union armies. Not only had deadly war depleted Hooker's grand army, but the expiration of enlistments would take away nearly thirty thousand more. Mr. Vosburgh was aware of this, and he also found the disloyal elements by which he was surrounded passing into every form of hostile activity possible within the bounds of safety. Men were beginning to talk of peace, at any cost, openly, and he knew that the Southern leaders were hoping for the beginning at any time of a counter-revolution at the North. The city was full of threatening rumors, intrigues, and smouldering rebellion.

Marian saw her father overwhelmed with labors and anxieties, and letters from her friends reflected the bitterness then felt by the army because the North appeared so half-hearted.

"Mr. Merwyn, meanwhile," she thought, "is interesting himself in landscape-gardening. If he has one spark of manhood or courage he will show it now."

The object of this reproach was living almost the life of a hermit at his country place, finding no better resource, in his desperate unrest and trouble, than long mountain rambles, which brought physical exhaustion and sleep.

He had not misunderstood Marian's final words and manner. Delicately, yet clearly, she had indicated the steps he must take to vindicate his character and win her friendship. He felt that he had become pale, that he had trembled in her presence. What but cowardice could explain his manner and account for his inability to confirm the good impression he had made by following the example of her other friends? From both his parents he had inherited a nature sensitive to the last degree to any imputation of this kind. To receive it from the girl he loved was a hundred-fold more bitter than death, yet he was bound by fetters which, though unseen by all, were eating into his very soul. The proud Mrs. Merwyn was a slave-holder herself, and the daughter of a long line of slave-owners; but never had a bondsman been so chained and crushed as was her son. For weeks he felt that he could not mingle with other men, much less meet the girl to whom manly courage was the corner-stone of character.

One evening in the latter part of May, as Mr. Vosburgh and his family were sitting down to dinner, Barney Ghegan, the policeman, appeared at their door with a decent-looking, elderly colored woman and her lame son. They were refugees, or "contrabands," as they were then called, from the South, and they bore a letter from Captain Lane.

It was a scrap of paper with the following lines pencilled upon it:--

"MR. VOSBURGH, No. -- -- ST.: I have only time for a line. Mammy Borden will tell you her story and that of her son. Their action and other circumstances have enlisted my interest. Provide them employment, if convenient. At any rate, please see that they want nothing, and draw on me. Sincere regard to you all.--In haste,

"LANE, Captain.-- --U.S. Cav."

CHAPTER XXVII.
"DE HEAD LINKUM MAN WAS CAP'N LANE."

It can be well understood that the two dusky strangers, recommended by words from Lane, were at once invested with peculiar interest to Marian. Many months had elapsed since she had seen him, but all that he had written tended to kindle her imagination. This had been the more true because he was so modest in his accounts of the service in which he had participated. She had learned what cavalry campaigning meant, and read more meaning between the lines than the lines themselves conveyed. He was becoming her ideal knight, on whom no shadow rested. From first to last his course had been as open as the day, nor had he, in any respect, failed to reach the highest standard developed by those days of heroic action.

If this were true when "Mammy Borden" and her son appeared, the reader can easily believe that, when they completed their story, Captain Lane was her Bayard sans peur et sans reproche.

Barney explained that they had met him in the street and asked for Mr. Vosburgh's residence; as it was nearly time for him to be relieved of duty he told them that in a few moments he could guide them to their destination. Marian's thanks rewarded him abundantly, and Mrs. Vosburgh told him that if he would go to the kitchen he should have a cup of coffee and something nice to take home to his wife. They both remained proteges of the Vosburghs, and received frequent tokens of good-will and friendly regard. While these were in the main disinterested, Mr. Vosburgh felt that in the possibilities of the future it might be to his advantage to have some men in the police force wholly devoted to his interests.

The two colored refugees were evidently hungry and weary, and, eager as Marian was to learn more of her friend when informed that he had been wounded, she tried to content herself with the fact that he was doing well, until the mother and son had rested a little and had been refreshed by an abundant meal. Then they were summoned to the sitting-room, for Mr. and Mrs. Vosburgh shared in Marian's deep solicitude and interest.

It was evident that their humble guests, who took seats deferentially near the door, had been house-servants and not coarse plantation slaves, and in answer to Mr. Vosburgh's questions they spoke in a better vernacular than many of their station could employ.

"Yes, mass'r," the woman began, "we seed Mass'r Lane,--may de Lord bress 'im,--and he was a doin' well when we lef. He's a true Linkum man, an' if all was like him de wah would soon be ended an' de cullud people free. What's mo', de white people of de Souf wouldn't be so bitter as dey now is."

"Tell us your story, mammy," said Marian, impatiently; "tell us everything you know about Captain Lane."

A ray of intelligence lighted up the woman's sombre eyes, for she believed she understood Marian's interest, and at once determined that Lane's action should lose no embellishment which she could honestly give.

"Well, missy, it was dis away," she said. "My mass'r and his sons was away in de wah. He own a big plantation an' a great many slabes. My son, Zeb dar, an' I was kep' in de house. I waited on de missus an' de young ladies, an' Zeb was kep' in de house too, 'kase he was lame and 'kase dey could trus' him wid eberyting an' dey knew it.

"Well, up to de time Cap'n Lane come we hadn't seen any ob de Linkum men, but we'd heared ob de prockermation an' know'd we was free, far as Mass'r Linkum could do it, an' Zeb was jus' crazy to git away so he could say, 'I'se my own mass'r.' I didn't feel dat away, 'kase I was brought up wid my missus, an' de young ladies was a'most like my own chillen, an' we didn't try to get away like some ob de plantation han's do.

"Well, one ebenin', short time ago, a big lot ob our sogers come marchin' to our house--dey was hoss sogers--an' de missus an' de young ladies knew some of de ossifers, an' dey flew aroun' an' got up a big supper fo' dem. We all turned in, an' dar was hurry-skurry all ober de big house, fo' de ossifers sed dey would stay all night if de sogers ob you-uns would let dem. Dey said de Linkum sogers was comin' dat away, but dey wouldn't be 'long afore de mawnin', an' dey was a-gwine to whip dem. All was light talk an' larfin' an' jingle ob sabres. De house was nebber so waked up afo'. De young ladies was high-strung an' beliebed dat one ob our sogers could whip ten Linkum men. In de big yard betwixt de house an' de stables de men was feedin' dere hosses, an' we had a great pot ob coffee bilin' fo' dem, too, an' oder tings, fo' de missus sed dere sogers mus' hab eberyting she had.

"Well, bimeby, as I was helpin' put de tings on de table, I heared shots way off at de foot ob de lawn. Frontin' de house dar was a lawn mos' half a mile long, dat slope down to de road, and de Linkum sogers was 'spected to come dat away, an' dere was a lookout for dem down dar. As soon as de ossifers heared de shots dey rush out an' shout to dere men, an' dey saddle up in a hurry an' gallop out in de lawn in front of de house an' form ranks."

"How many were there?" Marian asked, her cheeks already burning with excitement.

"Law, missy, I doesn't know. Dere was a right smart lot--hundreds I should tink."

"Dere was not quite two hundred, missy," said Zeb; "I counted dem;" and then he looked towards his mother, who continued.

"De young ladies an' de missus went out on de verandy dat look down de lawn, and Missy Roberta, de oldest one, said, 'Now, maumy, you can see the difference between our sogers an' de Linkum men, as you call dem.' Missy Roberta had great black eyes an' was allus a-grievin' dat she wasn't a man so she could be a soger, but Missy S'wanee had blue eyes like her moder, an' was as full ob frolic as a kitten. She used ter say, 'I doesn't want ter be a man, fer I kin make ten men fight fer me.' So she could, sho' 'nuff, fer all de young men in our parts would fight de debil hisself for de sake ob Missy S'wanee."

"Go on, go on," cried Marian; "the Northern soldiers were coming--"

"Deed, an' dey was, missy,--comin' right up de lawn 'fore our eyes, an' dribin' in a few ob our sogers dat was a-watchin' fer dem by de road; dey come right 'long too. I could see dere sabres flashin' in de sunset long way off. One ossifer set dere men in ranks, and den de oder head ossifer come ridin' up to de verandy, an' Missy Roberta gave de ribbin from her ha'r to de one dey call cunnel, an' de oder ossifer ask Missy S'wanee fer a ribbin, too. She larf an' say, 'Win it, an' you shall hab it.'

Den off dey gallop, Missy Roberta cryin' arter dem, 'Don't fight too fa' away; I want to see de Linkum hirelin's run.' Den de words rung out, 'For'ard, march, trot,' an' down de lawn dey went. De Linkum men was now in plain sight. Zeb, you tell how dey look an' what dey did. I was so afeard fer my missus and de young ladies, I was 'mos' out ob my mind."

"Well, mass'r and ladies," said Zeb, rising and making a respectful bow, "I was at an upper window an' could see eberyting. De Linkum men was trottin' too, an' comin' in two ranks, one little way 'hind de toder. Right smart way afore dese two ranks was a line of calvary-men a few feet apart from each oder, an' dis line reach across de hull lawn to de woods on de oder side. I soon seed dat dere was Linkum sogers in de woods, too. Dey seemed sort ob outside sogers all aroun' de two ranks in de middle. Dey all come on fas', not a bit afeard, an' de thin line in front was firin' at our sogers dat had been a-watchin' down by de road, an' our sogers was a-firin' back.

"Bimeby, soon, bofe sides come nigh each oder, den de thin line ob Linkum men swept away to de lef at a gallop, an' our sogers an' de fust rank ob Linkum men run dere hosses at each oder wid loud yells. 'Clar to you, my heart jus' stood still. Neber heard such horrid noises, but I neber took my eyes away, for I beliebed I saw my freedom comin'. Fer a while I couldn't tell how it was gwine; dere was nothin' but clash ob sabres, an' bofe sides was all mixed up, fightin' hand ter hand.

"I was wonderin' why de second rank of Linkum men didn't do nothin', for dey was standin' still wid a man on a hoss, out in front ob dem. Suddenly I heard a bugle soun', an' de Linkum men dat was fightin' gave way to right an' lef, an' de man on de hoss wave his sword an' start for'ard at a gallop wid all his men arter him. Den our sogers 'gan to give back, fightin' as dey came. Dey was brave, dey was stubborn as mules, but back dey had to come. De head Linkum ossifer was leadin' all de time. I neber seed such a man, eberyting an' eberybody guv way afo' him. De oder Linkum sogers dat I thought was whipped wasn't whipped at all, fer dey come crowdin' aroun' arter de head ossifer, jes' as peart as eber.

"Front ob de house our ossifers an' sogers made a big stan', fer de missus an' de young ladies stood right dar on de verandy, wabin' dere hankerchiefs an' cryin' to dem to dribe de Yankee back. I knowed my moder was on de verandy, an' I run to her, an' sho' 'nuff, dar she was stan'in' right in front of Missy S'wanee an' 'treating de missus an' de young ladies ter go in, fer de bullets was now flyin' tick. But dey wouldn't go in, an' Missy Roberta was wringin' her han's, an' cryin', 'Oh, dat I was a man!' De cunnel, de oder ossifer, an' a lot ob our sogers wouldn't give back an inch. Dar dey was, fightin' right afore our eyes. De rest ob dere sogers was givin' way eb'rywhar. De Linkum sogers soon made a big rush togedder. De cunnel's hoss went down. In a minute dey was surrounded; some was killed, some wounded, an' de rest all taken, 'cept de young ossifer dat Missy S'wanee tole to win her colors. He was on a po'ful big hoss, an' he jes' break right through eb'ryting, an' was off wid de rest. De Linkum sogers followed on, firin' at 'em.

"De missus fainted dead away, an' my moder held her in her arms. De head Linkum ossifer now rode up to de verandy an' took off his hat, an' he say: 'Ladies, I admire your co'age, but you should not 'spose yourselves so needlessly. Should de vict'ry still remain wid our side, I promise you 'tection an 'munity from 'noyance!'

"Den he bow an' gallop arter his men dat was chasin' our sogers, leabin' anoder ossifer in charge ob de pris'ners. De head Linkum man was Cap'n Lane."

"I knew it, I knew it," cried Marian. "Ah! he's a friend to be proud of."

Her father and mother looked at her glowing cheeks and flashing eyes, and dismissed Merwyn from the possibilities of the future.

CHAPTER XXVIIL
The Signal Light.

The colored woman again took up the thread of the story which would explain her presence and her possession of a note from Captain Lane, recommending her and her son to Mr. Vosburgh's protection.

"Yes, missy," she said, "Cap'n Lane am a fren' ter be proud ob. I tinks he mus' be like Mass'r Linkum hisself, fer dere nebber was a man more braver and more kinder. Now I'se gwine ter tell yer what happen all that drefful night, an' Zeb will put in his word 'bout what he knows. While de cap'n was a-speakin' to de young ladies, de missus jes' lay in my arms as ef she was dead. Missy Roberta, as she listen, stand straight and haughty, an' give no sign she hear, but Missy S'wanee, she bow and say, 'Tank you, sir!' Zeb called some ob de house-servants, an' we carry de missus to her room, an' de young ladies help me bring her to. Den I stayed wid her, a-fannin' her an' a-cheerin' an' a-tellin' her dat I knew Cap'n Lane wouldn't let no harm come ter dem. Now, Zeb, you seed what happen downstars."

"Yes, mass'r an' ladies, I kep' my eyes out, fer I tinks my chance is come now, if eber. Cap'n Lane soon come back an' said to de ossifer in charge ob de pris'ners,--an' dere was more pris'ners bein' brought in all de time,--sez Cap'n Lane, 'De en'my won't stand agin. I'se sent Cap'n Walling in pursuit, an' now we mus' make prep'rations fer de night.' Den a man dey call a sergeant, who'd been a spyin' roun' de kitchen, an' lookin' in de dinin'-room winders, come up an' say something to Cap'n Lane; an' he come up to de doah an' say he like ter see one ob de ladies. I call Missy S'wanee, an' she come, cool an' lady-like, an' not a bit afeard, an' he take off his hat to her, an' say:--

"'Madam, I'se sorry all dis yer happen 'bout yer house, but I'se could not help it. Dere's a good many woun'ed, an' our surgeon is gwine ter treat all alike. I'se tole dat yer had coffee a-bilin' an' supper was ready. Now all I ask is, dat de woun'ed on bofe sides shall have 'freshments fust, an' den ef dere's anyting lef', I'd like my ossifers to have some supper.' Den he kinder smile as he say, 'I know you 'spected oder company dis ebenin', an' when de woun'ed is provided fer, de ossifers on your side can hab supper too. I hab ordered de hospital made in de out-buildin's, an' de priv'cy ob your home shall not be 'truded on.'

"'Cunnel,' say Missy S'wanee. 'Plain Cap'n,' he say, interrupting--'Cap'n Lane.'

"'Cap'n Lane, she goes on, 'I tanks you fer your courtesy, an 'sideration. I did not 'spect it. Your wishes shall be carried out.' Den she says, 'I'se'll hab more supper pervided, an' we'll 'spect you wid your ossifers;' for she wanted ter make fren's wid him, seein' we was all in his po'er. He says, 'No, madam, I'se take my supper wid my men. I could not be an unwelcome gues' in any house, What I asks for my ossifers, I asks as a favor; I doesn't deman' it.' Den he bows an' goes away. Missy S'wanee, she larf--she was allus a-larfin' no matter what happen--an' she says, 'I'se'll get eben wid him.' Well, de cap'n goes an' speaks to de cunnel, an' de oder captured ossifers ob our sogers, an' dey bow to him, an' den dey comes up an' sits on de verandy, an' Missy Roberta goes out, and dey talk in low tones, an' I couldn't hear what dey say. I was a-helpin' Missy S'wanee, an' she say to me, 'Zeb, could you eber tink dat a Yankee cap'n could be such a gemlin?' I didn't say nuffin', fer I didn't want anybody ter'spect what was in my min', but eb'ry chance I git I keep my eye on Cap'n Lane, fer I believed he could gib us our liberty. He was aroun' 'mong de woun'ed, an' seein' ter buryin' de dead, an' postin' an' arrangin' his men; deed, an' was all ober eberywhar.

"By dis time de ebenin' was growin' dark, de woun'ed and been cared for, an' our ossifers an' de Linkum ossifers sat down to supper; an' dey talk an' larf as if dey was good fren's. Yer'd tink it was a supper-party, ef dere hadn't been a strappin' big soger walkin' up an' down de verandy whar he could see in de winders. I help waits on de table, an' Missy Roberta, she was rudder still an' glum-like, but Missy S'wanee, she smiles on all alike, an' she say to de Linkum ossifers, 'I 'predate de court'sy ob your cap'n, eben do' he doesn't grace our board. I shall take de liberty, howsemeber, ob sendin' him some supper;' an' she put a san'wich an' some cake an' a cup ob coffee on a waiter an' sen' me out to him whar he was sittin' by de fire in de edge ob de woods on de lawn. He smile an' say, 'Tell de young lady dat I drink to her health an' happier times.' Den I gits up my co'age an' says, 'Cap'n Lane, I wants ter see yer when my work's done in de house.' He say, 'All right, come ter me here.' Den he look at me sharp an' say, 'Can I trus' yer?' An' I say, 'Yes, Mass'r Cap'n; I'se Linkum, troo an' troo.' Den he whisper in my ear de password, 'White-rose.'"

Marian remembered that she had given him a white rose when he had asked for her colors. He had made it his countersign on the evening of his victory.

"Arter supper our ossifers were taken down ter de oder pris'ners, an' guards walk aroun dem all night. I help clar up de tings, an' watch my chance ter steal away. At las' de house seem quiet. I tought de ladies had gone ter dere rooms, an' I put out de light in de pantry, an' was watchin' an' waitin' an' listenin' to be sho' dat no one was 'roun, when I heared a step in de hall. De pantry doah was on a crack, an' I peeps out, an' my bref was nigh took away when I sees a rebel ossifer, de one dat got away in de fight. He give a long, low whistle, an' den dere was a rustle in de hall above, an' Missy Roberta came flyin' down de starway. I know den dat dere was mischief up, an' I listen wid all my ears. She say to him, 'How awfully imprudent!' An' she put de light out in de hall, les' somebody see in. Den she say, 'Shell we go in de parlor?' He say, 'No, dere's two doahs here, each end de hall, an' a chance ter go out de winders, too. I mus' keep open ebery line ob retreat. Are dere any Yanks in de house?' She say, 'No,'--dat de Union cap'n very 'sid'rate. 'Curse him!' sed de reb; 'he spoil my ebenin' wid Miss S'wanee, but tell her I win her colors yet, an' pay dis Yankee cap'n a bigger interest in blows dan he eber had afo.' Den he 'splain how he got his men togedder, an' he foun' anoder 'tachment ob rebs, an' how dey would all come in de mawnin', as soon as light, an' ride right ober eberyting, an' 'lease de cunnel an' all de oder pris'ners. Den he says, 'We'se a-comin' on de creek-road. Put a dim light in de winder facin' dat way, an' as long as we see it burnin' we'll know dat all's quiet an' fav'able, an' tell Missy S'wanee to hab her colors ready. Dey tought I was one oh de Yanks in de dark, when I come in, but gettin' away'll be more tick'lish.' Den she say, 'Don't go out ob de doah. Drap from de parlor winder inter de shrub'ry, an' steal away troo de garden.' While dey was gone ter de parlor, I step out an' up de starway mighty sudden. Den I whip aroun' to de beginnin' ob de garret starway an' listen. Soon Missy Roberta come out de parlor an' look in de pantry an' de oder rooms, an' she sof'ly call me, 'kase she know I was las' up 'round de house; but I'se ain't sayin' nuffin'. Den she go in de missus room, whar my moder was, an' soon she and Missy S'wanee came out an' whisper, an' Missy S'wanee was a-larfin' how as ef she was pleased. Den Missy S'wanee go back to de missus, an' Missy Roberta go to her room.

"Now was my chance, an' I tuck off'n my shoes an' carried dem, an' I tank de Lord I heared it all, fer I says, 'Cap'n Lane'll give me my liberty now sho' 'nuff, when I tells him all.' I'se felt sho' he'd win de fight in de mawnin', fer he seemed ob de winnin' kine. I didn't open any ob de doahs on de fust floah, but stole down in de cellar, 'kase I knowed ob a winder dat I could creep outen. I got away from de house all right, an' went toward de fire where I lef Cap'n Lane. Soon a gruff voice said, 'Halt!' I guv de password mighty sudden, an' den said, 'I want to see Cap'n Lane.' De man call anoder soger, an' he come an' question me, an' den took me ter de cap'n. An' he was a-sleepin' as if his moder had rocked 'im! But he was on his feet de moment he spoke to. He 'membered me, an' ask ef de mawnin' wouldn't answer. I say, 'Mass'r Cap'n, I'se got big news fer yer.' Den he wide awake sho' 'nuff, an' tuck me one side, an' I tole him all. 'What's yer name?' he says. 'Zeb Borden,' I answers. Den he say: 'Zeb, you've been a good fren'. Ef I win de fight in de mawnin' you shell hab your liberty. It's yours now, ef you can get away.' I says I'se lame an' couldn't get away unless he took me, an' dat I wanted my moder ter go, too. Den he tought a minute, an' went back ter de fire an' tore out a little book de paper we brought, an' he says, 'What your moder's name?' An' I says, 'Dey call her Maumy Borden.' Den he wrote de lines we bring, an' he says: 'No tellin' what happen in de mawnin'. Here's some money dat will help you 'long when you git in our lines. Dis my fust inderpendent comman', an' ef yer hadn't tole me dis I might a' los' all I gained. Be faithful, Zeb; keep yer eyes an' ears open, an' I'll take care ob yer. Now slip back, fer yer might be missed.'"

"I got back to my lof' mighty sudden, an' I was jis' a-shakin' wid fear, for I beliebe dat Missy Roberta would a' killed me wid her own hands ef she'd knowed. She was like de ole mass'r, mighty haughty an' despit-like, when she angry. I wasn't in de lof' none too soon, fer Missy Roberta was 'spicious and uneasy-like, an' she come to de head ob de gerret starway an' call my name. At fust I ain't sayin' suffin', an' she call louder. Den I say, 'Dat you, Missy Roberta?' Den she seem to tink dat I was all right. I slipped arter her down de starway an' listen, an' I know she gwine ter put de light in de winder. Den she go to her room again.

"A long time pass, an' I hear no soun'. De house was so still dat I done got afeard, knowin' dere was mischief up. Dere was a little winder in my lof lookin' toward de creek-road, an' on de leabes ob some trees I could see a little glimmer ob de light dat Missy Roberta had put dar as a signal. Dat glimmer was jes' awful, fer I knowed it mean woun's and death to de sogers, an' liberty or no liberty fer me. Bimeby I heared steps off toward de creek-road, but dey soon die away. I watched an' waited ter'ble long time, an' de house an' all was still, 'cept de tread ob de guards. Mus' a' been about tree in de mawnin' when I heared a stir. It was very quiet-like, an' I hear no words, but now an' den dere was a jingle like a sabre make when a man walk. I stole down de starway an' look outen a winder in de d'rection whar Cap'n Lane was, an' I see dat de Linkum men had let all dere fires go out. It was bery dark. Den I hear Missy Roberta open her doah, an' I whip back ter my lof. She come soon an' had a mighty hard time wakin' me up. an' den she say: 'Zeb, dere's sumpen goin' on 'mong de Yankee sogers. Listen.' I says, 'I doesn't hear nuffin'.' She says: 'Dere is; dey's a-saddlin' up, an' movin' roun'. I want you ter steal outen an' see what dey is doin', an' tell me.' I says, 'Yes, missy.' I tought de bole plan would be de bes' plan now, an' I put on my shoes an' went out. Putty soon I comes back and says to her, 'I axed a man, an' he tole me dey was changin' de guard.'--'Did de res' seem quiet?'--'Yes, missy, dey is sleepin' 'round under de trees.' She seemed greatly 'lieved, an' says, 'You watch aroun' an' tell me ef dere's any news.' I stole out again an' crep' up 'hind some bushes, an' den I sho' dat de Linkum men was a-slippin' away toward de creek-road, but de guards kep' walkin' 'roun de pris'ners, jes' de same. On a sudden dere was a man right 'longside ob me, an' he say, 'Make a noise or move, an' you are dead. What are you doin' here?' I gasp out, 'White-rose, Cap'n Lane.'--'Oh, it's you,' he say, wid a low larf. Fo' I could speak dere come a scream, sich as I neber heared, den anoder an' anoder. 'Dey comes from de missus' room.' Den he say, 'Run down dar an' ask de sergeant ob de guard to send tree men wid you, an' come quick!' Now moder kin tell yer what happened. I had lef de back hall doah unlocked, an' de cap'n went in like a flash."

"De good Lor' bress Cap'n Lane," began the colored woman, "fer he come just in time. De missus had been wakin' an' fearful-like mos' ob de night, but at las' we was all a-dozin'. I was in a char by her side, an' Missy S'wanee laid on a lounge. She hadn't undress, an' fer a long time seemed as if listenin'. At las' dere come a low knock, an' we all started up. I goes to de doah an' say, 'Who's dar?'--'A message from Cap'n Lane,' says a low voice outside. 'Open de doah,' says Missy S'wanee; 'I'se not afeard ob him.' De moment I slip back de bolt, a big man, wid a black face, crowds in an' say, 'Not a soun', as you valley your lives: I want yer jewelry an' watches;' an' he held a pistol in his hand. At fust we tought it was a plantation han', fer he tried ter talk like a cullud man, an' Missy S'wanee 'gan ter talk ter him; but he drew a knife an' says, 'Dis won't make no noise, an' it'll stop yer noise ef yer make any. Not a word, but gib up eberyting.' De missus was so beat out wid fear, dat she say, 'Gib him eberyting.' An' Missy S'wanee, more'n half-dead, too, began to gib dere watches an' jewels. De man put dem in his pocket, an' den he lay his hands on Missy S'wanee, to take off her ring. Den she scream, an' I flew at 'im an' tried to tear his eyes out. Missy Roberta 'gan screamin', so we knowed she was 'tacked too. De man was strong an' rough, an' whedder he would a' killed us or not de Lord only knows, fer jes' den de doah flew wide open, an' Cap'n Lane stood dere wid his drawn sword. In a secon' he seed what it all meant, an' sprung in an' grabbed de robber by de neck an' jerked him outen inter de hall. Den de man 'gan ter beg fer mercy, an' tole his name. It was one of Cap'n Lane's own sogers. At dis moment Missy Roberta rush outen her room, cryin', 'Help! murder!' Den we heared heaby steps rushing up de starway, an' tree ob Cap'n Lane's sogers dash for'ard. As soon as Missy Roberta see de cap'n wid de light from de open doah shinin' on his face, she comes an' ask, 'What does dis outrage mean?'--'It mean dat dis man shell be shot in de mawnin', he say, in a chokin' kind ob voice, fer he seem almost too angry to speak. Den he ask, 'Were you 'tacked also?'--'Yes,' she cried, 'dere's a man in my room.'--'Which room?' An' she pointed to de doah. De fus' robber den made a bolt ter get away, but de cap'n's men cotch 'im. 'Tie his han's 'hind his back, an' shoot him if he tries to run agin,' said de cap'n; den he say to Missy Roberta: 'Go in your moder's room. Don't leave it without my permission. Ef dere is a man in your room, he shall shar de fate ob dat villain dat I've 'spected ob bein' a tief afore.' An' he went an' looken in Missy Roberta's room. In a few moments he come back an' say, 'Dere was a man dar, but he 'scape troo de winder on de verandy-roof. Ef I kin discober 'im he shall die too.' Den he say, grave an' sad-like: 'Ladies, dere is bad men in eb'ry army. I'se deeply mort'fied dat dis should happen. You'll bar me witness dat I tried to save you from all 'noyance. I know dis man,' pointin' to a soger dat stood near, 'an' I'll put him in dis hall on guard. His orders are--you hear dem--not to let any one come in de hall, an' not to let any one leabe dis room. As long as yer all stay in dis room, you are safe, eben from a word.' Missy S'wanee rush for'ard an' take his han', an' say, 'Eben ef you is my en'my you'se a gallant soger an' a gemlin, an' I tanks you.' De cap'n smile an' bow, an' say, 'In overcomin' your prej'dice I'se 'chieved my bes' vict'ry.' An' he gib her back all de jewels an' watches, an' drew de doah to, an' lef us to ourselves. Den we hear 'im go to a wes' room back ob de house wid anoder soger, an' soon he come back alone, an' den de house all still 'cept de eben tread ob de man outside. Missy Roberta clasp her han's an' look wild. Den she whisper to Missy S'wanee, an' dey seem in great trouble. Den she go an' open de doah an' say to de soger dat she want ter go ter her room. 'You cannot, lady,' said de soger. 'You heared my orders.'--'I'll only stay a minute,' she say. 'You cannot pass dat doah,' said de soger. 'But I mus' an' will,' cried Missy Roberta, an' she make a rush ter get out. De soger held her still. 'Unhan' me!' she almost screamed. He turn her 'roun' an' push her back in de room, an' den says: 'Lady, does you tink a soger can disobey orders? Dere ain't no use ob your takin' on 'bout dat light. We'se watch it all night as well as your fren's, an' de cap'n has lef' a soger guardin' it, to keep it burnin'. Ef I should let yer go, yer couldn't put it out, an' ef it had been put out any time, we'd a' lighted it agin. So dere's nuffin' fer yer to do but 'bey orders an' shut de doah. Den no one will say a word to yer, as de cap'n said.' Den he pulled de doah to hisself.

"Missy Roberta 'gan to wring her han's an' walk up an' down like a caged tiger, an' Missy S'wanee larf and cry togedder as she say, 'Cap'n Lane too bright fer us.'--'No,' cries Missy Roberta, 'somebody's 'trayed me, an' I could strike a knife inter dere heart fer doin' it. O S'wanee, S'wanee, our fren's is walkin' right inter a trap.' Den she run to de winder an' open it ter see ef she couldn't git down, an' dere in de garden was a soger, a-walkin' up an' down a-watchin'. 'We jes' can't do nuffin',' she said, an' she 'gan to sob an' go 'sterical-like. Missy S'wanee tole de missus, an' she wrung her han's an' cry, too; an' Missy S'wanee, she was a-larfin' an' a-cryin', an' a-prayin' all ter once. Suddenly dere was a shot off toward de creek-road, an' den we was bery still. Now. Zeb, you know de res'!"

CHAPTER XXIX.
MARIAN CONTRASTS LANE AND MERWYN.

O
h, come, this won't do at all," said Mr. Vosburgh, as Zeb was about to continue the story. "It's nearly midnight now. Marian, dear, your cheeks and eyes look as if you had a fever. Let us wait and hear the rest of the story in the morning, or you'll be ill, your mother will have a headache, and I shall be unfit for my work to-morrow."

"Papa, papa, in pity don't stop them till we know all. If Captain Lane could watch all night and fight in the morning, can't we listen for an hour longer?"

"Oh, yes," cried Mrs. Vosburgh, "let them finish. It's like a story, and I never could sleep well till I knew how a story was going to turn out."

"Wait a moment and I'll bring everybody something nice from the sideboard, and you, also, papa, a cigar from the library," cried the young girl.

Her father smiled his acquiescence, and in a few moments they were all ready to listen to the completion of a tragedy not without its dash of comedy.

"Arter Cap'n Lane posted his guards in de house an' sent de robber off," Zeb resumed, "he jump on a hoss an' gallop toward de creek-road. De light in de winder kep' a-burnin'! I foun' arterwards dat he an' his ossifers had been down on de creek-road and studied it all out. At one place--whar it was narrer' wid tick woods on bofe sides--dey had built a high rail-fence. Den below dat he had put sogers in de woods each side widout dere hosses, an' farder down still he had hid a lot of men dat was mounted. Sho' 'nuff, wid de fust light of de mawnin', de rebs come ridin' toward de light in de winder. I'd run out to de hill, not far away, ter see what would happen, an' it was so dark yet dat eb'ryting was mixed up wid shadders. When de rebs was a-comin' by de Linkum men in de woods a shot was fired. Den I s'pose de rebs tought it would gib de 'larm, fer dey began ter run dere hosses for'ard. An' den de Linkum men let dem hab it on bofe sides ob de road, but dey kep' on till dey come to de fence 'cross de road, an' den dey git a volley in front. Dis skeered 'em, for dey knowed dat de Linkum men was ready, an' dey tried to git back. Den I heared a great tramplin' an' yellin', an' dere was Cap'n Lane a-leadin' his men an' hosses right in ahind dem. Dere was orful fightin' fer a while, an' de men widout dere hosses leap outen de woods and shot like mad. It was flash! bang! on eb'ry side. At las' de Linkum men won de day, an' some ob de rebs burst troo de woods an' run, wid Cap'n Lane's men arter dem, an' dey kep' a-chasin' till a bugle call dem back. Den I run to de house, fer dey was bringin' in de pris'ners. Who should I see 'mong dese but de bery ossifer dat was wid Missy Roberta de night afore, de one dat wanted de light in de winder, an' he look bery mad, I can tell you.

"It was now gettin' broad day, an' de light at las' was outen de winder. Dere was nuffin' mo' fer it to do. De Linkum soger dat had been in de house was now helpin' guard de pris'ners, an' Missy Roberta an' Missy S'wanee run up to de ossifer dat had been so fooled an' say: 'We'se couldn't help it. Somebody 'trayed us. We was kep' under guard, an' dere was a Yankee soger a-keepin' de light burnin' arter we knew Cap'n Lane was aroun' an' ready.' Missy Roberta look sharp at me, but I 'peared innercent as a sheep. Missy S'wanee say: 'No matter, Major Denham, you did all dat a brave man could do, an' dar's my colors. You hab won dem.' An' den he cheer up 'mazin'ly.

"Den I hear somebody say Cap'n Lane woun'ed, an' I slip out toward de creek-road, an' dar I see dem a-carryin Cap'n Lane, an' de surgeon walkin' 'longside ob him. My heart jes' stood still wid fear. His eyes was shut, an' he look bery pale-like. Dey was a-carryin' him up de steps ob de verandy when Missy S'wanee came runnin' ter see what was de matter. Den Cap'n Lane open his eyes an' he say: 'Not in here. Put me wid de oder woun'ed men; but Missy S'wanee say, 'No; he protec' us an' act like a gemlin, an' he shall learn dat de ladies ob de Souf will not be surpassed.' De missus say de same, but Missy Roberta frown an' say nuffin'. She too much put out yet 'bout dat light in de winder an' de 'feat it brought her fren's. De cap'n was too weak an' gone-like ter say anyting mo', an' dey carry him up ter de bes' company room. I goes up wid dem ter wait on de surgeon, an' he 'zamin' de woun' an' gib de cap'n brandy, an' at las' say dat de cap'n get well ef he keep quiet a few weeks,--dat he weak now from de shock an' loss ob blood.

"In de arternoon hundreds more Linkum men come, an' Cap'n Lane's cunnel come wid dem, an' he praise de cap'n an' cheer him up, an' de cap'n was bery peart an' say he feel better. Mos' ob de ossifers take supper at de house. De missus an' Missy Roberta were perlite but bery cold-like, but Missy S'wanee, while she show dat she was a reb down to de bottom ob her good, kine heart, could smile an' say sunshiny tings all de same. Dis night pass bery quiet, an' in de mawnin' de Linkum cunnel say he hab orders ter 'tire toward de Union lines. He feel bery bad 'bout leabin' Cap'n Lane, but de surgeon say he mus' not be moved. He say, too, dat he stay wid de cap'n an' de oder badly woun'ed men. De cap'n tell his cunnel 'bout me an' my moder an' what he promise us, an' de cunnel say he take us wid him an' send us to Washin'on. De missus an' de young ladies take on dreful 'bout our gwine, but I say, 'I mus' hab my liberty,' an' moder say she can't part wid her own flesh an' blood--"

"Yes, yes, but what did 'Cap'n' Lane say?" interrupted Marian.

"He tole me ter say ter you, missy, dat he was gwine ter git well, an' dat you mus'n't worry 'kase you didn't hear from him, an' dat he know you'd be kine to us, 'kase I'd help him win de vict'ry. De surgeon wrote some letters, too, an' gib dem to de Linkum cunnel. P'raps you git one ob dem. Dey put us in an army wagon, an' bimeby we reach a railroad, an' dey gib us a pass ter Washin'on, an' we come right on heah wid Cap'n Lane's money. I doesn't know what dey did with de robber--"

"Oh, oh," cried Marian, "it may be weeks before I hear from my friend again, if I 'ever do."

"Marian, dear," said her father, "do not look on the dark side; it might have been a hundred-fold worse. 'Cap'n' Lane was in circumstances of great comfort, with his own surgeon in care of his wound. Think how many poor fellows were left on the field of Chancellorsville to Heaven only knows what fate. In such desperate fighting as has been described we have much reason to be thankful that he was not killed outright. He has justly earned great credit with his superiors, and I predict that he will get well and be promoted. I think you will receive a letter in a day or two from the surgeon. I prescribe that you and mamma sleep in the morning till you are rested. I won't grumble at taking my coffee alone." Then, to the colored woman and her son: "Don't you worry. We'll see that you are taken care of."

Late as it was, hours still elapsed before Marian slept. Her hero had become more heroic than ever. She dwelt on his achievements with enthusiasm, and thought of his sufferings with a tenderness never before evoked, while the possibility that "Missy S'wanee" was his nurse produced twinges approaching jealousy.

As was expected, the morning post brought a letter from the surgeon confirming the account that had been given by the refugees, and full of hope-inspiring words. Then for weeks there were no further tidings from Lane.

Meanwhile, events were culminating with terrible rapidity, and their threatening significance electrified the North. The Southern people and their sympathizers everywhere were jubilant over the victory of Chancellorsville, and both demanded and expected that this success should be followed by decisive victories. Lee's army, General Longstreet said, was "in a condition of strength and morale to undertake anything," and Southern public sentiment and the needs of the Richmond government all pointed towards a second and more extended invasion of the North. The army was indeed strong, disciplined, a powerful instrument in the hands of a leader like General Lee. Nevertheless, it had reached about the highest degree of its strength. The merciless conscription in the South had swept into its ranks nearly all the able-bodied men, and food and forage were becoming so scarce in war-wasted Virginia and other regions which would naturally sustain this force, that a bold, decisive policy had become a necessity. It was believed that on Northern soil the army could be fed, and terms of peace dictated.

The chief motive for this step was the hope of a counter-revolution in the North where the peace faction had grown bold and aggressive to a degree that only stopped short of open resistance. The draft or general conscription which the President had ordered to take place in July awakened intense hostility to the war and the government on the part of a large and rapidly increasing class of citizens. This class had its influential and outspoken leaders, who were evidently in league with a secret and disloyal organization known as the "Knights of the Golden Circle," the present object of which was the destruction of the Union and the perpetuation of slavery. In the city of New York the spirit of rebellion was as rampant in the breasts of tens of thousands as in Richmond, and Mr. Vosburgh knew it. His great sagacity and the means of information at his command enabled him to penetrate much of the intrigue that was taking place, and to guess at far more. He became haggard and almost sleepless from his labors and anxieties, for he knew that the loyal people of the North were living over a volcano.

Marian shared in this solicitude, and was his chief confidante. He wished her, with her mother, to go to some safe and secluded place in the country, and offered to lease again the cottage which they had occupied the previous summer, but Marian said that she would not leave him, and that he must not ask her to do so. Mrs. Vosburgh was eventually induced to visit relatives in New England, and then father and daughter watched events with a hundred-fold more anxiety than that of the majority, because they were better informed and more deeply involved in the issues at stake than many others. But beyond all thought of worldly interests, their intense loyal feeling burned with a pure, unwavering flame.

In addition to all that occupied her mind in connection with her father's cares and duties, she had other grounds for anxiety. Strahan wrote that his regiment was marching northward, and that he soon expected to take part in the chief battle of the war. Every day she hoped for some news from Lane, but none came. His wishes in regard to Mammy Borden and her son had been well carried out. Mr. Vosburgh had been led to suspect that the man in charge of his offices was becoming rather too curious in regard to his affairs, and too well informed about them. Therefore Zeb was installed in his place; and when Mrs. Vosburgh departed on her visit Marian dismissed the girl who had succeeded Sally Maguire, and employed the colored woman in her stead. She felt that this action would be pleasing to Lane, and that it was the very least that she could do.

Moreover, Mammy Borden was what she termed a "character," one to whom she could speak with something of the freedom natural to the ladies of the Southern household. The former slave could describe a phase of life and society that was full of novelty and romance to Marian, and "de young ladies," especially "Missy S'wanee," were types of the Southern girl of whom she never wearied of hearing. From the quaint talk of her new servant she learned to understand the domestic life of those whom she had regarded as enemies, and was compelled to admit that in womanly spirit and dauntless patriotism they were her equals, and had proved it by facing dangers and hardships from which she had been shielded. More than all, the old colored woman was a protegee of Captain Lane and was never weary of chanting his praises.

Marian was sincerely perplexed by the attitude of her mind towards this young officer. He kindled her enthusiasm and evoked admiration without stint. He represented to her the highest type of manhood in that period of doubt, danger, and strong excitement. Brave to the last degree, his courage was devoid of recklessness. The simple, untutored description of his action given by the refugees had only made it all the more clear that his mind was as keen and bright as his sword, while in chivalric impulses he had never been surpassed. Unconsciously Mammy Borden and her son had revealed traits in him which awakened Marian's deepest respect, suggesting thoughts of which she would not have spoken to any one. She had been shown his course towards beautiful women who were in his power, and who at the same time were plotting his destruction and that of his command. While he foiled their hostile purpose, no knight of olden times could have shown them more thoughtful consideration and respect. She felt that her heart ought to go out towards this ideal lover in utter abandon. Why did it not? Why were her pride, exultation, and deep solicitude too near akin to the emotions she would have felt had he been her brother? Was this the only way in which she could love? Would the sacred, mysterious, and irresistible impulses of the heart, of which she had read, follow naturally in due time?

She was inclined to believe that this was true, yet, to her surprise, the thought arose unbidden: "If Willard Merwyn were showing like qualities and making the same record--What absurdity is this!" she exclaimed aloud. "Why does this Mr. Merwyn so haunt me, when I could not give him even respect and friendship, although he sent an army into the field, yet was not brave enough to go himself? Where is he? What is he doing in these supreme hours of his country's history? Everything is at stake at the front, yes, and even here at the North, for I can see that papa dreads unspeakably what each day may bring forth, yet neither this terrible emergency nor the hope of winning my love can brace his timid soul to manly action. There is more manhood in one drop of the blood shed by Captain Lane than in Merwyn's whole shrinking body."

CHAPTER XXX.
THE NORTH INVADED.

Merwyn could scarcely have believed that he had sunk so low in Marian's estimation as her words at the close of the previous chapter indicated, yet he guessed clearly the drift of her opinion in regard to him, and he saw no way of righting himself. In the solitude of his country home he considered and dismissed several plans of action. He thought of offering his services to the Sanitary Commission, but his pride prevented, for he knew that she and others would ask why a man of his youth and strength sought a service in which sisters of charity could be his equals in efficiency. He also saw that joining a regiment of the city militia was but a half-way measure that might soon lead to the violation of his oath, since these regiments could be ordered to the South in case of an emergency.

The prospect before him was that of a thwarted, blighted life. He might live till he was gray, but in every waking moment he would remember that he had lost his chance for manly action, when such action would have brought him self-respect, very possibly happiness, and certainly the consciousness that he had served a cause which now enlisted all his sympathies.

At last he wrote to his mother an impassioned appeal to be released from his oath, assuring her that he would never have any part in the Southern empire that was the dream of her life. He cherished the hope that she, seeing how unalterable were his feelings and purposes, would yield to him the right to follow his own convictions, and with this kindling hope his mind grew calmer.

Then, as reason began to assert itself, he saw that he had been absent from the city too long already. His pride counselled: "The world has no concern with your affairs, disappointments, or sufferings. Be your father's son, and maintain your position with dignity. In a few short weeks you may be free. If not, your secret is your own, and no living soul can gossip about your family affairs, or say that you betrayed your word or your family interests. Meanwhile, in following the example of thousands of other rich and patriotic citizens, you can contribute more to the success of the Union cause than if you were in the field."

He knew that this course might not secure him the favor of one for whom he would face every danger in the world, but it might tend to disarm criticism and give him the best chances for the future.

He at once carried out his new purposes, and early in June returned to his city home. He now resolved no longer to shrink and hide, but to keep his own counsel, and face the situation like one who had a right to choose his own career. Mr. Bodoin, his legal adviser, received the impression that he had been quietly looking after his country property, and the lawyer rubbed his bloodless hands in satisfaction over a youthful client so entirely to his mind.

Having learned more fully what his present resources were, Merwyn next called on Mr. Vosburgh at his office. That gentleman greeted the young man courteously, disguising his surprise and curiosity.

"I have just returned from my country place," Merwyn began, "and shall not have to go there very soon again, Can I call upon you as usual?"

"Certainly," replied Mr. Vosburgh; but there was no warmth in his tone.

"I have also a favor to ask," resumed Merwyn, with a slight deepening of color in his bronzed face. "I have not been able to follow events very closely, but so far as I can judge there is a prospect of severe battles and of sudden emergencies. If there is need of money, such means as I have are at your disposal."

Even Mr. Vosburgh, at the moment, felt much of Marian's repulsion as he looked at the tall youth, with his superb physique, who spoke of severe battles and offered "money." "Truly," he thought, "she must be right. This man will part with thousands rather than risk one drop of blood."

But he was too good a patriot to reveal his impression, and said, earnestly: "You are right, Mr. Merwyn. There will be heavy fighting soon, and all the aid that you can give the Sanitary and Christian Commissions will tend to save life and relieve suffering."

Under the circumstances he felt that he could not use any of the young man's money, even as a temporary loan, although at times the employment of a few extra hundreds might aid him greatly in his work.

Merwyn went away chilled and saddened anew, yet feeling that his reception had been all that he had a right to expect.

There had been no lack of politeness on Mr. Vosburgh's part, but his manner had not been that of a friend.

"He has recognized that I am under some secret restraint," Merwyn thought, "and distrusts me at last. He probably thinks, with his daughter, that I am afraid to go. Oh that I had a chance to prove that I am, at least, not a coward! In some way I shall prove it before many weeks pass."

At dinner, that evening, Mr. Vosburgh smiled significantly at Marian, and said, "Who do you think called on me to-day?"

"Mr. Merwyn," she said, promptly.

"You are right. He came to offer--"

"Money," contemptuously completing her father's sentence.

"You evidently think you understand him. Perhaps you do; and I admit that I felt much as you do, to-day, when he offered his purse to the cause. I fear, however, that we are growing a little morbid on this subject, and inclined to judgments too severe. You and I have become like so many in the South. This conflict and its results are everything to us, and we forget that we are surrounded by hundreds of thousands who are loyal, but are not ready for very great sacrifices."

"We are also surrounded by millions that are, and I cast in my lot with these. If this is to be morbid, we have plenty of company."

"What I mean is, that we may be too hard upon those who do not feel, and perhaps are not capable of feeling, as we do."

"O papa! you know the reason why Mr. Merwyn takes the course he does."

"I know what you think to be the reason, and you may be right. Your explanation struck me with more force than ever to-day; and yet, looking into the young fellow's face, it seems impossible. He impresses me strangely, and awakens much curiosity as to his future course. He asked if he could call as usual, and I, with ordinary politeness, said, 'Certainly.' Indeed, there was a dignity about the fellow that almost compelled the word. I don't know that we have any occasion to regret it. He has done nothing to forfeit mere courtesy on our part."

"Oh, no," said Marian, discontentedly; "but he irritates me. I wish I had never known him, and that I might never meet him again. I am more and more convinced that my theory about him is correct, and while I pity him sincerely, the ever-present consciousness of his fatal defect is more distressing--perhaps I should say, annoying--than if he presented some strong physical deformity. He is such a superb and mocking semblance of a man that I cannot even think of him without exasperation."

"Well, my dear, perhaps this is one of the minor sacrifices that we must make for the cause. Until Merwyn can explain for himself, he has no right to expect from us more than politeness. While I would not take from him a loan for my individual work, I can induce him to give much material help. In aiding Strahan, and in other ways, he has done a great deal, and he is willing to do more. The prospects are that everything will be needed, and I do not feel like alienating one dollar or one bit of influence. According to your theory his course is due to infirmity rather than to fault, and so he should be tolerated, since he is doing the best he can. Politeness to him will not compromise either our principles or ourselves."

"Well, papa, I will do my best; but if he had a particle of my intuition he would know how I feel. Indeed, I believe he does know in some degree, and it seems to me that, if I were a man, I couldn't face a woman while she entertained such an opinion."

"Perhaps the knowledge that you are wrong enables him to face you."

"If that were true he wouldn't be twenty-four hours in proving it."

"Well," said her father, with a grim laugh, and in a low voice, "he may soon have a chance to show his mettle without going to the front. Marian, I wish you would join your mother. The city is fairly trembling with suppressed disloyalty. If Lee marches northward I shall fear an explosion at any time."

"Leave the city!" said the young girl, hotly. "That would prove that I possess the same traits that repel me so strongly in Mr. Merwyn. No, I shall not leave your side this summer, unless you compel me to almost by force. Have we not recently heard of two Southern girls who cheered on their friends in battle with bullets flying around them? After witnessing that scene, I should make a pitiable figure in Captain Lane's eyes should I seek safety in flight at the mere thought of danger. I should die with shame."

"It is well Captain Lane does not hear you, or the surgeon would have fever to contend with, as well as wounds."

"O dear!" cried the girl. "I wish we could hear from him."

Mr. Vosburgh had nearly reached the conclusion that if the captain survived the vicissitudes of the war he would not plead a second time in vain.

A few evenings later Merwyn called. Mr. Vosburgh was out, and others were in the drawing-room. Marian did not have much to say to him, but treated him with her old, distant politeness. He felt her manner, and saw the gulf that lay between them, but no one unacquainted with the past would have recognized any lack of courtesy on her part.

Among the exciting topics broached was the possibility of a counter-revolution at the North. Merwyn noticed that Marian was reticent in regard to her father and his opinions, but he was startled to hear her say that she would not be surprised if violent outbreaks of disloyalty took place any hour, and he recognized her courage in remaining in the city. One of the callers, an officer in the Seventh Regiment, also spoke of the possibility of all the militia being ordered away to aid in repelling invasion.

Merwyn listened attentively, but did not take a very active part in the conversation, and went away with the words "counter-revolution" and "invasion" ringing in his ears.

He became a close student of the progress of events, and, with his sensitiveness in regard to the Vosburghs, adopted a measure that taxed his courage. A day or two later he called on Mr. Vosburgh at his office, and asked him out to lunch, saying that he was desirous of obtaining some information.

Mr. Vosburgh complied readily, for he wished to give the young man every chance to right himself, and he could not disguise the fact that he felt a peculiar interest in the problem presented by his daughter's unfortunate suitor. Merwyn was rather maladroit in accounting for his questions in regard to the results of a counter revolution, and gave the impression that he was solicitous about his property.

Convinced that his entertainer was loyal from conviction and feeling, as well as from the nature of his pecuniary interests, Mr. Vosburgh spoke quite freely of the dangerous elements rapidly developing at the North, and warned his host that, in his opinion, the critical period of the struggle was approaching. Merwyn's grave, troubled face and extreme reticence in respect to his own course made an unfavorable impression, yet he was acting characteristically. Trammelled as he was, he could not speak according to his natural impulses. He felt that brave words, not enforced by corresponding action, would be in wretched taste, and his hope was that by deeds he could soon redeem himself. If there was a counter-revolution he could soon find a post of danger without wearing the uniform of a soldier or stepping on Southern soil, but he was not one to boast of what he would do should such and such events take place. Moreover, before the month elapsed he had reason to believe that he would receive a letter from his mother giving him freedom. Therefore, Mr. Vosburgh was left with all his old doubts and perplexities unrelieved, and Marian's sinister theory was confirmed rather than weakened.

Merwyn, however, was no longer despondent. The swift march of events might give him the opportunities he craved. He was too young not to seize on the faintest hope offered by the future, and the present period was one of reaction from the deep dejection that, for a time, had almost paralyzed him in the country.

Even as a boy he had been a sportsman, and a good shot with gun, rifle, and pistol, but now he began to perfect himself in the use of the last-named weapon. He arranged the basement of his house in such a way that he could practise with his revolvers, and he soon became very proficient in the accuracy and quickness of his aim.

According to the press despatches of the day, there was much uncertainty in regard to General Lee's movements and plans. Mr. Vosburgh's means of information led him to believe that the rebel army was coming North, and many others shared the fear; but as late as June 15, so skilfully had the Confederate leader masked his purposes, that, according to the latest published news, the indications were that he intended to cross the Rappahannock near Culpepper and inaugurate a campaign similar to the one that had proved so disastrous to the Union cause the preceding summer.

On the morning of the 16th, however, the head-lines of the leading journals startled the people through the North. The rebel advance had occupied Chambersburg, Pa. The invasion was an accomplished fact. The same journals contained a call from the President for 100,000 militia, of which the State of New York was to furnish 20,000. The excitement in Pennsylvania was intense, for not only her capital, but her principal towns and cities were endangered. The thick-flying rumors of the past few days received terrible confirmation, and, while Lee's plans were still shrouded in mystery, enough was known to awaken apprehension, while the very uncertainty proved the prolific source of the most exaggerated and direful stories. There was immense activity at the various armories, and many regiments of the city militia expected orders to depart at any hour. The metropolis was rocking with excitement, and wherever men congregated there were eager faces and excited tones.

Behind his impassive manner, when he appeared in the street, no one disguised deeper feeling, more eager hope, more sickening fear, than Willard Merwyn. When would his mother's letter come? If this crisis should pass and he take no part in it he feared that he himself would be lost.

Since his last call upon Marian he felt that he could not see her again until he could take some decided course; but if there were blows to be struck by citizens at the North, or if his mother's letter acceded to his wish, however grudgingly, he could act at once, and on each new day he awoke with the hope that he might be unchained before its close.

The 17th of June was a memorable day. The morning press brought confirmation of Lee's northward advance. The men of the Quaker City were turning out en masse, either to carry the musket or for labor on fortifications, and it was announced that twelve regiments of the New-York militia were under marching orders. The invasion was the one topic of conversation. There was an immense revival of patriotism, and recruiting at the armories went on rapidly. At this outburst of popular feeling disloyalty shrunk out of sight for a time, and apparently the invaders who had come north as allies of the peace party created an uprising, as they had expected, but it was hostile to them.

The people were reminded of the threats of the Southern leaders. The speech of Jeff Davis in the winter of 1860-61 was quoted: "If war should result from secession, it will not be our fields that will witness its ravages, but those of the North."

The fact that this prediction was already fulfilled stung even the half-hearted into action, and nerved the loyalty of others, and when it became known that the gallant Seventh Regiment would march down Broadway en route for Pennsylvania at noon, multitudes lined the thoroughfare and greeted their defenders with acclamations.

Merwyn knew that Marian would witness the departure, and he watched in the distance till he saw her emerge from her home and go to a building on Broadway in which her father had secured her a place. She was attended by an officer clad in the uniform of a service so dear to her, but which HE had sworn never to wear. He hastily secured a point of observation in a building opposite, for while the vision of the young girl awakened almost desperate revolt at his lot, he could not resist a lover's impulse to see her. Pale, silent, absorbed, he saw her wave her handkerchief and smile at her friends as they passed; he saw a white-haired old lady reach out her hands in yearning love, an eloquent pantomime that indicated that her sons were marching under her eyes, and then she sank back into Marian's arms.

"Oh," groaned Merwyn, "if that were my mother I could give her a love that would be almost worship."

CHAPTER XXXI.
"I'VE LOST MY CHANCE."

During the remainder of the 17th of June and for the next few days, the militia regiments of New York and Brooklyn were departing for the seat of war. The city was filled with conflicting rumors. On the 19th it was said that the invaders were returning to Virginia. The questions "Where is Lee, and what are his purposes? and what is the army of the Potomac about?" were upon all lips.

On the 20th came the startling tidings of organized resistance to the draft in Ohio, and of troops fired upon by the mob. Mr. Vosburgh frowned heavily as he read the account at the breakfast-table and said: "The test of my fears will come when the conscription begins in this city, and it may come much sooner. I wish you to join your mother before that day, Marian!"

"No," she said, quietly,--"not unless you compel, me to."

"I may be obliged to use my authority," said her father, after some thought. "My mind is oppressed by a phase of danger not properly realized. The city is being stripped of its loyal regiments, and every element of mischief is left behind."

"Papa, I entreat you not to send me away while you remain. I assure you that such a course would involve far greater danger to me than staying with you, even though your fears should be realized. If the worst should happen, I might escape all harm. If you do what you threaten, I could not escape a wounded spirit."

"Well, my dear," said her father, gently, "I appreciate your courage and devotion, and I should indeed miss you. We'll await further developments."

Day after day passed, bringing no definite information. There were reports of severe cavalry fighting in Virginia, but the position of the main body of Lee's army was still practically unknown to the people at large. On the 22d, a leading journal said, "The public must, with patience, await events in Virginia, and remain in ignorance until some decisive point is reached;" and on the 24th, the head-lines of the press read, in effect, "Not much of importance from Pennsylvania yesterday." The intense excitement caused by the invasion was subsiding. People could not exist at the first fever-heat. It was generally believed that Hooker's army had brought Lee to a halt, and that the two commanders were manoeuvring for positions. The fact was that the Confederates had an abundance of congenial occupation in sending southward to their impoverished commissary department the immense booty they were gathering among the rich farms and towns of Pennsylvania. Hooker was seeking, by the aid of his cavalry force and scouts, to penetrate his opponent's plans, meanwhile hesitating whether to fall on the rebel communications in their rear, or to follow northward.

Lee and his great army, flushed with recent victories, were not all that Hooker had to contend with, but there was a man in Washington, whose incapacity and ill-will threatened even more fatal difficulties. Gen. Halleck, Commander-in-Chief, hung on the Union leader like the "Old Man of the Sea." He misled the noble President, who, as a civilian. was ignorant of military affairs, paralyzed tens of thousands of troops by keeping them where they could be of no practical use, and by giving them orders of which General Hooker was not informed. The Comte de Paris writes, "Lee's projects could not have been more efficiently subserved," and the disastrous defeat of General Milroy confirms these words. It was a repetition of the old story of General Miles of the preceding year, with the difference that Milroy was a gallant, loyal man, who did all that a skilful officer could accomplish to avert the results of his superior's blundering and negligence.

Hooker was goaded into resigning, and of the army of the Potomac the gifted French author again writes, "Everything seemed to conspire against it, even the government, whose last hope it was;" adding later: "Out of the 97,000 men thus divided (at Washington, Frederick, Fortress Monroe, and neighboring points) there were 40,000, perfectly useless where they were stationed, that might have been added to the army of the Potomac before the 1st of July. Thus reinforced, the Union general could have been certain of conquering his adversary, and even of inflicting upon him an irreparable disaster."

The fortunes of the North were indeed trembling in the balance. We had to cope with the ablest general of the South and his great army, with the peace (?) faction that threatened bloody arguments in the loyal States, and with General Halleck.

The people were asking: "Where is the army of the Potomac? What can it be doing, that the invasion goes on so long unchecked?" At Gettysburg this patient, longsuffering army gave its answer.

Meanwhile the North was brought face to face with the direst possibilities, and its fears, which history has proved to be just, were aroused to the last degree. The lull in the excitement which had followed the first startling announcement of invasion was broken by the wildest rumors and the sternest facts. The public pulse again rose to fever-heat. Farmers were flying into Harrisburg, before the advancing enemy; merchants were packing their goods for shipment to the North; and the panic was so general that the proposition was made to stop forcibly the flight of able-bodied men from the Pennsylvanian capital.

As Mr. Vosburgh read these despatches in the morning paper, Marian smiled satirically, and said: "You think that Mr. Merwyn is under some powerful restraint. I doubt whether he would be restrained from going north, should danger threaten this city."

And many believed, with good reason, that New York City was threatened. Major-General Doubleday, in his clear, vigorous account of this campaign writes: "Union spies who claimed to have counted the rebel forces as they passed through Hagerstown made their number to be 91,000 infantry and 280 guns. This statement, though exaggerated, gained great credence, and added to the excitement of the loyal people throughout the Northern States, while the disloyal element was proportionately active and jubilant." Again he writes: "There was wild commotion throughout the North, and people began to feel that the boast of the Georgia Senator, Toombs, that he would call the roll of his slaves at the foot of Bunker Hill Monument, might soon be realized. The enemy seemed very near and the army of the Potomac far away." Again: "The Southern people were bent upon nothing else than the entire subjugation of the North and the occupation of our principal cities."

These statements of sober history are but the true echoes of the loud alarms of the hour. On the morning of the 20th of June, such words as these were printed as the leading editorial of the New York Tribune: "The rebels are coming North.

All doubt seems at length dispelled. Men of the North, Pennsylvanians, Jersey-men, New-Yorkers, New-Englanders, the foe is at your doors! Are you true men or traitors? brave men or cowards? If you are patriots, resolved and deserving to be free, prove it by universal rallying, arming, and marching to meet the foe. Prove it NOW!"

Marian, with flashing eyes and glowing cheeks, read to her father this brief trumpet call, and then exclaimed: "Yes, the issue is drawn so sharply now that no loyal man can hesitate, and to-day Mr. Merwyn cannot help answering the question, 'Are you a brave man or a coward?' O papa, to think that a MAN should be deaf to such an appeal and shrink in such an emergency!"

At that very hour Merwyn sat alone in his elegant home, his face buried in his hands, the very picture of dejection. Before him on the table lay the journal from which he had read the same words which Marian had applied to him in bitter scorn. An open letter was also upon the table, and its contents had slain his hope. Mrs. Merwyn had answered his appeal characteristically. "You evidently need my presence," she wrote, "yet I will never believe that you can violate your oath, unless your reason is dethroned. When you forget that you have sworn by your father's memory and your mother's honor, you must be wrecked indeed. I wonder at your blindness to your own interests, and can see in it the influence which, in all the past, has made some weak men reckless and forgetful of everything except an unworthy passion. The armies of your Northern friends have been defeated again and again. I have means of communication with my Southern friends, and before the summer is over our gallant leaders will dictate peace in the city where you dwell. What then would become of the property which you so value, were it not for my influence? My hope still is, that your infatuation will pass away with your youth, and that your mind will become clear, so that you can appreciate the future that might be yours. If I can only protect you against yourself and designing people, all may yet be well; and when our glorious South takes the foremost place among the nations of the earth, my influence will be such that I can still obtain for you rank and title, unless you now compromise yourself by some unutterable folly. The crisis is approaching fast, and the North will soon learn that, so far from subduing the South, it will be subjugated and will gladly accept such terms as we may deem it best to give. I have fulfilled my mission here. The leading classes are with us in sympathy, and it will require but one or two more victories like that of Chancellorsville to make England our open ally. Then people of our birth and wealth will be the equals of the English aristocracy, and your career can be as lofty as you choose to make it. Then, with a gratitude beyond words, you will thank me for my firmness, for you can aspire to the highest positions in an empire such as the world has not seen before."

"No," said Merwyn, sternly, "if there is a free State left at the North, I will work there with my own hands for a livelihood, rather than have any part or lot in this Southern empire. Yet what can I ever appear to be but a shrinking coward? An owner of slaves all her life, my mother has made a slave of me. She has fettered my very soul. Oh! if there are to be outbreaks at the North, let them come soon, or I shall die under the weight of my chains."

The dark tide of invasion rose higher and higher. At last the tidings came that Lee's whole army was in Pennsylvania, that Harrisburg would be attacked before night, and that the enemy were threatening Columbia on the northern bank of the Susquehanna, and would have crossed the immense bridge which there spans the river, had it not been burned.

On the 27th, the Tribune contained the following editorial words: "Now is the hour. Pennsylvania is at length arousing, we trust not too late. We plead with the entire North to rush to the rescue; the whole North is menaced through this invasion. It we do not stop it at the Susquehanna, it will soon strike us on the Delaware, then on the Hudson."

"My chance is coming," Merwyn muttered, grimly, as he read these words. "If the answering counter-revolution does not begin during the next few days, I shall take my rifle and fight as a citizen as long as there is a rebel left on Northern soil."

The eyes of others were turned towards Pennsylvania; he scanned the city in which he dwelt. He had abandoned all morbid brooding, and sought by every means in his power to inform himself in regard to the seething, disloyal elements that were now manifesting themselves. From what Mr. Vosburgh had told him, and from what he had discovered himself, he felt that any hour might witness bloody co-operation at his very door with the army of invasion.

"Should this take place," he exclaimed, as he paced his room, "oh that it might be my privilege, before I died, to perform some deed that would convince Marian Vosburgh that I am not what she thinks me to be!"

Each new day brought its portentous news. On the 30th of June, there were accounts of intense excitement at Washington and Baltimore, for the enemy had appeared almost at the suburbs of these cities. In Baltimore, women rushed into the streets and besought protection. New York throbbed and rocked with kindred excitement.

On July 3d, the loyal Tribune again sounded the note of deep alarm: "These are times that try men's souls! The peril of our country's overthrow is great and imminent. The triumph of the rebels distinctly and unmistakably involves the downfall of republican and representative institutions."

By a strange anomaly multitudes of the poor, the oppressed in other lands, whose hope for the future was bound up in the cause of the North, were arrayed against it. Their ignorance made them dupes and tools, and enemies of human rights and progress were prompt to use them. On the evening of this momentous 3d of July, a manifesto, in the form of a handbill, was extensively circulated throughout the city. Jeff Davis himself could not have written anything more disloyal, more false, of the Union government and its aims, or better calculated to incite bloody revolution in the North.

For the last few days the spirit of rebellion had been burning like a fuse toward a vast magazine of human passion and intense hatred of Northern measures and principles. If from Pennsylvania had come in electric flash the words, "Meade defeated," the explosion would have come almost instantly; but all now had learned that the army of the Potomac had emerged from its obscurity, and had grappled with the invading forces. Even the most reckless of the so-called peace faction could afford to wait a few hours longer. As soon as the shattered columns of Meade's army were in full retreat, the Northern wing of the rebellion could act with confidence.

The Tribune, in commenting on the incendiary document distributed on the evening of the 3d, spoke as follows: "That the more determined sympathizers, in this vicinity, with the Southern rebels have, for months, conspired and plotted to bring about a revolution is as certain as the Civil War. Had Meade been defeated," etc.

The dramatic culmination of this awful hour of uncertainty may be found in the speeches, on July 4th, of ex-President Franklin Pierce, at Concord, N.H., and of Governor Seymour, in the Academy of Music, at New York. The former spoke of "the mailed hand of military usurpation in the North, striking down the liberties of the people and trampling its foot on a desecrated Constitution." He lauded Vallandigham, who was sent South for disloyalty, as "the noble martyr of free speech." He declared the war to be fruitless, and exclaimed: "You will take care of yourselves. With or without arms, with or without leaders, we will at least, in the effort to defend our rights, as a free people, build up a great mausoleum of hearts, to which men who yearn for liberty will, in after years, with bowed heads reverently resort as Christian pilgrims to the shrines of the Holy Land."

Such were the shrines with which this man would have filled New England. There is a better chance now, that a new and loyal Virginia will some day build a monument to John Brown.

Governor Seymour's speech was similar in tenor, but more guarded. In words of bitter irony toward the struggling government, whose hands the peace faction were striving to paralyze, he began: "When I accepted the invitation to speak with others, at this meeting, we were promised the downfall of Vicksburg, the opening of the Mississippi, the probable capture of the Confederate capital, and the exhaustion of the rebellion. By common consent, all parties had fixed upon this day when the results of the campaign should be known. But, in the moment of expected victory, there came a midnight cry for help from Pennsylvania, to save its despoiled fields from the invading foe; and, almost within sight of this metropolis, the ships of your merchants were burned to the water's edge. Parties are exasperated and stand in almost defiant attitude toward each other."

"At the very hour," writes the historian Lossing, "when this ungenerous taunt was uttered, Vicksburg and its dependences and vast spoils, with more than thirty thousand Confederate captives, were in the possession of General Grant; and the discomfited army of Lee, who, when that sentence was written, was expected to lead his troops victoriously to the Delaware, and perhaps to the Hudson, was flying from Meade's troops, to find shelter from utter destruction beyond the Potomac."

Rarely has history reached a more dramatic climax, and seldom have the great scenes of men's actions been more swiftly shifted.

Merwyn attended this great mass-meeting, and was silent when the thousands applauded. In coming out he saw, while unobserved himself, Mr. Vosburgh, and was struck by the proud, contemptuous expression of his face. The government officer had listened with a cipher telegram in his pocket informing him of Lee's repulse.

For the last twenty-four hours Merwyn had watched almost sleeplessly for the outburst to take place. That strong, confident face indicated no fears that it would ever take place.

A few hours later, he, and all, heard from the army of the Potomac.

When at last it became known that the Confederate army was in full retreat, and, as the North then believed, would be either captured or broken into flying fragments before reaching Virginia, Merwyn faced what he believed to be his fate.

"The country is saved," he said. "There will be no revolution at the North. Thank God for the sake of others, but I've lost my chance."

CHAPTER XXXII.
BLAUVELT.

In June, especially during the latter part of the month, Strahan and Blauvelt's letters to Marian had been brief and infrequent. The duties of the young officers were heavy, and their fatigues great. They could give her little information forecasting the future. Indeed, General Hooker himself could not have done this, for all was in uncertainty. Lee must be found and fought, and all that any one knew was that the two great armies would eventually meet in the decisive battle of the war.

The patient, heroic army of the Potomac, often defeated, but never conquered, was between two dangers that can be scarcely overestimated, the vast, confident hosts of Lee in Pennsylvania, and Halleck in Washington. General Hooker was hampered, interfered with, deprived of reinforcements that were kept in idleness elsewhere, and at last relieved of command on the eve of battle, because he asked that 11,000 men, useless at Harper's Ferry, might be placed under his orders. That this was a mere pretext for his removal, and an expression of Halleck's ill-will, is proved by the fact that General Meade, his successor, immediately ordered the evacuation of Harper's Ferry and was unrestrained and unrebuked. Meade, however, did not unite these 11,000 men to his army, where they might have added materially to his success, but left them far in his rear, a useless, half-way measure possibly adopted to avoid displeasing Halleck.

It would seem that Providence itself assumed the guidance of this longsuffering Union army, that had been so often led by incompetence in the field and paralyzed by interference at Washington. Even the philosophical historian, the Comte de Paris, admits this truth in remarkable language.

Neither Lee nor Meade knew where they should meet, and had under consideration various plans of action, but, writes the French historian, "The fortune of war cut short all these discussions by bringing the two combatants into a field which neither had chosen." Again, after describing the region of Gettysburg, he concludes: "Such is the ground upon which unforeseen circumstances were about to bring the two armies in hostile contact. Neither Meade nor Lee had any personal knowledge of it."

Once more, after a vivid description of the first day's battle, in which Buford with his cavalry division, Doubleday with the First Corps, and Howard with the Eleventh, checked the rebel advance, but at last, after heroic fighting, were overwhelmed and driven back in a disorder which in some brigades resembled a rout, the Comte de Paris recognizes, in the choice of position on which the Union troops were rallied, something beyond the will and wisdom of man.

"A resistless impulse seems to spur it (the rebel army) on to battle. It believes itself invincible. There is scorn of its adversary; nearly all the Confederate generals have undergone the contagion. Lee himself, the grave, impassive man, will some day acknowledge that he has allowed himself to be influenced by these common illusions. It seems that the God of Armies had designated for the Confederates the lists where the supreme conflict must take place: they cheerfully accept the alternative, without seeking for any other."

All the world knows now that the position in the "lists" thus "designated" to the Union army was almost an equivalent for the thousands of men kept idle and useless elsewhere. To a certain extent the conditions of Fredericksburg are reversed, and the Confederates, in turn, must storm lofty ridges lined with artillery.

Of those days of awful suspense, the 3d, 4th, and 5th of July, the French historian gives but a faint idea in the following words: "In the mean while, the North was anxiously awaiting for the results of the great conflict. Uneasiness and excitement were perceptible everywhere; terror prevailed in all those places believed to be within reach of the invaders. Rumors and fear exaggerated their number, and the remembrance of their success caused them to be deemed invincible."

When, therefore, the tidings came, "The rebel army totally defeated," with other statements of the victory too highly colored, a burden was lifted from loyal hearts which the young of this generation cannot gauge; but with the abounding joy and gratitude there were also, in the breasts of hundreds of thousands, sickening fear and suspense which must remain until the fate of loved ones was known.

In too vivid fancy, wives and mothers saw a bloody field strewn with still forms, and each one asked herself, "Could I go among these, might I not recognize HIS features?"

But sorrow and fear shrink from public observation, while joy and exultation seek open expression. Before the true magnitude of the victory at Gettysburg could be realized, came the knowledge that the nation's greatest soldier, General Grant, had taken Vicksburg and opened the Mississippi.

Marian saw the deep gladness in her father's eyes and heard it in his tones, and, while she shared in his gratitude and relief, her heart was oppressed with solicitude for her friends. To her, who had no near kindred in the war, these young men had become almost as dear as brothers. She was conscious of their deep affection, and she felt that there could be no rejoicing for her until she was assured of their safety. All spoke of the battle of Gettysburg as one of the most terrific combats of the world. Two of her friends must have been in the thick of it. She read the blood-stained accounts with paling cheeks, and at last saw the words, "Captain Blauvelt, wounded; Major Strahan, wounded and missing."

This was all. There was room for hope; there was much cause to fear the worst. From Lane there were no tidings whatever. She was oppressed with the feeling that perhaps the frank, true eyes of these loyal friends might never again look into her own. With a chill of unspeakable dread she asked herself what her life would be without these friends. Who could ever take their place or fill the silence made by their hushed voices?

Since reading the details of the recent battle her irritation against Merwyn had passed away, and she now felt for him only pity. Her own brave spirit had been awed and overwhelmed by the accounts of the terrific cannonade and the murderous hand-to-hand struggles. At night she would start up from vivid dreams wherein she saw the field with thousands of ghastly faces turned towards the white moonlight. In her belief Merwyn was incapable of looking upon such scenes. Therefore why should she think of him with scorn and bitterness? She herself had never before realized how terrible they were. Now that the dread emergency, with its imperative demand for manhood and action, had passed, her heart became softened and chastened with thoughts of death. She was enabled to form a kinder judgment, and to believe it very possible that Merwyn, in the consciousness of his weakness, was suffering more than many a wounded man of sterner mettle.

On the evening of the day whereon she had read the ominous words in regard to her friends, Merwyn's card was handed to her, and, although surprised, she went down to meet him without hesitation. His motives for this call need brief explanation.

For a time he had given way to the deepest dejection in regard to his own prospects. There seemed nothing for him to do but wait for the arrival of his mother, whom he could not welcome. He still had a lingering hope that when she came and found her ambitious dreams of Southern victory dissipated, she might be induced to give him back his freedom, and on this hope he lived. But, in the main, he was like one stunned and paralyzed by a blow, and for a time he could not rally. He had been almost sleepless for days from intense excitement and expectation, and the reaction was proportionately great. At last he thought of Strahan, and telegraphed to Mrs. Strahan, at her country place, asking if she had heard from her son. Soon, after receiving a negative answer, he saw, in the long lists of casualties, the brief, vague statement that Marian had found. The thought then occurred to him that he might go to Gettysburg and search for Strahan. Anything would be better than inaction. He believed that he would have time to go and return before his mother's arrival, and, if he did not, he would leave directions for her reception. The prospect of doing something dispelled his apathy, and the hope of being of service to his friend had decided attractions, for he had now become sincerely attached to Strahan. He therefore rapidly made his preparations to depart that very night, but decided first to see Marian, thinking it possible that she might have received some later intelligence. Therefore, although very doubtful of his reception, he had ventured to call, hoping that Marian's interest in her friend might secure for him a slight semblance of welcome. He was relieved when she greeted him gravely, quietly, but not coldly.

He at once stated his purpose, and asked if she had any information that would guide him in his search. Although she shook her head and told him that she knew nothing beyond what she had seen in the paper, he saw with much satisfaction that her face lighted up with hope and eagerness, and that she approved of his effort. While explaining his intentions he had not sat down, but now she cordially asked him to be seated and to give his plans more in detail.

"I fear you will find fearful confusion and difficulty in reaching the field," she said.

"I have no fears," he replied. "I shall go by rail as far as possible, then hire or purchase a horse. The first list of casualties is always made up hastily, and I have strong hopes of finding Strahan in one of the many extemporized hospitals, or, at least, of getting some tidings of him."

"One thing is certain," she added, kindly,--"you have proved that if you do find him, he will have a devoted nurse."

"I shall do my best for him," he replied, quietly. "If he has been taken from the field and I can learn his whereabouts, I shall follow him."

The color caused by his first slight embarrassment had faded away, and Marian exclaimed, "Mr. Merwyn, you are either ill or have been ill."

"Oh, no," he said, carelessly; "I have only shared in the general excitement and anxiety. I am satisfied that we have but barely escaped a serious outbreak in this city."

"I think you are right," she answered, gravely, and her thought was: "He is indeed to be pitied if a few weeks of fearful expectation have made him so pale and haggard. It has probably cost him a tremendous effort to remain in the city where he has so much at stake."

After a moment's silence Merwyn resumed: "I shall soon take my train. Would you not like to write a few lines to Strahan? As I told you, in effect, once before, they may prove the best possible tonic in case I find him."

Marian, eager to comply with the suggestion, excused herself. In her absence her father entered. He also greeted the young man kindly, and, learning of his project, volunteered some useful instructions, adding, "I can give you a few lines that may be of service."

At last Merwyn was about to depart, and Marian, for the first time, gave him her hand and wished him "God-speed." He flushed deeply, and there was a flash of pleasure in his dark eyes as he said, in a low tone, that he would try to deserve her kindness.

At this moment there was a ring at the door, and a card was brought in. Marian could scarcely believe her eyes, for on it was written, "Henry Blauvelt."

She rushed to the door and welcomed the young officer with exclamations of delight, and then added, eagerly, "Where is Mr. Strahan?"

"I am sorry indeed to tell you that I do not know," Blauvelt replied, sadly. Then he hastily added: "But I am sure he was not killed, for I have searched every part of the field where he could possibly have fallen. I have visited the hospitals, and have spent days and nights in inquiries. My belief now is that he was taken prisoner."

"Then there is still hope!" exclaimed the young girl, with tears in her eyes. "You surely believe there is still hope?"

"I certainly believe there is much reason for hope. The rebels left their own seriously wounded men on the field, and took away as prisoners only such of our men as were able to march. It is true I saw Strahan fall just as we were driven back; but I am sure that he was neither killed nor seriously wounded, for I went to the spot as soon as possible afterwards and he was not there, nor have I been able, since, to find him or obtain tidings of him. He may have been knocked down by a piece of shell or a spent ball. A moment or two later the enemy charged over the spot where he fell, and what was left of our regiment was driven back some distance. From that moment I lost all trace of him. I believe that he has only been captured with many other prisoners, and that he will be exchanged in a few weeks."

"Heaven grant that it may be so!" she breathed, fervently. "But, Mr. Blauvelt, YOU are wounded. Do not think us indifferent because we have asked so eagerly after Major Strahan, for you are here alive and apparently as undaunted as ever."

"Oh, my wounds are slight. Carrying my arm in a sling gives too serious an impression. I merely had one of the fingers of my left hand shot away, and a scratch on my shoulder."

"But have these wounds been dressed lately?" Mr. Vosburgh asked, gravely.

"And have you had your rations this evening?" Marian added, with the glimmer of a smile.

"Thanks, yes to both questions. I arrived this afternoon, and at once saw a good surgeon. I have not taken time to obtain a better costume than this old uniform, which has seen hard service."

"Like the wearer," said Marian. "I should have been sorry indeed if you had changed it."

"Well, I knew that you would be anxious to have even a negative assurance of

Strahan's safety."

"And equally so to be positively assured of your own."

"I hoped that that would be true to some extent. My dear old mother, in New Hampshire, to whom I have telegraphed, is eager to see me, and so I shall go on in the morning."

"You must be our guest, then, to-night," said Mr. Vosburgh, decisively. "We will take no refusal, and I shall send at once to the hotel for your luggage."

"It is small indeed," laughed Blauvelt, flushing with pleasure, "for I came away in very light marching order."

Marian then explained that Merwyn, who, after a brief, polite greeting from Blauvelt, had been almost forgotten, was about to start in search of Strahan.

"I would not lay a straw in his way, and possibly he may obtain some clue that escaped me," said the young officer.

"Perhaps, if you feel strong enough to tell us something of that part of the battle in which you were engaged, and of your search, Mr. Merwyn may receive hints which will be of service to him," Mr. Vosburgh suggested.

"I shall be very glad to do so, and feel entirely equal to the effort. Indeed, I have been resting and sleeping in the cars nearly all day, and am so much better that I scarcely feel it right to be absent from the regiment."

They at once repaired to the library, Marian leaving word with Mammy Borden that they were engaged, should there be other callers.

CHAPTER XXXIII.
A GLIMPSE OF WAR.

aptain Blauvelt," said Marian, when they were seated in the library, "I have two favors to ask of you. First, that you will discontinue your story as soon as you feel the least weakness, and, second, that you will not gloss anything over. I wish a life-picture of a soldier's experience. You and Mr. Strahan have been inclined to give me the brighter side of campaigning. Now, tell us just what you and Mr. Strahan did. I've no right to be the friend of soldiers if I cannot listen to the tragic details of a battle, while sitting here in this quiet room, and I wish to realize, as I never have done, what you and others have passed through. Do not be so modest that you cannot tell us exactly what you did. In brief, a plain, unvarnished tale unfold, and I shall be content."

"Now," she thought, "Mr. Merwyn shall know to whom I can give my friendship. I do not ask him, or any one, to face these scenes, but my heart is for a man who can face them."

Blauvelt felt that he was fortunate indeed. He knew that he had fair powers as a raconteur, and he was conscious of having taken no unworthy part in the events he was about to describe, while she, who required the story, was the woman whom he most admired, and whose good opinion was dear to him.

Therefore, after a moment's thought, he began: "In order to give you a quiet, and therefore a more artistic prelude to the tragedy of the battle, I shall touch lightly on some of the incidents of our march to the field. I will take up the thread of our experiences on the 15th of June, for I think you were quite well informed of what occurred before that date. The 15th was one of the hottest days that I remember. I refer to this fact because of a pleasant incident which introduces a little light among the shadows, and suggests that soldiers are not such bad fellows after all, although inclined to be a little rough and profane. Our men suffered terribly from the heat, and some received sunstrokes. Many were obliged to fall out of the ranks, but managed to keep up with the column. At noon we were halted near a Vermont regiment that had just drawn a ration of soft bread and were boiling their coffee. As our exhausted men came straggling and staggering in, these hospitable Vermonters gave them their entire ration of bread and the hot coffee prepared for their own meal; and when the ambulances brought in the men who had been sun-struck, these generous fellows turned their camp into a temporary hospital and themselves into nurses.

"I will now give you a glimpse of a different experience. Towards evening on the 19th a rain-storm began, and continued all night. No orders to halt came till after midnight. On we splashed, waded, and floundered along roads cut up by troops in advance until the mud in many places reached the depth of ten inches. It was intensely dark, and we could not see to pick our way. Splashed from head to foot, and wet through for hours, we had then one of the most dismal experiences I remember. I had not been well since the terrible heat of the 15th, and Strahan, putting on the air of a martinet, sternly ordered me to mount his horse while he took charge of my company."

Marian here clapped her hands in applause.

"At last we were ordered to file to the right into a field and bivouac for the night. The field proved to be a marshy meadow, worse than the road. But there was no help for it, and we were too tired to hunt around in the darkness for a better place. Strahan mounted again to assist in giving orders for the night's arrangement, and to find drier ground if possible. In the darkness he and his horse tumbled into a ditch so full of mire and water that he escaped all injury. We sank half-way to our knees in the swampy ground, and the horses floundered so that one or two of the officers were thrown, and all were obliged to dismount. At last, by hallooing, the regiment formed into line, and then came the unique order from the colonel, 'Squat, my bull-frogs.' There was nothing for us to do but to lie down on the swampy, oozing ground, with our shelter tents and blankets wrapped around and under us. You remember what an exquisite Strahan used to be. I wish you could have seen him when the morning revealed us to one another. He was of the color of the sacred soil from crown to toe. When we met we stood and laughed at each other, and I wanted him to let me make a sketch for your benefit, but we hadn't time.

"I will now relate a little incident which shows how promptly pluck and character tell. During the 25th we were pushed forward not far from thirty miles. On the morning of this severe march a young civilian officer, who had been appointed to the regiment by the Governor, joined us, and was given command of Company I. When he took his place in the march there was a feeling of intense hostility toward him, as there ever is among veterans against civilians who are appointed over them. If he had fallen out of the ranks and died by the roadside I scarcely believe that a man would have volunteered to bury him. But, while evidently unaccustomed to marching, he kept at the head of his company throughout the entire day, when every step must have been torture. He uttered not a word of complaint, and at night was seen, by the light of a flaring candle, pricking the blisters on his swollen feet; then he put on his shoes, and walked away as erect as if on parade. In those few hours he had won the respect of the entire regiment, and had become one of us. Poor fellow! I may as well mention now that he was killed, a few days later, with many of the company that he was bravely leading. His military career lasted but little over a week, yet he proved himself a hero.

"Now I will put in a few high lights again. On the 28th we entered Frederick City. Here we had a most delightful experience. The day was warm and all were thirsty. Instead of the cold, lowering glances to which we had been accustomed in Virginia, smiling mothers, often accompanied by pretty daughters, stood in the gateways with pails and goblets of cool, sparkling water. I doubt whether the same number of men ever drank so much water before, for who could pass by a white hand and arm, and a pretty, sympathetic face, beaming with good-will? Here is a rough sketch I made of a Quaker matron, with two charming daughters, and an old colored man, 'totin'' water at a rate that must have drained their well."

Marian praised the sketch so heartily that Merwyn knew she was taking this indirect way to eulogize the soldier as as well as the artist, and he groaned inwardly as he thought how he must suffer by contrast.

"I will pass over what occurred till the 1st of July. Our march lay through a country that, after desolated Virginia, seemed like paradise, and the kind faces that greeted us were benedictions. July 1st was clear, and the sun's rays dazzling and intense in their heat. Early in the afternoon we were lying around in the shade, about two miles from the State line of Pennsylvania. Two corps had preceded us. Some of our men, with their ears on the ground, declared that they could hear the distant mutter of artillery. The country around was full of troops, resting like ourselves.

"Suddenly shrill bugle-blasts in every direction called us into line. We were moved through Emmetsburg, filed to the left into a field until other troops passed, and then took our place in the column and began a forced march to Gettysburg. Again we suffered terribly from the heat and the choking clouds of dust raised by commands in advance of us. The sun shone in the west like a great, angry furnace. Our best men began to stagger from the ranks and fall by the wayside, while every piece of woods we passed was filled with prostrate men, gasping, and some evidently dying. But on, along that white, dusty road, the living torrent poured. Only one command was heard. 'Forward! Forward!'

"First, like a low jar of thunder, but with increasing volume and threatening significance, the distant roar of artillery quickened the steps of those who held out. Major Strahan was again on his feet, with other officers, their horses loaded down with the rifles of the men. Even food and blankets, indeed almost everything except ammunition, was thrown away by the men, for, in the effort to reach the field in time, an extra pound became an intolerable burden.

"At midnight we were halted on what was then the extreme left of Meade's position. When we formed our regimental line, as usual, at the close of the day, not over one hundred men and but five or six officers were present. Over one hundred and fifty had given out from the heat and fatigue. The moment ranks were broken the men threw themselves down in their tracks and slept with their loaded guns by their sides. Strahan and I felt so gone that we determined to have a little refreshment if possible. Lights were gleaming from a house not far away, and we went thither in the hope of purchasing something that would revive us. We found the building, and even the yard around it, full of groaning and desperately wounded men, with whom the surgeons were busy. This foretaste of the morrow took away our appetites, and we returned to our command, where Strahan was soon sleeping, motionless, as so many of our poor fellows would be on the ensuing night.

"Excessive fatigue often takes from me the power to sleep, and I lay awake, listening to the strange, ominous sounds off to our right. There were the heavy rumble of artillery wheels, the tramp of men, and the hoarse voices of officers giving orders. In the still night these confused sounds were wonderfully distinct near at hand, but they shaded off in the northeast to mere murmurs. I knew that it was the army of the Potomac arriving and taking its positions. The next day I learned that General Meade had reached the field about one A.M., and that he had spent the remaining hours of the night in examining the ground and in making preparations for the coming struggle. The clear, white moonlight, which aided him in his task, lighted up a scene strange and beautiful beyond words. It glinted on our weapons, gave to the features of the sleepers the hue of death, and imparted to Strahan's face, who lay near me, almost the delicacy and beauty of a girl. I declare to you, that when I remembered the luxurious ease from which he had come, the hero he was now, and all his many acts of kindness to me and others,--when I thought of what might be on the morrow, I'm not ashamed to say that tears came into my eyes."

"Nor am I ashamed," faltered Marian, "that you should see tears in mine. Oh, God grant that he may return to us again!"

"Well," resumed Blauvelt, after a moment of thoughtful hesitation, "I suppose I was a little morbid that night. Perhaps one was excusable, for all knew that we were on the eve of the most desperate battle of the war. I shall not attempt to describe the beauty of the landscape, or the fantastic shapes taken by the huge boulders that were scattered about. My body seemed almost paralyzed with fatigue, but my mind, for a time, was preternaturally active, and noted every little detail. Indeed, I felt a strange impulse to dwell upon and recall everything relating to this life, since the chances were so great that we might, before the close of another day, enter a different state of existence. You see I am trying, as you requested, to give you a realistic picture."

"That is what I wish," said the young girl; but her cheeks were pale as she spoke.

"In the morning I was awakened by one of my men bringing me a cup of hot coffee, and when I had taken it, and later a little breakfast of raw pork and hardtack, I felt like a new man. Nearly all of our stragglers had joined us during the night, or in the dawn, and our regiment now mustered about two hundred and forty rifles in line, a sad change from the time when we marched a thousand strong. But the men now were veterans, and this almost made good the difference.

"When the sun was a few hours high we were moved forward with the rest of our brigade; then, later, off to the left, and placed in position on the brow of a hill that descended steeply before us, and was covered with rocks, huge boulders, and undergrowth. The right of our regiment was in the edge of a wood with a smoother slope before it. I and my company had no other shelter than the rocks and boulders, which formed a marked feature of the locality, and protruded from the soil in every imaginable shape. If we had only thrown the smaller stones together and covered them with earth we might have made, during the time we wasted, a line of defence from which we could not have been driven. The 2d of July taught us that we had still much to learn. As it was, we lounged about upon the grass, seeking what shade we could from the glare of another intensely hot day, and did nothing.

"A strange, ominous silence pervaded the field for hours, broken only now and then by a shell screaming through the air, and the sullen roar of the gun from which it was fired. The pickets along our front would occasionally approach the enemy too closely, and there would be brief reports of musketry, again followed by oppressive silence. A field of wheat below us undulated in light billows as the breeze swept it. War and death would be its reapers. The birds were singing in the undergrowth; the sun lighted up the rural landscape brilliantly, and it was almost impossible to believe that the scenes of the afternoon could, take place. By sweeping our eyes up and down our line, and by resting them upon a battery of our guns but a few yards away, we became aware of the significance of our position. Lee's victorious army was before us. Sinister rumors of the defeat of Union forces the previous day had reached us, and we knew that the enemy's inaction did not indicate hesitation or fear, but rather a careful reconnaissance of our lines, that the weakest point might be discovered. Every hour of delay, however, was a boon to us, for the army of the Potomac was concentrating and strengthening its position.

"We were on the extreme left of the Union army; and, alas for us! Lee first decided to turn and crush its left. As I have said, we were posted along the crest of a hill which sloped off a little to the left, then rose again, and culminated in a wild, rocky elevation called the Devil's Den,--fit name in view of the scenes it witnessed. Behind us was a little valley through which flowed a small stream called Plum Run. Here the artillery horses, caissons, and wagons were stationed, that they might be in partial shelter. Across the Run, and still further back, rose the rocky, precipitous heights of Little Round Top, where, during the same afternoon, some of the severest fighting of the battle is said to have taken place. Please give me a sheet of paper, and I can outline the nature of the ground just around us. Of the general battle of that day I can give you but a slight idea. One engaged in a fight sees, as a rule, only a little section of it; but in portraying that he gives the color and spirit of the whole thing."

Rapidly sketching for a few minutes, Blauvelt resumed: "Here we are along the crest of this hill, with a steep, broken declivity in front of us, extending down a few hundred yards to another small stream, a branch of Plum Run. Beyond this branch the ground rises again to some thick woods, which screened the enemy's movements.

"At midday clouds of dust were seen rising in the distance, and we at last were told that Sedgwick's corps had arrived, and that the entire army of the Potomac was on the ground. As hours still elapsed and no attack was made, the feeling of confidence grew stronger. Possibly Lee had concluded that our position was unassailable, or something had happened. The soldier's imagination was only second to his credulity in receiving the rumors which flew as thick as did the bullets a little later.

"Strahan and I had a quiet talk early in the day, and said what we wished to each other. After that he became dreamy and absorbed in his own thoughts as we watched for signs of the enemy through hours that seemed interminable. Some laughing, jesting, and card-playing went on among the men, but in the main they were grave, thoughtful, and alert, spending the time in discussing the probabilities of this conflict, and in recalling scenes of past battles.

"Suddenly--it could not have been much past three o'clock--a dozen rebel batteries opened upon us, and in a second we were in a tempest of flying, bursting shells. Our guns, a few yards away, and other batteries along our line, replied. The roar of the opening battle thundered away to the right as far as we could hear. We were formed into line at once, and lay down upon the ground. A few of our men were hit, however, and frightful wounds were inflicted. After this iron storm had raged for a time we witnessed a sight that I shall never forget. Emerging from the woods on the slope opposite to us, solid bodies of infantry, marching by columns of battalion, came steadily toward us, their bayonets scintillating in the sunlight as if aflame. On they came till they crossed the little stream before us, and then deployed into four distinct lines of battle as steadily as if on parade. It was hard to realize that those men were marching towards us in the bright sunlight with deadly intent. Heretofore, in Virginia, the enemy had been partially screened in his approaches, but now all was like a panorama spread before us. We could see our shells tearing first through their column, then through the lines of battle, making wide gaps and throwing up clouds of dust. A second later the ranks were closed again, and, like a dark tide, on flowed their advance.

"We asked ourselves, 'What chance have our thin ranks against those four distinct, heavy battle lines advancing to assault us?' We had but two ranks of men, they eight. But not a man in our regiment flinched. When the enemy reached the foot of the hill our cannon could not be so depressed as to harm them. The time had come for the more deadly small arms. After a momentary halt the Confederates rushed forward to the assault with loud yells.

"Strahan's face was flushed with excitement and ardor. He hastened to the colonel on the right of the line and asked him to order a charge. The colonel coolly and quietly told him to go back to his place. A crash of musketry and a line of fire more vivid than July sunshine breaks out to the right and left as far as we can hear. Our men are beginning to fall. Again the impetuous Strahan hastens to the colonel and entreats for the order to charge, but our commander, as quiet and as impassive as the boulder beside which he stands, again orders him back. A moment later, however, their horses are brought, and they mount in spite of my remonstrances and those of other officers. Strahan's only answer was, "The men must see us to-day;" and he slowly rode to the rear and centre of the regiment, wheeled his horse, and, with drawn sword, fixed his eyes on the colonel, awaiting his signal. Supreme as was the moment of excitement, I looked for a few seconds at my gallant friend, for I wished to fix his portrait at that moment forever in my mind."

"Merciful Heaven!" said Marian, in a choking voice, "I thought I appreciated my friends before, but I did not."

Mr. Vosburgh's eyes rested anxiously on his daughter, and he asked, gravely, "Marian, is it best for you to hear more of this to-night?"

"Yes, papa. I must hear it all, and not a detail must be softened or omitted. Moreover," she added, proudly, dashing her tears right and left, "I am not afraid to listen."

Merwyn had shifted his seat, and was in deep shadow. He was pale and outwardly impassive, but there was torture in his mind. She thought, pityingly, "In spite of my tears I have a stouter heart than he."

CHAPTER XXXIV.
A GLIMPSE OF WAR, CONTINUED.

Miss Marian," resumed Blauvelt, "the scenes I am now about to describe are terrible in the extreme, even in their baldest statement. I cannot portray what actually took place; I doubt whether any one could; I can only give impressions of what I saw and heard when nearly all of us were almost insane from excitement. There are men who are cool in battle,--our colonel was, outwardly,--but the great majority of men must be not only veterans, but also gifted with unusual temperaments, to be able to remain calm and well balanced in the uproar of a bloody battle.

"In a sense, our men were veterans, and were steady enough to aim carefully as the enemy advanced up the steep hill. Our shots told on them more fatally than theirs on us. The greater number of us shared Strahan's impatience, and we longed for the wild, forward dash, which is a relief to the tremendous nervous strain at such a time. After a moment or two, that seemed ages, the colonel quietly nodded to Strahan, who waved his sword, pointed towards the enemy, and shouted, 'Charge!'

"You know him well enough to be sure that this was not an order for the men to fulfil while he looked on. In a second his powerful bay sprung through the centre of our line, and to keep up with him we had to follow on a run. There was no hesitation or flagging. Faces that had been pale were flushed now. As I turned my eyes from moment to moment back to my company, the terrible expression of the men's eyes impressed me even then. The colonel watched our impetuous rush with proud satisfaction, and then spurred his horse to the very midst of our advance. The lieutenant-colonel, undaunted by a former wound, never flinched a second, but wisely fought on foot.

"The first battle-line of the enemy seemed utterly unable to stand before our fierce onset. Those who were not shot fled.

"Again I saw Strahan waving his sword and shouting; 'Victory! Forward, men! forward!'

"He was in the very van, leading us all. At this moment the second rebel line fired a volley, and the bullets swept by like an autumn gust through a tree from which the leaves, thinned by former gales, are almost stripped. It seemed at the moment as if every other man went down. Wonder of wonders, as the smoke lifted a little, I saw to the right the tall form of our colonel still on his gray horse, pointing with his sword to the second rebel line, and shouting, 'Forward, my men! forward!'

"As the order left his lips, his sword fell, point-downward, and, with a headlong curve, he went over his horse upon the rocks below. Even in his death he went towards the enemy. His horse galloped in the same direction, but soon fell. I thought that Strahan was gone also, for he was hidden by smoke. A second later I heard his voice: 'Forward! Charge!'

"The men seemed infuriated by the loss of the colonel, and by no means daunted. Our next mad rush broke the second line of the enemy.

"The scene now defies all my powers of description. The little handful of men that was left of my company were almost beyond control. Each soldier was acting under the savage impulse to follow and kill some rebel before him. I shared the feeling, yet remained sane enough to thank God when I saw Strahan leap lightly down from his staggering horse, yet ever crying, 'Forward!' A second later the poor animal fell dead.

"Our own cannons were bellowing above us; the shells of the enemy were shrieking over our heads. There was a continuous crash of musketry that sounded like a fierce, devouring flame passing through dry thorns, yet above all this babel of horrid sounds could be heard the shouts and yells of the combatants and the shrieks and groans of wounded and dying men. Then remember that I saw but a little section, a few yards in width, of a battle extending for miles.

"In our mad excitement we did not consider the odds against us. The two remaining lines of battle were advancing swiftly through the fugitives, and we struck the first with such headlong impetuosity that it was repulsed and gave back; but the fourth and last line passing through, and being reinforced by the other broken lines, came unfaltering, and swept us back from sheer weight of numbers. We were now reduced to a mere skirmish line. It was at this moment that I saw Strahan fall, and it seemed but a second later that the enemy's advance passed over the spot. It was impossible then to rescue him, for the lieutenant-colonel had given orders for all to fall back and rally behind the guns that it was our duty to protect. Indeed, the difficult thing, now, was to get back. The Union regiment, on our right, had given way, after a gallant fight, earlier than we had, and the rebels were on our flank and rear. A number of our men going to the ridge, from which they had charged, ran into the enemy and were captured. There were desperate hand-to-hand encounters, hair-breadth escapes, and strange episodes.

"One occurs to me which I saw with my own eyes. It happened a little earlier in the fight. We were so close to the enemy that a man in my company had not time to withdraw his ramrod, and, in his instinctive haste to shoot first at a rebel just before him, sent ramrod and all through the Confederate's body, pinning him to the ground. The poor fellow stretched out his hands and cried for mercy. My man not only wished to recover his rod, but was, I believe, actuated by a kindly impulse, for he ran to the 'Johnny," pulled out the rod, jerked the man to his feet, and started him on a run to our rear as prisoner.

"When at last what was left of the regiment reached its original position it numbered no more than a full company. Scarcely a hundred were in line. Over one hundred of our men and the majority of the officers were either killed or wounded. While the lieutenant-colonel was rallying us near the battery, a shell struck a gun-carriage, hurling it against him, and he was home senseless from the field. The command now devolved on the senior captain left unwounded.

"One of my men now said to me, 'Captain, why don't you go to the rear? Your face is so covered with blood that you must be badly hurt.'

"It was only at that moment that I became conscious of my wound. In my intense anxiety about Strahan, in the effort to get my men back in something like order, and in the shock of seeing the lieutenant-colonel struck down, my mind seemed almost unaware of the existence of the body. In the retreat I had felt something sting my hand like a nettle, and now found one of the fingers of my left hand badly shattered. With this hand I had been wiping my brow, for it was intensely hot. I therefore was the most sanguineous-looking man of our number.

"Of course I did not go to the rear because of a wound of so slight a nature, and my earnest hope was that reinforcements would enable us to drive the enemy back so that I could go to the spot where I had seen Strahan fall.

"What I have vainly attempted to describe occurred in less time than I have taken in telling about it. I think it would have been much better if we had never left the line which we now occupied, and which we still held in spite of the overwhelming superiority, in numbers, of the enemy. If, instead of wasting the morning hours, we had fortified this line, we never could have been driven from it.

"Our immediate foes, in front of us did not at that time advance much farther than the point of our repulse, and, like ourselves, sought cover from which to fire. We now had a chance to recover a little from our wild excitement, and to realize, in a slight degree, what was taking place around us. Information came that our corps-commander had been seriously wounded. Our own colonel lay, with other dead officers, a little in our rear, yet in plain sight. We could only give them a mournful glance, for the battle was still at its height, and was raging in our front and for miles to the right. The thunder of three hundred or more guns made the very earth tremble, while the shrieking and bursting of the shells above us filled the air with a din that was infernal.

"But we had little chance to observe or think of anything except the enemy just below us. With wolfish eyes they were watching every chance to pick off our men. Many of our killed and wounded on the bloody declivity were in plain view, and one poor fellow, desperately hurt, would often raise his hand and wave it to us.

"Our men acted like heroes, and took deliberate aim before they fired. When a poor fellow dropped, one of our officers picked up the rifle and fired in his place."

"Did you do that?" Marian asked.

"Yes; my sword was of no service, and my handful of men needed no orders. Anything at such a time is better than inaction, and we all felt that the line must be held. Every bullet counted, you know.

"Some of our boys did very brave things at this time. For instance: rifles, that had become so clogged or hot as to be unserviceable, were dropped, and the men would say to their immediate companions, 'Be careful how you fire,' and then rush down the slope, pick up the guns of dead or wounded comrades, and with these continue the fight.

"At last the enemy's fire slackened a little, and I went to take my farewell look at our colonel and others of our officers whose bodies had been recovered. These were then carried to the rear, and I never saw their familiar faces again.

"The horses now came up at a gallop to take away the battery near us, and I saw a thing which touched me deeply. As the horses were turning that a gun might be limbered up, a shot, with a clean cut, carried away a leg from one of the poor animals. The faithful, well-trained beast, tried to hobble around into his place on three legs. He seemed to have caught the spirit which animated the entire army that day.

"As I turned toward the regiment, the cry went up, 'They are flanking us!'

"The brief slackening of the enemy's fire had only indicated preparations for a general forward movement. An aid now galloped to us with orders to fall back instantly. A few of my men had been placed, for the sake of cover, in the woods on the right, and I hastened over to them to give the order. By the time I had collected them, the enemy had occupied our old position and we barely escaped capture. When we caught up with the regiment, our brigade-commander had halted it and was addressing it in strong words of eulogy; adding, however, that he still expected almost impossible things of his troops.

"It was pleasant to know that our efforts had been recognized and appreciated, but our hearts were heavy with the thoughts of those we had lost. We were now sent to a piece of woods about a mile to the rear, as a part of the reserve, and it so happened that we were not again called into the fight, which ended, you know, the next day.

"I had bound up my fingers as well as I could, and now, in reaction and from loss of blood, felt sick and faint. I did not wish to go to our field hospital, for I knew the scenes there were so horrible that I should not be equal to witnessing them. Our surgeon came and dressed my finger for me, and said that it would have to come off in the morning, and I now found that my shoulder also had been slightly cut with a bullet. These injuries on that day, however, were the merest trifles.

"Our supper was the dreariest meal I ever took. The men spoke in subdued tones, and every now and then a rough fellow would draw his sleeve across his eyes, as so many things brought to mind those who had breakfasted with us. We were like a household that had returned from burying the greater part of its number. Yes, worse than this, for many, suffering from terrible wounds, were in the hands of the enemy.

"Of course I grieved for the loss of men and officers, but I had come to feel like a brother towards Strahan, and, fatigued as I was, solicitude on his account kept me awake for hours. The battle was still raging on our extreme right, and I fell asleep before the ominous sounds ceased.

"Waking with the dawn, I felt so much better and stronger that I took a hasty cup of coffee, and then started toward the spot where I had seen Strahan fall, in the hope of reaching it. The surgeon had ordered that I should be relieved from duty, and told me to keep quiet. This was impossible with my friend's fate in such uncertainty. I soon found that the enemy occupied the ground on which we had fought, and that to go beyond a certain point would be death or captivity. Therefore I returned, the surgeon amputated my finger, and then I rested with the regiment several hours. With the dawn, heavy fighting began again on the extreme right, but we knew at the time little of its character or object.

"After an early dinner I became restless and went to our corps-hospitals to look after such of the wounded of my company as had been carried thither. It was situated in a grove not far away. I will not describe the scenes witnessed there, for it would only give you useless pain. The surgeons had been at work all the night and morning around the amputation tables, and our doctor and chaplain had done about all that could be accomplished for our poor fellows. There were hundreds of men lying on the ground, many of whom were in the agonies of death even as I passed.

"I again went back to see if there had been any change in our front which would enable me to reach Strahan. This still being impossible, I continued along our lines to the right at a slow pace, that I might gain some idea of our position and prospects. My hope now of reaching Strahan lay in our defeating Lee and gaining the field. Therefore I had a double motive to be intensely interested in all I saw. Since nine in the morning a strange silence had settled on the field, but after yesterday's experience it raised no delusive hopes. With the aid of a small field-glass that I carried, I could see the enemy's batteries, and catch glimpses of their half-concealed infantry, which were moving about in a way that indicated active preparation for something. Our officers had also made the most of this respite, and there had been a continuous shifting of troops, strengthening of lines, and placing of artillery in position since the dawn. Now, however, the quiet was wonderful, in view of the vast bodies of men which were hi deadly array. Even the spiteful picket-firing had ceased.

"I had barely reached a high point, a little in the rear of the Second Corps, commanded by General Hancock, when I saw evidences of excitement and interest around me. Eyes and field-glasses were directed towards the enemy's lines nearly opposite. Springing on a rock near me, I turned my glass in the same direction, and saw that Lee was massing his artillery along the edge of the woods on the ridge opposite. The post of observation was a good one, and I determined to maintain it. The rock promised shelter when the iron tempest should begin.

"Battery after battery came into position, until, with my glass, I could count nearly a hundred guns. On our side batteries were massing also, both to the right and the left of where I stood. Experience had so taught me what these preparations meant that I fairly trembled with excitement and awe. It appeared as if I were about to witness one of the most terrific combats of the world, and while I might well doubt whether anything could survive the concentrated fire of these rebel guns, I could not resist the desire to see out what I felt must be the final and supreme effort of both armies. Therefore I stuck to my rock and swept with my glass the salient points of interest. I dreaded the effect of the awful cannonade upon our lines of infantry that lay upon the ground below me, behind such slight shelter as they could find. Our position at this point was commanding, but many of the troops were fearfully exposed, while our artillerymen had to stand in plain view. Over all this scene, so awfully significant and unnaturally quiet, the scorching July sun sent down its rays like fiery darts, which everywhere on the field scintillated as if they were kindling innumerable fires.

"At last the enemy fired a single gun. Almost instantly a flashing line of light swept along the massed Confederate batteries, I sprung down behind my rock as a perfect storm of iron swept over and around me, and my heart stood almost still at the deep reverberations which followed. This was but the prelude to the infernal symphony that followed. With remarkable rapidity and precision of aim the enemy continued firing, not irregularly, but in immense thundering volleys, all together. There would be a moment's pause, and then would come such a storm of iron that it seemed to me that even my sheltering rock would be cut away, and that everything exposed must be annihilated.

"At first I was exceedingly troubled that our guns did not reply. Could it be possible that the enemy's fire was so destructive that our forces were paralyzed? I was learning to distinguish between the measured cadences of the enemy's firing. After a hurtling shower flew over, I sprung out, took a survey, and was so filled with exultation and confidence, that I crept back again with hope renewed. Our men were standing at the guns, which officers were sighting in order to get more accurate range, and the infantry had not budged. Of course there were streams of wounded going to the rear, but this is true of every battle.

"I now had to share my slight cover with several others, and saw that if I went out again I should lose it altogether. So I determined to wait out the artillery duel quietly. I could see the effects of the enemy's shells in the rear, if not in front, and these were disastrous enough. In the depression behind the ridge on which were our guns and infantry, there were ammunition-wagons, ambulances, and caissons. Among these, shells were making havoc. Soon a caisson exploded with a terrific report and a great cloud of smoke, which, clearing, revealed many prostrate forms, a few of which were able to crawl away.

"Minutes, which seemed like ages, had passed, and the horrible din was then doubled by the opening of all our batteries. The ground beneath me trembled, but as time passed and our guns kept up their steady fire, and the infantry evidently remained unshaken in their lines of defence, my confidence became stronger. By degrees you grow accustomed to almost anything, and I now found leisure to observe my companions behind the rock. I instantly perceived that two of them were press-correspondents, young, boyish-looking fellows, who certainly proved themselves veterans in coolness and courage. Even in that deadly tempest they were alert and busy with their note-books.

"When the caisson exploded, each swiftly wrote a few cabalistic symbols. There was a house to the left, as we sat feeing our rear, and I saw that they kept their eyes on that almost continually. Curious to know why, I shouted in the ear of one, asking the reason. He wrote, 'Meade's headquarters,' and then I shared their solicitude. That it was occupied by some general of high rank, was evident from the number of horses tied around it, and the rapid coming and going of aids and orderlies; but it seemed a terrible thing that our commander-in-chief should be so exposed. Shells flew about the little cottage like angry hornets about their nest, and every few minutes one went in. The poor horses, tied and helpless, were kicking and plunging in their terror, and one after another went down, killed or wounded. I was told that General Meade and staff were soon compelled to leave the place.

"The hours of the cannonade grew monotonous and oppressive. Again and again caissons were exploded and added to the terrible list of casualties. Wagons and ambulances--such of them as were not wrecked--were driven out of range. Every moment or two the ground shook with the recoil and thunder of our batteries, while the air above and around us seemed literally filled with shrieking, moaning, whistling projectiles of almost every size and pattern in present use. From them came puffs of smoke, sharp cracks, heard above the general din, as they exploded and showered around us pieces of jagged iron. When a shell bursts, its fragments strike the ground obliquely, with a forward movement; therefore our comparative safety behind our rock, which often shook from the terrific impact of missiles on its outer side. So many had now sought its shelter that some extended beyond its protection, and before the cannonade was over two were killed outright, almost within reach of my arm. Many of the wounded, in going to the rear, were struck down before reaching a place of safety. The same was true of the men bringing ammunition from the caissons in the depression beneath us. Every few minutes an officer of some rank would be carried by on a stretcher, with a man or two in attendance. I saw one of these hastily moving groups prostrated by a shell, and none of them rose again or struggled. I only tell you of these scenes in compliance with your wish, Miss Marian, and because I see that you have the spirit of a soldier. I was told that, in the thickest of the fight, the wife of a general came on the field in search of her husband, who was reported wounded. I believe that you could have done the same."

"I don't know," she replied, sadly,--"I don't know, for I never realized what war was before;" and she looked apprehensively at Merwyn, fearing to see traces of weakness. His side face, as he sat in the shadow, was pale indeed, but he was rigid and motionless. She received the impression that he was bracing himself by the whole strength of his will to listen through the dreadful story.

Again Mr. Vosburgh suggested that these details were too terrific for his daughter's nerves, but she interrupted him almost sternly, saying: "No, papa, I intend to know just what my friends have passed through. I feel that it is due to them, and, if I cannot hear quietly, I am not worthy to be their friend. I can listen to words when Southern girls can listen to bullets. Captain Blauvelt, you are describing the battle exactly as I asked and wished. My only fear is that you are going beyond your strength;" and she poured him out a glass of light wine.

"When you come to hear all I passed through after leaving that rock, you will know that this story-telling is not worth thinking about," said Blauvelt, with a slight laugh, "All my exposure was well worth the risk, for the chance of telling it to a woman of your nerve. My hope now is that Strahan may some day learn how stanch was our 'home support,' as we were accustomed to call you. I assure you that many a man has been inspired to do his best because of such friendship and sympathy. I am now about to tell you of the grandest thing I ever saw or expect to see, and shall not abate one jot of praise because the heroic act was performed by the enemy."

CHAPTER XXXV.
THE GRAND ASSAULT.

After seeming ages had passed," Blauvelt resumed, having taken a few moments of rest, "the fire of our artillery slackened and soon ceased, and that of the rebete also became less rapid and furious. We saw horses brought up, and some of our batteries going to the rear at a gallop. Could our guns have been silenced? and was disaster threatening us? Our anxiety was so great that the two correspondents and I rushed out and were speedily reassured. There was our infantry, still in line, and we soon saw that reserve batteries were taking the place of those withdrawn. We afterward learned that General Meade and brave General Hunt, Chief of Artillery, had ordered our guns to be quiet and prepare for the assault which they knew would follow the cannonade.

"The wind blew from us towards the enemy, and our unbroken lines were in view. All honor to the steadfast men who had kept their places through the most awful artillery combat ever known on this continent. For nearly two mortal hours the infantry had been obliged to lie still and see men on every side of them torn and mangled to death; but like a wide blue ribbon, as far as the eye could reach, there they lay with the sunlight glittering on their polished muskets. The rebels' fire soon slackened also. We now mounted the friendly rock, and I was busy with my glass again. As the smoke lifted, which had covered the enemy's position, I saw that we had not been the only sufferers. Many of their guns were overturned, and the ground all along their line was thick with prostrate men.

"But they and their guns were forgotten. Their part in the bloody drama was to be superseded, and we now witnessed a sight which can scarcely ever be surpassed. Emerging from the woods on the opposite ridge, over a mile away, came long lines of infantry. Our position was to be assaulted. I suppose the cessation of our firing led the enemy to think that our batteries had been silenced and the infantry supports driven from the hill. The attacking column was forming right under our eyes, and we could see other Confederate troops moving up on the right and left to cover the movement and aid in carrying it out.

"There was bustle on our side also, in spite of the enemy's shells, which still fell thickly along our line. New batteries were thundering up at a gallop; those at the front, which had horses left, were withdrawn; others remained where they had been shattered and disabled, fresh pieces taking position beside them. The dead and wounded were rapidly carried to the rear, and the army stripped itself, like an athlete, for the final struggle.

"Our batteries again opened with solid shot at the distant Confederate infantry, but there was only the hesitation on their part incident to final preparation. Soon on came their centre rapidly, their flank supports, to right and left, moving after them. It proved to be the launching of a human thunderbolt, and I watched its progress, fascinated and overwhelmed with awe."

"Were you exposed at this time to the enemy's shells?" Marias asked.

"Yes, but their fire was not so severe as it had been, and my interest in the assault was so absorbing that I could scarcely think of anything else. I could not help believing that the fate of our army, perhaps of the country, was to be decided there right under my eyes, and this by an attack involving such deadly peril to the participants that I felt comparatively safe.

"The scene during the next half-hour defies description. All ever witnessed in Roman amphitheatres was child's play in comparison. The artillery on both sides had resumed its heavy din, the enemy seeking to distract our attention and render the success of their assault more probable, and we concentrating our fire on that solid attacking column. As they approached nearer, our guns were shotted with shells that made great gaps in their ranks, but they never faltered. Spaces were closed instantly, and on they still came like a dark, resistless wave tipped with light, as the sun glinted on their bayonets through rifts of smoke.

"As they came nearer, our guns in front crumbled and decimated the leading ranks with grape and canister, while other batteries farther away to the right and left still plowed red furrows with shot and shell; but the human torrent, although shrinking and diminishing, flowed on. I could not imagine a more sublime exhibition of courage. Should the South rear to the skies a monument to their soldiers, it would be insignificant compared with that assaulting column, projected across the plain of Gettysburg.

"At the foot of the ridge the leaders of this forlorn hope, as it proved, halted their troops for a moment. As far as the smoke permitted me to see, it seemed that the supporting Confederate divisions had not kept pace with the centre. Would the assault be made? The familiar rebel yell was a speedy answer, as they started up the acclivity, firing as they came. Now, more vivid than the sunlight, a sheet of fire flashed out along our line, and the crash of musketry drowned even the thunder of the cannon.

"The mad impulse of battle was upon me, as upon every one, and I rushed down nearer our lines to get a better view, also from the instinctive feeling that that attack must be repulsed, for it aimed at nothing less than the piercing of the centre of our army. The front melted away as if composed of phantoms, but other spectral men took their place, the flashes of their muskets outlining their position. On, on they came, up to our front line and over it. At the awful point of impact there was on our side a tall, handsome brigadier, whose black eyes glowed like coals. How he escaped so long was one of the mysteries of battle. His voice rang out above the horrid din as he rallied his men, who were not retreating, but were simply pushed back by the still unspent impetus of the rebel charge. I could not resist his appeal, or the example of his heroism, and, seizing a musket and some cartridges belonging to a fallen soldier, I was soon in the thick of it. I scarcely know what happened for the next few moments, so terrible were the excitement and confusion. Union troops and officers were rushing in on all sides, without much regard to organization, under the same impulse which had actuated me. I found myself firing point-blank at the enemy but a few feet away. I saw a rebel officer waving his hat upon his sword, and fired at him. Thank Heaven I did not hit him! for, although he seemed the leading spirit in the charge, I would not like to think I had killed so brave a man. In spite of all our efforts, they pushed us back, back past the battery we were trying to defend. I saw a young officer, not far away, although wounded, run his gun a little forward with the aid of the two or three men left on their feet, fire one more shot, and fall dead. Then I was parrying bayonet thrusts and seeking to give them. One fierce-looking fellow was making a lunge at me, but in the very act fell over, pierced by a bullet. A second later the rebel officer, now seen to be a general, had his hand on a gun and was shouting, 'Victory!' but the word died on his lips as he fell, for at this moment there was a rush in our rear. A heavy body of men burst, like a tornado, through our shattered lines, and met the enemy in a hand-to-hand conflict.

"I had been nearly run over in this charge, and now regained my senses somewhat. I saw that the enemy's advance was checked, that the spot where lay the Confederate general would mark the highest point attained by the crimson wave of Southern valor, for Union troops were concentrating in overwhelming numbers. The wound in my hand had broken out afresh. I hastened to get back out of the melee, the crush, and the 'sing' of bullets, and soon reached my old post of observation, exhausted and panting. The correspondents were still there, and one of them patted me on the shoulder in a way meant to be encouraging, and offered to put my name in his paper, an honor which I declined. We soon parted, unknown to each other. I learned, however, that the name of the gallant brigadier was Webb, and that he had been wounded. So also was General Hancock at this point.

"The enemy's repulse was now changed into a rout. Prisoners were brought in by hundreds, while those retreating across the plain were followed by death-dealing shot and shell from our lines. As I sat resting on my rock of observation, I felt that one could not exult over such a foe, and I was only conscious of profound gratitude over my own and the army's escape. Certainly if enough men, animated by the same desperate courage, had taken part in the attack, it would have been irresistible.

"As soon as I saw that the battle at this point was practically decided, I started back towards our left with the purpose of finding my regiment and our surgeon, for my hand had become very painful. I was so fortunate as to meet with my command as it was being moved up within a few rods of the main line of the Third Corps, where we formed a part of the reserve. Joining my little company and seeing their familiar faces was like coming home. Their welcome, a cup of coffee, and the redressing of my wound made me over again. I had to answer many questions from the small group of officers remaining, for they, kept in the rear all day, had not yet learned much about the battle or its results.

"While I gladdened their hearts with the tidings of our victory, our surgeon growled: 'I'll have you put under arrest if you don't keep quiet. You've been doing more than look on, or your hand would not be in its present condition.'

"Soon after I fell asleep, with my few and faithful men around me, and it was nearly midnight when I wakened."

"It's very evident that none of your present audience is inclined to sleep," Marian exclaimed, with a deep breath.

"And yet it's after midnight," Mr. Vosburgh added. "I fear we are taxing you, captain, far beyond your strength. Your cheeks, Marian, are feverish."

"I do not feel weary yet," said the young officer, "if you are not. Imagine that I have just waked up from that long nap of which I have spoken. Miss Marian was such a sympathetic listener that I dwelt much longer than I intended on scenes which impressed me powerfully. I have not yet described my search for Strahan, or given Mr. Merwyn such hints as my experience affords. Having just come from the field, I do not see that he could gain much by undue haste. He can accomplish quite as much by leaving sometime tomorrow. To be frank, I believe that the only place to find Strahan is under a rebel guard going South. Our troops may interpose in time to release him; if not, he will be exchanged before long."

"In a matter of this kind there should be no uncertainty which can possibly be removed," Merwyn said, in a husky voice. "I shall now save time by obtaining the information you can give, for I shall know better how to direct my search. I shall certainly go in the morning."

"Yes, captain," said Marian, eagerly. "Since you disclaim weariness we could listen for hours yet. You are a skilful narrator, for, intensely as your story has interested me, you have reserved its climax to the last, even though your search led you only among woful scenes in the hospitals."

"On such scenes I will touch as lightly as possible, and chiefly for Mr. Merwyn's benefit; for if Strahan had been left on the field, either killed or wounded, I do not see how he could have escaped me." Then, with a smile at the young girl, he added: "Since you credit me with some skill as a story-teller, and since my story is so long, perhaps it should be divided. In that case what I am now about to relate should be headed with the words, 'My search for Strahan.'"

CHAPTER XXXVI.
BLAUVELT'S SEARCH FOR STRAHAN.

Y ou will remember," said the captain, after a moment's pause, that he might take up the thread of his narrative consecutively, "that I awoke a little before midnight. At first I was confused, but soon all that had happened came back to me. I found myself a part of a long line of sleeping men that formed the reserve. Not farther than from here across the street was another line in front of us. Beyond this were our vigilant pickets, and then the vedettes of the enemy. All seemed strangely still and peaceful, but a single shot would have brought thousands of men to their feet. The moon poured a soft radiance over all, and gave to the scene a weird and terrible beauty. The army was like a sleeping giant. Would its awakening be as terrible as on the last three mornings? Then I thought of that other army sleeping beyond our lines,--an army which neither bugle nor the thunder of all our guns could awaken.

"I soon distinguished faint, far-off sounds from the disputed territory beyond our pickets. Rising, I put my hand to my ear, and then heard the words, 'Water! water!'

"They were the cries of wounded men entreating for that which would quench their intolerable thirst. The thought that Strahan might be among this number stung me to the very quick, and I hastened to the senior captain, who now commanded the regiment. I found him alert and watchful, with the bugle at his side, for he felt the weight of responsibility so suddenly thrust upon him.

"'Captain Markham,' I said, 'do you hear those cries for water?'

"'Yes,' he replied, sadly; 'I have heard them for hours,

"'Among them may be Strahan's voice,' I said, eagerly.

"'Granting it, what could we do? Our pickets are way this side of the spot where he fell.'

"'Captain,' I cried, 'Strahan was like a brother to me. I can't rest here with the possibility that he is dying yonder for a little water. I am relieved from duty, you know. If one of my company will volunteer to go with me, will you give him your permission? I know where Strahan fell, and am willing to try to reach him and bring him in.'

"'No,' said the captain, 'I can't give such permission. You might be fired on and the whole line aroused. You can go to our old brigade-commander, however--he now commands the division,--and see what he says. He's back there under that tree. Of course, you know, I sympathize with your feeling, but I cannot advise the risk. Good heavens, Blauvelt! we've lost enough officers already.'

"'I'll be back soon,' I answered.

"To a wakeful aid I told my errand, and he aroused the general, who was silent after he had been made acquainted with my project.

"'I might bring in some useful information,' I added, hastily.

"The officer knew and liked Strahan, but said: 'I shall have to put my permission on the ground of a reconnoissance. I should be glad to know if any changes are taking place on our front, and so would my superiors. Of course you understand the risk you run when once beyond our pickets?'

"'Strahan would do as much and more for me,' I replied.

"'Very well;' and he gave me permission to take a volunteer, at the same time ordering me to report to him on my return.

"I went back to our regimental commander, who growled, 'Well, if you will go I suppose you will; but it would be a foolhardy thing for even an unwounded man to attempt.'

"I knew a strong, active young fellow in my company who would go anywhere with me, and, waking him up, explained my purpose. He was instantly on the qui vive. I procured him a revolver, and we started at once. On reaching our pickets we showed our authority to pass, and were informed that the enemy's vedettes ran along the ridge on which we had fought the day before. Telling our pickets to pass the word not to fire on us if we came in on the run, we stole down into the intervening valley.

"The moon was now momentarily obscured by clouds, and this favored us.

My plan was to reach the woods on which the right of our regiment had rested. Here the shadows would be deep, and our chances better. Crouching and creeping silently from bush to bush, we made our gradual progress until we saw a sentinel slowly pacing back and forth along the edge of the woods. Most of his beat was in shadow, and there were bushes and rocks extending almost to it. We watched him attentively for a time, and then my companion whispered: 'The Johnny seems half dead with sleep. I believe I can steal up and capture him without a sound. I don't see how we can get by him as long as he is sufficiently wide awake to walk.'

"'Very well. You have two hands, and my left is almost useless,' I said. 'Make your attempt where the shadow is deepest, and if he sees you, and is about to shoot, see that you shoot first. I'll be with you instantly if you succeed, and cover your retreat in case of failure."

"In a moment, revolver in hand, he was gliding, like a shadow, from cover to cover, and it was his good fortune to steal up behind the sleepy sentinel, grasp his musket, and whisper, with his pistol against his head, 'Not a sound, or you are dead.'

"The man was discreet enough to be utterly silent. In a moment I was by Rush's side--that was the name of the brave fellow who accompanied me--and found that he had disarmed his prisoner. I told Rush to take the rebel's musket and walk up and down the beat, and especially to show himself in the moonlight. I made the Johnny give me his word not to escape, telling him that he would be shot instantly if he did. I gave him the impression that others were watching him. I then tied his hands behind him and fastened him to a tree in the shade. Feeling that I had not a moment to lose, I passed rapidly down through the woods bearing to the left. The place was only too familiar, and even in the moonlight I could recognize the still forms of some of my own company. I found two or three of our regiment still alive, and hushed them as I pressed water to their lips. I then asked if they knew anything about Strahan. They did not. Hastening on I reached the spot, by a large boulder, where I had seen Strahan fall. He was not there, or anywhere near it. I even turned up the faces of corpses in my wish to assure myself; for our dead officers had been partially stripped. I called his name softly, then more distinctly, and at last, forgetful in my distress, loudly. Then I heard hasty steps, and crouched down behind a bush, with my hand upon my revolver. But I had been seen.

"A man approached rapidly, and asked, in a gruff voice, 'What the devil are you doing here?'

"'Looking for a brother who fell hereabouts,' I replied, humbly.

"'You are a--Yankee,' was the harsh reply, 'and a prisoner; I know your Northern tongue.'"

"I fired instantly, and wounded him, but not severely, for he fired in return, and the bullet whizzed by my ear. My next shot brought him down, and then I started on a dead run for the woods, regained Rush, and, with our prisoner, we stole swiftly towards our lines. We were out of sure range before the startled pickets of the enemy realized what was the matter. A few harmless shots were sent after us, and then we gained our lines. I am satisfied that the man I shot was a rebel officer visiting the picket line. Our firing inside their lines could not be explained until the gap caused by the missing sentinel we had carried off was discovered.

"Then they knew that 'Yanks,' as they called us, had been within their lines. Rush, taking the sentinel's place while I was below the hill, had prevented an untimely discovery of our expedition. Perhaps it was well that I met the rebel officer, for he was making directly towards the spot where I had left my companion.

"The poor fellow we had captured was so used up that he could scarcely keep pace with us. He said he had not had any rest worth speaking of for forty-eight hours. I passed through our lines, now alert, and reported at Division Headquarters. The general laughed, congratulated us, and said he was glad we had not found Strahan among the dead or seriously wounded, for now there was a good chance of seeing him again.

"I turned over our prisoner to him, and soon all was quiet again. Captain Markham, of our regiment, greeted us warmly, but I was so exhausted that I contented him with a brief outline of what had occurred, and said I would tell him the rest in the morning. Satisfied now that Strahan was not crying for water, I was soon asleep again by the side of Rush, and did not waken till the sun was well above the horizon.

"I soon learned that the vedettes of the enemy had disappeared from before our lines, and that our skirmishers were advancing. After a hasty breakfast I followed them, and soon reached again the ground I had visited in the night. On the way I met two of our men to whom I had given water. The other man had meanwhile died. The survivors told me positively that they had not seen or heard of Strahan after he had fallen. They also said that they had received a little food and water from the rebels, or they could not have survived.

"The dead were still unburied, although parties were sent out within our picket line during the day to perform this sad duty, and I searched the ground thoroughly for a wide distance, acting on the possibility that Strahan might have crawled away somewhere.

"I shall not describe the appearance of the field, or speak of my feelings as I saw the bodies of the brave men and officers of our regiment who had so long been my companions.

"The rest of my story is soon told. From our surgeon I had positive assurance that Strahan had not been brought to our corps hospital. Therefore, I felt driven to one of two conclusions: either he was in a Confederate hospital on the field beyond our lines, or else he was a prisoner.

"As usual, the heavy concussion of the artillery produced a rain-storm, which set in on the afternoon of the 4th, and continued all night. As the enemy appeared to be intrenching in a strong position, there seemed no hope of doing any more that day, and I spent the night in a piece of woods with my men.

"On the dark, dreary morning of the 5th, it was soon discovered that the Confederate army had disappeared. As the early shades of the previous stormy evening had settled over the region, its movement towards Virginia had begun. I became satisfied before night that Strahan also was southward bound, for, procuring a horse, I rode all day, visiting the temporary Confederate hospitals. Since they had left their own severely wounded men, they certainly would not have taken Union soldiers unable to walk. Not content with my first search, I spent the next two days in like manner, visiting the houses in Gettysburg and vicinity, until satisfied that my effort was useless. Then, availing myself of a brief leave of absence, I came north."

Blauvelt then gave Merwyn some suggestions, adding: "If you find no trace of him on the field, I would advise, as your only chance, that you follow the track of Lee's army, especially the roads on which their prisoners were taken. Strahan might have given out by the way, and have been left at some farmhouse or in a village. It would be hopeless to go beyond the Potomac."

Rising, he concluded: "Mark my words, and see if I am not right. Strahan is a prisoner, and will be exchanged." Then with a laugh and a military salute to Marian, he said, "I have finished my report."

"It is accepted with strong commendation and congratulations," she replied. "I shall recommend you for promotion."

"Good-by, Miss Vosburgh," said Merwyn, gravely. "I shall start in the morning, and I agree with Captain Blauvelt that my best chance lies along the line of Lee's retreat."

Again she gave him her hand kindly in farewell; but her thought was: "How deathly pale he is! This has been a night of horrors to him,--to me also; yet if I were a man I know I could meet what other men face."

"She was kind," Merwyn said to himself, as he walked through the deserted streets; "but I fear it was only the kindness of pitiful toleration. It is plainer than ever that she adores heroic action, that her ardor in behalf of the North is scarcely less than that of my mother for the South, and yet she thinks I am not brave enough to face a musket What a figure I make beside the men of whom we have heard to-night! Well, to get away, to be constantly employed, is my only hope. I believe I should become insane if I brooded much longer at home."

In spite of his late hours, he ordered an early breakfast, proposing to start without further delay.

The next morning, as he sat down to the table, the doorbell rang, there was a hasty step down the hall, and Strahan, pale and gaunt, with his arm in a sling, burst in upon him, and exclaimed, with his old sang froid and humor: "Just in time. Yes, thanks; I'll stay and take a cup of coffee with you."

Merwyn greeted him with mingled wonder and gladness, yet even at that moment the thought occurred to him: "Thwarted on every side! I can do absolutely nothing."

After Strahan was seated Merwyn said: "Half an hour later I should have been off to Gettysburg in search of you. Blauvelt is here, and says he saw you fall, and since a blank, so far as you are concerned."

"Thank God! He escaped then?"

"Yes; but is wounded slightly. What is the matter with your arm?"

"Only a bullet-hole through it. That's nothing for Gettysburg. I was captured, and escaped on the first night's march. Dark and stormy, you know. But it's a long story, and I'm hungry as a wolf. Where's Blauvelt?"

"He's a guest at Mr. Vosburgh's."

"Lucky fellow!" exclaimed Strahan; and for some reason the edge of his appetite was gone.

"Yes, he IS a lucky fellow, indeed; and so are you," said Merwyn, bitterly. "I was there last evening till after midnight;" and he explained what had occurred, adding, "Blauvelt trumpeted your praise, and on the night of the 3d he went inside the enemy's picket line in search of you, at the risk of his life.'

"Heaven bless the fellow! Wait till I spin my yarn. I shall give him credit for the whole victory."

"Write a note to Miss Vosburgh, and I'll send it right down."

"Confound it, Merwyn! don't you see I'm winged? You will even have to cut my food for me as if I were a baby."

"Very well, you dictate and I'll write. By the way, I have a note for you in my pocket."

Strahan seized upon it and forgot his breakfast. Tears suffused his blue eyes before he finished it, and at last he said, "Well, if you HAD found me in some hospital this would have cured me, or else made death easy."

Merwyn's heart grew heavy, in spite of the fact that he had told himself so often that there was no hope for him, and he thought, "In the terrible uncertainty of Strahan's fate she found that he was more to her than she had supposed, and probably revealed as much in her note, which she feared might reach him only when death was sure."

The glad intelligence was despatched, and then Merwyn said: "After you have breakfasted I will send you down in my coupe."

"You will go with me?"

"No. There is no reason why I should be present when Miss Vosburgh greets her friends. I remained last night by request, that I might be better informed in prosecuting my search."

Strahan changed the subject, but thought: "She's loyal to her friends. Merwyn, with all his money, has made no progress. Her choice will eventually fall on Lane, Blauvelt, or poor little me. Thank Heaven I gave the Johnnies the slip! The other fellows shall have a fair field, but I want one, too."

Before they had finished their breakfast Blauvelt came tearing in, and there was a fire of questions between the brother-officers.

Tears and laughter mingled with their words; but at last they became grave and quiet as they realized how many brave comrades would march with them no more.

In a few moments Blauvelt said, "Come; Miss Marian said she would not take a mouthful of breakfast till you returned with me."

Merwyn saw them drive away, and said, bitterly, "Thanks to my mother, I shall never have any part in such greetings."

CHAPTER XXXVII.
STRAHAN'S ESCAPE.

AFTER Blauvelt had left Mr. Vosburgh's breakfast-table in obedience to his own and Marian's wish to see Strahan at once, the young girl laughed outright--she would laugh easily to-day--and exclaimed:--

"Poor Mr. Merwyn! He is indeed doomed to inglorious inaction. Before he could even start on his search, Strahan found him. His part in this iron age will consist only in furnishing the sinews of war and dispensing canned delicacies in the hospitals. I do feel sorry for him, for last night he seemed to realize the fact himself. He looked like a ghost, back in the shadow that he sought when Captain Blauvelt's story grew tragic. I believe he suffered more in hearing about the shells than Mr. Blauvelt did in hearing and seeing them."

"It's a curious case," said her father, musingly. "He was and has been suffering deeply from some cause. I have not fully accepted your theory yet."

"Since even your sagacity can construct no other, I am satisfied that I am right. But I have done scoffing at Mr. Merwyn, and should feel as guilty in doing so as if I had shown contempt for physical deformity. I have become so convinced that he suffers terribly from consciousness of his weakness, that I now pity him from the depths of my heart. Just think of a young fellow of his intelligence listening to such a story as we heard last night and of the inevitable contrasts that he must have drawn!"

"Fancy also," said her father, smiling, "a forlorn lover seeing your cheeks aflame and your eyes suffused with tears of sympathy for young heroes, one of whom was reciting his epic. Strahan is soon to repeat his; then Lane will appear and surpass them all."

"Well," cried Marian, laughing, "you'll admit they form a trio to be proud of."

"Oh, yes, and will have to admit more, I suppose, before long. Girls never fall in love with trios."

"Nonsense, papa, they are all just like brothers to me." Then there was a rush of tears to her eyes, and she said, brokenly, "The war is not over yet, and perhaps not one of them will survive."

"Come, my dear," her father reassured her, gently, "you must imitate your soldier friends, and take each day as it comes. Remembering what they have already passed through, I predict that they all survive. The bravest men are the most apt to escape."

Marian's greeting of Strahan was so full of feeling, and so many tears suffused her dark blue eyes, that they inspired false hopes in his breast and unwarranted fears in that of Blauvelt. The heroic action and tragic experience of the young and boyish Strahan had touched the tenderest chords in her heart. Indeed, as she stood, holding his left hand in both her own, they might easily have been taken for brother and sister. His eyes were almost as blue as hers, and his brow, where it had not been exposed to the weather, as fair. She knew of his victory over himself. Almost at the same time with herself, he had cast behind him a weak, selfish, frivolous life, assuming a manhood which she understood better than others. Therefore, she had for him a tenderness, a gentleness of regard, which her other friends of sterner natures could not inspire. Indeed, so sisterly was her feeling that she could have put her arms about his neck and welcomed him with kisses, without one quickening throb of the pulse. But he did not know this then, and his heart bounded with baseless hopes.

Poor Blauvelt had never cherished many, and the old career with which he had tried to be content defined itself anew. He would fight out the war, and then give himself up to his art.

He could be induced to stay only long enough to finish his breakfast, and then said: "Strahan can tell me the rest of his story over the camp-fire before long. My mother has now the first claim, and I must take a morning train in order to reach home to-night."

"I also must go," exclaimed Mr. Vosburgh, looking at his watch, "and shall have to hear your story at second hand from Marian. Rest assured," he added, laughing, "it will lose nothing as she tells it this evening."

"And I order you, Captain Blauvelt, to make this house your headquarters when you are in town," said Marian, giving his hand a warm pressure in parting. Strahan accompanied his friend to the depot, then sought his family physician and had his wound dressed.

"I advise that you reach your country home soon," said the doctor; "your pulse is feverish."

The young officer laughed and thought he knew the reason better than his medical adviser, and was soon at the side of her whom he believed to be the exciting cause of his febrile symptoms.

"Oh," he exclaimed, throwing himself on a lounge, "isn't this infinitely better than a stifling Southern prison?" and he looked around the cool, shadowy drawing-room, and then at the smiling face of his fair hostess, as if there were nothing left to be desired.

"You have honestly earned this respite and home visit," she said, taking a low chair beside him, "and now I'm just as eager to hear your story as I was to listen to that of Captain Blauvelt, last night."

"No more eager?" he asked, looking wistfully into her face.

"That would not be fair," she replied, gently. "How can I distinguish between my friends, when each one surpasses even my ideal of manly action?"

"You will some day," he said, thoughtfully. "You cannot help doing so. It is the law of nature. I know I can never be the equal of Lane and Blauvelt."

"Arthur," she said, gravely, taking his hand, "let me be frank with you. It will be best for us both. I love you too dearly, I admire and respect you too greatly, to be untrue to your best interests even for a moment. What's more, I am absolutely sure that you only wish what is right and best for me. Look into my eyes. Do you not see that if your name was Arthur Vosburgh, I could scarcely feel differently? I do love you more than either Mr. Lane or Mr. Blauvelt. They are my friends in the truest and strongest sense of the word, but--let me tell you the truth--you have come to seem like a younger brother. We must be about the same age, but a woman is always older in her feelings than a man, I think. I don't say this to claim any superiority, but to explain why I feel as I do. Since I came to know--to understand you--indeed, I may say, since we both changed from what we were, my thoughts have followed you in a way that they would a brother but a year or two younger than myself,--

that is, so far as I can judge, having had no brother. Don't you understand me?"

"Yes," he replied, laughing a little ruefully, "up to date."

"Very well," she added, with an answering laugh, "let it be then to date. I shall not tell you that I feel like a sister without being as frank as one. I have never loved any one in the way--Oh, well, you know. I don't believe these stern times are conducive to sentiment. Come, tell me your story."

"But you'll give me an equal chance with the others," he pleaded.

She now laughed outright. "How do I know what I shall do?" she asked. "I may come to you some day for sympathy and help. According to the novels, people are stricken down as if by one of your hateful shells and all broken up. I don't know, but I'm inclined to believe that while a girl can withhold her love from an unworthy object, she cannot deliberately give it here or there as she chooses. Now am I not talking to you like a sister?"

"Yes, too much so--"

"Oh, come, I have favored you more highly than any one."

"Do not misunderstand me," he said, earnestly, "I'm more grateful than I can tell you, but--"

"But tell me your story. There is one thing I can give you at once,--the closest attention."

"Very well. I only wish you were like one of the enemy's batteries, so I could take you by storm. I'd face all the guns that were at Gettysburg for the chance."

"Arthur, dear Arthur, I do know what you have faced from a simple sense of duty and patriotism. Blauvelt was a loyal, generous friend, and he has told us."

"You are wrong. 'The girl I left behind me' was the corps-de-reserve from which I drew my strength. I believe the same was true of Blauvelt, and a better, braver fellow never drew breath. He would make a better officer than I, for he is cooler and has more brains."

"Now see here, Major Strahan," cried Marian, in mock dignity, "as your superior officer, I am capable of judging of the merits of you both, and neither of you can change my estimate. You are insubordinate, and I shall put you under arrest if you don't tell me how you escaped at once. You have kept a woman's curiosity in check almost as long as your brave regiment held the enemy, and that's your greatest achievement thus far. Proceed. Captain Blauvelt has enabled me to keep an eye on you till you fell and the enemy charged over you. Now you know just where to begin."

"My prosaic story is soon told. Swords and pike-staffs! what a little martinet you are! Well, the enemy was almost on me. I could see their flushed, savage faces. Even in that moment I thought of you and whispered, 'Good-by,' and a prayer to God for your happiness flashed through my mind."

"Arthur, don't talk that way. I can't stand it;" and there was a rush of tears to her eyes.

"I'm beginning just where you told me to. The next second there was a sting in my right arm, then something knocked me over and I lost consciousness for a few moments. I am satisfied, also, that I was grazed by a bullet that tore my scabbard from my side. When I came to my senses, I crawled behind a rock so as not to be shot by our own men, and threw away my sword. I didn't want to surrender it, you know. Soon after a rebel jerked me to my feet.

"'Can you stand?' he asked.

"'I will try,' I answered.

"'Join that squad of prisoners, then, and travel right smart.'

"I staggered away, too dazed for many clear ideas, and with others was hurried about half a mile away to a place filled with the rebel wounded. Here a Union soldier, who happened to have some bandages with him, dressed my arm. The Confederate surgeons had more than they could do to look after their own men. Just before dark all the prisoners who were able to walk were led into a large field, and a strong guard was placed around us.

"Although my wound was painful, I obtained some sleep, and awoke the next morning with the glad consciousness that life with its chances was still mine. We had little enough to eat that day, and insufficient water to drink. This foretaste of the rebel commissariat was enough for me, and I resolved to escape if it were a possible thing."

"You wanted to see me a little, too, didn't you? Nevertheless, you shall have a good lunch before long."

"Such is my fate. First rebel iron and now irony. I began to play the role of feebleness and exhaustion, and it did not require much effort. Of course we were all on the qui vive to see what would happen next, and took an intense interest in the fight of the 3d, which Blauvelt has described. The scene of the battle was hidden from us, but we gathered, from the expression of our guards' faces and the confusion around us, that all had not gone to the enemy's mind, and so were hopeful. In the evening we were marched to the outskirts of Gettysburg and kept there till the afternoon of the 4th, when we started towards Virginia. I hung back and dragged myself along, and so was fortunately placed near the rear of the column, and we plodded away. I thanked Heaven that the night promised to be dark and stormy, and was as vigilant as an Indian, looking for my chance. It seemed long in coming, for at first the guards were very watchful. At one point I purposely stumbled and fell, hoping to crawl into the bushes, but a rebel was right on me and helped me up with his bayonet."

"O Arthur!"

"Yes, the risks were great, for we had been told that the first man who attempted to leave the line would be shot. I lagged behind as if I could not keep up, and so my vigilant guard got ahead of me, and I proposed to try it on with the next fellow. I did not dare look around, for my only chance was to give the impression that I fell from utter exhaustion. We were winding around a mountain-side and I saw some dark bushes just beyond me. I staggered towards them and fell just beside them, and lay as if I were dead.

"A minute passed, then another, and then there was no other sound than the tramp and splash in the muddy road. I edged still farther and farther from this, my head down the steep bank, and soon found myself completely hidden. The comrade next to me either would not tell if he understood my ruse, or else was so weary that he had not noticed me. If the guard saw me, he concluded that I was done for and not worth further bother.

"After the column had passed, I listened to hear if others were coming, then stumbled down the mountain, knowing that my best chance was to strike some stream and follow the current. It would take me into a valley where I would be apt to find houses. At last I became so weary that I lay down in a dense thicket and slept till morning. I awoke as hungry as a famished wolf, and saw nothing but a dense forest on every side. But the brook murmured that it would guide me, and I now made much better progress in the daylight. At last I reached a little clearing and a wood-chopper's cottage. The man was away, but his wife received me kindly and said I was welcome to such poor fare and shelter as they had. She gave me a glass of milk and some fried bacon and corn-bread, and I then learned all about the nectar and ambrosia of the gods. In the evening her husband came home and said that Lee had been whipped by the Yanks, and that he was retreating rapidly, whereon I drank to the health of my host nearly all the milk given that night by his lean little cow. He was a good-natured, loutish sort of fellow, and promised to guide me in a day or two to the west of the line of retreat. He seemed very tearful of falling in with the rebels, and I certainly had seen all I wished of them for the present, so I was as patient as he desired. At last he kept his word and guided me to a village about six miles away. I learned that Confederate cavalry had been there within twenty-four hours, and, tired as I was, I hired a conveyance and was driven to another village farther to the northwest, for I now had a morbid horror of being recaptured. After a night's rest in a small hamlet, I was taken in a light wagon to the nearest railway station, and came on directly, arriving here about six this morning. Finding our house closed, I made a descent on Merwyn. I telegraphed mother last evening that I should be home this afternoon."

"You should have telegraphed me, also," said Marian, reproachfully. "You would have saved me some very sad hours. I did not sleep much last night."

"Forgive me. I thoughtlessly wished to give you a surprise, and I could scarcely believe you cared so much."

"You will always believe it now, Arthur. Merciful Heaven! what risks you have had!"

"You have repaid me a thousand-fold. Friend, sister, or wife, you will always be to me my good genius."

"I wish the war was over," she said, sadly. "I have not heard from Captain Lane for weeks, and after the battle the first tidings from Blauvelt was that he was wounded and that you were wounded and missing. I can't tell you how oppressed I was with fear and foreboding."

"How about Lane?" Strahan asked, with interest.

She told him briefly the story she had heard and of the silence which had followed.

"He leads us all," was his response. "If he survives the war, he will win you, Marian."

"You suggest a terrible 'if' and there may be many others. I admit that he has kindled my imagination more than any man I ever saw, but you, Arthur, have touched my heart. I could not speak to him, had he returned, as I am now speaking to you. I have the odd feeling that you and I are too near of kin to be anything to each other except just what we are. You are so frank and true to me, that I can't endure the thought of misleading you, even unintentionally."

"Very well, I'll grow up some day, and as long as you remain free, I'll not give up hope."

"Foolish boy! Grow up, indeed! Who mounted his horse in that storm of shells and bullets in spite of friendly remonstrances, and said, 'The men must see us to-day'? What more could any man do? I'm just as proud of you as if my own brother had spoken the words;" and she took his hand caressingly, then exclaimed, "You are feverish."

A second later her hand was on his brow, and she sprung up and said, earnestly, "You should have attention at once."

"I fancy the doctor was right after all," said Strahan, rising also. "I'll take the one o'clock train and be at home in a couple of hours."

"I wish you would stay. You can't imagine what a devoted nurse I'll be."

"Please don't tempt me. It wouldn't be best. Mamma is counting the minutes before my return now, and it will please her if I come on an earlier train. Mountain air and rest will soon bring me around, and I can run down often. I think the fever proceeds simply from my wound, which hasn't had the best care. I don't feel seriously ill at all."

She ordered iced lemonade at once, lunch was hastened, and then she permitted him to depart, with the promise that he would write a line that very night.

CHAPTER XXXVIII.
A LITTLE REBEL.

THE next day Marian received a note from Strahan saying that some bad symptoms had developed in connection with his wound, but that his physician had assured him that if he would keep absolutely quiet in body and mind for a week or two they would pass away, concluding with the words: "I have promised mother to obey orders, and she has said that she would write you from time to time about me. I do not think I shall be very ill."

"O dear!" exclaimed Marian to her father at dinner, "what times these are! You barely escape one cause of deep anxiety before there is another. Now what is troubling you, that your brow also is clouded?"

"Is it not enough that your troubles trouble me?"

"There's something else, papa."

"Well, nothing definite. The draft, you know, begins on Saturday of this week. I shall not have any rest of mind till this ordeal is over. Outwardly all is comparatively quiet. So is a powder magazine till a spark ignites it. This unpopular measure of the draft is to be enforced while all our militia regiments are away. I know enough about what is said and thought by thousands to fear the consequences. I wish you would spend a couple of weeks with your mother in that quiet New-England village."

"No, papa, not till you tell me that all danger is past. How much I should have missed during the past few days if I had been away! But for my feeling that my first duty is to you, I should have entreated for your permission to become a hospital nurse. Papa, women should make sacrifices and take risks in these times as well as men."

"Well, a few more days will tell the story. If the draft passes off quietly and our regiments return, I shall breathe freely once more."

A letter was brought in, and she exclaimed, "Captain Lane's handwriting!" She tore open the envelope and learned little more at that time than that he had escaped, reached our lines, and gone to Washington, where he was under the care of a skilful surgeon. "In escaping, my wound broke out again, but I shall soon be able to travel, and therefore to see you."

In order to account for Lane's absence and silence we must take up the thread of his story where Zeb had dropped it. The cavalry force of which Captain Lane formed a part retired, taking with it the prisoners and such of the wounded as could bear transportation; also the captured thief. Lane was prevented by his wound from carrying out his threat, which his position as chief officer of an independent command would have entitled him to do. The tides of war swept away to the north, and he was left with the more seriously wounded of both parties in charge of the assistant surgeon of his regiment. As the shades of evening fell, the place that had resounded with war's loud alarms, and had been the scene of so much bustle and confusion, resumed much of its old aspect of quiet and seclusion. The marks of conflict, the evidence of changes, and the new conditions under which the family would be obliged to live, were only too apparent. The grass on the lawn was trampled down, and there were new-made graves in the edge of the grove. Fences were prostrate, and partly burned. Horses and live stock had disappeared. The negro quarters were nearly empty, the majority of the slaves having followed the Union column. Confederate officers, who were welcome, honored guests but a few hours before, were on their way to Washington as prisoners. Desperately wounded and dying men were in the out-buildings, and a Union officer, the one who had led the attacking party and precipitated these events, had begun his long fight for life in the mansion itself,--a strange and unexpected guest.

Mrs. Barkdale, the mistress of the house, could scarcely rally from her nervous shock or maintain her courage, in view of the havoc made by the iron heel of war. Miss Roberta's heart was full of bitterness and impotent revolt. She had the courage and spirit of her race, but she could not endure defeat, and she chafed in seclusion and anger while her mother moaned and wept. Miss Suwanee now became the leading spirit.

"We can't help what's happened, and I don't propose to sit down and wring my hands or pace my room in useless anger. We were all for war, and now we know what war means. If I were a man I'd fight; being only a woman, I shall do what I can to retrieve our losses and make the most of what's left. After all, we have not suffered half so much as hundreds of other families. General Lee will soon give the Northerners some of their own medicine, and before the summer is over will conquer a peace, and then we shall be proud of our share in the sacrifices which so many of our people have made."

"I wouldn't mind any sacrifice,--no, not of our home itself,--if we had won the victory," Roberta replied. "But to have been made the instrument of our friends' defeat! It's too cruel. And then to think that the man who wrought all this destruction, loss, and disgrace is under this very roof, and must stay for weeks, perhaps!"

"Roberta, you are unjust," cried Suwanee. "Captain Lane proved himself to be a gallant, considerate enemy, and you know it. What would you have him do? Play into our hands and compass his own defeat? He only did what our officers would have done. The fact that a Northern officer could be so brave and considerate was a revelation to me. We and all our property were in his power, and his course was full of courtesy toward all except the armed foes who were seeking to destroy him. The moment that even these became unarmed prisoners he treated them with great leniency. Because we had agreed to regard Northerners as cowards and boors evidently doesn't make them so."

"You seem wonderfully taken with this Captain Lane."

"No," cried the girl, with one of her irresistible laughs; "but our officer friends would have been taken with him if he had not been wounded. I'm a genuine Southern girl, so much so that I appreciate a brave foe and true gentleman. He protected us and our home as far as he could, and he shall have the best hospitality which this home can now afford. Am I not right, mamma?"

"Yes, my dear, even our self-respect would not permit us to adopt any other course."

"You will feel as I do, Roberta, after your natural grief and anger pass;" and she left the room to see that their wounded guest had as good a supper as she could produce from diminished resources.

The surgeon, whom she met in the hall, told her that his patient was feverish and a "little flighty" at times, but that he had expected this, adding: "The comfort of his room and good food will bring him around in time. He will owe his life chiefly to your hospitality, Miss Barkdale, for a little thing would have turned the scale against him. Chicken broth is all that I wish him to have to-night, thanks."

And so the process of care and nursing began. The Union colonel had left a good supply of coffee, sugar, and coarse rations for the wounded men, and Suwanee did her best to supplement these, accomplishing even more by her kindness, cheerfulness, and winsome ways than by any other means. She became, in many respects, a hospital nurse, and visited the wounded men, carrying delicacies to all alike. She wrote letters for the Confederates and read the Bible to those willing to listen. Soon all were willing, and blessed her sweet, sunny face. The wounds of some were incurable, and, although her lovely face grew pale indeed in the presence of death, she soothed their last moments with the gentlest ministrations. There was not a man of the survivors, Union or rebel, but would have shed his last drop of blood for her. Roberta shared in these tasks, but it was not in her nature to be so impartial. Even among her own people she was less popular. Among the soldiers, on both sides, who did the actual fighting, there was not half the bitterness that existed generally among non-combatants and those Southern men who never met the enemy in fair battle; and now there was a good-natured truce between the brave Confederates and those who had perhaps wounded them, while all fought a battle with the common foe,--death. Therefore the haggard faces of all lighted up with unfeigned pleasure when "Missy S'wanee," as they had learned from the negroes to call her, appeared among them.

But few slaves were left on the place, and these were old and feeble ones who had not ventured upon the unknown waters of freedom. The old cook remained at her post, and an old man and woman divided their time between the house and the garden, Suwanee's light feet and quick hands relieving them of the easier labors of the mansion.

Surgeon McAllister was loud in his praises of her general goodness and her courtesy at the table, to which he was admitted; and Lane, already predisposed toward a favorable opinion, entertained for her the deepest respect and gratitude, inspired more by her kindness to his men than by favors to himself. Yet these were not few, for she often prepared delicacies with her own hands and brought them to his door, while nearly every morning she arranged flowers and sent them to his table.

Thus a week passed away. The little gathering of prostrate men, left in war's trail, was apparently forgotten except as people from the surrounding region came to gratify their curiosity.

Lane's feverish symptoms had passed away, but he was exceedingly weak, and the wound in his shoulder was of a nature to require almost absolute quiet. One evening, after the surgeon had told him of Suwanee's ministrations beside a dying Union soldier, he said, "I must see her and tell her of my gratitude."

On receiving his message she hesitated a single instant, then came to his bedside. The rays of the setting sun illumined her reddish-brown hair as she stood before him, and enhanced her beauty in her simple muslin dress. Her expression towards him, her enemy, was gentle and sympathetic.

He looked at her a moment in silence, almost as if she were a vision, then began, slowly and gravely: "Miss Barkdale, what can I say to you? I'm not strong enough to say very much, yet I could not rest till you knew. The surgeon here has told me all,--no, not all. Deeds like yours can be told adequately only in heaven. You are fanning the spark of life in my own breast. I doubt whether I should have lived but for your kindness. Still more to me has been your kindness to my men, the poor fellows that are too often neglected, even by their friends. You have been like a good angel to them. These flowers, fragrant and beautiful, interpret you to me. You can't know what reverence--"

"Please stop, Captain Lane," said Suwanee, beginning to laugh, while tears stood in her eyes. "Why, I'm only acting as any good-hearted Southern girl would act. I shall not permit you to think me a saint when I am not one. I've a little temper of my own, which isn't always sweet. I like attention and don't mind how many bestow it--in brief, I am just like other girls, only more so, and if I became what you say I shouldn't know myself. Now you must not talk any more. You are still a little out of your head. You can only answer one question. Is there anything you would like,--anything we can do for you to help you get well?"

"No; I should be overwhelmed with gratitude if you did anything more. I am grieved enough now when I think of all the trouble and loss we have caused you."

"Oh, that's the fortune of war," she said, with a light, deprecatory gesture. "You couldn't help it any more than we could."

"You are a generous enemy, Miss Barkdale."

"I'm no wounded man's enemy, at least not till he is almost well. Were I one of my brothers, however, and you were on your horse again with your old vigor--" and she gave him a little, significant nod.

He now laughed responsively, and said, "I like that." Then he added, gravely: "Heaven grant I may never meet one of your brothers in battle. I could not knowingly harm him."

"Thank you for saying that," she said, gently. "Now, tell me truly, isn't there anything you wish?"

"Yes, I wish to get better, so that I may have a little of your society. These days of inaction are so interminably long, and you know I've been leading a very active life."

"I fear you wouldn't enjoy the society of such a hot little rebel as I am."

"We should differ, of course, on some things, but that would only give zest to your words. I'm not so stupid and prejudiced, Miss Barkdale, as to fail to see that you are just as sincere and patriotic as I am. I have envied the enlisted men when I have heard of your attentions to them."

"Now," she resumed, laughing, "I've found out that the 'good angel' is not treating you as well as the common soldiers. Men always let out the truth sooner or later. If Surgeon McAllister will permit, I'll read and talk to you also."

"I not only give my permission," said the surgeon, "but also assure you that such kindness will hasten the captain's recovery, for time hangs so heavily on his hands that he chafes and worries."

"Very well," with a sprightly nod at the surgeon, "since we've undertaken to cure the captain, the most sensible thing for us to do IS to cure him. You shall prescribe when and how the doses of society are to be administered." Then to Lane, "Not another word; good-night;" and in a moment she was gone.

Suwanee never forgot that interview, for it was the beginning of a new and strange experience to her. From the first, her high, chivalric spirit had been compelled to admire her enemy. The unknown manner in which he had foiled her sister's strategy showed that his mind was equal to his courage, while his hot indignation, when he found them threatened by a midnight marauder, had revealed his nature. Circumstances had swiftly disarmed her prejudices, and her warm heart had been full of sympathy for him as he lay close to the borders of death. All these things tended to throw down the barriers which would naturally interpose between herself and a Northern man. When, therefore, out of a full heart, he revealed his gratitude and homage, she had no shield against the force of his words and manner, and was deeply touched. She had often received gallantry, admiration, and even words of love, but never before had a man looked and acted as if he reverenced her and the womanhood she represented. It was not a compliment that had been bestowed, but a recognition of what she herself had not suspected. By her family or acquaintances she had never been thought or spoken of as an especially good girl. Hoydenish in early girlhood, leading the young Southern gallants a chase in later years, ever full of frolic and mischief, as fond of the dance as a bird of flying, she was liked by every one, but the graver members of the community were accustomed to shake their heads and remark, "She is a case; perhaps she'll sober down some day." She had hailed the war with enthusiasm, knowing little of its meaning, and sharing abundantly in rural Virginia's contempt for the North. She had proved even a better recruiting officer than her stately sister, and no young fellow dared to approach her until be had donned the gray. When the war came she met it with her own laughing philosophy and unconquerable buoyancy, going wild over Southern victories and shrugging her plump shoulders over defeats, crying: "Better luck next time. The Yankees probably had a hundred to one. It won't take long for Southerners to teach Northern abolitionists the difference between us." But now she had seen Northern soldiers in conflict, had witnessed the utmost degree of bravery on her side, but had seen it confronted by equal courage, inspired by a leader who appeared irresistible.

This Northern officer, whose eyes had flashed like his sabre in battle, whose wit had penetrated and used for his own purpose the scheme of the enemy, and whose chivalric treatment of women plotting against him had been knightly,--this man who had won her respect by storm, as it were, had followed her simple, natural course during the past week, and had metaphorically bowed his knee to her in homage. What did it mean? What had she done? Only made the best of things, and shown a little humanity toward some poor fellows whose sufferings ought to soften hearts of flint.

Thus the girl reasoned and wondered. She did not belong to that class who keep an inventory of all their good traits and rate them high. Moulded in character by surrounding influences and circumstances, her natural, unperverted womanhood and her simple faith in God found unconscious expression in the sweet and gracious acts which Lane had recognized at their true worth. The most exquisite music is but a little sound; the loveliest and most fragrant flower is but organized matter. True, she had been engaged in homely acts,--blessing her enemies as the Bible commanded and her woman's heart dictated,--but how were those acts performed? In her unaffected manner and spirit consisted the charm which won the rough men's adoration and Lane's homage. That which is simple, sincere, spontaneous, ever attains results beyond all art and calculation.

"Missy S'wanee" couldn't understand it. She had always thought of herself as "that child,", that hoyden, that frivolous girl who couldn't help giggling even at a funeral, and now here comes a Northern man, defeats and captures her most ardent admirer, and bows down to her as if she were a saint!

"I wish I were what he thinks me to be," she laughed to herself. "What kind of girls have they in the North, anyway, that he goes on so? I declare, I've half a mind to try to be good, just for the novelty of the thing. But what's the use? It wouldn't last with me till the dew was off the grass in the morning.

"Heigho! I suppose Major Denham is thinking of me and pining in prison, and I haven't thought so very much about him. That shows what kind of an 'angel' I am. Now if there were only a chance of getting him out by tricking his jailers and pulling the wool over the eyes of some pompous old official, I'd take as great a risk as any Southern--'Reverence,' indeed! Captain Lane must be cured of his reverence, whatever becomes of his wound."

CHAPTER XXXIX.
THE CURE OF CAPTAIN LANE.

A DAINTIER bouquet than usual was placed on Lane's table next morning, and the piece of chicken sent to his breakfast was broiled to the nicest turn of brown. The old colored cook was friendly to the "Linkum ossifer," and soon discovered that "Missy S'wanee" was not averse to a little extra painstaking.

After the surgeon had made his morning rounds the young girl visited the men also. She found them doing well, and left them doing better; for, in rallying the wounded, good cheer and hopefulness can scarcely be over-estimated.

As she was returning the surgeon met her, and said, "Captain Lane is already better for your first visit and impatient for another."

"Then he's both patient and impatient. A very contradictory and improper condition to remain in. I can read to him at once, after I have seen if mamma wishes anything."

"Please do; and with your permission I'll take a little walk, for I, too, am restless from inaction."

"I don't think it's nice for you to read alone with that officer," said Roberta.

"I see no impropriety at all," cried Suwanee. "Yours and mamma's rooms are but a few yards away, and you can listen to all we say if you wish. If your colonel was sick and wounded at the North wouldn't you like some woman to cheer him up?"

"No, not if she were as pretty as you are," replied Roberta, laughing.

"Nonsense," said Suwanee, flushing. "For all I know this captain is married and at the head of a large family.

"But I'm going to find out," she assured herself. "I shall investigate this new species of genus homo who imagines me to be a saint. He wasn't long in proving that Northern men were not what I supposed. Now I shall give him the harder task of proving me to be an angel;" and she walked demurely in, leaving the door open for any espionage that her mother and sister might deem proper.

Lane's face lighted up the moment he saw her, and he said: "You have robbed this day of its weariness already. I've had agreeable anticipations thus far, and I'm sure you will again leave pleasant memories."

"Then you are better?"

"Yes; thanks to you."

"You are given to compliments, as our Southern men are."

"I should be glad to equal them at anything in your estimation. But come, such honest enemies as we are should be as sincere as friends. I have meant every word I have said to you. You are harboring me, an entire stranger, who presented my credentials at first very rudely. Now you can ask me any questions you choose. You have proved yourself to be such a genuine lady that I should be glad to have you think that I am a gentleman by birth and breeding."

"Oh, I was convinced of that before you put your sabre in its scabbard on the evening of your most unwelcome arrival, when you spoiled our supper-party. You have since been confirming first impressions. I must admit, however, that I scarcely 'reverence' you yet, nor have I detected anything specially 'angelic.'"

"Your failure in these respects will be the least of my troubles. I do not take back what I have said, however."

"Wait; perhaps you will. You are very slightly acquainted with me, sir."

"You are much less so with me, and can't imagine what an obstinate fellow I am."

"Oh, if I have to contend with obstinacy rather than judgment--"

"Please let us have no contentions whatever. I have often found that your Southern men out-matched me, and not for the world would I have a dispute with a woman of your mettle. I give you my parole to do all that you wish, as far as it is within my power, while I am helpless on your hands."

"And when I have helped to make you well you will go and fight against the South again?"

"Yes, Miss Barkdale," gravely, "and so would your officers against the North."

"Oh, I know it. I sha'n't put any poison in your coffee."

"Nor will you ever put poison in any man's life. The most delightful thing about you, Miss Barkdale," he continued, laughing, "is that you are so genuinely good and don't know it."

"Whatever happens," she said, almost irritably, "you must be cured of that impression. I won't be considered 'good' when I'm not. Little you know about me, indeed! Good heavens, Captain Lane! what kind of women have you been accustomed to meet in the North? Would they put strychnine in a wounded Southerner's food, and give him heavy bread, more fatal than bullets, and read novels while dying men were at their very doors?"

"Heaven help them! I fear there are many women the world over who virtually do just those things."

"They are not in the South," she replied, hotly.

"They are evidently not in this house," he replied, smiling. "You ask what kind of women I am accustomed to meet. I will show you the shadow of one of my friends;" and he took from under his pillow a photograph of Marian.

"Oh, isn't she lovely!" exclaimed the girl.

"Yes, she is as beautiful as you are; she is as brave as you are, and I've seen you cheering on your friends when even in the excitement of the fight my heart was filled with dread lest you or your mother or sister might be shot. She is just as ardent for the North as you are for the South, and her influence has had much place in the motives of many who are now in the Union army. If wounded Confederates were about her door you could only equal--you could not surpass--her in womanly kindness and sympathy. The same would be true of my mother and sisters, and millions of others. I know what you think of us at the North, but you will have to revise your opinions some day."

Her face was flushed, a frown was upon her brow, a doubtful smile upon her lips, and her whole manner betokened her intense interest. "You evidently are seeking to revise them," she said, with a short laugh, "much as you charged our cavalry the other evening. I think you are a dangerous man to the South, Captain Lane, and I don't know whether I should let you get well or not."

He reached out his hand and took hers, as he said, laughingly: "I should trust you just the same, even though Jeff Davis and the whole Confederate Congress ordered you to make away with me."

"Don't you call our President 'Jeff,'" she snapped, but did not withdraw her hand.

"I beg your pardon. That was just as rude in me as if you had called Mr. Lincoln 'Abe.'"

She now burst out laughing. "Heaven knows we do it often enough," she said.

"I was aware of that."

"This won't do at all," she resumed. "Your hand is growing a little feverish, and if my visits do not make you better I shall not come. I think we have defined our differences sufficiently. You must not 'reverence' me any more. I couldn't stand that at all. I will concede at once that you are a gentleman, and that this lovely girl is my equal; and when our soldiers have whipped your armies, and we are free, I shall be magnanimous, and invite you to bring this girl here to visit us on your wedding trip. What is her name?"

"Marian Vosburgh. But I fear she will never take a wedding trip with me. If she did I would accept your invitation gratefully after we had convinced the South that one flag must protect us all."

"We won't talk any more about that. Why won't Miss Vosburgh take a wedding trip with you?"

"For the best of reasons,--she doesn't love me well enough."

"Stupid! Perhaps she loves some one else?"

"No, I don't think so. She is as true a friend as a woman can be to a man, but there it ends."

"With her."

"Certainly, with her only. She knows that I would do all that a man can to win her."

"You are frank."

"Why should I not be with one I trust so absolutely? You think us Northmen cold, underhanded. I do not intend virtually to take my life back from your hands, and at the same time to keep that life aloof from you as if you had nothing to do with it. If I survive the war, whichever way it turns, I shall always cherish your memory as one of my ideals, and shall feel honored indeed if I can retain your friendship. To make and keep such friends is to enrich one's life. Should I see Miss Vosburgh again

I shall tell her about you, just as I have told you about her."

"You were born on the wrong side of the line, Captain Lane. You are a Southerner at heart."

"Oh, nonsense! Wait till you visit us at the North. You will find people to your mind on both sides of the line. When my mother and sisters have learned how you have treated me and my men they will welcome you with open arms."

She looked at him earnestly a moment, and then said: "You make me feel as if the North and South did not understand each other." Then she added, sadly: "The war is not over. Alas! how much may happen before it is. My gray-haired father and gallant brothers are marching with Lee, and while I pray for them night and morning, and often through the day, I fear--I FEAR inexpressibly,--all the more, now that I have seen Northern soldiers fight. God only knows what is in store for us all. Do not think that because I seem light-hearted I am not conscious of living on the eve of a tragedy all the time. Tears and laughter are near together in my nature. I can't help it; I was so made."

"Heaven keep you and yours in safety," said Lane, earnestly; and she saw that his eyes were moist with feeling.

"This won't answer," she again declared, hastily. "We must have no more such exciting talks. Shall I read to you a little while, or go at once?"

"Read to me, by all means, if I am not selfishly keeping you too long. Your talk has done me good rather than harm, for you are so vital yourself that you seem to give me a part of your life and strength. I believe I should have died under the old dull monotony."

"I usually read the Bible to your men," she said, half humorously, half questioningly.

"Read it to me. I like to think we have the same faith. That book is the pledge that all differences will pass away from the sincere."

He looked at her wonderingly as she read, in her sweet, girlish voice, the sacred words familiar since his childhood; and when she rose and said, "This must do for to-day," his face was eloquent with his gratitude. He again reached out his hand, and said, gently, "Miss Suwanee, Heaven keep you and yours from all harm."

"Don't talk to me that way," she said, brusquely. "After all, we are enemies, you know."

"If you can so bless your enemies, what must be the experience of your friends, one of whom I intend to be?"

"Roberta must read to you, in order to teach you that the South cannot be taken by storm."

"I should welcome Miss Roberta cordially. We also shall be good friends some day."

"We must get you well and pack you off North, or there's no telling what may happen," she said, with a little tragic gesture. "Good-by."

This was the beginning of many talks, though no other was of so personal a nature. They felt that they understood each other, that there was no concealment to create distrust. She artlessly and unconsciously revealed to him her life and its inspirations, and soon proved that her mind was as active as her hands. She discovered that Lane had mines of information at command, and she plied him with questions about the North, Europe, and such parts of the East as he had visited. Her father's library was well stored with standard works, and she made him describe the scenes suggested by her favorite poets. Life was acquiring for her a zest which it had never possessed before, and one day she said to him, abruptly, "How you have broadened my horizon!"

He also improved visibly in her vivacious society, and at last was able to come down to his meals and sit on the piazza. Mrs. Barkdale's and Roberta's reserve thawed before his genial courtesy, and all the more readily since a letter had been received from Colonel Barkdale containing thanks to Lane for the consideration that had been shown to his family, and assuring his wife that the Barkdale mansion must not fail in hospitality either to loyal friends or to worthy foes.

Roberta was won over more completely than she had believed to be possible. Her proud, high spirit was pleased with the fact that, while Lane abated not one jot of his well-defined loyalty to the North and its aims, he also treated her with respect and evident admiration in her fearless assertion of her views. She also recognized his admirable tact in preventing their talk from verging towards a too-earnest discussion of their differences. Suwanee was delighted as she saw him disarm her relatives, and was the life of their social hours. She never wearied in delicately chaffing and bewildering the good-natured but rather matter-of-fact Surgeon McAllister, and it often cost Lane much effort to keep from exploding in laughter as he saw the perplexed and worried expression of his friend. But before the meal was over she would always reassure her slow-witted guest by some unexpected burst of sunshine, and he afterwards would remark, in confidence: "I say, Lane, that little 'Missy S'wanee' out-generals a fellow every time. She attacks rear, flank, and front, all at once, and then she takes your sword in such a winsome way that you are rather glad to surrender."

"Take care, McAllister,--take care, or you may surrender more than your sword."

"I think you are in the greater danger."

"Oh, no, I'm forearmed, and Miss Suwanee and I understand each other."

But he did not understand her, nor did she comprehend herself. Her conversation seemed as open, and often as bright as her Southern sunshine, and his mind was cheered and delighted with it. He did not disguise his frank, cordial regard for her, even before her mother and sister, but it was ever blended with such a sincere respect that she was touched and surprised by it, and they were reassured. She had told them of the place possessed by Marian in his thoughts, and this fact, with his manner, promised immunity from all tendencies towards sentiment. Indeed, that Suwanee should bestow anything more upon the Northern officer than kindness, a certain chivalric hospitality, and some admiration, was among the impossibilities in their minds.

This, at the time, seemed equally true to the young girl herself. Not in the least was she on her guard. Her keen enjoyment of his society awakened no suspicions, for she enjoyed everything keenly. His persistence in treating her, in spite of all her nonsense and frolicsomeness, as if she were worthy of the deepest respect and honor which manhood can pay to womanhood, ever remained a bewildering truth, and touched the deepest chords in her nature. Sometimes when they sat in the light of the young moon on the veranda she revealed thoughts which surprised him, and herself even more. It appeared to her as if a new and deeper life were awakening in her heart, full of vague beauty and mystery. She almost believed that she was becoming good, as he imagined. Why otherwise should she be so strangely happy and spiritually exalted? He was developing in her a new self-respect. She now knew that he was familiar with standards of comparison at the North of which she need not be ashamed. Even her mother and sister had remarked, in effect, "It is evident that Captain Lane has been accustomed to the best society." His esteem was not the gaping admiration of a boor to whom she had been a revelation.

"No," she said, "he is a revelation to me. I thought my little prejudices were the boundaries of the world. He, who has seen the world, walks right over my prejudices as if they were nothing, and makes me feel that I am his friend and equal, because he fancies I possess a true, noble womanhood; and now I mean to possess it. He has made his ideal of me seem worthy and beautiful, and it shall be my life effort to attain it. He doesn't think me a barbarian because I am a rebel and believe in slavery. He has said that his mother and sisters would receive me with open arms. It seems to me that I have grown years older and wiser during the last few weeks."

She did not know that her vivid, tropical nature was responding to the influence which is mightiest even in colder climes.

CHAPTER XL.
LOVE'S TRIUMPH.

THE month of June was drawing to a close. Captain Lane, his surgeon, and a little company of wounded men, equally with the Confederates, were only apparently forgotten. They were all watched, and their progress towards health was noted. Any attempt at escape would have been checked at once. The majority of the Federal soldiers could now walk about slowly, and were gaining rapidly. Although they were not aware of the fact, the Confederate wounded, who had progressed equally far in convalescence, were their guards, and the residents of the neighborhood were allies in watchfulness. The Southerners were only awaiting the time, near at hand, when they could proceed to Richmond with their prisoners. This purpose indicated no deep hostility on the part of the rebels. Companionship in suffering had banished this feeling. A sergeant among their number had become their natural leader, and he was in communication with guerilla officers and other more regular authorities. They had deemed it best to let events take their course for a time. Lee's northward advance absorbed general attention, although little as yet was known about it on that remote plantation. The Union men were being healed and fed at no cost to the Confederates, and could be taken away at the time when their removal could be accomplished with the least trouble.

Lane himself was the chief cause of delay. He was doing well, but his wound was of a peculiar nature, and any great exertion or exposure might yet cause fatal results. This fact had become known to the rebel sergeant, and since the captain was the principal prize, and they were all very comfortable, he had advised delay. It had been thought best not to inform the family as to the state of affairs, lest it should in some way become known to Lane and the surgeon, and lead to attempted escape. The Barkdales, moreover, were high-strung people, and might entertain some chivalric ideas about turning over their guests to captivity.

"They might have a ridiculous woman's notion about the matter," said one of these secret advisers.

Lane and McAllister, however, were becoming exceedingly solicitous concerning the future. The former did not base much hope on Suwanee's evident expectation that when he was well enough he would go to his friends as a matter of course. He knew that he and his men were in the enemy's hands, and that they would naturally be regarded as captives. He had a horror of going to a Southern prison and of enduring weeks and perhaps months of useless inactivity. He and McAllister began to hold whispered consultations. His mind revolted at the thought of leaving his men, and of departing stealthily from the family that had been so kind. And yet if they were all taken to Richmond he would be separated from the men, and could do nothing for them. Matter-of-fact McAllister had no doubts or scruples.

"Of course we should escape at once if your wound justified the attempt"

On the 29th of June Lane and the surgeon walked some little distance from the house, and became satisfied that they were under the surveillance of the rebel sergeant and his men. This fact so troubled Lane that Suwanee noticed his abstraction and asked him in the evening what was worrying him. The moonlight fell full on her lovely, sympathetic face.

"Miss Suwanee," he said, gravely, "I've been your guest about a month. Are you not tired of me yet?"

"That's a roundabout way of saying you are tired of us."

"I beg your pardon: it is not. But, in all sincerity, I should be getting back to duty, were it possible."

"Your wound is not sufficiently healed," she said, earnestly, wondering at the chill of fear that his words had caused. "The surgeon says it is not."

"Don't you know?" he whispered.

"Know what?" she almost gasped.

"That I'm a prisoner."

She sprung to her feet and was about to utter some passionate exclamation; but he said, hastily, "Oh, hush, or I'm lost. I believe that eyes are upon me all the time."

"Heigho!" she exclaimed, walking to the edge of the veranda, "I wish I knew what General Lee was doing. We are expecting to hear of another great battle every day;" and she swept the vicinity with a seemingly careless glance, detecting a dark outline behind some shrubbery not far away. Instantly she sprung down the steps and confronted the rebel sergeant.

"What are you doing here?" she asked, indignantly.

"My duty," was the stolid reply.

"Find duty elsewhere then," she said, haughtily.

The man slunk away, and she returned to Lane, who remarked, significantly, "Now you understand me."

It was evident that she was deeply excited, and immediately she began to speak in a voice that trembled with anger and other emotions. "This is terrible. I had not thought--indeed it cannot be. My father would not permit it. The laws of war would apply, I suppose, to your enlisted men, but that you and Surgeon McAllister, who have been our guests and have sat at our table, should be taken from our hospitality into captivity is monstrous. In permitting it, I seem to share in a mean, dishonorable thing."

"How characteristic your words and actions are!" said Lane, gently. "It would be easy to calculate your orbit. I fear you cannot help yourself. You forget, too, that I was the means of sending to prison even your Major Denham."

"Major Denham is nothing--" she began, impetuously, then hesitated, and he saw the rich color mantling her face even in the moonlight. After a second or two she added: "Our officers were captured in fair fight. That is very different from taking a wounded man and a guest."

"Not a guest in the ordinary sense of the word. You see I can be fair to your people, unspeakably as I dread captivity. It will not be so hard for McAllister, for surgeons are not treated like ordinary prisoners. His remaining, however, was a brave, unselfish act;" and Lane spoke in tones of deep regret.

"It must not be," she said, sternly.

"Miss Suwanee,"--and his voice was scarcely audible,--"do you think we can be overheard?"

"No," she replied, in like tones. "Roberta and mamma are incapable of listening."

"I was not thinking of them. I must speak quickly. I don't wish to involve you, but the surgeon and I must try to escape, for I would almost rather die than be taken prisoner. Deep as is my longing for liberty I could not leave you without a word, and my trust in the chivalric feeling that you have just evinced is so deep as to convince me that I can speak to you safely. I shall not tell you anything to compromise you. You have only to be blind and deaf if you see or hear anything."

Her tears were now falling fast, but she did not move, lest observant eyes should detect her emotion.

"Heaven bless your good, kind heart!" he continued, in a low, earnest tone. "Whether I live or die, I wish you to know that your memory will ever be sacred to me, like that of my mother and one other. Be assured that the life you have done so much to save is always at your command. Whenever I can serve you or yours you can count on all that I am or can do. Suwanee, I shall be a better man for having known you. You don't half appreciate yourself, and every succeeding day has only proved how true my first impressions were."

She did not answer, and he felt that it would be dangerous to prolong the interview. They entered the house together. As they went up the stairs she pressed her handkerchief to her eyes, he wondering at her silence and emotion. At the landing in the dusky hall-way he raised her hand to his lips.

There was not a trace of gallantry in the act, and she knew it. It was only the crowning token of that recognition at which she had wondered from the first. She realized that it was only the homage of a knightly man and the final expression of his gratitude; but it overwhelmed her, and she longed to escape with the terrible revelation which had come to her at last. She could not repress a low sob, and, giving his hand a quick, strong pressure, she fled to her room.

"Can it be possible?" he thought. "Oh! if I have wounded that heart, however unintentionally, I shall never forgive myself."

"Lane," whispered McAllister, when the former entered his room, "there are guards about the house."

"I'm not surprised," was the despondent reply. "We are prisoners."

"Does the family know it?"

He told him how Suwanee had detected the espionage of the rebel sergeant.

"Wouldn't she help us?"

"I shall not ask her to. I shall not compromise her with her people."

"No, by thunder! I'd rather spend my life in prison than harm her. What shall we do?"

"We must put our light out soon, and take turns in watching for the slightest opportunity. You lie down first. I do not feel sleepy."

After making some slight preparations the doctor slept, and it was well on towards morning before Lane's crowding thoughts permitted him to seek repose. He then wakened McAllister and said, "There has been a stealthy relief of guards thus far, and I've seen no chance whatever."

The doctor was equally satisfied that any attempt to escape would be fruitless.

Suwanee's vigil that night was bitter and terrible, indeed. Her proud, passionate nature writhed under the truth that she had given her heart, unsought, to a Northern officer,--to one who had from the first made it clear that his love had been bestowed on another. She felt that she could not blame him. His frankness had been almost equal to that of her own brothers, and he had satisfied her that they could scarcely be more loyal to her than he would be. She could detect no flaw in his bearing towards her. He had not disguised his admiration, his abundant enjoyment of her society, but all expression of his regard had been tinged with respect and gratitude rather than gallantry. He perhaps had thought that her knowledge of his attitude towards Miss Vosburgh was an ample safeguard, if any were needed. Alas! it had been the chief cause of her fatal blindness. She had not dreamed of danger for him or herself in their companionship. Nothing was clearer than that he expected and wished no such result. It was well for Lane that this was true, for she would have been a dangerous girl to trifle with.

But she recognized the truth. Before, love had been to her a thing of poetry, romance, and dreams. Now it was a terrible reality. Her heart craved with intense longing what she felt it could never possess.

At last, wearied and exhausted by her deep emotion, she sighed: "Perhaps it is better as it is. Even if he had been a lover, the bloody chasm of war would have separated us, but it seems cruel that God should permit such an overwhelming misfortune to come upon an unsuspecting, inexperienced girl. Why was I so made that I could, unconsciously, give my very soul to this stranger? yet he is not a stranger. Events have made me better acquainted with him than with any other man. I know that he has kept no secrets from me. There was nothing to conceal. All has been simple, straightforward, and honorable. It is to the man himself, in his crystal integrity, that my heart has bowed, and then--that was his chief power--he made me feel that I was not unworthy. He taught me to respect my own nature, and to aspire to all that was good and true.

"After all, perhaps I am condemning myself too harshly,--perhaps the truth that my heart acknowledged such a man as master is proof that his estimate of me is not wholly wrong. Were there not some kinship of spirit between us, this could not be; but the secret must remain between me and God."

Lane, tormented by the fear suggested by Suwanee's manner on the previous evening, dreaded to meet her again, but at first he was reassured. Never had she been more brilliant and frolicsome than at the breakfast-table that morning. Never had poor McAllister been more at his wits' end to know how to reply to her bewildering sallies of good-natured badinage. Every vulnerable point of Northern character received her delicate satire. Lane himself did not escape her light shafts. He made no defence, but smiled or laughed at every palpable hit. The girl's pallor troubled him, and something in her eyes that suggested suffering. There came a time when he could scarcely think of that day without tears, believing that no soldier on either side ever displayed more heroism than did the wounded girl.

He and the surgeon walked out again, and saw that they were watched. He found that his men had become aware of the truth and had submitted to the inevitable. They were far from the Union lines, and not strong enough to attempt an escape through a hostile country. Lane virtually gave up, and began to feel that the best course would be to submit quietly and look forward to a speedy exchange. He longed for a few more hours with Suwanee, but imagined that she avoided him. There was no abatement of her cordiality, but she appeared preoccupied.

After dinner a Confederate officer called and asked for Miss Roberta, who, after the interview, returned to her mother's room with a troubled expression. Suwanee was there, calmly plying her needle. She knew what the call meant.

"I suppose it's all right, and that we can't help ourselves," Roberta began, "but it annoys me nevertheless. Lieutenant Macklin, who has just left, has said that our own men and the Union soldiers are now well enough to be taken to Richmond, and that he will start with them to-morrow morning. Of course I have no regrets respecting the enlisted men, and am glad they are going, for they are proving a heavy burden to us; but my feelings revolt at the thought that Captain Lane and the surgeon should be taken to prison from our home."

"I don't wonder," said Suwanee, indignantly; "but then what's the use? we can't help ourselves. I suppose it is the law of war."

"Well, I'm glad you are so sensible about it. I feared you would feel a hundred-fold worse than I, you and the captain have become such good friends. Indeed, I have even imagined that he was in danger of becoming something more. I caught him looking at you at dinner as if you were a saint 'whom infidels might adore.' His homage to our flirtatious little Suwanee has been a rich joke from the first. I suppose, however, there may have been a vein of calculation in it all, for I don't think any Yankee--"

"Hush," said Suwanee, hotly; "Captain Lane is still our guest, and he is above calculation. I shall not permit him to be insulted because he has over-estimated me."

"Why, Suwanee, I did not mean to insult him. You have transfixed him with a dozen shafts of satire to-day, and as for poor Surgeon McAllister--"

"That was to their faces," interrupted Suwanee, hastily.

"Suwanee is right," said Mrs. Barkdale, smiling. "Captain Lane has had the sense to see that my little girl is good-hearted in spite of her nonsense."

The girl's lip was quivering but she concealed the fact by savagely biting off her thread, and then was impassive again.

"I sincerely regret with you both," resumed their mother, "that these two gentlemen must go from our home to prison, especially so since receiving a letter from Captain Lane, couched in terms of the strongest respect and courtesy, and enclosing a hundred dollars in Northern money as a slight compensation--so he phrased it--for what had been done for his men. Of course he meant to include himself and the surgeon, but had too much delicacy to mention the fact. He also stated that he would have sent more, but that it was nearly all they had."

"You did not keep the money!" exclaimed the two girls in the same breath.

"I do not intend to keep it," said the lady, quietly, "and shall hand it back to him with suitable acknowledgments. I only mention the fact to convince Roberta that Captain Lane is not the typical Yankee, and we have much reason to be thankful that men of a different stamp were not quartered upon us. And yet," continued the matron, with a deep sigh, "you little know how sorely we need the money. Your father's and brothers' pay is losing its purchasing power. The people about here all profess to be very hot for the South, but when you come to buy anything from them what they call 'Linkum money' goes ten times as far. We have never known anything but profusion, but now we are on the verge of poverty."

"Oh, well," said Suwanee, recklessly, "starving isn't the worst thing that could happen."

"Alas! my child, you can't realize what poverty means. Your heart is as free from care as the birds around us, and, like them, you think you will be provided for."

The girl sprung up with a ringing laugh, and kissed her mother as she exclaimed, "I'll cut off my hair, put on one of brother Bob's old suits, and enlist;" and then she left the room.

At supper there was a constraint on all except Suwanee. Mrs. Barkdale and Roberta felt themselves to be in an embarrassing position. The men at the table, who had been guests so long, would be marched away as prisoners from their door in the morning. The usages of war could not satisfy their womanly and chivalric natures, or make them forget the courtesy and respect which, in spite of prejudices, had won so much good-will. Lane scarcely sought to disguise his perplexity and distress. Honest Surgeon McAllister, who knew that they all had been an awful burden, was as troubled as some men are pleased when they get much for nothing. Suwanee appeared in a somewhat new role. She was the personification of dignity and courtesy. She acted as if she knew all and was aware that their guests did. Therefore levity would be in bad taste, and their only resource was the good breeding which ignores the disagreeable and the inevitable. Her mother looked on her with pride, and wondered at so fine an exibition of tact. She did not know that the poor girl had a new teacher, and that she was like an inexorable general who, in a desperate fight, summons all his reserve and puts forth every effort of mind and body.

Lane had not found a chance to say one word to Suwanee in private during the day, but after supper she went to the piano and began to play some Southern airs with variations of her own improvising. He immediately joined her and said, "We shall not attempt to escape; we are too closely watched."

She did not reply.

"Miss Suwanee," he began again, and distress and sorrow were in his tones, "I hardly know how to speak to you of what troubles me more than the thought of captivity. How can I manage with such proud, chivalric women as you and your mother and sister? But I am not blind, nor can I ignore the prosaic conditions of our lot. I respect your pride; but have a little mercy on mine,--nay, let me call it bare self-respect. We have caused you the loss of your laborers, your fields are bare, and you have emptied your larder in feeding my men, yet your mother will not take even partial compensation. You can't realize how troubled I am."

"You, like ourselves, must submit to the fortunes of war," she replied, with a sudden gleam of her old mirthfulness.

"A bodily wound would be a trifle compared with this," he resumed, earnestly. "O Miss Suwanee, have I won no rights as a friend? rather, let me ask, will you not generously give me some rights?"

"Yes, Captain Lane," she said, gently, "I regard you as a friend, and I honor you as a true man. Though the war should go on forever I should not change in these respects unless you keep harping on this financial question."

"Friends frankly accept gifts from friends; let it be a gift then, by the aid of which you can keep your mother from privation. Suwanee, Suwanee, why do you refuse to take this dross from me when I would give my heart's blood to shield you from harm?"

"You are talking wildly, Captain Lane," she said, with a laugh. "Your heart belongs to Miss Vosburgh, and therefore all its blood."

"She would be the first to demand and expect that I should risk all and give all for one to whom I owe so much and who is so deserving."

"I require of her no such sacrifice," Suwanee replied, coldly, "nor of you either, Captain Lane. Unforeseen circumstances have thrown us together for a time. We have exchanged all that is possible between those so divided,--esteem and friendship. If my father thinks it best he will obtain compensation from our government. Perhaps, in happier times, we may meet again," she added, her tone and manner becoming gentle once more; "and then I hope you will find me a little more like what you have thought me to be."

"God grant that we may meet again. There, I can't trust myself to speak to you any more. Your unaffected blending of humility and pride with rare, unconscious nobility touches my very soul. Our leave-taking in the morning must be formal. Good-by, Suwanee Barkdale. As sure as there is a God of justice your life will be filled full with happiness."

Instead of taking his proffered hand, she trembled, turned to the piano, and said hastily between the notes she played: "Control yourself and listen. We may be observed. You and the surgeon be ready to open your door and follow me at any time to-night. Hang your sword where it may be seen through the open window. I have contrived a chance--a bare chance--of your escape. Bow and retire."

He did so. She bent her head in a courtly manner towards him, and then went on with her playing of Southern airs.

A moment later the rebel sergeant disappeared from some shrubbery a little beyond the parlor window, and chuckled, "The Yankee captain has found out that he can't make either an ally or a sweetheart out of a Southern girl; but I suspicioned her a little last night."

At two o'clock that night there was an almost imperceptible tap at Lane's door. He opened it noiselessly, and saw Suwanee with her finger on her lips.

"Carry your shoes in your hands," she said, and then led the way down the stairs to the parlor window. Again she whispered: "The guard here is bribed,--bribed by kindness. He says I saved his life when he was wounded. Steal through the shrubbery to the creek-road; continue down that, and you'll find a guide. Not a word. Good-by."

She gave her hand to the surgeon, whose honest eyes were moist with feeling, and then he dropped lightly to the ground.

"Suwanee," began Lane.

"Hush! Go."

Again he raised her hand to his lips, again heard that same low, involuntary sob that had smote his heart the preceding night; and then followed the surgeon. The guard stood out in the garden with his back towards them, as, like shadows, they glided away.

On the creek-road the old colored man who worked in the garden joined them, and led the way rapidly to the creek, where under some bushes a skiff with oars was moored. Lane slipped twenty dollars into the old man's hand, and then he and his companion pushed out into the sluggish current, and the surgeon took the oars and pulled quietly through the shadows of the overhanging foliage. The continued quiet proved that their escape had not been discovered. Food had been placed in the boat. The stream led towards the Potomac. With the dawn they concealed themselves, and slept during the day, travelling all the following night. The next day they were so fortunate as to fall in with a Union scouting party, and so eventually reached Washington; but the effort in riding produced serious symptoms in Lane's wound, and he was again doomed to quiet weeks of convalescence, as has already been intimated to the reader.

When Mrs. Barkdale and Roberta came down the next morning they found Suwanee in the breakfast room, fuming with apparent irritability.

"Here is that Lieutenant Macklin again," she said, "and he is very impatient, saying that his orders are imperative, and that he is needed on some special duty. His orders are to convey the prisoners to the nearest railroad station, and then report for some active service. From all I can gather it is feared that the Yankees propose an attack on Richmond, now that General Lee is away."

"It's strange that Captain Lane and the surgeon don't come down," Roberta remarked. "I truly wish, however, that we had not to meet them again."

"Well, since it must be, the sooner the ordeal is over the better," said Suwanee, with increasing irritation. "Captain Lane has sense enough to know that we are not responsible for his being taken away."

"Hildy," said Mrs. Barkdale, "go up and tell the gentlemen that breakfast is ready."

In a few moments the old woman returned in a fluster and said, "I knock on de doah, and dey ain't no answer."

"What!" exclaimed Suwanee, in the accents of surprise; then, sharply, "go and knock louder, and wake them up," adding, "it's very strange."

Hildy came back with a scared look, and said, "I knock and knock; den I open de doah, and der' ain't no one dere."

"They must be out in the grounds for a walk," exclaimed Roberta. "Haven't you seen them this morning?"

"I ain't seen nuffin' nor heard nuffin'," protested the old woman.

"Girls, this is serious," said Mrs. Barkdale, rising; and she summoned Lieutenant Macklin, who belonged to a class not received socially by the family.

"We have but this moment discovered," said the lady, "that Captain Lane and Surgeon McAllister are not in their room. Therefore we suppose they are walking in the grounds. Will you please inform them that breakfast is waiting?"

"Pardon me, madam, they cannot be outside, or I should have been informed."

"Then you must search for them, sir. The house, grounds, and buildings are open to you."

The fact of the prisoners' escape soon became evident, and there were haste, confusion, and running to and fro to no purpose. Suwanee imitated Roberta so closely that she was not suspected. Lieutenant Macklin and the rebel sergeant at last returned, giving evidence of strong vexation.

"We don't understand this," began the lieutenant.

"Neither do we," interrupted Mrs. Barkdale, so haughtily that they were abashed, although they directed keen glances towards Suwanee, who met their scrutiny unflinchingly.

The Barkdales were not people to be offended with impunity, and the lieutenant knew it. He added, apologetically: "You know I must do my duty, madam. I fear some of your servants are implicated, or that guards have been tampered with."

"You are at liberty to examine any one you please."

They might as well have examined a carved, wrinkled effigy as old Cuffy, Lane's midnight guide. "I don' know nuffin' 'tall 'bout it," he declared. "My ole woman kin tell yo' dat I went to bed when she did and got up when she did."

The guard, bought with kindness, was as dense in his ignorance as any of the others. At last Macklin declared that he would have to put citizens on the hunt, for his orders admitted of no delay.

The Union prisoners, together with the Confederates, when formed in line, gave a ringing cheer for "Missy S'wanee and the ladies," and then the old mansion was left in more than its former isolation, and, as the younger girl felt, desolation.

She attended to her duties as usual, and then went to her piano. The words spoken the previous evening would ever make the place dear to her. While she was there old Hildy crept in, with her feeble step, and whispered, "I foun' dis un'er Cap'n Lane's piller."

It was but a scrap of paper, unaddressed; but Suwanee understood its significance. It contained these words: "I can never repay you, but to discover some coin which a nature like yours can accept has become one of my supreme ambitions. If I live, we shall meet again."

Those words formed a glimmering hope which grew fainter and fainter in the dark years which followed.

She did not have to mask her trouble very long, for another sorrow came like an avalanche. Close to the Union lines, on Cemetery Ridge, lay a white-haired colonel and his two tall sons. They were among the heroes in Pickett's final charge, on the 3d of July. "Missy S'wanee" laughed no more, even in self-defence.

CHAPTER XLI.
SUNDAY'S LULL AND MONDAY'S STORM.

SUNDAY, the 12th of July, proved a long, restful sabbath to Marian and her father, and they spent most of its hours together. The great tension and strain of the past weeks appeared to be over for a time. The magnificent Union victories had brought gladness and hopefulness to Mr. Vosburgh, and the return of her friends had relieved his daughter's mind. He now thought he saw the end clearly. He believed that hereafter the tide of rebellion would ebb southward until all the land should be free.

"This day has been a godsend to us both," he said to Marian, as they sat together in the library before retiring. "The draft has begun quietly, and no disturbances have followed. I scarcely remember an evening when the murmur of the city was so faint and suggestive of repose. I think we can both go to the country soon, with minds comparatively at rest. I must admit that I expected no such experience as has blessed us to-day. We needed it. Not until this respite came did I realize how exhausted from labor and especially anxiety I had become. You, too, my little girl, are not the blooming lassie you were a year ago."

"Yet I think I'm stronger in some respects, papa."

"Yes, in many respects. Thank God for the past year. Your sympathy and companionship have made it a new era in my life. You have influenced other lives, also, as events have amply proved. Are you not satisfied now that you can be unconventional without being queer? You have not been a colorless reflection of some social set; neither have you left your home for some startling public career; and yet you have achieved the distinct individuality which truthfulness to nature imparts. You have simply been developing your better self naturally, and you have helped fine fellows to make the best of themselves."

"Your encouragement is very sweet, papa. I'm not complacent over myself, however; and I've failed so signally in one instance that I'm vexed and almost saddened. You know what I mean."

"Yes, I know," with a slight laugh. "Merwyn is still your unsolved problem, and he worries you."

"Not because he is unsolved, but rather that the solution has proved so disappointing and unexpected. He baffles me with a trait which I recognize, but can't understand, and only admit in wonder and angry protest. Indeed, from the beginning of our acquaintance he has reversed my usual experiences. His first approaches incensed me beyond measure,--all the more, I suppose, because I saw in him an odious reflection of my old spirit. But, papa, when to his condescending offer I answered from the full bitterness of my heart, he looked and acted as if I had struck him with a knife."

Her father again laughed, as he said: "You truly used heroic surgery, and to excellent purpose. Has he shown any conceit, complacency, or patronizing airs since?"

"No, I admit that, at least."

"In destroying some of his meaner traits by one keen thrust, you did him a world of good. Of course he suffered under such a surgical operation, but he has had better moral health ever since."

"Oh, yes," she burst out, "he has become an eminently respectable and patriotic millionnaire, giving of his abundance to save the nation's life, living in a palace meanwhile. What did he mean by his passionate words, 'I shall measure everything hereafter by the breadth of your woman's soul'? What have the words amounted to? You know, papa, that nothing but my duty and devotion to you keeps me from taking an active part in this struggle, even though a woman. Indeed, the feeling is growing upon me that I must spend part of my time in some hospital. A woman can't help having an intense conviction of what she would do were she a man, and you know what I would have done, and he knows it also. Therefore he has not kept his word, for he fails at the vital point in reaching my standard. I have no right to judge men in Mr. Merwyn's position because they do not go to the front. Let them do what they think wise and prudent; let them also keep among their own kind. I protest against their coming to me for what I give to friends who have already proved themselves heroes. But there, I forgot. He looks so like a man that I can't help thinking that he is one,--that he could come up to my standard if he chose to. He still seeks me--"

"No, he has not been here since he heard Blauvelt's story."

"He passed the house once, hesitated, and did not enter. Papa, he has not changed, and you know it. He has plainly asked for a gift only second to what I can give to God. With a tenacity which nothing but his will can account for, perhaps, he seeks it still. Do you think his distant manner deceives me for a moment? Nor has my coldness any influence on him. Yet it has not been the coldness of indifference, and he knows that too. He has seen and felt, like sword-thrusts, my indignation, my contempt. He has said to my face, 'You think me a coward.' He is no fool, and has fully comprehended the situation. If he had virtually admitted, 'I am a coward, and therefore can have no place among the friends who are surpassing your ideal of manly heroism,' and withdrawn to those to whom a million is more than all hero-ism, the affair would have ended naturally long ago. But he persists in bringing me a daily sense of failure and humiliation. He says: 'My regard for you is so great I can't give you up, yet not so great as to lead me to do what hundreds of thousands are doing. I can't face danger for your sake.' I have tried to make the utmost allowance for his constitutional weakness, yet it has humiliated me that I had not the power to enable him to overcome so strange a failing. Why, I could face death for you, and he can't stand beside one whom he used to sneer at as 'little Strahan.' Yet, such is his idea of my woman's soul that he still gives me his thoughts and therefore his hopes;" and she almost stamped her foot in her irritation.

"Would you truly give your life for me?" he asked, gently.

"Yes, I know I could, and would were there necessity; not in callous disregard of danger, but because the greater emotion swallows up the less. Faulty as I am, there would be no bargainings and prudent reservations in my love. These are not the times for half-way people. Oh think, papa, while we are here in the midst of every comfort, how many thousands of mutilated, horribly wounded men are dying in agony throughout the South! My heart goes out to them in a sympathy and hom-age I can't express. Think how Lane and even Strahan may be suffering to-night, with so much done for them, and then remember the prisoners of war and the poor unknown enlisted men, often terribly neglected, I fear. Papa, won't you let me go as a nurse? The ache would go out of my own heart if I tried to reduce this awful sum of anguish a little. He whose word and touch always banished pain and disease would surely shield me in such labors. As soon as danger no longer threatens you, won't you let me do a little, although I am only a girl?"

"Yes, Marian," her father replied, gravely; "far be it from me to repress such heaven-born impulses. You are now attaining the highest rank reached by humanity. All the avenues of earthly distinction cannot lead beyond the spirit of self-sacrifice for others. This places you near the Divine Man, and all grow mean and plebeian to the degree that they recede from him. You see what comes of developing your better nature. Selfishness and its twin, cowardice, are crowded out."

"Please don't praise me any more. I can't stand it," faltered the girl, tearfully. A moment later her laugh rang out. "Hurrah!" she cried, "since Mr. Merwyn won't go to the war, I'm going myself."

"To make more wounds than you will heal," her father added. "Remember the circumstances under which you go will have to receive very careful consideration, and I shall have to know all about the matron and nurses with whom you act. Your mother will be horrified, and so will not a few of your acquaintances. Flirting in shadows is proper enough, but helping wounded soldiers to live--But we understand each other, and I can trust you now."

The next morning father and daughter parted with few misgivings, and the latter promised to go to her mother in a day or two, Mr. Vosburgh adding that if the week passed quietly he could join them on Saturday evening.

So they quietly exchanged their good-by kiss on the edge of a volcano already in eruption.

An early horseback ride in Central Park had become one of Merwyn's habits of late. At that hour he met comparatively few abroad, and the desire for solitude was growing upon him. Like Mr. Vosburgh, he had watched with solicitude the beginning of the draft, feeling that if it passed quietly his only remaining chance would be to wring from his mother some form of release from his oath. Indeed, so unhappy and desperate was he becoming that he had thought of revealing everything to Mr. Vosburgh. The government officer, however, might feel it his duty to use the knowledge, should there come a time when the authorities proceeded against the property of the disloyal. Moreover, the young man felt that it would be dishonorable to reveal the secret.

Beyond his loyal impulses he now had little motive for effort. Marian's preju-dices against him had become too deeply rooted, and her woman's honor for the knightly men her friends had proved too controlling a principle, ever to give him a chance for anything better than polite tolerance. He had discovered what this meant so fully, and in Blauvelt's story had been shown the inevitable contrast which she must draw so vividly, that he had decided:--

"No more of Marian Vosburgh's society until all is changed. Therefore no more forever, probably. If my mother proves as obdurate as a Southern jailer, I suppose I'm held, although I begin to think I have as good cause to break my chains as any other Union man. She tricked me into captivity, and holds me remorselessly,--not like a mother. Miss Vosburgh did show she had a woman's heart, and would have given me her hand in friendship had I not been compelled to make her believe that I was a coward. If in some way I can escape my oath, and my reckless courage at the front proves her mistaken, I may return to her. Otherwise it is a useless humiliation and pain to see her any more."

Such had been the nature of his musings throughout the long Sunday whose quiet had led to the belief that the draft would scarcely create a ripple of overt hos-tility. During his ride on Monday morning he nearly concluded to go to his country place again. He was growing nervous and restless, and he longed for the steadying influence of his mountain rambles before meeting his mother and deciding ques-tions which would involve all their future relations.

As with bowed head, lost in thought, he approached the city by one of the park entrances, he heard a deep, angry murmur, as if a storm-vexed tide was coming in. Spurring his horse forward, he soon discovered, with a feeling like an electric shock, that a tide was indeed rising. Was it a temporary tidal wave of human pas-sion, mysterious in its origin, soon to subside, leaving such wreckage as its senseless fury might have caused? Or was it the beginning of the revolution so long feared, but not now guarded against?

Converging from different avenues, men, women, and children were pouring by the thousand into a vacant lot near the park. Their presence seemed like a dream. Why was this angry multitude gathering here within a few rods of rural loveliness, their hoarse cries blending with the songs of robins and thrushes? It had been expected that the red monster would raise its head, if at all, in some purlieu of the east side. On the contrary its segregate parts were coming together at a distance from regions that would naturally generate them, and were forming under his very eyes the thing of which he had read, and, of late, had dreamed night and day,--a mob.

To change the figure, the vacant space, unbuilt upon as yet, was becoming an immense human reservoir, into which turgid streams with threatening sounds were surging from the south. His eyes could separate the tumultuous atoms into ragged forms, unkempt heads, inflamed faces, animated by some powerful destructive impulse. Arms of every description proved that the purpose of the gathering was not a peaceful one. But what was the purpose?

Riding closer he sought to question some on the outskirts of the throng, and so drew attention to himself. Volleys of oaths, stones, and sticks, were the only answers he received.

"Thank you," Merwyn muttered, as he galloped away. "I begin to comprehend your meaning, but shall study you awhile before I take part in the controversy. Then there shall be some knock-down arguments."

As he drew rein at a short distance the cry went up that he was a "spy," and another rush was made for him; but he speedily distanced his pursuers. To his surprise the great multitude turned southward, pouring down Fifth and Sixth avenues. After keeping ahead for a few blocks, he saw that the mob, now numbering many thousands, was coming down town with some unknown purpose and destination.

Two things were at least clear,--the outbreak was unexpected, and no preparation had been made for it. As he approached his home on a sharp trot, a vague air of apprehension and expectation was beginning to manifest itself, and but little more. Policemen were on their beats, and the city on the fashionable avenues and cross-streets wore its midsummer aspect. Before entering his own home he obeyed an impulse to gallop by the Vosburgh residence. All was still quiet, and Marian, with surprise, saw him clattering past in a way that seemed reckless and undignified.

On reaching his home he followed his groom to the stable, and said, quietly: "You are an old family servant, but you must now give me positive assurance that I can trust you. There is a riot in the city, and there is no telling what house will be safe. Will you mount guard night and day in my absence?"

"Faix, sur, I will. Oi'll sarve ye as I did yer fayther afore ye."

"I believe you, but would shoot you if treacherous. You know I've been expecting this trouble. Keep the horse saddled. Bar and bolt everything. I shall be in and out at all hours, but will enter by the little side-door in the stable. Watch for my signal, and be ready to open to me only any door, and bolt it instantly after me. Leave all the weapons about the house just where I have put them. If any one asks for me, say I'm out and you don't know when I'll be back. Learn to recognize my voice and signal, no matter how disguised I am."

The faithful old servant promised everything, and was soon executing orders. Before their neighbors had taken the alarm, the heavy shutters were closed, and the unusual precautions that in the family's absence had been adopted rendered access possible only to great violence. On reaching his room Merwyn thought for a few moments. He was intensely excited, and there was a gleam of wild hope in his eyes, but he felt with proud exultation that in his manner he was imitating his father. Not a motion was hasty or useless. Right or wrong, in the solitude of his room or in the midst of the mob, his brain should direct his hand.

"And now my hand is free!" he exclaimed, aloud; "my oath cannot shackle it now."

His first conclusion was to mingle with the mob and learn the nature and objects of the enemy. He believed the information would be valuable to Mr. Vosburgh and the police authorities. Having accomplished this purpose he would join any organized resistance he could find, at the same time always seeking to shield Marian from the possibility of danger.

He had already been shown that in order to understand the character and aims of the mob he must appear to be one of them, and he decided that he could carry off the disguise of a young city mechanic better than any other.

This plan he carried out by donning from his own wardrobe a plain dark flannel suit, which, when it had been rolled in dust and oil, and received a judicious rip here and there, presented the appearance of a costume of a workman just from his shop. With further injunctions to Thomas and the old serving-woman, he made his way rapidly to the north-east, where the smoke of a conflagration proved that the spirit of mischief was increasing.

One would not have guessed, as he hurried up Third Avenue, that he was well armed, but there were two small, yet effective revolvers and a dirk upon his person.

As has been related before, he had practised for this emergency, and could be as quick as a flash with his weapon.

He had acted with the celerity of youth, guided by definite plans, and soon began to make his way quietly through the throng that blocked the avenue, gradually approaching the fire at the corner of 45th Street. At first the crowd was a mystery to him, so orderly, quiet, and inoffensive did it appear, although composed largely of the very dregs of the slums. The crackling, roaring flames, devouring tenement-houses, were equally mysterious. No one was seeking to extinguish them, although the occupants of the houses were escaping for their lives, dragging out their humble effects. The crowd merely looked on with a pleased, satisfied expression. After a moment's thought Merwyn remembered that the draft had been begun in one of the burning houses, and was told by a bystander, "We smashed the ranch and broke some jaws before the bonfire."

That the crowd was only a purring tiger was soon proved, for some one near said, "There's Kennedy, chief of the cops;" and it seemed scarcely a moment before the officer was surrounded by an infuriated throng who were raining curses and blows upon him.

Merwyn made an impulsive spring forward in his defence, but a dozen forms intervened, and his effort was supposed to be as hostile as that of the rioters. The very numbers that sought to destroy Kennedy gave him a chance, for they impeded one another, and, regaining his feet, he led a wild chase across a vacant lot, pursued by a hooting mob as if he were a mad dog. The crowd that filled the street almost as far as eye could reach now began to sway back and forth as if coming under the influence of some new impulse, and Merwyn was so wedged in that he had to move with the others. Being tall he saw that Kennedy, after the most brutal treatment, was rescued almost by a miracle, apparently more dead than alive. It also became clear to him that the least suspicion of his character and purpose would cost him his life instantly. He therefore resolved on the utmost self-control. He was ready to risk his life, but not to throw it away uselessly,--not at least till he knew that Marian was safe. It was his duty now to investigate the mob, not fight it.

The next excitement was caused by the cry, "The soldiers are coming!"

These proved to be a small detachment of the invalid corps, who showed their comprehension of affairs by firing over the rioters' heads, thinking to disperse them by a little noise. The mob settled the question of noise by howling as if a menagerie had broken loose, and, rushing upon the handful of men, snatched their muskets, first pounding the almost paralyzed veterans, and then chasing them as a wilderness of wolves would pursue a small array of sheep.

As Merwyn stepped down from a dray, whereon he had witnessed the scene, he muttered, indiscreetly, "What does such nonsense amount to!"

A big hulking fellow, carrying a bar of iron, who had stood beside him, and who apparently had had his suspicions, asked, fiercely, "An' what did ye expect it wud amount to? An' what's the nonsense ye're growlin' at? By the holy poker oi belave you're a spy."

"Yis, prove that, and I'll cut his heart out," cried an inebriated woman, brandishing a knife a foot long.

"Yes, prove it, you thunderin' fool!" cried Merwyn.

"The cops are comin' now, and you want to begin a fight among ourselves."

True enough, the cry came ringing up the avenue, "The cops comin.'"

"Oh, an' ye's wan uv us, oi'll stan' by ye; but oi've got me eye on ye, and 'ud think no more o' brainin' ye than a puppy."

"Try brainin' the cops first, if yer know when yer well off," replied Merwyn, drawing a pistol. "I didn't come out to fight bullies in our crowd."

The momentary excitement caused by this altercation was swallowed up by the advent of a squad of police, which wheeled into the avenue from 43d Street, and checked the pursuit of the bleeding remnants of the invalid corps. Those immediately around the young man pressed forward to see what took place, he following, but edging towards the sidewalk, with the eager purpose to see the first fight between the mob and the police.

CHAPTER XLII.
THAT WORST OF MONSTERS, A MOB.

AFTER reaching the sidewalk Merwyn soon found a chance to mount a dry-goods box, that he might better observe the action of the police and form an idea of their numbers. The moment he saw the insignificant band he felt that they were doomed men, or else the spirit abroad was not what he thought it to be, and he had been witnessing some strong indications of its ruthless nature.

It was characteristic of the young fellow that he did not rush to the aid of the police. He was able, even in that seething flood of excitement, to reason coolly, and his thoughts were something to this effect: "I'm not going to throw away my life and all its chances and duties because the authorities are so ignorant as to sacrifice a score or two of their men. I shall not fight at all until I have seen Marian and Mr. Vosburgh. When I have done something to insure their safety, or at least to prove that I am not a coward, I shall know better what to do and how to do it. This outbreak is not an affair of a few hours. She herself may be exposed to the fury of these fiends, for I believe her father is, or will be, a marked man."

Seeing, farther up the avenue, a small balcony as yet unoccupied, he pushed his way towards it, that he might obtain one more view of the drift of affairs before taking his course. The hall-door leading to the second story was open and filled with a crowd of frightened, unkempt women and children, who gave way before him. The door of the room opening on the balcony was locked, and, in response to his repeated knockings, a quavering voice asked what was wanted.

"You must open instantly," was his reply.

A trembling, gray-haired woman put the door ajar, and he pushed in at once, saying: "Bolt the door again, madam. I will do you no harm, and may be able to save you from injury;" and he was out in the balcony before his assurances were concluded.

"Indeed, sir, I've done no one any wrong, and therefore need no protection. I only wish to be let alone with my children."

"That you cannot expect with certainty, in view of what is going on to-day. Do you not know that they are burning houses? As long as I'm here I'll be a protection. I merely wish the use of this little outlook for a brief time. So say nothing more, for I must give my whole attention to the fight."

"Well then, since you are so civil, you can stay; but the street is full of devils."

He paid no heed to her further lamentations, and looking southward saw that the police had formed a line across the avenue, and that such battered remnants of the invalid corps as had escaped were limping off behind their cover as fast as possible. The presence of the city's guardians had caused a brief hesitation in the approaching and broken edge of the rabble. Seeing this the brave sergeant ordered a charge, which was promptly and swiftly made, the mob recoiling before it more and more slowly as under pressure it became denser. There was no more effort to carry out the insane, rather than humane, tactics of the invalid corps, who had either fired high or used blank cartridges, for now the police struck for life with their locust clubs, and the thud of the blows could often be heard even above the uproar. Every one within reach of their arms went down, and the majority lay quietly where they fell, as the devoted little band pressed slowly forward. With regret Merwyn saw Barney Ghegan among the foremost, his broad red face streaming with perspiration, and he wielding his club as if it were the deadliest of shillalahs.

They did indeed strike manfully, and proved what an adequate force could do. Rioters fell before them on every side. But hopeless reaping was theirs, with miles of solid, bloodthirsty humanity before them. Slowly and more falteringly they made their way three blocks, as far as 46th Street, sustained by the hope of finding reinforcements there. Instead of these, heavier bodies of the enemy poured in from the side-streets upon the exhausted men, and the mob closed behind them from 45th Street, like dark, surging waves. Then came a mad rush upon the hemmed-in officers, who were attacked in front and in the rear, with clubs, iron-bars, guns, and pistols. Tom, bruised, bleeding, the force that had fought so gallantly broke, each man striking out for his own life. The vast heterogeneous crowd now afforded their chief chance for escape. Dodging behind numbers, taking advantage of the wild confusion of the swaying, trampling masses, and striking down some direct opponent, a few got off with slight bruises. There were wonderful instances of escape. The brave sergeant who had led the squad had his left wrist broken by an iron bar, but, knocking down two other assailants, he sprung into a house and bolted the door after him. An heroic German girl, with none of the stolid phlegm attributed to her race, lifted the upper mattress of her bed. The sergeant sprung in and was covered up without a word. There was no time then for plans and explanations. A moment later the door was broken, and a score of fierce-visaged men streamed in. Now the girl was stolidity itself.

"Der cop run out der back door," was all that she could be made to say in answer to fierce inquiries. Every apartment was examined in vain, and then the roughs departed in search of other prey. Brave, simple-hearted girl! She would have been torn to pieces had her humane strategy been discovered.

But a more memorable act of heroism was reserved for another woman, Mrs. Eagan, the wife of the man who had rescued Superintendent Kennedy a short time before. A policeman was knocked down with a hay-bale rung, and fell at her very feet. In a moment more he would have been killed, but this woman instantly covered his form with her own, so that no blow could reach him unless she was first struck. Then she begged for his life. Even the wild-beast spirit of the mob was touched, and the pursuers passed on. A monument should have been built to the woman who, in that pandemonium of passion, could so risk all for a stranger.

I am not defending Merwyn's course, but sketching a character. His spirit of strategical observation would have forsaken him had he witnessed that scene, and indeed it did forsake him as he saw Barney Ghegan running and making a path for himself by the terrific blows of his club. Three times he fell but rose again, with the same indomitable pluck which had won his suit to pretty Sally Maguire. At last the brave fellow was struck down almost opposite the balcony. Merwyn knew the man was a favorite of the Vosburghs, and he could not bear that the brave fellow should be murdered before his very eyes; yet murdered he apparently was ere Merwyn could reach the street. Like baffled fiends his pursuers closed upon the unfortunate man, pounding him and jumping upon him. And almost instantly the vile hags that followed the marauders like harpies, for the sake of plunder began stripping his body.

"Stop!" thundered Merwyn, the second he reached the scene, and, standing over the prostrate form, he levelled a pistol at the throng. "Now, listen to me," he added. "I don't wish to hurt anybody. You've killed this man, so let his body alone. I know his wife, an Irishwoman, and she ought at least to have his body for decent burial."

"Faix, an he's roight," cried one, who seemed a leader. "We've killed the man. Let his woife have what's left uv 'im;" and the crowd broke away, following the speaker.

This was one of the early indications of what was proved afterwards,--that the mob was hydra-headed, following either its own impulses or leaders that sprung up everywhere.

An abandoned express-wagon stood near, and into this Merwyn, with the help of a bystander, lifted the insensible man. The young fellow then drove, as rapidly as the condition of the streets permitted, to the nearest hospital. A few yards carried him beyond those who had knowledge of the affair, and after that he was unmolested. It was the policy of the rioters to have the bodies of their friends disappear as soon as possible. Poor Ghegan had been stripped to his shirt and drawers, and so was not recognized as a "cop."

Leaving him at the hospital, with brief explanations, Merwyn was about to hasten away, when the surgeon remarked, "The man is dead, apparently."

"I can't help it," cried Merwyn. "I'll bring his wife as soon as possible. Of course you will do all in your power;" and he started away on a run.

A few moments later Barney Ghegan was taken to the dead-house.

CHAPTER XLIII.
THE "COWARD."

MERWYN now felt that he had carried out the first part of his plan. He had looked into the murderous eyes of the mob, and learned its spirit and purpose. Already he reproached himself for leaving Marian alone so long, especially as columns of smoke were rising throughout the northern part of the city. It seemed an age since he had seen that first cloud of the storm, as he emerged from the park after his quiet ride, but it was not yet noon.

As he sped through the streets, running where he dared, and fortunately having enough of the general aspect of a rioter to be unmolested, he noticed a new feature in the outbreak, one that soon became a chief characteristic,--the hatred of negroes and the sanguinary pursuit of them everywhere.

"Another danger for the Vosburghs," he groaned. "They have a colored servant, who must be spirited off somewhere instantly."

Avoiding crowds, he soon reached the quiet side-street on which Marian lived, and was overjoyed to find it almost deserted. Mammy Borden herself answered his impatient ring, and was about to shut the door on so disreputable a person as he now appeared to be, when he shouldered it open, turned, locked and chained it with haste.

"What do you mean, sir? and who are you?" Marian demanded, running from the parlor on hearing the expostulations of her servant.

"Have patience, Miss Vosburgh."

"Oh, it is you, Mr. Merwyn. Indeed I have need of patience. An hour ago papa sent a message from down town, saying: 'Don't leave the house to-day. Serious trouble on foot.' Since then not a word, only wild-looking people running through the street, the ringing of fire-bells, and the sounds of some kind of disturbance.

What does it all mean? and why do you bar and bolt everything so timidly?" and the excited girl poured out her words in a torrent.

Merwyn's first words were exasperating, and the girl had already passed almost beyond self-control. "Has any one seen your colored servant to-day?"

"What if they have? What does your unseemly guise mean? Oh that my brave friends were here to go out and meet the rabble like soldiers! There's an outbreak, of course; we've been expecting it; but certainly MEN should not fear the canaille of the slums. It gives me a sickening impression, Mr. Merwyn, to see you rush in, almost force your way in, and disguised too, as if you sought safety by identifying yourself with those who would quail before a brave, armed man. Pardon me if I'm severe, but I feel that my father is in danger, and if I don't hear from him soon I shall take Mammy Borden as escort and go to his office. Whoever is abroad, they won't molest women, and I'M NOT AFRAID."

"By so doing you would disobey your father, who has told you not to leave the house to-day."

"But I can't bear inaction and suspense at such a time."

"You must bear it, Miss Vosburgh. Seeing the mood you are in, I shall not permit that door to be opened to any one except your father or some one that you recognize."

"You cannot help yourself," she replied, scornfully, approaching the door.

He was there before her, and, taking out the key, put it in his pocket.

"Oh, this is shameful!" she cried, blushing scarlet "Can your fears carry you so far?"

"Yes, and much farther, if needful," he replied, with a grim laugh. "When you are calm enough to listen to me, to be sane and just, I'll explain. Until you are I shall remain master here and protect you and your home." Then, in a tone of stern authority, he added: "Mrs. Borden, sit yonder in that darkened parlor, and don't move unless I tell you to hide. Then hide in earnest, as you value your life."

"Would you not also like a hiding-place provided, Mr. Merwyn?" Marian asked, almost beside herself with anger and anxiety.

His reply was to go to the window and look up and down the still quiet street.

"A respite," he remarked, then turned to the colored woman, and in a tone which she instantly obeyed, said, "Go to that parlor, where you cannot be seen from the street." Then to Marian, "I have no authority over you."

"No, I should hope not. Is there no escape from this intrusion?"

"None for the present," he replied, coldly. "You settled it long since that I was a coward, and now that I am not a gentleman. I shall make no self-defence except to your father, whom I expect momentarily. He cannot leave you alone to-day an instant longer than is unavoidable. I wish to remind you of one thing, however: your soldier friends have long been your pride."

"Oh that these friends were here to day!"

"They would be surprised at your lack of quiet fortitude."

"Must I be humiliated in my own home?"

"You are humiliating yourself. Had you treated me with even your old cool toleration and civility, I would have told you all that has happened since morning; but you have left me no chance for anything except to take the precautions heedful to save your home and yourself. You think I fled here as a disguised fugitive. When shall I forget this crowning proof of your estimate and esteem? You see I did not come unarmed," partially drawing a revolver. "I repeat, you are proud of your soldier friends. You have not learned that the first duty of a soldier is to obey orders; and you have your father's orders. Obey them quietly, and you are under no necessity to speak to me again. When your father comes I will relieve you of my hated presence. If he wishes it, I will still serve you both for his sake, for he always kept a little faith and fairness for me. Now, regard me as a sentinel, a common soldier, to whom you need not speak until your father comes;" and he turned to the windows and began fastening them.

He, too, was terribly incensed. He had come to interpose his life between her and danger, and her words and manner had probed a deep wound that had long been bleeding. The scenes he had witnessed had wrought him up to a mood as stern and uncompromising as the death he soon expected to meet. When utterly off her guard she had shown him, as he believed, her utter contempt and detestation, and at that moment there was not a more reckless man in the city.

But his bitter words and indomitable will had quieted her As he stood motionless upon guard by the window, his was not the attitude of a cowering fugitive. She now admitted that her wild excitement and her disposition to rush to her father, contrary to his injunction, were unworthy of her friends and of herself.

There had been panic that morning in the city, and she had caught the contagion in a characteristic way. She had had no thought of hiding and cowering, but she had been on the eve of carrying out rash impulses. She had given way to uncontrollable excitement; and if her father should learn all she feared he would send her from the city as one not to be trusted. What should she think of that silent, motionless sentinel at the window? Suppose, after all, she had misunderstood and misjudged him,--suppose he HAD come for her protection. In view of this possibility which she had now to entertain, how grossly she had insulted him! If her father came and approved of his course, how could she ever look one so wronged in the face again? She must try to soften her words a little. Woman-like, she believed that she could certainly soothe a man as far as she deemed it judicious, and then leave the future for further diplomacy. Coward, or not, he had now made her afraid of him.

"Mr. Merwyn," she began.

He made no response whatever.

Again, in a lower and more timid voice, she repeated his name.

Without turning, he said: "Miss Vosburgh, I'm on guard. You interfere with my duty. There is no reason for further courtesies between us. If you are sufficiently calm, aid Mrs. Borden in packing such belongings as she actually needs. She must leave this house as soon as possible."

"What!" cried the girl, hotly, "send this faithful old woman out into the streets? Never."

"I did not say, 'out into the streets.' When your father comes one of his first efforts will be to send her to a place of safety. No doubt he has already warned her son to find a hiding-place."

"Great heavens! why don't you explain?"

"What chance have I had to explain? Ah! come here, and all will be plain enough."

She stood at his side and saw a gang of men and boys' chasing a colored man, with the spirit of bloodhounds in their tones and faces.

"Now I'se understan', too, Mass'r Merwyn," said the trembling colored woman, looking over their shoulders.

"Go back," he said, sternly. "If you were seen, that yelling pack of fiends would break into this house as if it were paste-board. Obey orders, both of you, and keep out of sight."

Awed, overwhelmed, they stole to the back parlor; but Marian soon faltered, "O Mr. Merwyn, won't you forgive me?"

He made no reply, and a moment later he stepped to the door. Mr. Vosburgh hastily entered, and Marian rushed into his arms.

"What, Merwyn! you here? Thank God my darling was not alone! Well, Merwyn, you've got to play the soldier now, and so have we all."

"I shall not 'play the soldier';" was the reply, in quick, firm utterance. "But no matter about me, except that my time is limited. I wish to report to you certain things which I have seen, and leave it to your decision whether I can serve you somewhat, and whether Miss Vosburgh should remain in the city. I would also respectfully suggest that your colored servant be sent out of town at once. I offer my services to convey her to New Jersey, if you know of a near refuge there, or else to my place in the country."

"Good God, Merwyn! don't you know that by such an act you take your life in your hand?"

"I have already taken it in my hand, an open hand at that. It has become of little value to me. But we have not a second to lose. I have a very sad duty to perform at once, and only stayed till you came. If you have learned the spirit abroad to-day, you know that your household was and is in danger."

"Alas! I know it only too well. The trouble had scarcely begun before I was using agents and telegraph wires. I have also been to police headquarters. Only the sternest sense of duty to the government kept me so long from my child; but a man at Washington is depending on me for information."

"So I supposed. I may be able to serve you, if you can bring yourself to employ a coward. I shall be at police headquarters, and can bring you intelligence. When not on duty you should be in the streets as little as possible. But, first, I would respectfully suggest that Miss Vosburgh retire, for I have things to say to you which she should not hear."

"This to me, who listened to the story of Gettysburg?"

"All was totally different then."

"And I, apparently, was totally different. I deserve your reproach; I should be sent to the nursery."

"I think you should go and help Mrs. Borden," said Merwyn, quietly.

"It's impossible to send Mammy Borden away just yet,--not till darkness comes to aid our effort," said Mr. Vosburgh, decisively. "You can serve me greatly, Merwyn, and your country also, if you have the nerve. It will require great risks. I tell you so frankly. This is going to prove worse than open battle. O Marian, would to God you were with your mother!"

"In that case I would come to you if I had to walk. I have wronged and insulted you, Mr. Merwyn; I beg your pardon. Now don't waste another moment on me, for I declare before God I shall remain with my father unless taken away by force; and you would soon find that the most fatal course possible."

"Well, these are lurid times. I dreaded the thing enough, but now that it has come so unexpectedly, it is far worse--But enough of this. Mr. Merwyn, are you willing to take the risks that I shall?"

"Yes, on condition that I save you unnecessary risks."

"Oh what a fool I've been!" Marian exclaimed, with one of her expressive gestures.

"Mr. Vosburgh," said Merwyn, "there is one duty which I feel I ought to perform first of all. Mrs. Ghegan, your old waitress, should be taken to her husband."

"What! Barney? What has happened to him?"

"I fear he is dead. I disguised myself as you see--"

"Yes, sensibly. No well-dressed man is safe on some streets."

"Certainly not where I've been. I determined to learn the character of the mob, and I have mingled among them all the morning. I saw the invalid corps put to flight instantly, and the fight with a handful of police that followed. I looked on, for to take part was to risk life and means of knowledge uselessly. The savage, murderous spirit shown on every side also proved that your household might be in danger while you were absent. The police fought bravely and vainly. They were overpowered as a matter of course, and yet the police will prove the city's chief defence. When I saw Barney running and fighting heroically for his life, I couldn't remain spectator any longer, but before I could reach him he was prostrate, senseless, and nearly stripped. With my revolver and a little persuasion I secured his body, and took it to a hospital. A surgeon thought he was dead. I don't know, but that his wife should be informed and go to him seems only common humanity."

"Well, Merwyn, I don't know," said Mr. Vosburgh, dubiously; "we are in the midst of a great battle, and when one is down--Well, the cause must be first, you know. Whether this is a part of the rebellion or not, it will soon be utilized by the Confederate leaders. What I say of Barney I would say of myself and mine,--all private considerations must give--"

"I understand," interrupted Merwyn, impatiently. "But in taking Mrs. Ghegan across town I could see and learn as much as if alone, and she would even be a protection to me. In getting information one will have to use every subterfuge. I think nothing will be lost by this act. From the hospital I will go direct to police headquarters, and stipulate as to my service,--for I shall serve in my own way,--and then, if there is no pressing duty, I will report to you again."

Mr. Vosburgh sprung up and wrung the young fellow's hand as he said: "We have done you great wrong. I, too, beg your pardon. But more than all the city to me is my duty to the general government. To a certain extent I must keep aloof from the actual scenes of violence, or I fail my employers and risk vast interests. If consistently with your ideas of duty you can aid me now, I shall be more grateful than if you saved my life. Information now may be vital to the nation's safety. You may find me at police headquarters an hour or two hence."

"It is settled then, and events will shape future action;" and he was turning hastily away.

A hand fell upon his arm, and never had he looked upon a face in which shame and contrition were so blended.

"What will be your future action towards me?" Marian asked, as she detained him. "Will you have no mercy on the girl who was so weak as to be almost hysterical?"

"You have redeemed your weakness," he replied, coldly. "You are your old high-bred, courageous self, and you will probably cease to think of me as a coward before the day is over. Good-afternoon;" and in a moment he was gone.

"I have offended him beyond hope," she said, as she turned, drooping, to her father.

"Never imagine it, darling," her father replied, with a smile. "His lip quivered as you spoke, and I have learned to read the faintest signs in a man. You have both

been overwrought and in no condition for calm, natural action. Mervvyn will relent. You lost your poise through excitement, not cowardice, and he, young and all
undisciplined, has witnessed scenes that might appall a veteran. But now all must
be courage and action. Since you will remain with me you must be a soldier, and be
armed like one. Come with me to my room, and I will give you a small revolver. I
am glad that you have amused yourself with the dangerous toy, and know how to
use it. Then you must help me plan a disguise which will almost deceive your eyes.
Keeping busy, my dear, will prove the best tonic for your nerves. Mammy Borden,
you must go to your room and stay there till we find a way of sending you to a place
of safety. After you have disappeared for a time I'll tell the other servant that you
have gone away. I sent your son home before I left the office, and he, no doubt, is
keeping out of harm's way."

The old woman courtesied, but there was a dogged, hunted look in her eyes as
she crept away, muttering, "Dis is what Zeb call de 'lan' ob de free!'"

CHAPTER XLIV.
A WIFE'S EMBRACE.

O PAPA," cried Marian, after reaching the library, "we let Mr. Merwyn go without a lunch, and it's nearly two o'clock. Nor do I believe you have had a mouthful since breakfast, and I've forgotten all about providing anything. Oh, how signally I have failed on the first day of battle!"

"You are not the first soldier, by untold millions, who has done so; but you have not shown the white feather yet."

"When I do that I shall expire from shame. You rummage for a disguise, and I'll be back soon."

She hastened to the kitchen, and at a glance saw that the Irish cook had fled, taking not a little with her. The range fire was out, and the refrigerator and the store-closet had been ravaged. She first barred and bolted all the doors, and then the best she could bring her father was crackers and milk and some old Sherry wine; but she nearly dropped these when she saw a strange man, as she supposed, emerge from his bedroom.

Mr. Vosburgh's laugh reassured her, and he said: "I fancy I shall pass among strangers, since you don't know me. Nothing could be better than the milk and crackers. No wine. My head must be clearer to-day than it ever was before. So the Irish Biddy has gone with her plunder? Good riddance to her. She would have been a spy in the camp. I'll bring home food that won't require cooking, and you'll have to learn to make coffee, for Merwyn and others will, no doubt, often come half dead from fatigue. All we can do is to forage in such shops as are open, and you'll have to take the office of commissary at once. You must also be my private secretary. As fast as I write these despatches and letters copy them. I can eat and write at the same time. In an hour I must go out."

"I won't play the fool again," said the girl, doggedly.

"Drink this glass of milk first, while I run down for more, and satisfy my mind as to the fastenings, etc."

"But, papa--"

"Marian," he said, gravely, "you can stay with me only on one condition: you must obey orders."

"That is what Mr. Merwyn said. Oh what a credit I've been to my military friends!" and with difficulty she drank the milk.

"You are a promising young recruit," was the smiling reply. "We'll promote you before the week's out."

In five minutes he was back, cool, yet almost as quick as light in every movement.

The despatches she copied were unintelligible to Marian, but the one to whom they were addressed had the key. The copies of the letters were placed in a secret drawer.

When their tasks were finished, Mr. Vosburgh looked up and down the street and was glad to find it comparatively empty. The storm of passion was raging elsewhere.

He closed all the shutters of the house, giving it a deserted aspect, then said to his daughter. "You must admit no one in my absence, and parley with no one who does not give the password, 'Gettysburg and Little Round Top.' If men should come who say these words, tell them to linger near without attracting attention, and come again after I return. Admit Merwyn, of course, for you know his voice. It is a terrible trial to leave you alone, but there seems to be no prospect of trouble in this locality. At all events, I must do my duty, cost what it may. Be vigilant, and do not worry unnecessarily if I am detained."

"I am bent on retrieving myself, papa; and I'd rather die than be so weak again."

"That's my brave girl. You won't die. After this venture, which I must make at once, I shall be able to take greater precautions;" and with a fond look and kiss, he hastened away through the basement entrance, Marian fastening it securely after him.

We must now follow Merwyn's fortunes for a time. Rapidly, yet vigilantly he made his way up town and crossed Third Avenue. He soon observed that the spirit of lawlessness was increasing. Columns of smoke were rising from various points, indicating burning buildings, and in Lexington Avenue he witnessed the unblushing sack of beautiful homes, from which the inmates had been driven in terror for their lives.

"It will be strange if Mr. Vosburgh's home escapes," he thought. "Some one must know enough of his calling to bring upon him and his the vengeance of the mob. I shall do the best I can for him and his daughter, but to-day has slain the last vestige of hope beyond that of compelling her respect. Wholly off her guard, she showed her deep-rooted detestation, and she can never disguise it again. Regret and mortification at her conduct, a wish to make amends and to show gratitude for such aid as I may give her father, will probably lead her to be very gracious; at the same time I shall ever know that in her heart is a repugnance which she cannot overcome. A woman can never love a man towards whom she has entertained thoughts like hers;" and with much bitter musings, added to his reckless impulses, he made his way to the region in which Mrs. Ghegan had her rooms.

Finding a livery stable near he hired a hack, securing it by threats as well as money, and was soon at the door of the tenement he sought.

Mrs. Ghegan showed her scared, yet pretty face in response to his knock.

"Ye's brought me bad news," she said, instantly, beginning to sob.

"Yes, Mrs. Ghegan; but if you love your husband you will show it now. I have come to take you to him. He has been wounded."

"Is it Mr. Merwyn?"

"Yes; I've just come from Mr. Vosburgh, and he will do what he can for you when he has a chance. They know about your trouble. Now make haste, for we've not a moment to lose in reaching the hospital."

"The Lord knows I love Barney as me loife, an' that I'd go to him through fire and blood. Oi'll kape ye no longer than to tie me bonnet on;" and this she was already doing with trembling fingers.

Locking the door, she took the key with her, and was soon in the hack. Merwyn mounted the box with the driver, knowing that openness was the best safeguard against suspicions that might soon prove fatal. At one point they were surrounded and stopped by the rioters, who demanded explanations.

"Clear out, ye bloody divils!" cried Sally, who did not count timidity among her foibles; "wud ye kape a woman from goin' to her husband, a-dyin' beloikes?"

"Oh, let us pass," said Merwyn, in a loud tone. "A cop knocked her husband on the head, and we are taking her to him."

"Och! ye are roight, me mon. We'll let onybody pass who spakes in her swate brogue;" and the crowd parted.

Reaching the hospital, Sally rushed into the office with the breathless demand, "Where's Barney?"

Merwyn recognized the surgeon he had met before, and said: "You know the man I brought a few hours since. This is his wife."

The surgeon looked grave and hesitated.

"What have ye done wid him?" Sally almost screamed. "Are ye no better than the bloody villains in the strates?"

"My good woman," began the surgeon, "you must be more composed and reasonable. We try to save life when there is life--"

"Where is he?" shrieked the woman.

The surgeon, accustomed to similar scenes, nodded to an attendant, and said, gravely, "Show her."

Merwyn took the poor woman's hand to restrain as well as to reassure her, saying, with sympathies deeply touched, "Mrs. Ghegan, remember you are not friendless, whatever happens."

"Quick! quick!" she said to her guide. "Och! what's a wurld uv frin's if I lose Barney? Poor man! poor man! He once said I blew hot and could, but oi'd give him me loife's blood now."

To Merwyn's sorrow they were led to the dead-house, and there lay the object of their quest, apparently lifeless, his battered face almost past recognition. But Sally knew him instantly, and stared for a moment as if turned to stone; then, with a wild cry, she threw herself upon him, moaning, sobbing, and straining his unconscious form to her breast.

Merwyn felt that it would be best to let her paroxysm of grief expend itself unrestrained; but a bitter thought crossed his mind,--"I may be in as bad a plight as poor Barney before the day closes, yet no one would grieve for me like that."

Suddenly Mrs. Ghegan became still. In her embrace her hand had rested over her husband's heart, and had felt a faint pulsation. A moment later she sprung up and rushed back to the office. Merwyn thought that she was partially demented, and could scarcely keep pace with her.

Bursting in at the door, she cried: "Och! ye bloody spalpanes, to put a loive man where ye did! Come wid me, an' oi'll tache ye that I knows more than ye all."

"Please satisfy her," said Merwyn to the surgeon, who was inclined to ignore what he regarded as the wild ravings of a grief-crazed woman.

"Well, well, if it will do any good; but we have too much to do to-day for those who have a chance--"

"Come on, or oi'll drag ye there," the wife broke in.

"When I've satisfied you, my good woman, you must become quiet and civil. Other wives have lost their husbands--"

But Sally was already out of hearing. Reaching the supposed corpse, the deeply excited woman said, with eyes blazing through her tears, "Put yez hand on his heart."

The surgeon did so, and almost instantly the expression of his face changed, and he said sharply to the attendant, "Bring a stretcher with bearers at once." Then to Sally: "You are right; he is alive, but there was no such pulsation as this when he was brought here. Now be quiet and cheer up, and we may help you save his life. You can stay and take care of him."

Merwyn again took the wife's trembling hand and said, earnestly: "Mrs. Ghegan, obey the surgeon's orders exactly. Be quiet, gentle, and self-controlled, and Barney may outlive us all."

"Faix, Mr. Merwyn, now that oi've hope I'll be whist as a baby asleep. Ye knew me onst as a light, giddy gurl, but oi'll watch over Barney wid such a slapeless eye as wud shame his own mither." And she kept her word. For days and nights her husband remained unconscious, wavering between life and death. The faithful woman, as indifferent to the tumult and havoc in the city as if it were in another land, sat beside him and furthered all efforts in a winning fight.

Merwyn saw him in a hospital ward, surrounded by skilful hands, before he took his leave.

"God bless ye!" Sally began. "If yez hadn't brought me--"

But, pressing her hand warmly, he did not wait to hear her grateful words.

CHAPTER XLV.
THE DECISIVE BATTLE.

MERWYN was now very anxious to reach police headquarters in Mulberry Street, for he felt that the safety of the city, as well as all personal interests dear to him, depended upon adequate and well-organized resistance.

The driver, having been promised a handsome reward to remain, still waited. Indeed, he had gained the impression that Merwyn was in sympathy with the ruthless forces then in the ascendant, and he felt safer in his company than if returning alone.

Mounting the box again, Merwyn directed the driver to make his way through the more open streets to Broadway and 14th Street.

They had not gone far through the disturbed districts when four rough-looking men stopped them, took possession of the hack, and insolently required that they should be driven to Union Square. The last ugly-visaged personage to enter the vehicle paused a moment, drew a revolver, and said, "An' ye don't 'bey orders, this little bull-dog will spake to ye next."

The Jehu looked with a pallid face at Merwyn, who said, carelessly: "It's all right. They are going in my direction."

The quartet within soon began to entertain suspicions of Merwyn, and the one who had last spoken, apparently the leader, thrust his head out of the window and shouted: "Shtop! Who the divil is that chap on the box wid ye?"

"I'll answer for myself," said Merwyn, seeking to employ the vernacular as well as the appearance of an American mechanic. "The driver don't know anything about me. A cop knocked a friend of mine on the head this morning, and I've been taking his wife to him."

The driver now took his cue, and added, "Faix, and a nice, dacent little Irish-woman she was, bedad."

"Then ye're wan wid us?" cried the leader of the gang.

"It looks mighty like it," was the laughing reply. "This would be a poor place for me to hang out, if I was afraid of you or your friends."

"Yez may bet your loife on that. How cooms it ye're so hand-and-glove wid an Irishman, when ye spake no brogue at all?"

"Thunder! man, do you think no one but Irishmen are going to have a fist in this scrimmage? I'm as ready to fight as you are, and am only going down town to join my own gang. Why shouldn't I have an Irishman for a friend, if he's a good fellow, I'd like to know?"

"Beloikes they'll be yez best frin's. All roight. Dhrive on and moind your eye, or the bull-dog will bark."

They ordered a halt several times, while one and another went to a saloon for a drink. It was fast becoming evident that, should there be any want of courage or recklessness, whiskey would supply the lack.

Merwyn preserved nonchalant indifference, even when his disreputable companions were approached by those with whom they were in league, and information and orders were exchanged which he partially overheard. Although much was said in a jargon that he scarcely understood, he gathered that nothing less was on foot than an attack on police headquarters, in the hope of crushing at the start the power most feared. Therefore, while he maintained his mask, every sense was on the alert.

At length they reached Union Square, and the occupants of the hack alighted. Two went east and one west, while the leader said to Merwyn, who had also jumped down: "Take me to your gang. We're afther needing ivery divil's son of 'im widin the next hour or so. It's a big game we're playin' now, me lad, an' see that ye play square and thrue, or your swateheart'll miss ye the noight."

"You'll have to have a bigger crowd on Broadway before you'll get our fellows out," Merwyn replied. "We're not going to face the cops until there's enough on hand to give us a livin' chance."

"There'll be plenty on hand--more'n ye ever seed in yer loife--before ye're an hour older. So lead on, and shtop your palaver. I'm not quite sure on ye yet."

"You soon will be," replied Merwyn, with his reckless and misleading laugh. "My course is down Broadway to Bleecker Street and then west. I can show you as pretty a lot of fellows as you'll want to see, and most of us are armed."

"All roight. Broadway suits me. I want to see if the coast is clear."

"So do I, and what the cops are about in these diggin's. The right thing to do is for all hands to pitch right on to them in Mulberry Street, and then the game's in our own hands."

"If that's the lark we have on foot, can ye promise that yer gang'll join us?"

"Yes, sir, for we'd know that meant business."

"How many could ye muster?"

"I hardly know. We were a-growin' fast when I left."

"Well, lead on loively. Ivery minute now should give me a dozen men, an' we want to start the blaze down this way. I tell ye it's a burning-up town."

"So I should guess from the smoke we see," said Merwyn, with his old laugh. "Jupiter! there comes a squad of cops."

"Well, what do we care? We're two paceable, dacent citizens, a-strollin' down Broadway."

"Oh, I'm not afraid," was the careless reply. "I'm going to see this scrimmage out, and I like the fun. Let's watch the cops cross the street, and see how they are armed."

As the little squad approached Broadway from a side-street, hastening to headquarters, the Hibernian firebrand and his supposed ally stood on the curbstone, A moment later Merwyn struck his companion such a powerful blow on the temple that he fell in the street, almost in front of the officers of the law. The young fellow then sprung upon the stunned and helpless man, and took away his weapons, at the same time, crying: "Secure him. He's a leader of the mob."

"Yes, and you too, my hard hitter," said the sergeant in command.

"I'll go quietly enough, so long as you take him with me. Be quick about it, too, for I have news that should be known at headquarters as soon as possible."

The police now supposed that they recognized one of a band of detectives, everywhere busy about the city in all kinds of disguises,--men of wonderful nerve, who rendered the authorities very important services, and often captured the most dangerous of the ruffianly leaders.

The fellow in question was hustled to his feet, having discovered Merwyn's gang sooner than he desired. The squad pushed through the fast-gathering and bewildered crowd, and soon reached headquarters. The young fellow told his story in the presence of Mr. Vosburgh, who evidently had credentials which secured for him absolute confidence on the part of the authorities.

Merwyn soon learned to recognize in his interlocutor, the superintendent of the metropolitan police, a man to whose active brain, iron will, and indomitable courage, the city chiefly owed its deliverance,--Thomas C. Acton.

Confirmation of the sinister tidings was already coming in fast. The brutal mob that had sacked and burned the Colored Orphan Asylum was moving southward, growing with accessions from different quarters, like a turbulent torrent. Its destination was well understood, and Acton knew that the crisis had come thus early. He frequently conferred with Chief Clerk Seth C. Hawley, upon whom, next to himself, rested the heaviest burdens of those terrific days.

Merwyn offered his services on the force, stipulating, however, that he might be in a measure his own master, since he had other duties to perform, at the same time promising to do his share of the fighting.

Mr. Vosburgh drew Acton to one side, and made a few whispered explanations. Merwyn's request was granted at once, Acton adding, "There will be a general call in the morning papers for the enrolment of citizens as policemen."

The moments were crowded with preparations, counsels, and decisions. The telegraph wires, concentring there from all parts of the city, were constantly ticking off direful intelligence; but the most threatening fact was the movement down Broadway of unknown thousands, maddened by liquor, and confident from their unchecked excesses during the day. They knew that they had only to destroy the handful of men at police headquarters and the city was theirs to plunder and destroy with hyena-like savagery.

Acton, now cognizant of the worst, went to the police commissioners' room and said: "Gentlemen, the crisis has come. A battle must be fought now, and won, too, or all is lost."

None doubted the truth of his word; but who should lead the small force at hand? Inspector Carpenter's name was suggested, for he was known to be a man of great resolution and courage, and leadership naturally fell to him as one of the oldest and most experienced members of the force. Acton instructed him not only that a battle must be fought immediately, but also that it MUST be successful.

Carpenter listened quietly, comprehending both the peril and the necessity; then after a moment's hesitation he rose to his full height, and with an impressive gesture and a terrible oath said, "I will go, and I'll win that fight, or Daniel Carpenter will never come back a live man."

He instantly summoned his insignificant force, and the order, "Fall in, men," resounded through the street.

Merwyn, with a policeman's coat buttoned over his blouse, avowed his purpose of going with them; and his exploit of the afternoon, witnessed and bruited by members of the force, made his presence welcome.

It was now between five and six in the evening. The air was hot and sultry, and in the west lowered heavy clouds, from which the thunder muttered. Emblematic they seemed to such as heeded them in the intense excitement.

Few in the great city at that hour were so deeply stirred as Merwyn. The tremendous excitements of the day, to which his experience at Mr. Vosburgh's residence had chiefly contributed, were cumulative in their effect. Now he had reached the goal of his hope, and had obtained an opportunity, far beyond his wildest dreams, to redeem his character from the imputation of cowardice. He was part of the little force which might justly be regarded as a "forlorn hope." The fate of the city depended upon its desperate valor, and no one knew this better than he, who, from early morning, had witnessed the tiger-spirit of the mob. If the thousands, every minute approaching nearer, should annihilate the handful of men who alone were present to cope with them, that very night the city would be at the mercy of the infuriated rioters, and not a home would be secure from outrage.

The column of police was formed scarcely two hundred strong. Merwyn, as a new recruit, was placed in its rear, a position that he did not mean to keep when the fight should begin. Like the others, he was armed with a locust-club, but he had two revolvers on his person, and these he knew how to use with fatal precision. From an open window Superintendent Acton shouted, "Inspector Carpenter, my orders are, Make no arrests, bring no prisoners, but kill--kill every, time."

It was to be a life-and-death struggle. The mob would have no mercy: the officers of the law were commanded to show none.

As Carpenter went forward to the head of his column, his face as dark with his sanguinary puipose as the lowering west, Merwyn saw that Mr. Vosburgh, quiet and observant, was present.

The government officer, with his trained instincts, knew just where to be, in order to obtain the most vital information. He now joined Merwyn, and was struck by his extreme pallor, a characteristic of the young fellow under extreme emotion.

"Mr. Merwyn," he said, hastily, "you have done enough for two to-day, You need rest. This is going to be a desperate encounter."

"Forward!" shouted Carpenter.

A proud smile lighted up Merwyn's features, as he said: "Good-by. Thank you for such faith as you have had in me;" and he moved off with the others.

Mr. Vosburgh muttered, "I shall see this fight, and I shall solve that embodied mystery whom we have thought a coward;" and he followed so near as to keep Merwyn under his eye.

A black, sulphurous cloud was rising in the west. This little dark blue column approaching from the east, marching down Bleecker Street, was insignificant in comparison, yet it was infinitely the more dangerous, and charged with forces that would scatter death and wounds such as the city had never witnessed.

No words were spoken by the resolute men. The stony pavement echoed their measured, heavy tread. Turning into Broadway they saw the enemy but a block and a half away, a howling mob, stretching northward as far as the eye could reach. It was sweeping the thoroughfare, thousands in line. Pedestrians, stages, vehicles of all kinds, were vanishing down side-streets. Pallid shopkeepers were closing their stores as sailors take in sail before a cyclone.

Carpenter halted his command, and sent small detachments up parallel side-streets, that they might come around and fall upon the flanks of the mob.

As these men were moving off on the double-quick, Merwyn left his squad and said to Carpenter: "I am a citizen, and I stipulated that I should fight as I chose. I choose to fight with you."

"Well, well, so long as you fight," was the hasty answer. "You shall have plenty of it, if you keep near me." Then he added, sternly: "Mark you, young fellow, if you show the white feather I'll knock you over myself. Those devils yonder must be taught that the one thing this force can't do is run."

"Brain me if I do not do my whole duty," was the firm reply; and he took his place at the right of the front rank.

A moment later he was startled by Mr. Vosburgh, who seized his hand and said, earnestly: "Merwyn, no man ever did a braver thing than you are doing now. I can't forgive myself that I wronged you in my thoughts."

"You had reason. I'm doing no better than these other men, and I have a thousand-fold their motive." Then he added, gravely, "I do not think you ought to be here and your daughter alone."

"I know my duty," was the quiet reply; "and there are those who must be informed of the issue of this fight as soon as it is over. Once more, farewell, my brave friend;" and he disappeared.

Carpenter was holding his force until his flanking detachments should reach their co-operative points. When the mob saw the police, it advanced more slowly, as if it, too, instinctively recognized that the supreme crisis was near. In the van of the dense mass a large board was borne aloft, inscribed with the words, "No Draft!" and beside it, in mocking irony, floated the stars and stripes.

The hesitation of the rioters was but brief. They mistook the inaction of the few policemen opposed to them for timidity, and the immense masses behind pushed them forward. Therefore, with a new impetus, the howling, yelling throng approached, and Merwyn could distinguish the features of the liquor-inflamed, maddened faces that were already becoming familiar to him. In the sultry July evening the greater part of the rioters were in their shirt-sleeves, and they were armed with every description of weapon, iron bars, clubs, pitchforks, barrel-staves, and not a few with guns and pistols.

Carpenter stood out before his men, watching the approach of his victims with an expression which only the terrible excitement of battle can produce. His men, behind him, were like statues. Suddenly his stentorian command rang out,--

"BY THE RIGHT FLANK, COMPANY FRONT! DOUBLE-QUICK! CHARGE!"

As if the lever of a powerful engine had been pressed, all clubs were raised aloft, and with swift, even tread the trained, powerful men rushed after their leader, who kept several paces ahead.

When such a disciplined force, with such a leader, have resolved to fight till they die, their power is not to be estimated by numbers. They smote the astonished van of the mob like a thunderbolt, Carpenter leading by several steps, his face aflame with his desperate resolve. He dealt the first blow, sending down, bleeding and senseless, a huge ruffian who was rushing upon him with a club. A second later the impetuous officer was in the midst of the mob, giving deadly blows right and left.

His men closed up with him instantly, Merwyn being among the first to reach his side, and for a few moments the thud of clubs on human skulls was heard above every other sound. Mr. Vosburgh, keeping a little to the rear on the sidewalk, watched Merwyn, who held his attention almost equally with the general issues of this decisive battle. The youth was dealing blows like an athlete, and keeping pace with the boldest. The windows of the buildings on Broadway were now crowded by thousands witnessing the conflict, while Mr. Vosburgh, following closely, heard the ominous "sing" of more than one bullet. The man who had come that day to the protection of his home and child should not be left to the mercy of strangers, should he fall. To his surprise he soon saw that Merwyn had shifted his club to his left hand, and that he was fighting with a revolver. He watched the young fellow with renewed interest, and observed that his aim was as deliberate as it was quick, and that often when he fired some prominent figure in the mob dropped.

"By all the powers! if he is not coolly shooting the leaders, and picking out his man every time!" ejaculated the astonished officer.

The police made a clean sweep of the street, and only prostrate forms were left in their rear. Therefore Mr. Vosburgh could almost keep pace with Merwyn.

The rioters soon became appalled at their punishment. Like a dark blue wave, with bloody clubs forming a crimson crest, that unfaltering rank of men steadily advanced and ingulfed them. All within reach went down. Those of the police who were wounded still fought on, or, if disabled, the ranks closed up, and there was no cessation in the fatal hail of blows. The rioters in front would have given way, had not the thousands in their rear pressed them forward to their fate.

The judicious Carpenter had provided for this feature of the strife, for now his detachments were smiting both flanks of the human monster with the same terrific vengeance dealt upon its head. The undisciplined herd fought desperately for a time, then gave way to panic and the wild effort to escape. Long since a policeman had seized the national flag, and bore it triumphantly with his left hand while he fought with his right. The confusion and uproar were beyond description. The rioters were yelling their conflicting views as to what ought to be done, while others were shouting to those in their rear to cease crowding forward. The pressure down Broadway now came from a desire to escape the police. In brief, a large section of the mob was hemmed in, and it surged backwards and forwards and up against the stores, while hundreds, availing themselves of the side-streets, ran for their lives. In a very short time what had been a compact, threatening mass was flying in fragments, as if disrupted by dynamite, but the pursuing clubs of Carpenter's men never ceased their levelling blows while a rioter's head was in reach. Far northward the direful tidings of defeat spread through the ragged hosts as yet unharmed, and they melted away, to come together again and again during the lurid days and nights which followed.

The Gettysburg of the conflict had been fought and won. Unspeakable outrages and heavy battles were yet to come; but this decisive victory gave the authorities advantage which they never lost, and time to organize more effective resistance with the aid of the military. The police saved the city.

Broadway looked like a battle-field, prostrate forms strewing its crimsoned pavement throughout the area of the conflict. The majority were left where they fell, and were carried off by their friends.

As the melee was drawing to a close, Mr. Vosburgh saw Merwyn chasing a man who apparently had had much influence with his associates, and had been among the last to yield. After a brief pursuit the young fellow stopped and fired. The man struggled on a few steps, then fell. Merwyn, panting, sat down on the curbstone, and here Mr. Vosburgh joined him with radiant face, exclaiming, as he wrung the young man's hand: "I've seen it all,--seen how you smote them hip and thigh. Never has my blood been so stirred. The city is saved. When a mob is thus dealt with it soon gives up. Come, you have done more than your part. Go with me, and as soon as I have sent a despatch about this glorious victory, we'll have supper and a little rest."

"Impossible, Mr. Vosburgh. The inspector has heard that the mob is sacking the mayor's house, and we have orders to march there at once. I'll get my wind in a moment."

"But you are not under obligations, in view of all you have done."

"I'm going to see this fight out. If the force were ordered back to headquarters I'd go with you."

"But you will come soon?"

"Yes; when the fighting is over for the night I'll bring the latest news. There, the men are falling in for their march up Broadway, and I must go."

"Well, I congratulate you. No soldier ever won greener laurels in so short a time. What's more, you were cool enough to be one of the most effective of the force. I saw you picking off the leaders. Good-by;" and he hastened away, while Merwyn followed Carpenter and the captured flag to a new scene of battle.

CHAPTER XLVI.
"I HAVE SEEN THAT YOU DETEST ME."

After her father had left her on that eventful afternoon, Marian felt as if alone in a beleaguered fortress. The familiar streets in which she had trundled her hoop as a child, and until to-day walked without fear, were now filled with nameless terrors. She who had been so bent on going out in the morning would now as readily stroll in a tiger-infested jungle as to venture from her door. When men like her father used such language and took such precautions as she had anxiously noted, she knew that dangers were manifold and great, that she was in the midst of the most ruthless phase of war.

But her first excitement had passed, and it had brought her such lessons that now her chief thought was to retrieve herself. The one who had dwelt in her mind as so weak and unmanly as to be a constant cause of irritation had shown himself to be her superior, and might even equal the friends with whom she had been scornfully contrasting him. That she should have spoken to him and treated him as she had done produced boundless self-reproach, while her egregious error in estimating his character was humiliating in the last degree.

"Fool! fool!" she said, aloud, "where was your woman's intuition?"

Marian had much warm blood in her veins and fire in her spirit, and on provocation could become deeply incensed at others, as we have seen; but so devoid of petty vanity was she that she could be almost equally angry at herself. She did not share her father's confidence that Merwyn would relent under a few smiles, for she knew how deeply she had wounded and wronged him, and she believed that he possessed a will as steadfast as fate. The desire to test her father's theory, the hope to atone for her wrong judgment, grew so strong and absorbing as to make the awful fact of the riot secondary in her thoughts.

To get through the hours she felt that she must keep incessantly busy. She first went to her own room, packed valuables and jewels in a convenient form to carry if there should be cause for a hasty exit, then concealed them. Going to her mother's and father's room, she acted in view of the same possible necessity, all the while carrying on the distinct process of thought in regard to Merwyn, dwelling on their past relations, but above all questioning his course when they should meet again.

Suddenly she reproached herself with forgetfulness of Mammy Borden. True, not much time had passed; but the poor creature, after what she had heard, should be reassured frequently. She went to the attic room, but it was empty. On inspection it became evident that the colored woman had made up her little bundle and departed. Calling as she went down through the house, Marian reached the basement and saw that its door had been unfastened.

"She has gone to join her son," said the girl, as she hastily rebolted and barred the door. "Oh what awful imprudence! Perhaps she also wished to relieve us of the danger of her presence. Well, I am now alone in very truth. I could now give Mr. Merwyn a very different reception. He and papa will be here soon perhaps. Oh, I wish I knew how to make coffee, but I can't even kindle a fire in the range. I have proved myself to-day a fine subject for a soldier. My role is to listen, in elegant costume, to heroic deeds, and to become almost hysterical in the first hour of battle. O 'Missy S'wanee,' I make a sorry figure beside you, facing actual war and cheering on your friends!"

Thus she passed the time in varied and bitter soliloquy while putting the kitchen and closets in order, and in awkward attempts to remove the debris of the last fire from the range. The gas gave light for her efforts, for the closed shutters darkened the apartment.

She was startled by a tap at the door.

"Well?" she faltered, after a moment's hesitation.

"'Gettysburg and Little Round Top,'" was the response.

"Mr. Vosburgh is out, and left word that you should linger near till he returned and then come again."

"I cannot do that. It would not be safe for either him or me. He does not realize. Can you be trusted?"

"I am his daughter."

"Say, then, terrible work up town. The orphan asylum sacked and burned. Many private residences also. The mob having its own way. A crowd is coming, and I must not be seen here. Will be back to-night if possible;" and the unseen communicator of dismal intelligence went westward with hasty steps.

Marian trembled as she heard the confused, noisy tread of many feet. Hastening to the second story, she peeped through the blinds, and shuddered as she saw a fragment of the mob which had been defeated on Broadway, returning to their haunts on the west side. Baffled and infuriated, they made the street echo with their obscene words and curses. Her heart almost stood still as they approached her door, and with white, compressed lips she grasped her revolver; but the rioters passed on like a flock of unclean birds, and the street became quiet again.

She was now so anxious about her father that she maintained her position of observation. The coming storm lowering in the west oppressed her with its terrible symbolism. Already the street was darkening, while from other parts of the city came strange sounds.

"Oh, if papa should never come back,--if the mob should have its own way everywhere! To think of staying here alone to-night! Would HE come again after my treatment this morning?"

She was aroused from her deep and painful revery by a knocking on the basement door. Hastening down she was overjoyed to hear her father's voice, and when he entered she clung to him, and kissed him with such energy that his heavy beard came off, and his disguising wig was all awry.

"O papa!" she cried, "I'm so glad you are back safe! A body of rioters passed through the street, and the thought of your falling into such hands sickened me with fear;" and then she breathlessly told him of all that had occurred, and of Mammy Borden's disappearance.

He reassured her gently, yet strongly, and her quick ear caught the ring of truth in his words.

"I, too, have much to tell you," he said, "and much to do; so we must talk as we work. First help me to unpack and put away these provisions. This evening I must get a stout German woman that I know of to help you. You must not be left alone again, and I have another plan in mind for our safety. I think the worst is over, but it is best not to entertain a sense of false security for a moment in these times. The mob has been thoroughly whipped on Broadway. I'll tell you all about it after we have had a good cup of coffee and a little supper. Now that there is a respite I find I'm almost faint myself from reaction and fatigue."

"Have you seen--do you think Mr. Merwyn will be here again?"

"I've seen him, and so have others, to their sorrow. 'Coward,' indeed!" He threw back his head and laughed. "I only wish I had a regiment of such cowards, and I could abolish the mob in twenty-four hours. But I'll tell you the whole story after supper is ready, and will show how quickly a soldier can get up a meal in an emergency. You must go into training as a commissary at once."

Her father seemed so genuinely hopeful and elated that Marian caught his spirit and gave every faculty to the task of aiding him. Now that he was with her, all fears and forebodings passed; the nearer roll of the thunder was unheeded except as it called out the remark, "It will be too bad if Mr. Merwyn is out in the storm."

Again her father laughed, as he said, "All the thunder gusts that have raged over the city are nothing to the storm which Merwyn has just faced."

"O papa, you make me half wild with curiosity and impatience. Must I wait until the coffee boils?"

"No," was the still laughing reply. "What is more, you shall have another surprising experience; you shall eat your supper--for the first time, I imagine--in the kitchen. It will save time and trouble, and some of my agents may appear soon. Well, well, all has turned out, so far, better than I ever hoped. I have been able to keep track of all the most important movements; I have seen a decisive battle, and have sent intelligence of everything to Washington. A certain man there cannot say that I have failed in my duty, unexpected and terrible as has been the emergency. By morning the military from the forts in the harbor will be on hand. One or two more such victories, and this dragon of a mob will expire."

"Papa, should not something be done to find and protect Mammy Borden?"

"Yes, as soon as possible; but we must make sure that the city's safe, and our own lives secure before looking after one poor creature. She has undoubtedly gone to her son, as you suggest. After such a scare as she has had she will keep herself and him out of sight. They are both shrewd and intelligent for their race, and will, no doubt, either hide or escape from the city together. Rest assured she went out heavily veiled and disguised. She would have said good-by had she not feared you would detain her, and, as you say, her motive was probably twofold. She saw how she endangered us, and, mother-like, she was determined to be with her son."

"Come, papa, the coffee's boiled, and supper, such as it is, is on the table. Hungry as I am, I cannot eat till you have told me all."

"All about the fight?"

"Yes, and--and--Well, what part did Mr. Merwyn take in it?"

"Ah, now I am to recite MY epic. How all is changed since Blauvelt kindled your eyes and flushed your cheeks with the narration of heroic deeds! Then we heard of armies whose tread shook the continent, and whose guns have echoed around the world. Men, already historic for all time, were the leaders, and your soldier friends were clad in a uniform which distinguished them as the nation's defenders. My humble hero had merely an ill-fitting policeman's coat buttoned over his soiled, ragged blouse. Truly it is fit that I should recite his deeds in a kitchen and not in a library. When was the heroic policeman sung in homeric verse before? When--"

"O papa, papa! don't tantalize me. You cannot belittle this struggle or its consequences. Our enemies are at our very doors, and they are not soldiers. I would rather face scalping Indians than the wretches that I saw an hour since. If Merwyn will do a man's part to quell this mob I shall feel honored by his friendship. But he never will forgive me, never, never."

"We'll see about that," was Mr. Vosburgh's smiling reply. Then his face became grave, and he said: "You are right, Marian. The ruffians who filled the streets to-day, and who even now are plundering and burning in different parts of the city, are not soldiers. They are as brutal as they are unscrupulous and merciless. I can only tell you what has occurred in brief outline, for the moment I am a little rested and have satisfied hunger I must be at work."

He then rapidly narrated how Merwyn had been brought in at police headquarters with one of the leaders of the riot whom he had beguiled and helped to capture. A graphic account of the battle followed, closing with the fact that he had left the "coward" marching up Broadway to engage in another fight.

The girl listened with pale cheeks and drooping head.

"He will never forgive me," she murmured; "I've wronged him too deeply."

"Be ready to give him a generous cup of coffee and a good supper," her father replied. "Men are animals, even when heroes, and Merwyn will be in a condition to bless the hand that feeds him to-night. Now I must carry out my plans with despatch. Oh, there is the rain. Good. Torrents, thunder, and lightning will keep away more dangerous elements. Although I have but a slight acquaintance with the Erkmanns, whose yard abuts upon ours, I hope, before the evening is over, to have a door cut in the fence between us, and a wire stretched from our rear windows to theirs. It will be for our mutual safety. If attacked we can escape through their house or they through ours. I'll put on my rubber suit and shall not be gone long now at any one time. You can admit Merwyn or any of my agents who give the password. Keep plenty of coffee and your own courage at boiling-point. You will next hear from me at our back door."

In less than half an hour she again admitted her father, who said: "It's all arranged. I have removed a couple of boards so that they can be replaced by any one who passes through the opening. I have some fine wire which I will now stretch from my library to Mr. Erkmann's sleeping-apartment."

When he again entered the house two of his agents whom Marian had admitted were present, dripping wet, hungry, and weary. They had come under cover of the storm and darkness. While they gave their reports Mr. Vosburgh made them take a hearty supper, and Marian waited on them with a grace that doubled their incentive to serve their chief. But more than once she sighed, "Merwyn does not come."

Then the thought flashed upon her: "Perhaps he cannot come. He may be battered and dying in the muddy streets."

The possibility of this made her so ill and faint that she hastily left the apartment and went up to the darkened drawing-room, where her father found her a moment later seeking to stifle her sobs.

"Why, Marian, darling, you who have kept up so bravely are not going to give way now."

"I'm not afraid for myself," she faltered, "but Mr. Merwyn does not come. You said he was marching to another fight. He may be wounded; he may be--" her voice fell to a whisper--"he may be dead."

"No, Marian," replied her father, confidently, "that young fellow has a future. He is one of those rare spirits which a period like this develops, and he'll take no common part in it. He has probably gone to see if his own home is safe. Now trust God and be a soldier, as you promised."

"I couldn't bear to have anything happen to him and I have no chance to make amends, to show I am not so weak and silly as I appeared this morning."

"Then let him find you strong and self-controlled when he appears. Come down now, for I must question my agents while they are yet at supper; then I must go out, and I'll leave them for your protection till I return."

He put his arm about her, and led her to the stairway, meanwhile thinking, "A spell is working now which she soon will have to recognize."

By the time his agents had finished their meal, Mr. Vosburgh had completed his examination of them and made his notes. He then placed a box of cigars on the table, instructed them about admitting Merwyn should he come, and with his daughter went up to the library, where he wrote another long despatch.

"After sending this," he said, "and getting the woman I spoke of, I will not leave you again to-night, unless there should be very urgent necessity. You can sit in the darkened front room, and watch till either I or Merwyn returns."

This she did and listened breathlessly.

The rain continued to pour in torrents, and the lightning was still so vivid as to blind her eyes at times, while the crashes of thunder often drowned the roar of the unquiet city; but undaunted, tearless, motionless, she watched the deserted street and listened for the footfall of one whom she had long despised, as she had assured herself.

An hour passed. The storm was dying away, and still he did not come. "Alas!" she sighed, "he is wounded; if not by the rabble, certainly by me. I know now what it has cost him to be thought a coward for months, and must admit that I don't understand him at all. How vividly come back the words he spoke last December, 'What is the storm, and what the danger, to that which I am facing?' What was he facing? What secret and terrible burden has he carried patiently through all my coldness and scorn? Oh, why was I such an idiot as to offend him mortally just as he was about to retrieve himself and render papa valuable assistance,--worse still, when he came to my protection!"

The gloomy musings were interrupted by the sound of a carriage driven rapidly up town in a neighboring street. It stopped at the corner to the east, and a man alighted and came towards the Vosburgh residence. A moment later Marian whispered, excitedly, "It's Mr. Merwyn."

He approached slowly and she thought warily, and began mounting the steps.

"Is it Mr. Merwyn?;" she called.

"Yes."

"I will admit you at the basement door;" and she hastened down. She meant to give her hand, to speak in warm eulogy of his action, but his pale face and cold glance as he entered chilled her. She felt tongue-tied in the presence of the strangers who sat near the table smoking.

Merwyn started slightly on seeing them, and then she explained, hastily, "These gentlemen are assisting my father in a way you understand."

He bowed to them, then sank into a chair, as if too weary to stand.

"Mr. Merwyn," she began, eagerly, "let me make you some fresh coffee. That on the range is warm, but it has stood some little time."

"Please do not take the slightest trouble," he said, decidedly. "That now ready will answer. Indeed, I would prefer it to waiting. I regret exceedingly that Mr. Vosburgh is not at home, for I am too exhausted to wait for him. Can I not help myself?" and he rose and approached the range.

"Not with my permission," she replied, with a smile, but he did not observe it. She stole shy glances at him as she prepared the coffee. Truly, as he sat, drooping in his chair, wet, ragged, and begrimed, he presented anything but the aspect of a hero. Yet as such he appeared in her eyes beyond all other men whom she had ever seen.

She said, gently: "Let me put the coffee on the table, and get you some supper. You must need it sorely."

"No, I thank you. I could not eat anything to-night;" and he rose and took the coffee from her hand, and drank it eagerly. He then said, "I will thank you for a little more."

With sorrow she noted that he did not meet her eyes or relax his distant manner.

"I wish you could wait until papa returns," she said, almost entreatingly, as she handed him a second cup.

"I hope Mr. Vosburgh will pardon my seeming lack of courtesy, and that you will also, gentlemen. It has been a rather long, hard day, and I find that I have nearly reached the limit of my powers." With a short, grim laugh, he added: "I certainly am not fit to remain in the presence of a lady. I suppose, Miss Vosburgh, I may report what little I have to say in the presence of these gentlemen? I would write it out if I could, but I cannot to-night."

"I certainly think you may speak freely before these gentlemen," was her reply.

"Mr. Vosburgh trusts us implicitly, and I think we are deserving of it," said one of the agents.

"Why need you go out again when you are so weary?" Marian asked. "I am expecting papa every moment, and I know he would like you to stay with him."

"That would be impossible. Besides, I have some curiosity to learn whether I have a home left. My report in brief amounts to little more than this. Soon after our return from the mayor's residence on Broadway we were ordered down to Printing-House Square. Intelligence that an immense mob was attacking the Tribune Office had been received. Our hasty march thither, and the free use of the club on our arrival, must account for my present plight. You see, gentlemen, that I am not a veteran, only a raw recruit. In a day or two I shall be more seasoned to the work. You may say to your father, Miss Vosburgh, that the mob had been broken before we arrived. We met them on their retreat across City-Hall Park, and nothing was left for us but the heavy, stupid work of knocking a good many of the poor wretches on the head. Such fighting makes me sick; yet it is imperative, no doubt. Inspector Carpenter is at City Hall with a large force, and the rioters are thoroughly dispersed. I think the lower part of the city will be quiet for the night."

"You were wise, Mr. Merwyn, to ride up town," said Marian, gravely. "I know well that you have been taxed to-day beyond the strength of any veteran."

"How did you know that I rode up town?"

"I was watching for papa, and saw you leave your carriage."

"I could never have reached home had I not secured a cab, and that reminds me that it is waiting around the corner; at least, the driver promised to wait. I shall now say good-night. Oh, by the way, in the press of other things I forgot to say that Mrs. Ghegan reached her husband, and that her good nursing, with surgical help, will probably save his life."

Bowing to the agents, who had been listening and watching him with great curiosity, he turned to the door.

Marian opened it for him, and, stepping out into the dusky area, said, "I see that you do not forgive me."

"And I have seen, to-day, Miss Vosburgh, that you detest me. You showed the truth plainly when off your guard. Your own pride and sense of justice may lead you to seek to make amends for an error in your estimate of me. Having convinced you that I am not a coward, I have accomplished all that I can hope for, and I'm in no mood for hollow courtesies. I shall do everything in my power to aid your father until the trouble is over or I am disabled, and then will annoy you no more. Good-night;" and he strode away, with a firm, rapid step, proving that his pride for a moment had mastered his almost mortal weariness.

Marian returned to her post in the second story to watch for her father, her ears tingling, and every faculty confused, while excited, by the words Merwyn had spoken. He had revealed his attitude towards her clearly, and, as she grew calmer, she saw it was not a mere question of the offence she had given him that morning which she had to face, but rather a deep-rooted conviction that he was personally detested.

"If he knew how far this is from the truth NOW!" she thought, with a smile.

Then the query presented itself: "How far is it from the truth? Why am I thinking more of him than of the riot, our danger, yes, even my father?"

In the light of that lurid day much had been revealed to her, and before her revery ceased she understood her long months of irritation and anger at Merwyn's course; she saw why she had not dismissed him from her thoughts with contemptuous indifference and why she had ingeniously wrought the MacIan theory of constitutional timidity. When had she given so much thought to a man whom she had disliked? Even in her disapproval of him, even when her soldier friends appeared at their best and she was contrasting him with them to his fatal disadvantage as she believed, thoughts of him would pursue her constantly. Now that he had shown himself the peer of each and all in manhood and courage, it seemed as if feelings, long held in check, were released and were sweeping irresistibly towards one conclusion. Merwyn was more to her than any other man in the world. He had fulfilled her ideal, and was all the more attractive because he was capable of such deep, strong passion, and yet could be so resolute and cool.

"But how can I ever undeceive him?" was her most perplexing thought. "I cannot make advances. Well, well, the future must disentangle itself."

Now that she was beginning to understand herself, every instinct of her being led towards reserve. In a misunderstanding with her soldier friends she could easily and frankly effect a reconciliation, but she must be dumb with Merwyn, and distant in manner, to the degree that she was self-conscious.

Suddenly she became aware that it was growing late, and that her father had not returned, and for the next hour she suffered terribly from anxiety, as did many women in those days of strange vicissitudes.

At last, a little before midnight, he came, looking stern and anxious. "I will soon explain," he said to her. "Take this woman to her room." Then, to his aroused and sleepy agents: "You have had some rest and respite. Go to the nearest hotel and take a little more, but be up with the dawn and do your best, for to-morrow promises to be worse than to-day."

With a few further instructions he dismissed them.

Upon reaching the library he said to his daughter: "I've been at a conference in which the police, military, and state authorities took part, and things look gloomy. I have also sent further despatches. My dear child, I wish you were with your mother, but I'm too weary to think any more to-night."

"Papa, the question of my remaining has been settled. Now rest. Mr. Merwyn came and brought good news."

"Yes, I know all about it. Why did he not stay?"

"He naturally wished to return and look after his own home."

"True enough. I hope he found it unharmed. He has proved himself a grand, brave fellow to-day, and I only wish it was my privilege to fight at his side. It would be far easier than to carry my burden."

"Not another perplexing thought to-night, papa."

"Well, Marian, I must have some sleep, to be equal to to-morrow. You must obey orders and sleep also. I shall not take off my clothes, and shall be ready for any emergency; and do you also sleep in your wrapper."

He kissed her fondly, but with heavy eyes.

CHAPTER XLVII.
A FAIR FRIEND AND FOUL FOES.

THE reader has already discovered that I have not attempted anything approaching a detailed history of the dreadful days of the riot. I merely hope to give a somewhat correct impression of the hopes, fears, and passions which swayed men's minds and controlled or directed their action. Many of the scenes are too horrible to be described, and much else relating to the deeds and policy of recognized leaders belongs to the sober page of history. The city was in awful peril, and its destruction would have crippled the general government beyond all calculation. Unchecked lawlessness in New York would soon have spread to other centres. That cool, impartial historian, the Comte de Paris, recognized the danger in his words: "Turbulent leaders were present in the large cities of the East, which contained all the elements for a terrible insurrection. This insurrection was expected to break out in New York, despite Lee's defeat: one may judge what it might have been had Lee achieved a victory."

With the best intentions the administration had committed many grave errors,--none more so, perhaps, than that of ordering the draft to be inaugurated at a time when the city was stripped of its militia.

Now, however, it only remained for the police and a few hundreds of the military to cope with the result of that error,--a reckless mob of unnumbered thousands, governed by the instinct to plunder and destroy.

When the sun dawned in unclouded splendor on the morning of the 14th of July, a superficial observer, passing through the greater part of the city, would not have dreamed that it could become a battle-ground, a scene of unnumbered and untold outrages, during the day. It was hard for multitudes of citizens, acquainted with what had already taken place, to believe in the continuance of such lawlessness. In large districts there was an effort to carry on business as usual. In the early hours vehicles of every kind rattled over the stony pavement, and when at last Merwyn awoke, the sounds that came through his open windows were so natural that the events of the preceding day seemed but a distorted dream. The stern realities of the past and the future soon confronted him, however, and he rang and ordered breakfast at once.

Hastily disguising himself as he had done before, he again summoned his faithful servant. This man's vigilance had enabled him to admit his master instantly the night before. Beyond the assurance that all was well and safe Merwyn had not then listened to a word, yielding to the imperative craving for sleep and rest. These, with youth and the vigor of a strong, unvitiated constitution, had restored him wonderfully, and he was eager to enter on the perils and duties of the new day. His valet and man-of-all-work told him that he had been at pains to give the impression that the family was away and the house partially dismantled.

"It wouldn't pay ye," he had said to a band of plunderers, "to bother with the loikes of this house when there's plenty all furnished."

With injunctions to maintain his vigilance and not to be surprised if Merwyn's absence was prolonged, the young man hastened away, paving no heed to entreaties to remain and avoid risks.

It was still early, but the uneasy city was waking, and the streets were filling with all descriptions of people. Thousands were escaping to the country; thousands more were standing in their doors or moving about, seeking to satisfy their curiosity; while in the disaffected districts on the east and the west side the hosts of the mob were swarming forth for the renewal of the conflict, now inspired chiefly by the hope of plunder. Disquiet, anxiety, fear, anger, and recklessness characterized different faces, according to the nature of their possessors; but as a rule even the most desperate of the rioters were singularly quiet except when under the dominion of some immediate and exciting influence.

In order to save time, Merwyn had again hired a hack, and, seated with the driver, he proceeded rapidly, first towards the East River, and then, on another street, towards the Hudson. His eyes, already experienced, saw on every side the promise of another bloody day. He was stopped and threatened several times, for the rioters were growing suspicious, fully aware that detectives were among them, but he always succeeded in giving some plausible excuse. At last, returning from the west side, the driver refused to carry him any longer, and gave evidence of sympathy with the mob.

Merwyn quietly showed him the butt of a revolver, and said, "You will drive till I dismiss you."

The man yielded sullenly, and Merwyn alighted near Mr. Vosburgh's residence, saying to his Jehu, "Your course lies there," pointing east,--and he rapidly turned a corner.

As Merwyn had surmised, the man wheeled his horses with the purpose of following and learning his destination. Observing this eager quest he sprung out upon him from a doorway and said, "If you try that again I'll shoot you as I would a dog." The fellow now took counsel of discretion.

Going round the block to make sure he was not observed, Merwyn reached the residence of Mr. Vosburgh just as that gentleman was rising from his breakfast, and received a cordial welcome.

"Why, Merwyn," he exclaimed, "you look as fresh as a June daisy this morning."

The young fellow had merely bowed to Marian, and now said, "I cannot wonder at your surprise, remembering the condition in which I presented myself last night."

"Condition? I do not understand."

Marian laughed, as she said: "Papa came in about midnight in scarcely better plight. In brief, you were both exhausted, and with good reason."

"But you did not tell me, Marian--"

"No," she interrupted; "nothing but a life-and-death emergency should have made me tell you anything last night."

"Why, our little girl is becoming a soldier and a strategist. I think you had better make your report over again, Mr. Merwyn;" and he drew out a fuller account of events than had been given the evening before, also the result of the young man's morning observations.

Marian made no effort to secure attention beyond offering Merwyn a cup of coffee.

"I have breakfasted," he said, coldly.

"Take it, Merwyn, take it," cried Mr. Vosburgh. "Next to courage, nothing keeps up a soldier better than coffee. According to your own view we have another hard day before us."

Merwyn complied, and bowed his thanks.

"Now for plans," resumed Mr. Vosburgh. "Are you going to police headquarters again?"

"Direct from here."

"I shall be there occasionally, and if you learn anything important, leave me a note. If I am not there and you can get away, come here. Of course I only ask this as of a friend and loyal man. You can see how vitally important it is that the authorities at Washington should be informed. They can put forth vast powers, and will do so as the necessity is impressed upon them. If we can only hold our own for a day or two the city will be full of troops. Therefore remember that in aiding me you are helping the cause even more than by fighting with the best and bravest, as you did yesterday. You recognize this fact, do you not? I am not laying any constraint on you contrary to your sense of duty and inclination."

"No, sir, you are not. I should be dull indeed did I not perceive that you are burdened with the gravest responsibilities. What is more, your knowledge guides, in a measure, the strong national hand, and I now believe we shall need its aid."

"That's it, that's the point. Therefore you can see why I am eager to secure the assistance of one who has the brains to appreciate the fact so quickly and fully. Moreover, you are cool, and seem to understand the nature of this outbreak as if you had made a study of the mobs."

"I have, and I have been preparing for this one, for I knew that it would soon give me a chance to prove that I was not a coward."

Marian's cheeks crimsoned.

"No more of that, if you please," said Mr. Vosburgh, gravely. "While it is natural that you should feel strongly, you must remember that both I and my daughter have asked your pardon, and that you yourself admitted that we had cause for misjudging you. We have been prompt to make amends, and I followed you through yesterday's fight at some risk to see that you did not fall into the hands of strangers, if wounded. I could have learned all about the fight at a safer distance. You are now showing the best qualities of a soldier. Add to them a soldier's full and generous forgiveness when a wrong is atoned for,--an unintentional wrong at that. We trust you implicitly as a man of honor, but we also wish to work with you as a friend."

Mr. Vosburgh spoke with dignity, and the young fellow's face flushed under the reproof in his tone.

"I suppose I have become morbid on the subject," he said, with some embarrassment. "I now ask your pardon, and admit that the expression was in bad taste, to say the least."

"Yes, it was, in view of the evident fact that we now esteem and honor you as a brave man. I would not give you my hand in friendship and trust concerning matters vital to me were this not so."

Merwyn took the proffered hand with a deep flush of pleasure.

"Having learned the bitterness of being misjudged," said Marian, quietly, "Mr. Merwyn should be careful how he misjudges others."

"That's a close shot, Merwyn," said Mr. Vosburgh, laughing.

Their guest started and bent a keen glance on the girl's averted face, and then said, earnestly: "Miss Vosburgh, your father has spoken frankly to me and I believe him. Your words, also, are significant if they mean anything whatever. I know well what is before me to-day,--the chances of my never seeing you again. I can only misjudge you in one respect. Perhaps I can best make everything clear to your father as well as yourself by a single question. If I do my duty through these troubles, Mr. Vosburgh being the judge, can you give me some place among those friends who have already, and justly, won your esteem? I know it will require time. I have given you far more cause for offence than you have given me, but I would be glad to fight to-day with the inspiration of hope rather than that of recklessness."

Her lip trembled as she faltered: "You would see that you have such a place already were you not equally prone to misjudge. Do you think me capable of cherishing a petty spite after you had proved yourself the peer of my other friends?"

"That I have not done, and I fear I never can. You have seen that I have been under a strong restraint which is not removed and which I cannot explain. To wear, temporarily, a policeman's uniform is probably the best I can hope for."

"I was thinking of men, Mr. Merwyn, not uniforms. I have nothing whatever to do with the restraint to which you refer. If my father trusts you, I can. Do not think of me so meanly as to believe I cannot give honest friendship to the man who is risking his life to aid my father. Last evening you said I had been off my guard. I must and will say, in self-defence, that if you judge me by that hour of weakness and folly you misjudge me."

"Then we can be friends," he said, holding out his hand, his face full of the sunshine of gladness.

"Why not?" she replied, laughing, and taking his hand,--"that is, on condition that there is no more recklessness."

Mr. Vosburgh rose and said, with a smile: "Now that there is complete amity in the camp we will move on the enemy. I shall go with you, Merwyn, to police-headquarters;" and he hastily began his preparation.

Left alone with Marian a moment, Merwyn said, "You cannot know how your words have changed everything for me."

"I fear the spirit of the rioters is unchanged, and that you are about to incur fearful risks."

"I shall meet them cheerfully, for I have been under a thick cloud too long not to exult in a little light at last."

"Ready?" said Mr. Vosburgh.

Again Merwyn took her hand and looked at her earnestly as he said, "Good-by, Heaven bless you, whatever happens to me;" and he wondered at the tears that came into her eyes.

Making their way through streets which were now becoming thronged, Mr. Vosburgh and Merwyn reached police headquarters without detention. They found matters there vastly changed for the better: the whole police force well in hand; and General Harvey Brown, a most capable officer, in command of several hundred soldiers. Moreover, citizens, in response to a call from the mayor, were being enrolled in large numbers as special policemen. Merwyn was welcomed by his old companions under the command of Inspector Carpenter, and provided with a badge which would indicate that he now belonged to the police force.

Telegrams were pouring in announcing trouble in different sections. Troops were drawn up in line on Mulberry Street, ready for instant action, and were harangued by their officers in earnest words which were heeded and obeyed, for the soldiers vied with the police in courage and discipline.

Soon after his arrival Merwyn found himself marching with a force of policemen two hundred and fifty strong, led by Carpenter and followed by a company of the military. The most threatening gatherings were reported to be in Second and Third Avenues.

The former thoroughfare, when entered, was seen to be filled as far as the eye could reach, the number of the throng being estimated at not less than ten thousand. At first this host was comparatively quiet, apparently having no definite purpose or recognized leaders. Curiosity accounted for the presence of many, the hope of plunder for that of more; but there were hundreds of ferocious-looking men who thirsted for blood and lawless power. A Catholic priest, to his honor be it said, had addressed the crowd and pleaded for peace and order; but his words, although listened to respectfully, were soon forgotten. What this section of the mob, which was now mustering in a score of localities, would have done first it is impossible to say; for as it began to be agitated with passion, ready to precipitate its brutal force on any object that caught its attention, the cry, "Cops and soldiers coming," echoed up the avenue from block to block, a long, hoarse wave of sound.

Carpenter, with his force, marched quietly through the crowd from 21st to 32d Street, paying no heed to the hootings, yells, and vile epithets that were hurled from every side. Dirty, ragged women, with dishevelled hair and bloated faces, far exceeded the men in the use of Billingsgate; and the guardians of the law, as they passed through those long lines of demoniacal visages, scowling with hate, and heard their sulphurous invectives, saw what would be their fate if overpowered. It was a conflict having all the horrors of Indian warfare, as poor Colonel O'Brien, tortured to death through the long hot afternoon of that same day, learned in agony.

The mob in the street had not ventured on anything more offensive than jeers and curses, but when Carpenter's command reached 32d Street it was assailed in a new and deadly manner. Rioters, well provided with stones and brick-bats, had stationed themselves on the roofs, and, deeming themselves secure, began to rain the missiles on the column below, which formed but too conspicuous a mark. This was a new and terrible danger which Merwyn had not anticipated, and he wondered how Carpenter would meet the emergency. Comrades were falling around him, and a stone grazed his shoulder which would have brained him had it struck his head.

Their leader never hesitated a moment. The command, "Halt, charge those houses, brain every devil that resists," rang down the line.

The crowd on the sidewalk gave way before the deeply incensed and resolute officers of the law. Merwyn, with a half-dozen others, seized a heavy pole which had been cut down in order to destroy telegraphic communication, and, using it as a ram, crashed in the door of a tall tenement-house on the roof of which were a score of rioters, meantime escaping their missiles as by a miracle. Rushing in, paying no heed to protests, and clubbing those who resisted, he kept pace with the foremost. In his left hand, however, he carried his trusty revolver, for he did not propose to be assassinated by skulkers in the dark passage-ways. Seeing a man levelling a gun from a dusky corner, he fired instantly, and man and gun dropped. As the guardians of the law approached the scuttle, having fought their way thither, the ruffians stood ready to hurl down bricks, torn from the chimneys; but two or three well-aimed shots cleared the way, and the policemen were on the roof, bringing down a man with every blow. One brawny fellow rushed upon Merwyn, but received such a stroke on his temple that he fell, rolled off the roof, and struck the pavement, a crushed and shapeless mass.

The assaults upon the other houses were equally successful, but the fight was a severe one, and was maintained for nearly an hour. The mob was appalled by the fate of their friends, and looked on in sullen, impotent anger.

Having cleared the houses, the police re-formed in the street, and marched away to other turbulent districts.

Only the military were left, and had formed about a block further to the north. Beyond the feeble demonstration of the invalid corps the rioters, as yet, had had no experience with the soldiery. That policemen would use their clubs was to them a matter of course, but they scarcely believed that cannon and musketry would be employed. Moreover, they were maddened and reckless that so many of their best and bravest had been put hors de combat. The brief paralysis caused by the remorseless clubs of the police passed, and like a sluggish monster, the mob, aroused to sudden fury, pressed upon the soldiery, hurling not only the vilest epithets but every missile on which they could lay their hands. Colonel O'Brien, in command for the moment, rode through the crowd, supposing he could overawe them by his fearless bearing; but they only scoffed at him, and the attack upon his men grew more bold and reckless.

The limit of patience was passed. "Fire!" he thundered, and the howitzers poured their deadly canister point-blank into the throng. At the same time the soldiers discharged their muskets. Not only men, but women fell on every side, one with a child in her arms.

A warfare in which women stand an equal chance for death and wounds is a terrible thing, and yet this is usually an inseparable feature of mob-fighting. However, setting aside the natural and instinctive horror at injuring a woman, the depraved creatures in the streets were deserving of no more sympathy than their male abettors in every species of outrage. They did their utmost to excite and keep alive the passions of the hour. Many were armed with knives, and did not hesitate to use them, and when stronger hands broke in the doors of shops and dwellings they swarmed after,--the most greedy and unscrupulous of plunderers. If a negro man, woman, or child fell into their hands, none were more brutal than the unsexed hags of the mob.

If on this, and other occasions, they had remained in their homes they would not have suffered, nor would the men have been so ferocious in their violence. They were the first to yield to panic, however, and now their shrieks were the loudest and their efforts to escape out of the deadly range of the guns the most frantic. In a few moments the avenue was cleared, and the military marched away, leaving the dead and wounded rioters where they had fallen, as the police had done before. Instantly the friends of the sufferers gathered them up and carried them into concealment.

This feature, from the first, was one of the most marked characteristics of the outbreak. The number of rioters killed and wounded could be only guessed at approximately, for every effort was made to bury the bodies secretly, and keep the injured in seclusion until they either died or recovered. Almost before a fight was over the prostrate rioters would be spirited away by friends or relatives on the watch.

The authorities were content to have it so, for they had no place or time for the poor wretches, and the police understood that they were to strike blows that would incapacitate the recipients for further mischief.

In the same locality which had witnessed his morning fight, Colonel O'Brien, later in the day, met a fate too horrible to be described.

CHAPTER XLVIII.
DESPERATE FIGHTING.

HAVING again reached police headquarters, Merwyn rested but a short time and then joined a force of two hundred men under Inspector Dilkes, and returned to the same avenue in which he had already incurred such peril. The mob, having discovered that it must cope with the military as well as the police, became eager to obtain arms. It so happened that several thousand carbines were stored in a wire factory in Second Avenue, and the rioters had learned the fact. Therefore they swarmed thither, forced an entrance, and began to arm themselves and their comrades. A despatch to headquarters announced the attack at its commencement, and the force we have named was sent off in hot haste to wrest from the mob the means of more effective resistance. Emerging into the avenue from 21st Street, Dilkes found the thoroughfare solid with rioters, who, instead of giving way, greeted the police with bitter curses. Hesitating not a moment on account of vast inequality of numbers, the leader formed his men and charged. The mob had grown reckless with every hour, and it now closed on the police with the ferocity of a wild beast. A terrible hand-to-hand conflict ensued, and Merwyn found himself warding off and giving blows with the enemy so near that he could almost feel their hot, tainted breath on his cheek, while horrid visages inflamed with hate and fury made impressions on his mind that could not easily pass away. It was a close, desperate encounter, and the scorching July sun appeared to kindle passion on either side into tenfold intensity. While the police were disciplined men, obeying every order and doing nothing at random, they WERE men, and they would not have been human if anger and thoughts of vengeance had not nerved their arms as they struck down ruffians who would show no more mercy to the wounded or captured than would a man-eating tiger.

Since the mob would not give way, the police cut a bloody path through the throng, and forced their way like a wedge to the factory. Their orders were to capture all arms; and when a rioter was seen with a carbine or a gun of any kind, one or more of the police would rush out of the ranks and seize it, then fight their way back.

By the time they reached the factory so many of the mob had been killed or wounded, and so many of their leaders were dead or disabled, that it again yielded to panic and fled. One desperate leader, although already bruised and bleeding, had for a time inspired the mob with much of his own reckless fury, and was left almost alone by his fleeing companions. His courage, which should have been displayed in a better cause, cost him dear, for a tremendous blow sent him reeling against a fence, the sharp point of one of the iron pickets caught under his chin, and he hung there unheeded, impaled and dying. He was afterwards taken down, and beneath his soiled overalls and filthy shirt was a fair, white skin, clad in cassimere trousers, a rich waistcoat, and the finest of linen. His delicate, patrician features emphasized the mystery of his personality and action.

When all resistance in the street was overcome, there still remained the factory, thronged with armed and defiant rioters. Dilkes ordered the building to be cleared, and Merwyn took his place in the storming party. We shall not describe the scenes that followed. It was a strife that differed widely from Lane's cavalry charge on the lawn of a Southern plantation, with the eyes of fair women watching his deeds. Merwyn was not taking part with thousands in a battle that would be historic as Strahan and Blauvelt had done at Gettysburg. Every element of romance and martial inspiration was wanting. It was merely a life-and-death encounter between a handful of policemen and a grimy, desperate band of ruffians, cornered like rats, and resolved to sell their lives dearly.

The building was cleared, and at last Merwyn, exhausted and panting, came back with his comrades and took his place in the ranks. His club was bloody, and his revolver empty. The force marched away in triumph escorting wagons loaded with all the arms they could find, and were cheered by the better-disposed spectators that remained on the scene of action.

The desperate tenacity of the mob is shown by the fact that it returned to the wire factory, found some boxes of arms that had been overlooked, filled the great five-story building and the street about it, and became so defiant that the same battle had to be fought again in the afternoon with the aid of the military.

For the sake of making a definite impression we have touched upon the conflicts taking place in one locality. But throughout this awful day there were mobs all over the city, with fighting, plundering, burning, the chasing and murdering of negroes occurring at the same time in many and widely separated sections. Telegrams for aid were pouring into headquarters from all parts of the city, large tracts of which were utterly unprotected. The police and military could be employed only in bodies sufficiently large to cope with gatherings of hundreds or thousands. Individual outrages and isolated instances of violence and plunder could not be prevented.

But law-abiding citizens were realizing their danger and awakening to a sense of their duty. Over four hundred special policemen were sworn in. Merchants and bankers in Wall Street met and resolved to close business. Millionnaires vied with their clerks and porters in patriotic readiness to face danger. Volunteer companies were formed, and men like Hon. William E. Dodge, always foremost in every good effort in behalf of the city, left their offices for military duty. While thousands of citizens escaped from the city, with their families, not knowing where they would find a refuge, and obeying only the impulse to get away from a place apparently doomed, other thousands remained, determined to protect their hearths and homes and to preserve their fair metropolis from destruction. Terrible as was the mob, and tenfold more terrible as it would have been if it had used its strength in an organized effort and with definite purpose, forces were now awakening and concentrating against it which would eventually destroy every vestige of lawlessness. With the fight on Broadway, during Monday evening, the supreme crisis had passed. After that the mob fought desperate but losing battles. Acton, with Napoleonic nerve and skill, had time to plan and organize. General Brown with his brave troops reached him on Monday night, and thereafter the two men, providentially brought and kept together, met and overcame, in cordial co-operation, every danger as it arose. Their names should never be forgotten by the citizens of New York. Acton, as chief of police, was soon feared more than any other man in the city, and he began to receive anonymous letters assuring him that he had "but one more day to live." He tossed them contemptuously aside, and turned to the telegrams imploring assistance. In every blow struck his iron will and heavy hand were felt. For a hundred hours, through the storm, he kept his hand on the helm and never closed his eyes. He inspired confidence in the men who obeyed him, and the humblest of them became heroes.

The city was smitten with an awful paralysis. Stages and street cars had very generally ceased running; shops were closed; Broadway and other thoroughfares and centres usually so crowded were at times almost deserted; now and then a hack would whirl by with occupants that could not be classified. They might be leaders of the mob, detectives, or citizens in disguise bent on public or private business. On one occasion a millionnaire whose name is known and honored throughout the land, dressed in the mean habiliments of a laborer, drove a wagon up Broadway in which was concealed a load of arms and ammunition. In hundreds of homes fathers and sons kept watch with rifles and revolvers, while city and State authorities issued proclamations.

It was a time of strange and infinite vicissitude, yet apparently the mob steadily attained vaster and more terrible proportions, and everywhere lawlessness was on the increase, especially in the upper portions of the city.

Mr. Vosburgh, with stern and clouded brow, obtained information from all available sources, and flashed the vital points to Washington. He did not leave Marian alone very long, and as the day advanced kept one of his agents in the house during his absences. He failed to meet Merwyn at headquarters, but learned of the young man's brave action from one of his wounded comrades.

When Mr. Vosburgh told Marian of the risks which her new friend was incurring, and the nature of the fighting in which he was engaged, she grew so pale and agitated that he saw that she was becoming conscious of herself, of the new and controlling element entering into her life.

This self-knowledge was made tenfold clearer by a brief visit from Mrs. Ghegan.

"Oh! how dared you come?" cried Marian.

"The strates are safe enough for the loikes o' me, so oi kape out o' the crowds," was the reply, "but they're no place fer ye, Miss Marian. Me brogue is a password iverywhere, an' even the crowds is civil and dacent enough onless something wakes the divil in 'em;" and then followed a vivid account of her experiences and of the timely help Merwyn had given her.

"The docthers think me Barney'll live, but oi thank Misther Merwyn that took him out o' the very claws uv the bloody divils, and not their bat's eyes. Faix, but he tops all yez frin's, Miss Marian, tho' ye're so could to 'im. All the spalpanes in the strates couldn't make 'im wink, yet while I was a-wailin' over Barney he was as tender-feelin' as a baby."

The girl's heart fluttered strangely at the words of her former maid, but she tried to disguise her emotion. When again left alone she strained her ears for every sound from the city, and was untiring in her watch. From noon till evening she kept a dainty lunch ready for Merwyn, but he did not come.

After the young man's return from his second fight he was given some rest. In the afternoon, he, with others, was sent on duty to the west side, the force being carried thither in stages which Acton had impressed into the service. One driver refused to stir, saying, insolently, that he had "not been hired to carry policemen."

"Lock that man in cell No. 4," was Acton's answer, while, in the same breath, he ordered a policeman to drive.

That was the superintendent's style of arguing and despatching business.

Merwyn again saw plenty of service, for the spirit of pandemonium was present in the west side. Towards evening, however, the rioters ceased their aimless and capricious violence, and adopted in their madness the dangerous method of Parisian mobs. They began throwing up a series of barricades in Eighth Avenue. Vehicles of all kinds within reach, telegraph poles, boxes,--anything that would obstruct,-- were wired together. Barricades were also erected on cross-streets, to prevent flank movements. Captain Walling, of the police, who was on duty in the precinct, appreciated the importance of abolishing this feature from street fighting as speedily as possible, and telegraphed to headquarters for a co-operating military force. He also sent to General Sanford, at the arsenal, for troops. They were promised, but never sent. General Brown, fortunately, was a man of a very different stamp from Sanford, and he promptly sent a body of regulars.

Captain Slott took command of the police detailed to co-operate with the soldiers, and, with their officers, waited impatiently and vainly for the company promised by Sanford. Meanwhile the mob was strengthening its defences with breathless energy, and the sun was sinking in the west. As the difficult and dangerous work to be done required daylight it was at last resolved to wait no longer.

As the assailants drew near the barricade, they received a volley, accompanied by stones and other missiles. The police fell back a little to the left, and the troops, advancing, returned the fire. But the rioters did not yield, and for a time the crash of musketry resounded through the avenue, giving the impression of a regular pitched battle. The accurate aim of the soldiers, however, at last decided the contest, and the rioters fled to the second barricade, followed by the troops, while the police tore away the captured obstruction.

Obtaining a musket and cartridges from a wounded soldier, Merwyn, by explaining that he was a good marksman, obtained the privilege of fighting on the left flank of the military.

The mob could not endure the steady, well-directed fire of the regulars, and one barricade after another was carried, until the rioters were left uncovered when they fled, shrieking, yelling, cursing in their impotent rage,--the police with their clubs and the soldiers with their rifles following and punishing them until the streets were clear.

Merwyn, having been on duty all day, obtained a leave of absence till the following morning, and, availing himself of his old device to save time and strength, went to a livery stable near the station-house and obtained a hack by payment of double the usual fare. Mounting the box with the driver, and avoiding crowds, he was borne rapidly towards Mr. Vosburgh's residence. He was not only terribly exhausted, but also consumed with anxiety as to the safety of the girl who had never been absent long from his thoughts, even in moments of the fiercest conflict.

CHAPTER XLIX.
ONE FACING HUNDREDS.

THE evening was growing dusky when Merwyn dismissed his carriage and hastened to Mr. Vosburgh's residence. Marian and her father had waited for him until their faces were clouded with anxiety by reason of his long delay. The young girl's attempt to dine with her father was but a formal pretence.

At last she exclaimed, "Something must have happened to Mr. Merwyn!"

"Do not entertain gloomy thoughts, my dear. A hundred things besides an injury might have detained him. Keep a good dinner ready, and I think he'll do justice to it before the evening is over."

Even then the German servant announced his presence at the basement door, which, in view of the disguises worn, was still used as the place of ingress and egress.

Mr. Vosburgh hastened to welcome him, while Marian bustled around to complete her preparations. When he entered the dining-room he did indeed appear weary and haggard, a fair counterpart of the rioters whom he had been fighting.

"Only necessity, Miss Vosburgh, compels me to present myself in this scarecrow aspect," he said. "I've had no time or chance for anything better. I can soon report to your father all that is essential, and then can go home and return later."

"I shall be much hurt if you do so," said Marian, reproachfully. "I kept a lunch prepared for you during the afternoon, and now have a warm dinner all ready. It will be very ungracious in you to go away and leave it."

"But I look like a coal-heaver."

"Oh, I've seen well-dressed men before. They are no novelty; but a man direct from a field of battle is quite interesting. Will you please take this chair? You are not in the least like my other friends. They obey me without questionings."

"You must remember," he replied, "that the relation is to me as new and strange as it is welcome. I shall need a great deal of discipline."

"When you learn what a martinet I can be you may repent, like many another who has obtained his wish. Here we shall reverse matters. Everything is topsy-turvy now, you know, so take this coffee at the beginning of your dinner."

"I admit that your orders differ widely from those of police captains." Then he added, with quiet significance, "No; I shall not repent."

"Mr. Merwyn, will you take an older man's advice?"

"Certainly. Indeed, I am under your orders, also, for the night."

"I'm glad to hear it, for it will be a night of deep anxiety to me. Make a very light dinner, and take more refreshment later. You are too much exhausted to dine now. You need not tell me of your morning adventures. I learned about those at headquarters."

"I have heard about them too," Marian added, with a look that warmed the young fellow's soul. "I have also had a visit from Mrs. Ghegan, and her story was not so brief as yours."

"From what section have you just come?" Mr. Vosburgh asked.

Merwyn gave a brief description of the condition of affairs on the west side, ending with an account of the fight at the barricades.

"In one respect you are like my other friends, only more so," Marian said. "You are inclined to give me Hamlet with Hamlet left out. What part did you take at the barricades?"

He told her in a matter-of-fact way.

"Ah, yes, I understand. I am learning to read between the lines of your stories."

"Well, Heaven be thanked," ejaculated Mr. Vosburgh, "that you demolished the barricades! If the rioters adopt that mode of fighting us, we shall have far greater difficulty in coping with them."

At last Mr. Vosburgh said, "Will you please come with me to my library for a few minutes?"

On reaching the apartment he closed the door, and continued, gravely: "Mr. Merwyn, I am in sore straits. You have offered to aid me. I will tell you my situation, and then you must do as you think best. I know that you have done all a man's duty to-day and have earned the right to complete rest. You will also naturally wish to look after your own home. Nevertheless my need and your own words lead me to suggest that you stay here to-night, or at least through the greater portion of it. I fear that I have been recognized and followed,--that I have enemies on my track. I suspect the man whom I discharged from the care of my office. Yet I must go out, for I have important despatches to send, and--what is of more consequence--I must make some careful observations. The mob seems to be a mere lawless, floundering monster, bent chiefly on plunder; but the danger is that leaders are organizing its strength as a part of the rebellion. You can understand that, while I look upon the outbreak with the solicitude of a citizen whose dearest interests are at stake, I also, from habit of mind and duty, must study it as a part of the great campaign of the year. If there are organizers at work there will be signals to-night, and I can see them from a tall neighboring church-spire. Yet how can I leave my child alone? How--"

"Mr. Vosburgh," cried Merwyn, "what honor or privilege could I ask greater than that of being your daughter's protector during your absence? I understand you perfectly. You feel that you must do your duty at any cost to yourself. After what you have said, nothing could induce me to go away. Indeed, I would stand guard without your door, were there no place for me within."

"There, I won't thank you in words," said the elder man, wringing Merwyn's hand. "Will you do as I wish?"

"Yes, sir."

"Then lie down on the sofa in the front parlor and sleep while you can. The least disturbance in the street would waken you there. Marian will watch from an upper window and give you warning if anything occurs. It is possible that I may be set upon when returning home, but I think not, for I shall enter the house from the rear;" and he told the young man of the means of exit which he had secured in case the house was attacked. "Rather than permit my child to take any risks," concluded the father, solemnly, "fly with her and the woman who will be her companion till I return. Beyond the fact of general danger to all homes, she does not suspect anything, nor shall I increase her anxieties by telling her of my fears. She will be vigilant on general principles. Have you arms?"

"I have fired most of my cartridges to-day."

"Well here is a revolver and a repeating rifle that you can depend upon. Do you understand the latter weapon?"

"Yes, I have one like it."

"I will now tell Marian of my plans, so far as it is wise for her to know them, and then, God help and protect us all! Come, I wish you to lie down at once, for every moment of rest may be needed."

When they descended, Mr. Vosburgh said to his daughter, laughingly, "Mr. Merwyn is under orders, and can have nothing more to say to you to-night."

The young fellow, in like vein, brought the rifle to his shoulder, presented arms to her, wheeled, and marched to his station in the darkened front parlor. Before lying down, however, he opened one blind for an outlook.

"Do you fear any special danger to-night, papa?" Marian asked, quickly.

"I have been expecting special dangers from the first," replied her father, gently. "While I must do my duty I shall also take such precautions as I can. Merwyn will be your protector during my absence. Now take your station at your upper window and do your part." He explained briefly what he expected of her. "In case of an attack," he concluded, almost sternly, "you must fly before it is too late. I shall now go and prepare Mr. Erkmann for the possible emergency, and then go out through the basement door as usual, after giving our loyal German her directions."

A few moments later he had departed, all were at their posts, and the house was quiet.

Merwyn felt the necessity of rest, for every bone in his body ached from fatigue; but he did not dream of the possibility of sleep. His heart was swelling with pride and joy that he had become, not only the friend of the girl he loved, but also her trusted protector.

But at last Nature claimed her dues, and he succumbed and slept.

Mr. Vosburgh, unmolested, climbed to his lofty height of observation. The great city lay beneath him with its myriad lights, but on Third Avenue, from 40th Street northward for a mile, there was a hiatus of darkness. There the mob had begun, and there still dwelt its evil spirit uncurbed. The rioters in that district had cut off the supply of gas, feeling, as did the French revolutionists, that "Light was not in order."

Mr. Vosburgh watched that long stretch of gloom with the greatest anxiety. Suddenly from its mystery a rocket flamed into the sky. Three minutes elapsed and another threw far and wide its ominous light. Again there was an interval of three minutes, when a third rocket confirmed the watcher's fears that these were signals. Four minutes passed, and then, from the vicinity of Union Square, what appeared to be a great globe of fire rose to an immense height. A few seconds later there was an answering rocket far off in the eastern districts of Brooklyn.

These were indeed portents in the sky, and Mr. Vosburgh was perplexed as to their significance. Were they orders or at least invitations, for a general uprising against all authority? Was the rebellion against the government about to become general in the great centres of population? With the gloomiest of forebodings he watched for two hours longer, but only heard the hoarse murmur of the unquiet city, which occasionally, off to the west, became so loud as to suggest the continuance of the strife of the day. At last he went to the nearest available point and sent his despatches, then stole by a circuitous route to the dwelling of Mr. Erkmann, who was watching for him.

Marian's vigilance was sleepless. While she had been burdened throughout the day with the deepest anxieties, she had been engaged in no exhausting efforts, and the novelty of her present position and her new emotions banished the possibility of drowsiness. She felt as if she had lived years during the past two days. The city was full of dangers nameless and horrible, yet she was conscious of an exaltation of spirit and of a happiness such as she had never known.

The man whom she had despised as a coward was her protector, and she wondered at her sense of security. She almost longed for an opportunity to prove that her courage could now be equal to his, and her eyes flashed in the darkness as they glanced up and down the dusky street; again they became gentle in her commiseration of the weary man in the room below, and gratefully she thanked God that he had been spared through the awful perils of the day.

Suddenly her attention was caught by the distant tramp of many feet. She threw open a blind and listened with a beating heart. Yes, a mob was coming, nearer, nearer; they are at the corner. With a sudden outburst of discordant cries they are turning into this very street.

A moment later her hand was upon Merwyn's shoulder. "Wake, wake," she cried; "the mob is coming--is here."

He was on his feet instantly with rifle in hand. Through the window he saw the dusky forms gathering about the door. The German woman stood behind Marian, crying and wringing her hands.

"Miss Vosburgh, you and the woman do as I bid," Merwyn said, sternly. "Go to the rear of the hall, open the door, and if I say, 'Fly,' or if I fall, escape for your lives."

"But what will you--"

"Obey!" he cried, with a stamp of his foot.

They were already in the hall, and did as directed.

Imagine Marian's wonder as she saw him throw open the front door, step without, and fire instantly. Then, dropping his rifle on his arm, he began to use his revolver. She rushed to his side and saw the mob, at least three hundred strong, scattering as if swept away by a whirlwind.

Merwyn's plan of operations had been bold, but it proved the best one. In the streets he had learned the effect of fearless, decisive action, and he had calculated correctly on the panic which so often seized the undisciplined hordes. They probably believed that his boldness was due to the fact that he had plenty of aid at hand. So long as there was a man within range he continued to fire, then became aware of Marian's presence.

"O Miss Vosburgh," he said, earnestly, "you should not look on sights like these;" for a leader of the mob lay motionless on the pavement beneath them.

He took her hand, which trembled, led her within, and refastened the door. Her emotion was so strong that she dared not speak.

"Why did you take such a risk?" he asked, gravely. "What would your father have said to me if one of those wretches had fired and wounded you?"

"I--I only realized one thing--that you were facing hundreds all alone," she faltered.

"Why, Miss Marian, I was only doing my duty, and I took the safest way to perform it. I had learned from experience that the bluff game is generally the best. No doubt I gave those fellows the impression that there were a dozen armed men in the house."

But her emotion was too strong for control, and she sobbed: "It was the bravest thing I ever heard of. Oh! I have done you SUCH wrong! Forgive me. I--I--can't--" and she hastened up the dusky stairway, followed by her servant, who was profuse in German interjections.

"I am repaid a thousand-fold," was Merwyn's quiet comment. "My oath cannot blight my life now."

Sleep had been most effectually banished from his eyes, and as he stood in the unlighted apartment, motionless and silent, looking out upon the dusky street, but a few moments passed before a man and a woman approached cautiously, lifted the slain rioter, and bore him away.

In less than half an hour Mr. Vosburgh entered his house from the rear so silently that he was almost beside Merwyn before his approach was recognized.

"What, Merwyn!" he exclaimed, with a little chiding in his tone; "is this the way you rest? You certainly haven't stood here, 'like Patience on a monument,' since I left?"

"No, indeed. You are indebted to Miss Vosburgh that you have a home to come to, for I slept so soundly that the house might have been carried off bodily. The mob has been here."

"O papa!" cried Marian, clasping her arms about his neck, "thank God you are back safe! Oh, it was all so sudden and terrible!"

"But how, how, Merwyn? What has happened?"

"Well, sir, Miss Vosburgh was a better sentinel than I, and heard the first approach of the ruffians. I was sleeping like old Rip himself. She wakened me. A shot or two appeared to create a panic, and they disappeared like a dream, as suddenly as they had come."

"Just listen to him, papa!" cried the girl, now reassured by her father's presence, and recovering from her nervous shock. "Why shouldn't he sleep after such a day as he has seen? It was his duty to sleep, wasn't it? The idea of two sentinels in a small garrison keeping awake, watching the same points!"

"I'm very glad you obtained some sleep, Merwyn, and surely you had earned it; but as yet I have a very vague impression of this mob and of the fight. I looked down the street but a few moments ago, and it seemed deserted. It is quiet now. Have you not both slept and dreamed?"

"No, papa," said the girl, shudderingly; "there's a dead man at the foot of our steps even now."

"You are mistaken, Miss Vosburgh. As usual, his friends lost no time in carrying him off."

"Well, well," cried Mr. Vosburgh, "this is a longer story than I can listen to without something to sustain the inner man. "Riten,"--to the servant,--"some fresh coffee please. Now for the lighted dining-room,--that's hidden from the street,-- where we can look into each other's faces. So much has happened the last two days that here in the dark I begin to feel as if it all were a nightmare. Ah! how cosey and home-like this room seems after prowling in the dangerous streets with my hand on the butt of a revolver! Come now, Marian, sit down quietly and tell the whole story. I can't trust Merwyn at all when he is the hero of the tale."

"You may well say that. I hope, sir," with a look of mock severity at the young fellow, "that your other reports to papa are more accurate than the one I have heard. Can you believe it, papa? he actually threw open the front door and faced the entire mob alone."

"I beg your pardon, Miss Vosburgh, as I emptied my revolver and looked around, a lady stood beside me. I've seen men do heroic things to-day, but nothing braver than that."

"But I didn't think!" cried the girl; "I didn't realize--" and then she paused, while her face crimsoned. Her heart had since told her why she had stepped to his side.

"But you would have thought twice, yes, a hundred times," said Merwyn, laughing, "if you hadn't been a soldier. Jove! how Strahan will stare when he hears of it!"

"Please, never tell him," exclaimed the girl.

Her father now stood encircling her with his arm, and looking fondly down upon her. "Well, thank God we're all safe yet! and, threatening as is the aspect of affairs, I believe we shall see happy days of peace and security before very long."

"I am so glad that mamma is not in the city!" said Marian, earnestly.

"Oh that you were with her, my child!"

"I'm better contented where I am," said the girl, with a decided little nod.

"Yes, but great God! think of what might have happened if Merwyn had not been here,--what might still have happened had he not had the nerve to take, probably, the only course which could have saved you! There, there, I can't think of it, or I shall be utterly unnerved."

"Don't think of it, papa. See, I'm over the shock of it already. Now don't you be hysterical as I was yesterday."

He made a great effort to rally, but it was evident that the strong man was deeply agitated. They all, however, soon regained self-control and composure, and spent a genial half-hour together, Merwyn often going to the parlor, that he might scan the street. After a brief discussion of plans for the morrow they separated for the night, Merwyn resuming his bivouac in the parlor. After listening for a time he was satisfied that even mobs must rest, and, as the soldiers slept on their arms, he slumbered, his rifle in hand.

When Marian bade her father good-night he took her face in his hands and gazed earnestly down upon it. The girl understood his expression, and the color came into her fair countenance like a June dawn.

"Do you remember, darling, my words when I said, 'I do not know how much it might cost you in the end to dismiss Mr. Merwyn finally'?"

"Yes, papa."

"Are you not learning how much it might have cost you?"

"Yes, papa," with drooping eyes.

He kissed her, and nothing more was said.

CHAPTER L.
ZEB.

MERWYN awoke early, and, as soon as he heard the German servant coming down-stairs, wrote a line to Mr. Vosburgh saying that he would call on his way to headquarters, and then hastened through the almost deserted streets to his own home. To his great satisfaction he found everything unchanged there. After luxuriating in a bath and a bountiful breakfast he again instructed his man to be on the watch, and to keep up a fire throughout the coming night, so that a hot meal might be had speedily at any time.

More than once the thought had crossed his mind: "Unless we make greater headway with the riot, that attack on Mr. Vosburgh's house will be repeated. Vengeance alone would now prompt the act, and besides he is undoubtedly a marked man. There's no telling what may happen. Our best course is to fight, fight, knock the wretches on the head. With the quelling of the mob comes safety;" and, remembering the danger that threatened Marian, he was in a savage mood.

On this occasion, he went directly to Mr. Vosburgh's residence, resolving to take no risks out of the line of duty. His first thought now was the securing of Marian's safety. He had learned that there was no longer any special need for personal effort on his part to gain information, since the police authorities had wires stretching to almost every part of the city. An account of the risks taken to keep up this telegraphic communication would make a strange, thrilling chapter in itself. Moreover, police detectives were busy everywhere, and Mr. Vosburgh at headquarters and with the aid of his own agents could now obtain all the knowledge essential. Therefore the young fellow's plan was simple, and he indicated his course at once after a cordial greeting from Mr. Vosburgh and Marian.

"Hard fighting appears to me to be the way to safety," said he. "I can scarcely believe that the rioters will endure more than another day of such punishment as they received yesterday. Indeed, I should not be surprised if to-day was comparatively quiet."

"I agree with you," said Mr. Vosburgh, "unless the signals I saw last night indicate a more general uprising than has yet taken place. The best elements of the city are arming and organizing. There is a deep and terrible anger rising against the mob and all its abettors and sympathizers."

"I know it," cried Merwyn; "I feel it myself. When I think of the danger which threatened your home and especially Miss Vosburgh, I feel an almost ungovernable desire to be at the wretches."

"But that means greater peril for you," faltered the young girl.

"No, it means the shortest road to safety for us all. A mob is like fire: it must be stamped out of existence as soon as possible."

"I think Merwyn is right," resumed Mr. Vosburgh. "Another day of successful fighting will carry us to safety, for the general government is moving rapidly in our behalf, and our militia regiments are on their way home. I'll be ready to go to headquarters with you in a minute."

"Oh, please do not be rash to-day. If you had fallen yesterday think what might have happened," said Marian.

"Every blow I strike to-day, Miss Vosburgh, will be nerved by the thought that you have one enemy, one danger, the less; and I shall esteem it the greatest of privileges if I can remain here to-night again as one of your protectors."

"I cannot tell you what a sense of security your presence gives me," she replied. "You seem to know just what to do and how to do it."

"Well," he answered, with a grim laugh, "one learns fast in these times. A very stern necessity is the mother of invention."

"Yes," sighed the girl, "one learns fast. Now that I have seen war, it is no longer a glorious thing, but full of unspeakable horrors."

"This is not war," said Merwyn, a little bitterly. "I pity, while I detest, the poor wretches we knock on the head. Your friends, who have fought the elite of the South will raise their eyebrows if they hear us call this war."

"I have but one friend who has faced a mob alone," she replied, with a swift, shy glance.

"A friend whom that privilege made the most fortunate of men," he replied. "Had the rioters been Southern soldiers, they would have shot me instantly, instead of running away."

"All my friends soon learn that I am stubborn in my opinions," was her laughing reply, as her father joined them.

Mr. Erkmann on the next street north was a sturdy, loyal man, and he permitted Mr. Vosburgh and Merwyn to pass out through his house, so that to any one who was watching the impression would be given that at least two men were in the house. Burdened with a sense of danger, Mr. Vosburgh had resolved on brief absences, believing that at headquarters and through his agents he could learn the general drift of events.

Broadway wore the aspect of an early Sunday morning in quiet times. Pedestrians were few, and the stages had ceased running. The iron shutters of the great Fifth Avenue and other hotels were securely fastened. No street cars jingled along the side avenues; shops were closed; and the paralysis of business was almost complete in its greatest centres. At police headquarters, however, the most intense activity prevailed. Here were gathered the greater part of the police force and of the military co-operating with it The neighboring African church was turned into a barrack. Acton occupied other buildings, with or without the consent of the owners.

The top floor of the police building was thronged with colored refugees, thankful indeed to have found a place of safety, but many were consumed with anxiety on account of absent ones.

The sanguine hopes for a more quiet day were not fulfilled, but the severest fighting was done by the military, and cavalry now began to take part in the conflict. On the west side, Seventh Avenue was swept again and again with grape and canister before the mob gave way. On the east side there were several battles, and in one of them, fought just before night, the troops were compelled to retreat, leaving some of their dead and wounded in the streets. General Brown sent Captain Putnam with one hundred and fifty regulars to the scene of disaster and continued violence, and a sanguinary conflict ensued between ten and eleven o'clock at night. Putnam swept the dimly lighted streets with his cannon, and when the rioters fled into the houses he opened such a terrible fire upon them as to subdue all resistance.

The mob was at last learning that the authorities would neither yield nor scruple to make use of any means in the conflict.

In the great centres down town, things were comparatively quiet. The New York Times took matters into its own hands. A glare of light from the windows of its building was shed after night-fall over Printing-House Square, and editors and reporters had their rifles as readily within reach as their pens.

We shall not follow Merwyn's adventures, for that would involve something like a repetition of scenes already described. As the day was closing, however, he took part in an affair which explained the mystery of Mammy Borden's disappearance.

During the first day of the riot the colored woman had seen enough to realize her own danger and that of her son, and she was determined to reach him and share his fate, whatever it might be. She had no scruple in stealing away from Mr. Vosburgh's house, for by her departure she removed a great peril from her employers and friends. She was sufficiently composed, however, to put on a heavy veil and gloves, and so reached her son in safety. Until the evening of the third day of the riot, the dwelling in which they cowered escaped the fury of the mob, although occupied by several colored families. At last the hydra-headed monster fixed one of its baleful eyes upon the spot. Just as the occupants of the house were beginning to hope, the remorseless wretches came, and the spirit of Tophet broke loose. The door was broken in with axes, and savage men streamed into the dwelling. The poor victims tried to barricade themselves in the basement, but their assailants cut the water-pipes and would have drowned them. Driven out by this danger, the hunted creatures sought to escape through the yard. As Zeb was lifting his mother over the fence the rioters came upon her and dragged her back.

"Kill me, kill me," cried Zeb, "but spare my mother."

They seemed to take him at his word. Two of the fiends held his arms, while another struck him senseless and apparently dead with a crowbar. Then, not accepting this heroic self-sacrifice, they began to beat the grief-frenzied mother. But retribution was at hand. The cries of the victims and the absorption of the rioters in their brutal work prevented them from hearing the swift, heavy tread of the police. A moment later Merwyn and others rushed through the hallway, and the ruffians received blows similar to the one which had apparently bereft poor Zeb of life. The rioters were either dispersed or left where they fell, a wagon was impressed, and Zeb and his mother were brought to headquarters. Merwyn had soon recognized Mrs. Borden, but she could not be comforted. Obtaining leave of absence, the young man waited until the evening grew dusky; then securing a hack from a stable near headquarters, the proprietor of which was disposed to loyalty by reason of his numerous blue-coated neighbors, he took the poor woman and the scarcely breathing man to a hospital, and left money for their needs. The curtains of the carriage had been closely drawn; but if the crowds through which they sometimes passed had guessed its occupants, they would have instantly met a tragic fate, while Merwyn's and the driver's chances would have been scarcely better.

CHAPTER LI.
A TRAGEDY.

MR. VOSBURGH and his daughter had passed a very anxious day, the former going out but seldom. The information obtained from the city had not been reassuring, for while the authorities had under their direction larger bodies of men, and lawlessness was not so general, the mob was still unquelled and fought with greater desperation in the disaffected centres. In the after-part of the day Mr. Vosburgh received the cheering intelligence that the Seventh Regiment would arrive that night, and that other militia organizations were on their way home. Therefore he believed that if they escaped injury until the following morning all cause for deep anxiety would pass away. As the hours elapsed and no further demonstration was made against his home, his hopes grew apace, and now, as he and his daughter waited for Merwyn before dining, he said, "I fancy that the reception given to the mob last night has curbed their disposition to molest us."

"O papa, what keeps Mr. Merwyn?"

"Well, my dear, I know he was safe at noon."

"Oh, oh, I do hope that this will be the last day of this fearful suspense! Isn't it wonderful what Mr. Merwyn has done in the past few days?"

"Not so wonderful as it seems. Periods like these always develop master-spirits, or rather they give such spirits scope. How little we knew of Acton before this week! yet at the beginning he seized the mob by the throat and has not once relaxed his grasp. He has been the one sleepless man in the city, and how he endures the strain is almost beyond mortal comprehension. The man and the hour came together. The same is true of Merwyn in his sphere. He had been preparing for this, hoping that it would give him an opportunity to right himself. Fearless as the best of your friends, he combines with courage the singularly cool, resolute nature inherited from his father. He is not in the least ambitious for distinction, but is only bent on carrying out his own aims and purposes."

"And what are they, papa?"

"Sly fox! as if you did not know. Who first came to your protection?"

"And to think how I treated him!"

"Quite naturally, under the circumstances. The mystery of his former restraint is still unexplained, but I now think it due to family reasons. Yet why he should be so reluctant to speak of them is still another mystery. He has no sympathy with the South or his mother's views, yet why should he not say, frankly, 'I cannot fight against my mother's people'? When we think, however, that the sons of the same mother are often arrayed against each other in this war, such a reason as I have suggested appears entirely inadequate. All his interests are at the North, and he is thoroughly loyal; but when I intimated, last evening, that he might wish to spend the night in his own home to insure its protection, it seemed less than nothing to him compared with your safety. He has long had this powerful motive to win your regard, and yet there has been some restraint more potent."

"But you trust him now, papa?"

"Yes."

Thus they talked until the clock struck eight, and Marian, growing pallid with anxiety and fear, went to the darkened parlor window to watch for Merwyn, then returned and looked at her father with something like dismay on her face.

Before he could speak, she exclaimed, "Ah! there is his ring;" and she rushed toward the door, paused, came back, and said, blushingly, "Papa, you had better admit him."

Mr. Vosburgh smilingly complied.

The young fellow appeared in almost as bad a plight as when he had come in on Monday night and gone away with bitter words on his lips. He was gaunt from fatigue and long mental strain. His first words were: "Thank God you we still all safe! I had hoped to be here long before this, but so much has happened!"

"What!" exclaimed Marian, "anything worse than took place yesterday?"

"No, and yes." Then, with an appealing look; "Miss Marian, a cup of your good coffee. I feel as if a rioter could knock me down with a feather."

She ran to the kitchen herself to see that it was of the best possible quality, and Merwyn, sinking into a chair, looked gloomily at his host and said: "We have made little if any progress. The mob grows more reckless and devilish."

"My dear fellow," cried Mr. Vosburgh, "the Seventh Regiment will be here to-night, and others are on the way;" and he told of the reassuring tidings he had received.

"Thank Heaven for your news! I have been growing despondent during the last few hours."

"Take this and cheer up," cried Marian. "The idea of your being despondent! You are only tired to death, and will have a larger appetite for fighting to-morrow, I fear, than ever."

"No; I witnessed a scene this evening that made me sick of it all. Of course I shall do my duty to the end, but I wish that others could finish it up. More than ever I envy your friends who can fight soldiers;" and then he told them briefly of the scene witnessed in the rescue of Mammy Borden and her son.

"Oh, horrible! horrible!" exclaimed the girl. "Where are they now?"

"I took them from headquarters to a hospital. They both need the best surgical attention, though poor Zeb, I fear, is past help."

"Merwyn," said Mr. Vosburgh, gravely, "you incurred a fearful risk in taking those people through the streets."

"I suppose so," replied the young fellow, quietly; "but in a sense they were a part of your household, and the poor creatures were in such a desperate plight that--"

"Mr. Merwyn," cried Marian, a warm flush mantling her face, "you are a true knight. You have perilled your life for the poor and humble."

He looked at her intently a moment, and then said, quietly, "I would peril it again a thousand times for such words from YOU."

To hide a sudden confusion she exclaimed: "Great Heavens! what differences there are in men! Those who would torture and kill these inoffensive people have human forms."

"Men are much what women make them; and it would almost seem that women are the chief inspiration of this mob. The draft may have been its inciting cause, but it has degenerated into an insatiable thirst for violence, blood, and plunder. I saw an Irishwoman to-day who fought like a wild-cat before she would give up her stolen goods."

The German servant Riten now began to place dinner on the table, Mr. Vosburgh remarking, "We had determined to wait for you on this occasion."

"What am I thinking of?" cried Merwyn. "If this thing goes on I shall become uncivilized. Mr. Vosburgh, do take me somewhere that I may bathe my hands and face, and please let me exchange this horrid blouse, redolent of the riot, for almost any kind of garment. I could not sit at the table with Miss Vosburgh in my present guise."

"Yes, papa, give him your white silk waistcoat and dress-coat," added Marian, laughing.

"Come with me," said Mr. Vosburgh, "and I'll find you an outfit for the sake of your own comfort."

"I meant to trespass on your kindness when I first came in, but mind and body seemed almost paralyzed. I feel better already, however. While we are absent may I ask if you have your weapons ready?"

"Yes, I have a revolver on my person, and my rifle is in the dining-room."

A few moments later the gentlemen descended, Merwyn in a sack-coat that hung rather loosely on his person. Before sitting down he scanned the street, which was quiet.

"My former advice, Merwyn," said his host; "you must make a light meal and wait until you are more rested."

"O papa, what counsel to give a guest!"

"Counsel easily followed," said Merwyn. "I crave little else than coffee. Indeed, your kindness, Miss Vosburgh, has so heartened me, that I am rallying fast."

"Since everything is to be in such great moderation, perhaps I have been too prodigal of that," was the arch reply.

"I shall be grateful for much or little."

"Oh, no, don't put anything on the basis of gratitude. I have too much of that to be chary of it."

"A happy state of affairs," said Merwyn, "since what you regard as services on my part are priceless favors to me. I can scarcely realize it, and have thought of it all day, that I only, of all your friends, can be with you now. Strahan will be green with envy, and so I suppose will the others."

"I do not think any the less of them because it is impossible for them to be here," said the young girl, blushing.

"Of course not. It's only my immense good fortune. They would give their right eyes to stand in my shoes."

"I hope I may soon hear that they are all recovering. I fear that Mr. Lane's and Mr. Strahan's wounds are serious; and, although Mr. Blauvelt made light of his hurt, he may find that it is no trifle."

"It would seem that I am doomed to have no honorable scars."

"Through no fault of yours, Mr. Merwyn. I've thought so much of poor mamma to-day! She must be wild with anxiety about us."

"I think not," said Mr. Vosburgh. "I telegraphed to her yesterday and to-day. I admit they were rather misleading messages."

From time to time Mr. Vosburgh went to the outlook on the street, but all remained apparently quiet in their vicinity. Yet an hour of fearful peril was drawing near. A spirit of vengeance, and a desire to get rid of a most dangerous enemy, prompted another attack on Mr. Vosburgh's home that night; and, taught by former experience, the assailants had determined to approach quietly and fight till they should accomplish their purpose. They meant to strike suddenly, swiftly, and remorselessly.

The little group in the dining-room, however, grew confident with every moment of immunity; yet they could not wholly banish their fears, and Mr. Vosburgh explained to Merwyn how he had put bars on the outside of the doors opening into the back yard, a bolt also on the door leading down-stairs to the basement.

But they dined very leisurely, undisturbed; then at Marian's request the gentlemen lighted their cigars. Mr. Vosburgh strolled away to see that all was quiet and secure.

"I shouldn't have believed that I could rally so greatly in so short a time," said Merwyn, leaning back luxuriously in his chair. "Last night I was overcome with drowsiness soon after I lay down. I now feel as if I should never want to sleep again. It will be my turn to watch to-night, and you must sleep."

"Yes, when I feel like it," replied Marian.

"I think you bear the strain of anxiety wonderfully."

"I am trying to retrieve myself."

"You have retrieved yourself, Miss Vosburgh. You have become a genuine soldier. It didn't take long to make a veteran of you."

"So much for a good example, you see."

"Oh, well, it's easy enough for a man to face danger. Think how many thousands do it as a matter of course."

"And must women be timid as a matter of course?"

"Women do not often inspire men as you do, Miss Marian. I know I am different from what I was, and I think I always shall be different."

"I didn't treat you fairly, Mr. Merwyn, and I've grieved over the past more than I can tell you."

"And you won't mistrust me again?"

"Never."

"You make me very happy, and you will never know how unhappy I have been. Even before I left the country, last autumn, I envied the drummer-boys of Strahan's regiment. I don't wish to take advantage of your present feeling, or have you forget that I am still under a miserable restraint which I can't explain. I must probably resume my old inactive life, while your other friends win fame and rank in serving their country. Of course I shall give money, but bah! what's that to a girl like you? When all this hurly-burly in the streets is over, when conventional life begins again, and I seem a part of it, will you still regard me as a friend?"

His distrust touched her deeply, when she was giving him her heart's best love, and her strong feeling caused her to falter as she said, "Do you think I can grow cold towards the man who risked his life for me?"

"That is exaggerated gratitude. Any decent man would risk his life for you. Why, you were as brave as I. I often ask myself, can you be a friend for my own sake, because of some inherent congeniality? You have done more for your other friends than they for you, and yet they are very dear to you, because you esteem them as men. I covet a like personal regard, and I hope you will teach me to win it"

"You have won it,--that is--"

"That is--? There is a mental reservation, or you are too truthful for undoubted assurance when shown that gratitude has no place in this relation."

She averted her face from his searching eyes, and was deeply embarrassed.

"I feared it would be so," he said, sadly. "But I do not blame you. On the contrary I honor your sincerity. Very well, I shall be heartily glad of any regard that you can give me, and shall try to be worthy of it."

"Mr. Merwyn," she said, impetuously, "no friend of mine receives a stronger, better, or more sincere regard than I give you for your own sake. There now, trust me as I trust you;" and she gave him her hand.

He took it in his strong grasp, but she exclaimed, instantly: "You are feverish. You are ill. I thought your eyes were unnaturally bright."

"They should be so if it is in the power of happiness to kindle them!"

"Come now," she cried, assuming a little brusqueness of manner which became her well; "I've given you my word, and that's my bond. If you indulge in any more doubts I'll find a way to punish you. I'll take my 'affidavy' I'm just as good a friend to you as you are to me. If you doubt me, I shall doubt you."

"I beg your pardon; no you won't, or cannot, rather. You know well that I have my father's unchangeable tenacity. It's once and always with me."

"You are speaking riddles," she faltered, averting her face.

"Not at all. I am glad indeed that you can give me simple friendship, unforced, uncompelled by any other motive than that which actuates you in regard to the others. But you know well--your most casual glance would reveal it to you--that I, in whom you have inspired some semblance of manhood, can never dream of any other woman. When you see this truth, as you often will, you must not punish me for it. You must not try to cure me by coldness or by any other of the conventional remedies, for you cannot. When we meet, speak kindly, look kindly; and should it ever be not best or right that we should meet,--that is, often,--we shall not."

"You are scarcely speaking as a friend," she said, in a low voice.

"Will you punish me if I cannot help being far more?"

"No, since you cannot help it," she replied, with a shy laugh.

A new light, a new hope, began to dawn upon him, and he was about to speak impetuously when Mr. Vosburgh appeared and said, "Merwyn, I've been watching two men who passed and repassed the house, and who seem to be reconnoitring."

As Merwyn and Marian accompanied him to the parlor they heard the heavy booming of cannon off on the east side, and it was repeated again and again.

"Those are ominous sounds at this time of night," said Mr. Vosburgh.

"That they don't come from the rioters is a comfort," Merwyn replied; "but it proves what I said before,--they are becoming more bold and reckless."

"It may also show that the authorities are more stern and relentless in dealing with them."

At last the sounds of conflict died away, the street appeared quiet and deserted, and they all returned to the dining-room.

The light enabled Merwyn to look eagerly and questioningly at Marian. She smiled, flushed, and, quickly averting her eyes, began to speak on various topics in a way that warned Merwyn to restrain all further impatience; but she inspired so strong and delicious a hope that he could scarcely control himself. He even fancied that there was at times a caressing accent in her tone when she spoke to him.

"Surely," he thought, "if what I said were repugnant, she would give some hint of the fact; but how can it be possible that so soon--"

"Come, Marian, I think you may safely retire now," said her father; "I hear Riten coming up."

Even as he spoke, a front parlor window was crashed in. Merwyn and Mr. Vosburgh sprung into the hall, revolvers in hand; Riten instinctively fled back towards the stairs leading to the basement, in which she had extinguished the light, and Mr. Vosburgh told his daughter to follow the servant.

But she stood still, as if paralyzed, and saw a man rushing upon him with a long knife. Mr. Vosburgh fired, but, from agitation, ineffectually. Merwyn at the same moment had fired on another man, who fell. A fearful cry escaped from the girl's lips as she saw that her father was apparently doomed. The gleaming knife was almost above him. Then--how it happened she could never tell, so swift was the movement--Merwyn stood before her father. The knife descended upon his breast, yet at the same instant his pistol exploded against the man's temple, and the miscreant dropped like a log. There were sounds of other men clambering in at the window, and Mr. Vosburgh snatched Merwyn back by main force, saying to Marian, "Quick! for your life! down the stairs!"

The moment the door closed upon them all he slid the heavy bolt. Riten stood sobbing at the foot of the stairs.

"Hush!" said Mr. Vosburgh, sternly. "Each one obey me. Out through the area door instantly."

Across this he also let down a heavy bar, and, taking his daughter's hand, he hurried her to the fence, removed the boards, and, when all had passed through, replaced them. Mr. Erkmann, at his neighbor's request, had left his rear basement door open, and was on the watch. He appeared almost instantly, and counselled the fugitives to remain with him.

"No," said Mr. Vosburgh; "we will bring no more peril than we must on you. Let us out into the street at once, and then bar and bolt everything."

"But where can you go at this time?"

"To my house," said Merwyn, firmly. "Please do as Mr. Vosburgh asks. It will be safest for all."

"Well, since you will have it so."

"Hasten, hasten," Merwyn urged.

Mr. Erkmann unlatched the door and looked out. The street was quiet and deserted, and the fugitives rushed away with whispered thanks.

"Marian, tie Riten's apron over your head, so as to partially disguise your face," said her father.

Fortunately they met but few people, and no crowds whatever. As they approached Merwyn's home his steps began to grow unsteady.

"Papa," said Marian, in agitated tones, "Mr. Merwyn is wounded; he wants your support."

"Merciful Heaven, Merwyn! are you wounded?"

"Yes, hasten. I must reach home before giving out."

When they gained his door he had to be almost carried up the steps, and Mr. Vosburgh rang the bell furiously.

Only a moment or two elapsed before the scared face of Thomas appeared, but as Merwyn crossed the threshold he fainted.

They carried him to his room, and then Mr. Vosburgh said, "Bring a physician and lose not a second. Say it is a case of life and death. Hold! first bring me some brandy."

"Oh, oh!" Marian moaned, "I fear it's death! O papa he gave his life for you."

"No, no," was the hoarse response; "it cannot, shall not be. It's only a wound, and he has fainted from loss of blood. Show your nerve now. Moisten his lips with brandy. You, Riten, chafe his wrists with it, while I cut open his shirt and stanch the wound."

A second more and a terrible gash on Merwyn's breast was revealed. How deep it was they could not know.

Marian held out her handkerchief, and it was first used to stop the flow of blood. When it was taken away she put it in her bosom.

The old servant, Margy, now rushed in with lamentations.

"Hush!" said Mr. Vosburgh, sternly. "Chafe that other wrist with brandy."

But the swoon was prolonged, and Marian, pallid to her lips, sighed and moaned as she did her father's bidding.

Thomas was not very long in bringing a good physician, who had often attended the family. Marian watched his face as if she were to read there a verdict in regard to her own life, and Mr. Vosburgh evinced scarcely less solicitude.

"His pulse certainly shows great exhaustion; but I cannot yet believe that it is a desperate case. We must first tally him, and then I will examine his wound. Mr. Vosburgh, lift him up, and let me see if I cannot make him swallow a little diluted brandy."

At last Merwyn revived somewhat, but did not seem conscious of what was passing around him. The physician made a hasty examination of the wound and said, "It is not so severe as to be fatal in itself, but I don't like the hot, dry, feverish condition of his skin."

"He was feverish before he received the wound," said Marian, in a whisper. "I fear he has been going far beyond his strength."

"I entreat you, sir, not to leave him," said Mr. Vosburgh, "until you can give us more hope."

"Rest assured that I shall not. I am the family physician, and I shall secure for him in the morning the best surgical aid in the city. All that can be done in these times shall be done. Hereafter there must be almost absolute quiet, especially when he begins to notice anything. He must not be moved, or be allowed to move, until I say it is safe. Perhaps if all retire, except myself and Thomas, he will be less agitated when he recovers consciousness. Margy, you make good, strong coffee, and get an early breakfast."

They all obeyed his suggestions at once.

The servant showed Mr. Vosburgh and his daughter into a sitting-room on the same floor, and the poor girl, relieved from the necessity of self-restraint, threw herself on a lounge and sobbed and moaned as if her heart was breaking.

Wise Mr. Vosburgh did not at first restrain her, except by soothing, gentle words. He knew that this was nature's relief, and that she would soon be the better and calmer for it.

The physician wondered at the presence of strangers in the Merwyn residence, and speedily saw how Marian felt towards his patient; but he had observed professional reticence, knowing that explanations would soon come. Meanwhile he carefully sought to rally his patient, and watched each symptom.

At last Merwyn opened his eyes and asked, feebly: "Where am I? What has happened?"

"You were injured, but are doing well," was the prompt reply. "You know me, Dr. Henderson, and Thomas is here also. You are in your own room."

"Yes, I see," and he remained silent for some little time; then said, "I remember all now."

"You must keep quiet and try not to think, Mr. Merwyn. Your life depends upon it."

"My mind has a strong disposition to wander."

"The more need of quiet."

"Miss Vosburgh is here. I must see her."

"Yes, by and by."

"Doctor, I fear I am going to be out of my mind. I must see Miss Vosburgh. I will see her; and if you are wise you will permit me to do so. My life depends upon it more than upon your skill. Do what I ask, and I will be quiet"

"Very well, then, but the interview must be brief."

"It must be as I say."

Marian was summoned. Hastily drying her eyes, she tried to suppress her strong emotion.

Merwyn feebly reached out his hand to her, and she sat down beside him.

"Do not try to talk," she whispered, taking his hand.

"Yes, I must while I am myself. Dr. Henderson, I love and honor this girl, and would make her my wife should she consent. I may be dying, but if she is willing to stay with me, it seems as if I could live through everything, fever and all. If she is willing and you do not permit her to stay, I want you to know that my blood is on your hands! Marian, are you willing to stay?"

"Yes," she replied; and then, leaning down, she whispered: "I do love you; I have loved you ever since I understood you. Oh, live for my sake! What would life be now without you?"

"Now you shall stay."

"See, doctor, he is quiet while I am with him," she said, pleadingly.

"And only while you are with me. I know I should die if you were sent away."

"She shall stay with you, Mr. Merwyn, if you obey my orders in other respects. I give you my word," said Dr. Henderson.

"Very well. Now have patience with me."

"Thomas," whispered the physician, "have the strongest beef tea made, and keep it on hand."

Mr. Vosburgh intercepted the man, and was briefly told what had taken place. "Now there is a chance for them both," the agitated father muttered, as he restlessly paced the room. "Oh, how terribly clouded would our lives be, should he die!"

CHAPTER LII.
MOTHER AND SON.

FOR a time Merwyn did keep quiet, but he soon began to mutter brokenly and unintelligibly. Marian tried to remove her hand to aid the physician a moment, but she felt the feeble tightening of his clasp, and he cried, "No, no!"

This, for days, was the last sign he gave of intelligent comprehension of what was going on around him.

"We must humor him as far as we can in safety," the doctor remarked, in a low whisper, and so began the battle for life.

Day was now dawning, and Thomas was despatched for a very skilful surgeon, who came and gave the help of long experience.

At last Dr. Henderson joined Mr. Vosburgh in the breakfast-room, and the latter sent a cup of coffee to his daughter by the physician, who said, when he returned: "I think it would be well for me to know something about Mr. Merwyn's experience during the past few days. I shall understand his condition better if I know the causes which led to it."

Mr. Vosburgh told him everything.

"Well," said the doctor, emphatically, "we should do all within human effort to save such a young fellow."

"I feel that I could give my life to save him," Mr. Vosburgh added.

Hours passed, and Merwyn's delirium became more pronounced. He released his grasp on Marian's hand, and tossed his arms as if in the deepest trouble, his disordered mind evidently reverting to the time when life had been so dark and hopeless.

"Chained, chained," he would mutter. "Cruel, unnatural mother, to chain her son like a slave. My oath is eating out my very heart. SHE despises me as a coward. Oh if she knew what I was facing!" and such was the burden of all his broken words.

The young girl now learned the secret which had been so long unfathomed. Vainly, with streaming eyes, she tried at first to reassure him, but the doctor told her it was of no use, the fever must take its course. Yet her hand upon his brow and cheek often seemed to have a subtle, quieting spell.

Mr. Vosburgh felt that, whatever happened, he must attend to his duties. Therefore he went to headquarters and learned that the crisis of the insurrection had passed. The Seventh Regiment was on duty, and other militia organizations were near at hand.

He also related briefly how he had been driven from his home on the previous night, and was told that policemen were in charge of the building. Having received a permit to enter it, he sent his despatch to Washington, also a quieting telegram to his wife, assuring her that all danger was past.

Then he went to his abandoned home and looked sadly on the havoc that had been made. Nearly all light articles of value had been carried away, and then, in a spirit of revenge, the rioters had destroyed and defaced nearly everything. His desk had been broken, but the secret drawer remained undiscovered. Having obtained his private papers, he left the place, and, as it was a rented house, resolved that he would not reside there again.

On his return to Merwyn's home, the first one to greet him was Strahan, his face full of the deepest solicitude.

"I have just arrived," he said. "I first went to your house and was overwhelmed at seeing its condition; then I drove here and have only learned enough to make me anxious indeed. O my accursed wound and fever! They kept the fact of the riot from me until this morning, and then I learned of it almost by accident, and came instantly in spite of them."

"Mr. Strahan, I entreat you to be prudent. I am overwhelmed with trouble and fear for Merwyn, and I and mine must cause no more mischief. Everything is being done that can be, and all must be patient and quiet and keep their senses."

"Oh, I'm all right now. As Merwyn's friend, this is my place. Remember what he did for me."

"Very well. If you are equal to it I shall be glad to have you take charge here. As soon as I have learned of my daughter's and Merwyn's welfare I shall engage rooms at the nearest hotel, and, if the city remains quiet, telegraph for my wife;" and he sent Thomas to Dr. Henderson with a request to see him.

"No special change, and there cannot be very soon," reported the physician.

"But my daughter--she must not be allowed to go beyond her strength."

"I will look after her as carefully as after my other patient," was the reassuring reply.

"It's a strange story, Mr. Strahan," resumed Mr. Vosburgh, when they were alone. "You are undoubtedly surprised that my daughter should be one of Merwyn's watchers. He saved my life last night, and my daughter and home the night before. They are virtually engaged."

"Oh that I had been here!" groaned Strahan.

"Under the circumstances it was well that you were not. It would probably have cost you your life. Only the strongest and soundest men could endure the strain. Merwyn came to our assistance from the first;" and he told the young officer enough of what had occurred to make it all intelligible to him.

Strahan drew a long breath, then said: "He has won her fairly. I had suspected his regard for her; but I would rather have had his opportunity and his wound than be a major-general."

"I appreciate the honor you pay my daughter, but there are some matters beyond human control," was the kind response.

"I understand all that," said the young man, sadly; "but I can still be her loyal friend, and that, probably, is all that I ever could have been."

"I, at least, can assure you of our very highest esteem and respect, Mr. Strahan;" and after a few more words the gentlemen parted.

The hours dragged on, and at last Dr. Henderson insisted that Marian should go down to lunch. She first met Strahan in the sitting-room, and sobbed on his shoulder: "O Arthur! I fear he will die, and if he does I shall wish to die, too. You must stand by us both like a loyal brother."

"Marian, I will," he faltered; and he kept his word.

He made her take food, and at last inspired her with something of his own sanguine spirit.

"Oh, what a comfort it is to have you here!" she said, as she was returning to her post. "You make despair impossible."

Again the hours dragged slowly on, the stillness of the house broken only by Merwyn's delirious words. Then, for a time, there was disquiet in bitter truth.

All through the dreadful night just described, an ocean steamer had been ploughing its way towards the port of New York. A pilot had boarded her off Sandy Hook, and strange and startling had been his tidings to the homeward-bound Americans. The Battle of Gettysburg, the capture of Vicksburg, and, above all, the riots had been the burden of his narrations.

Among the passengers were Mrs. Merwyn and her daughters. Dwelling on the condition of her son's mind, as revealed by his letter, she had concluded that she must not delay her departure from England an hour longer than was unavoidable. "It may be," she thought, "that only my presence can restrain him in his madness; for worse than madness it is to risk all his future prospects in the South just when our arms are crowned with victories which will soon fulfil our hopes. His infatuation with that horrid Miss Vosburgh is the secret of it all."

Therefore, her heart overflowing with pride and anger, which increased with every day of the voyage, she had taken an earlier steamer, and was determined to hold her son to his oath if he had a spark of sanity left.

Having become almost a monomaniac in her dream of a Southern empire, she heard in scornful incredulity the rumor of defeat and disaster brought to her by her daughters. All the pride and passion of her strong nature was in arms against the bare thought. But at quarantine papers were received on board, their parallel columns lurid with accounts of the riot and aglow with details of Northern victories. It appeared to her that she had sailed from well-ordered England, with its congenial, aristocratic circles, to a world of chaos. When the steamer arrived at the wharf, many of the passengers were afraid to go ashore, but she, quiet, cold, silent, hiding the anger that raged in her heart, did not hesitate a moment. She came of a race that knew not what fear meant. At the earliest possible moment she and her daughters entered a carriage and were driven up town. The young girls stared in wonder at the troops and other evidences of a vast disturbance, and when they saw Madison Square filled with cavalry-horses they exclaimed aloud, "O mamma, see!"

"Yes," said their mother, sternly, "and mark it well. Even these Northern people will no longer submit to the Lincoln tyranny. He may win a few brief triumphs, but the day is near when our own princely leaders will dictate law and order everywhere. The hour has air passed when he will have the South only to fight;" and in her prejudice and ignorance she believed her words to be absolutely infallible.

Strahan met them as they entered, and received but a cold greeting from the lady.

"Where is Willard?" she asked, hastily.

"Mrs. Merwyn, you must prepare yourself for a great shock. Your son--"

Her mind was prepared for but one great disaster, and, her self-control at last giving way, she almost shrieked, "What! has he taken arms against the South?"

"Mrs. Merwyn," replied Strahan, "is that the worst that could happen?"

A sudden and terrible dread smote the proud woman, and she sunk into a chair, while young Estelle Merwyn rushed upon Strahan, and, seizing his hand, faltered in a whisper, "Is--is--" but she could proceed no further.

"No; but he soon will be unless reason and affection control your actions and words. Your family physician is here, Mrs. Merwyn, and I trust you will be guided by his counsel."

"Send him to me," gasped the mother.

Dr. Henderson soon came and explained in part what had occurred.

"Oh, those Vosburghs!" exclaimed Mrs. Merwyn, with a gesture of unspeakable revolt at the state of affairs. "Well," she added, with a stern face, "it is my place and not a stranger's to be at my son's side."

"Pardon me, madam; you cannot go to your son at all in your present mood. In an emergency like this a physician is autocrat, and your son's life hangs by a hair."

"Who has a better right--who can do more for a child than a mother?"

"That should be true, but--" and he hesitated in embarrassment, for a moment, then concluded, firmly: "Your son is not expecting you, and agitation now might be fatal to him. There are other reasons which you will soon understand."

"There is one thing I already understand,--a nameless stranger is with him, and I am kept away."

"Miss Vosburgh is not a nameless stranger," said Strahan; "and she is affianced to your son."

"O Heaven! I shall go mad!" the lady groaned, a tempest of conflicting emotions sweeping through her heart.

"Come, Mrs. Merwyn," said Dr. Henderson, kindly, yet firmly, "take the counsel of an old friend. Distracted as you naturally are with all these unexpected and terrible events, you must recognize the truth that you are in no condition to take upon you the care of your son now. He would not know you, I fear, yet your voice might agitate him fatally. I do not forbid you to see him, but I do forbid that you should speak to him now, and I shall not answer for the consequences if you do."

"Mamma, mamma, you must be patient and do as Dr. Henderson advises," cried Estelle. "When you are calm you will see that he is right. If anything should happen you would never forgive yourself."

The mother's bitter protest was passing into a deadlier fear, but she only said, coldly, "Very well; since such are your decrees I shall go to my room and wait till I am summoned;" and she rose and left the apartment, followed by her elder daughter, a silent, reticent girl, whose spirit her mother had apparently quenched.

Estelle lingered until they had gone, and then she turned to Strahan, who said, with an attempt at a smile, "I can scarcely realize that this is the little girl whom I used to play with and tease."

But she heeded not his words. Her large, lustrous eyes were dim with tears, as she asked, falteringly, "Tell me the truth, Mr. Strahan; do you think my brother is very ill?"

"Yes," he replied, sadly; "and I hope I may be permitted to remain as one of his watchers. He took care of me, last winter, in an almost mortal illness, and I would gladly do him a like service."

"But you are hurt. Your arm is in a sling."

"My wound is healing, and I could sit by your brother's side as well as elsewhere."

"You shall remain," said the girl, emphatically. "I have some of mamma's spirit, if not all her prejudices. Is this Miss Vosburgh such a fright?"

"I regard her as the noblest and most beautiful girl I ever saw."

"Oh, you do?"

"Yes."

"Well, I shall go and talk reason to mamma, for sister Berta yields to everything without a word. You must stay, and I shall do my share of watching as soon as the doctor permits."

Mrs. Merwyn thought she would remain in her room as she had said, but the fountains of the great deep in her soul were breaking up. She found that the mother in her heart was stronger than the partisan. She MUST see her son.

At last she sent Thomas for Dr. Henderson again, and obtained permission to look upon her child. Bitter as the physician knew the experience would be, it might be salutary. With noiseless tread she crossed the threshold, and saw Marian's pure, pale profile; she drew a few steps nearer; the young girl turned and bowed gravely, then resumed her watch.

For the moment Merwyn was silent, then in a voice all too distinct he said: "Cruel, unnatural mother, to rob me of my manhood, to chain me like one of her slaves. Jeff Davis and empire are more to her than husband or son."

The conscience-stricken woman covered her face with her hands and glided away. As by a lightning-flash the reason why she had forfeited her place by the couch of her son was revealed.

CHAPTER LIII.
"MISSY S'WANEE."

THERE is no need of dwelling long on subsequent events. Our story has already indicated many of them. Mrs. Merwyn's bitter lesson was emphasized through many weary days. She hovered about her son like a remorseful spirit, but dared not speak to him. She had learned too well why her voice might cause fatal agitation. For a time she tried to ignore Marian, but the girl's gentle dignity and profound sorrow, her untiring faithfulness, conquered pride at last, and the mother, with trembling lips, asked forgiveness and besought affection.

Blauvelt arrived in town on the evening of the day just described, proposing to offer his services to the city authorities, meanwhile cherishing the secret hope that he might serve Marian. He at last found Strahan at Merwyn's home. The brother officers talked long and earnestly, but, while both were reticent concerning their deeper thoughts, they both knew that a secret dream was over forever.

Marian came down and gave her hand to the artist soldier in warm pressure as she said, "My friends are loyal in my time of need."

He lingered a day or two in the city, satisfied himself that the insurrection was over, then went home, bade his old mother good-by, and joined his regiment. He was soon transferred to the staff of a general officer, and served with honor and distinction to the end of the war.

Mrs. Vosburgh joined her husband; and the awful peril through which he and her daughter had passed awakened in her a deeper sense of real life. In contemplation of the immeasurable loss which she might have sustained she learned to value better what she possessed. By Estelle's tact it was arranged that she could often see Marian without embarrassment. So far as her nature permitted she shared in her husband's boundless solicitude for Merwyn.

Warm-hearted Estelle was soon conscious of a sister's affection for the girl of her brother's choice, and shared her vigils. She became also a very good friend to Strahan, and entertained a secret admiration for him, well hidden, however, by a brusque, yet delicate raillery.

But Strahan believed that the romance of his life was over, and he eventually joined his regiment with some reckless hopes of "stopping a bullet" as he phrased it. Gloomy cynicism, however, was not his forte; and when, before the year was out, he was again promoted, he found that life was anything but a burden, although he was so ready to risk it.

At last the light of reason dawned in Merwyn's eyes. He recognized Marian, smiled, and fell into a quiet sleep. On awakening, he said to her: "You kept your word, my darling. You did not leave me. I should have died if you had. I think I never wholly lost the consciousness that you were near me."

The young girl soon brought about a complete reconciliation between mother and son, and Merwyn was absolved from his oath. Even as a devoted husband, which he became at Christmas-tide, she found him too ready to go to the front. He appeared, however, to have little ambition for distinction, and was satisfied to enter upon duty in a very subordinate position; but he did it so well and bravely that his fine abilities were recognized, and he was advanced. At last, to his mother's horror, he received a colonel's commission to a colored regiment.

Many of Mrs. Merwyn's lifelong prejudices were never overcome, and she remained loyal to the South; but she was taught that mother-love is the mightiest of human forces, and at last admitted that her son, as a man, had a right to choose and act for himself.

Mr. Vosburgh remained in the city as the trusted agent of the government until the close of the war, and was then transferred to Washington. Every year cemented his friendship with Merwyn, and the two men corresponded so faithfully that Marian declared she was jealous. Each knew, however, that their mutual regard and good-comradeship were among her deepest sources of happiness. While her husband was absent Marian made the country house on the Hudson her residence, but in many ways she sought opportunity to reduce the awful sum of anguish entailed by the war. She often lured Estelle from the city as her companion, even in bleak wintry weather. Here Strahan found her when on a leave of absence in the last year of the war, and he soon learned that he had another heart to lose. Marian was discreetly blind to his direct and soldier-like siege. Indeed, she proved the best of allies, aware that the young officer's time was limited.

Estelle was elusive as a mocking spirit of the air, until the last day of his leave was expiring, and then laughingly admitted that she had surrendered almost two years before.

Of the humble characters in my story it is sufficient to say that Zeb barely survived, and was helpless for life. Pensions from Merwyn and Lane secured for him and his mother every comfort. Barney Ghegan eventually recovered, and resumed his duties on the police force.

He often said, "Oi'm proud to wear the uniform that Misther Merwyn honored."

I have now only to outline the fortunes of Captain Lane and "Missy S'wanee," and then to take leave of my reader, supposing that he has had the patience to accompany me thus far.

Lane's wound, reopened by his exertions in escaping to Washington, kept him helpless on a bed of suffering during the riots and for weeks thereafter. Then he was granted a long furlough, which he spent chiefly with his family at the North. Like Strahan he felt that Merwyn had won Marian fairly. So far was he from cherishing any bitterness, that he received the successful rival within the circle of his nearest friends. By being sincere, true to nature and conscience, Marian retained, not only the friendship and respect of her lovers, but also her ennobling influence over them. While they saw that Merwyn was supreme, they also learned that they would never be dismissed with indifference from her thoughts,--that she would follow them through life with an affectionate interest and good-will scarcely less than she would bestow on brothers cradled in the same home with herself. Lane, with his steadfast nature, would maintain this relation more closely than the others, but the reader has already guessed that he would seek to give and to find consolation elsewhere. Suwanee Barkdale had awakened his strongest sympathy and respect, and the haunting thought that she, like himself, had given her love apparently where it could not be returned, made her seem akin to himself in the deepest and saddest experience. Gradually and almost unconsciously he gave his thoughts to her, and began to wonder when and how they should meet again, if ever. He wrote to her several times, but obtained no answer, no assurance that his letters were received. When he was fit for duty again his regiment was in the West, and it remained there until the close of the war, he having eventually attained to its command.

As soon as he could control his own movements he resolved to settle one question before he resumed the quiet pursuit of his profession,--he would learn the fate of "Missy S'wanee." Securing a strong, fleet horse, he left Washington, and rode rapidly through a region that had been trampled almost into a desert by the iron heel of war. The May sun was low in the west when he turned from the road into the extended lawn which led up to the Barkdale mansion. Little beyond unsightly stumps was left of the beautiful groves by which it had been bordered.

Vividly his memory reproduced the same hour, now years since, when he had ridden up that lawn at the head of his troopers, his sabre flashing in the last rays of the sun. It seemed ages ago, so much had happened; but through all the changes and perils the low sob of the Southern girl when she opened the way for his escape had been vibrating in stronger and tenderer chords in the depths of his soul. It had awakened dreams and imaginings which, if dissipated, would leave but a busy, practical life as devoid of romance as the law-tomes to which he would give his thoughts. It was natural, therefore, that his heart should beat fast as he approached the solution of a question bearing so vitally on all his future.

He concealed himself and his horse behind some low, shrubby trees that had been too insignificant for the camp fires, long since burned out, and scanned the battered dwelling. No sign of life was visible. He was about to proceed and end his suspense at once, when a lady, clad in mourning, came out and sat down on the veranda. He instantly recognized Suwanee.

For a few moments Lane could scarcely summon courage to approach. The surrounding desolation, her badges of bereavement and sorrow, gave the young girl the dignity and sacredness of immeasurable misfortune. She who had once so abounded in joyous, spirited life now seemed emblematical of her own war-wasted and unhappy land,--one to whom the past and the dead were more than the future and the living.

Would she receive him? Would she forgive him, one of the authors of her people's bleeding wounds? He determined to end his suspense, and rode slowly towards her, that she might not be startled.

At first she did not recognize the stranger in civilian dress, who was still more disguised by a heavy beard; but she rose and approached the veranda steps to meet him. He was about to speak, when she gave a great start, and a quick flush passed over her face.

Then, as if by the sternest effort, she resumed her quiet, dignified bearing, as she said, coldly, "You will scarcely wonder, Captain Lane, that I did not recognize you before." He had dismounted and stood uncovered before her, and she added, "I regret that I have no one to take your horse, and no place to stable him, but for yourself I can still offer such hospitality as my home affords."

Lane was chilled and embarrassed. He could not speak to her in like distant and formal manner, and he resolved that he would not. However it might end, he would be true to his own heart and impulses.

He threw the reins on the horse's neck, caring not what became of him, and stepping to her side, he said, impetuously, "I never doubted that I should receive hospitality at your home,--that is refused to no one,--but I did hope for a different greeting."

Again there was a quick, auroral flush, and then, with increased pallor and coldness, she asked, "Have I failed in courtesy?"

"No."

"What reason had you to expect more?"

"Because, almost from the first hour we met, I had given you esteem and reverence as a noble woman,--because I promised you honest friendship and have kept my word."

Still more coldly she replied: "I fear there can be no friendship between us. My father and brothers lie in nameless graves in your proud and triumphant North, and my heart and hope are buried with them. My mother has since died, broken-hearted; Roberta's husband, the colonel you sent to prison, is a crippled soldier, and both are so impoverished that they know not how to live. And you,--you have been so busy in helping those who caused these woes that you evidently forgot the once light-hearted girl whom you first saw on this veranda. Why speak of friendship, Captain Lane, when rivers of blood flow between us,--rivers fed from the veins of my kindred?"

Her words were so stern and sad that Lane sat down on the steps at her feet and buried his face in his hands. His hope was withering and his tongue paralyzed in the presence of such grief as hers.

She softened a little as she looked down upon him, and after a moment or two resumed: "I do not blame you personally. I must try to be just in my bitter sorrow and despair. You proved long ago that you were obeying your conscience; but you who conquer cannot know the hearts of the conquered. Your home does not look like mine; your kindred are waiting to welcome you with plaudits. You have everything to live for,--honor, prosperity, and love; for doubtless, long before this, the cold-hearted Northern girl has been won by the fame of your achievements. Think of me as a ghost, doomed to haunt these desolate scenes where once I was happy."

"No," he replied, springing to his feet, "I shall think of you as the woman I love. Life shall not end so unhappily for us both; for if you persist in your morbid enmity, my future will be as wretched as yours. You judge me unheard, and you wrong me cruelly. I have never forgotten you for an hour. I wrote to you again and again, and received no answer. The moment I was released from the iron rule of military duty in the West I sought you before returning to the mother who bore me. No river of blood flows between us that my love could not bridge. I admit that I was speechless at first before the magnitude of your sorrows; but must this accursed war go on forever, blighting life and hope? What was the wound you did so much towards healing compared to the one you are giving me now? Many a blow has been aimed at me, but not one has pierced my heart before."

She tried to listen rigidly and coldly to his impassioned utterance, but could not, and, as he ceased, she was sobbing in her chair. He sought with gentle words to soothe her, but by a gesture she silenced him. At last she said, brokenly: "For months I have not shed a tear. My heart and brain seemed bursting, yet I could get no relief. Were it not for some faith and hope in God, I should have followed my kindred. You cannot know, you never can know."

"I know one thing, Suwanee. You were once a brave, unselfish woman. I will not, I cannot believe that you have parted with your noble, generous impulses. You may remain cold to me if I merely plead my cause for your sake, that I may bring consolation and healing into your life; but I still have too much faith in your large, warm, Southern heart to believe that you will blight my life also. If you can never love me, give me the right to be your loyal and helpful friend. Giving you all that is best and most sacred in my nature how can you send me away as if I had no part or lot in your life? It is not, cannot be true. When I honor you and would give my life for you, and shall love you all my days, it is absurd to say that I am nothing to you. Only embodied selfishness and callousness could say that. You may not be able to give what I do, but you should give all you can. 'Rivers of blood flowing between us' is morbid nonsense. Forgive me that I speak strongly,--I feel strongly. My soul is in my words. I felt towards my cause as you towards yours, and had I not acted as I have, you would be the first to think me a craven. But what has all this to do with the sacred instinct, the pure, unbounded love which compels me to seek you as my wife?"

"You have spoken such words to another," she said, in a low tone.

"No, never such words as I speak to you. I could not have spoken them, for then I was too young and immature to feel them. I did love Miss Vosburgh as sincerely as I now respect and esteem her. She is the happy wife of another man. I speak to you from the depths of my matured manhood. What is more I speak with the solemnity and truth which your sorrows should inspire. Should you refuse my hand it will never be offered to another, and you know me well enough to be sure I will keep my word."

"Oh, can it be right?" cried the girl, wringing her hands.

"One question will settle all: Can you return my love?"

With that query light came into her mind as if from heaven. She saw that such love as theirs was the supreme motive, the supreme obligation.

She rose and fixed her lovely, tear-gemmed eyes upon him searchingly as she asked, "Would you wed me, a beggar, dowered only with sorrow and bitter memories?"

"I will wed you, Suwanee Barkdale, or no one."

"There," she said, with a wan smile, holding out her hand; "the North has conquered again."

"Suwanee," he said, gravely and gently, as he caressed the head bowed upon his breast, "let us begin right. For us two there is no North or South. We are one for time, and I trust for eternity. But do not think me so narrow and unreasonable as to expect that you should think as I do on many questions. Still more, never imagine that I shall chide you, even in my thoughts, for love of your kindred and people, or the belief that they honestly and heroically did what seemed to them their duty. When you thought yourself such a hopeless little sinner, and I discovered you to be a saint, did I not admit that your patriotic impulses were as sincere as my own? As it has often been in the past, time will settle all questions between your people and ours, and time and a better knowledge of each other will heal our mutual wounds. I wish to remove fear and distrust of the immediate future from your mind, however. I must take you to a Northern home, where I can work for you in my profession, but you can be your own true self there,--just what you were when you first won my honor and esteem. The memory of your brave father and brothers shall be sacred to me as well as to you. I shall expect you to change your feelings and opinions under no other compulsion than that of your own reason and conscience. Shall you fear to go with me now? I will do everything that you can ask if you will only bless me with your love."

"I never dreamed before that it could be so sweet to bless an enemy," she said, with a gleam of her old mirthfulness, "and I have dreamed about it. O Fenton, I loved you unsought, and the truth nearly killed me at first, but I came at last to be a little proud of it. You were so brave, yet considerate, so fair and generous towards us, that you banished my prejudices, and you won my heart by believing there was some good in it after all."

A white shock of wool surmounting a wrinkled, ebon visage appeared at the door, and the old cook said, "Missy S'wanee, dere's nuffin' in de house for supper but a little cawn-meal. Oh, bress de Lawd! if dere ain't Cap'n Lane!"

"Give us a hoe-cake, then," cried Lane, shaking the old woman's hand. "I'd rather sup with your mistress to-night on corn-meal than sit down to the grandest banquet you have ever prepared in the past. In the morning I'll forage for breakfast."

"Bress de Lawd!" said the old woman, as she hobbled away. "Good times comin' now. If I could jes' hear Missy S'wanee larf once mo';" and then she passed beyond hearing.

"Yes, Suwanee, if I could only hear your old sweet laugh once more!" Lane pleaded.

"Not yet, Fenton; not yet,--some day."

www.bookjungle.com *email: sales@bookjungle.com fax: 630-214-0564 mail: Book Jungle PO Box 2226 Champaign, IL 61825*

The Codes Of Hammurabi And Moses
W. W. Davies

QTY

The discovery of the Hammurabi Code is one of the greatest achievements of archaeology, and is of paramount interest, not only to the student of the Bible, but also to all those interested in ancient history...

Religion   **ISBN:** *1-59462-338-4*   **Pages:132**
MSRP $12.95

The Theory of Moral Sentiments
Adam Smith

QTY

This work from 1749. contains original theories of conscience amd moral judgment and it is the foundation for systemof morals.

Philosophy **ISBN:** *1-59462-777-0*   **Pages:536**
MSRP $19.95

Jessica's First Prayer
Hesba Stretton

QTY

In a screened and secluded corner of one of the many railway-bridges which span the streets of London there could be seen a few years ago, from five o'clock every morning until half past eight, a tidily set-out coffee-stall, consisting of a trestle and board, upon which stood two large tin cans, with a small fire of charcoal burning under each so as to keep the coffee boiling during the early hours of the morning when the work-people were thronging into the city on their way to their daily toil...

Childrens **ISBN:** *1-59462-373-2*   **Pages:84**
MSRP $9.95

My Life and Work
Henry Ford

QTY

Henry Ford revolutionized the world with his implementation of mass production for the Model T automobile. Gain valuable business insight into his life and work with his own auto-biography... "We have only started on our development of our country we have not as yet, with all our talk of wonderful progress, done more than scratch the surface. The progress has been wonderful enough but..."

Biographies/   **ISBN:** *1-59462-198-5*   **Pages:300**
MSRP $21.95

The Art of Cross-Examination
Francis Wellman

QTY

I presume it is the experience of every author, after his first book is published upon an important subject, to be almost overwhelmed with a wealth of ideas and illustrations which could readily have been included in his book, and which to his own mind, at least, seem to make a second edition inevitable. Such certainly was the case with me; and when the first edition had reached its sixth impression in five months, I rejoiced to learn that it seemed to my publishers that the book had met with a sufficiently favorable reception to justify a second and considerably enlarged edition. ...

Reference   ISBN: *1-59462-647-2*

Pages:412

MSRP $19.95

On the Duty of Civil Disobedience
Henry David Thoreau

QTY

Thoreau wrote his famous essay, On the Duty of Civil Disobedience, as a protest against an unjust but popular war and the immoral but popular institution of slave-owning. He did more than write—he declined to pay his taxes, and was hauled off to gaol in consequence. Who can say how much this refusal of his hastened the end of the war and of slavery ?

Law   ISBN: *1-59462-747-9*

Pages:48

MSRP $7.45

Dream Psychology Psychoanalysis for Beginners
Sigmund Freud

QTY

Sigmund Freud, born Sigismund Schlomo Freud (May 6, 1856 - September 23, 1939), was a Jewish-Austrian neurologist and psychiatrist who co-founded the psychoanalytic school of psychology. Freud is best known for his theories of the unconscious mind, especially involving the mechanism of repression; his redefinition of sexual desire as mobile and directed towards a wide variety of objects; and his therapeutic techniques, especially his understanding of transference in the therapeutic relationship and the presumed value of dreams as sources of insight into unconscious desires.

Psychology   ISBN: *1-59462-905-6*

Pages:196

MSRP $15.45

The Miracle of Right Thought
Orison Swett Marden

QTY

Believe with all of your heart that you will do what you were made to do. When the mind has once formed the habit of holding cheerful, happy, prosperous pictures, it will not be easy to form the opposite habit. It does not matter how improbable or how far away this realization may see, or how dark the prospects may be, if we visualize them as best we can, as vividly as possible, hold tenaciously to them and vigorously struggle to attain them, they will gradually become actualized, realized in the life. But a desire, a longing without endeavor, a yearning abandoned or held indifferently will vanish without realization.

Self Help   ISBN: *1-59462-644-8*

Pages:360

MSRP $25.45

www.bookjungle.com *email: sales@bookjungle.com fax: 630-214-0564 mail: Book Jungle PO Box 2226 Champaign, IL 61825*

QTY

The Rosicrucian Cosmo-Conception Mystic Christianity *by Max Heindel* ISBN: *1-59462-188-8* **$38.95**
The Rosicrucian Cosmo-conception is not dogmatic, neither does it appeal to any other authority than the reason of the student. It is: not controversial, but is: sent forth in the, hope that it may help to clear... New Age/Religion Pages 646

Abandonment To Divine Providence *by Jean-Pierre de Caussade* ISBN: *1-59462-228-0* **$25.95**
"The Rev. Jean Pierre de Caussade was one of the most remarkable spiritual writers of the Society of Jesus in France in the 18th Century. His death took place at Toulouse in 1751. His works have gone through many editions and have been republished... Inspirational/Religion Pages 400

Mental Chemistry *by Charles Haanel* ISBN: *1-59462-192-6* **$23.95**
Mental Chemistry allows the change of material conditions by combining and appropriately utilizing the power of the mind. Much like applied chemistry creates something new and unique out of careful combinations of chemicals the mastery of mental chemistry... New Age Pages 354

The Letters of Robert Browning and Elizabeth Barret Barrett 1845-1846 vol II ISBN: *1-59462-193-4* **$35.95**
by Robert Browning and Elizabeth Barrett Biographies Pages 596

Gleanings In Genesis (volume I) *by Arthur W. Pink* ISBN: *1-59462-130-6* **$27.45**
Appropriately has Genesis been termed "the seed plot of the Bible" for in it we have, in germ form, almost all of the great doctrines which are afterwards fully developed in the books of Scripture which follow... Religion/Inspirational Pages 420

The Master Key *by L. W. de Laurence* ISBN: *1-59462-001-6* **$30.95**
In no branch of human knowledge has there been a more lively increase of the spirit of research during the past few years than in the study of Psychology, Concentration and Mental Discipline. The requests for authentic lessons in Thought Control, Mental Discipline and... New Age/Business Pages 422

The Lesser Key Of Solomon Goetia *by L. W. de Laurence* ISBN: *1-59462-092-X* **$9.95**
This translation of the first book of the "Lernegton" which is now for the first time made accessible to students of Talismanic Magic was done, after careful collation and edition, from numerous Ancient Manuscripts in Hebrew, Latin, and French... New Age/Occult Pages 92

Rubaiyat Of Omar Khayyam *by Edward Fitzgerald* ISBN:*1-59462-332-5* **$13.95**
Edward Fitzgerald, whom the world has already learned, in spite of his own efforts to remain within the shadow of anonymity, to look upon as one of the rarest poets of the century, was born at Bredfield, in Suffolk, on the 31st of March, 1809. He was the third son of John Purcell... Music Pages 172

Ancient Law *by Henry Maine* ISBN: *1-59462-128-4* **$29.95**
The chief object of the following pages is to indicate some of the earliest ideas of mankind, as they are reflected in Ancient Law, and to point out the relation of those ideas to modern thought. Religion/History Pages 452

Far-Away Stories *by William J. Locke* ISBN: *1-59462-129-2* **$19.45**
"Good wine needs no bush, but a collection of mixed vintages does. And this book is just such a collection. Some of the stories I do not want to remain buried for ever in the museum files of dead magazine-numbers an author's not unpardonable vanity..." Fiction Pages 272

Life of David Crockett *by David Crockett* ISBN: *1-59462-250-7* **$27.45**
"Colonel David Crockett was one of the most remarkable men of the times in which he lived. Born in humble life, but gifted with a strong will, an indomitable courage, and unremitting perseverance... Biographies/New Age Pages 424

Lip-Reading *by Edward Nitchie* ISBN: *1-59462-206-X* **$25.95**
Edward B. Nitchie, founder of the New York School for the Hard of Hearing, now the Nitchie School of Lip-Reading, Inc, wrote "LIP-READING Principles and Practice". The development and perfecting of this meritorious work on lip-reading was an undertaking... How-to Pages 400

A Handbook of Suggestive Therapeutics, Applied Hypnotism, Psychic Science ISBN: *1-59462-214-0* **$24.95**
by Henry Munro Health/New Age/Health/Self-help Pages 376

A Doll's House: and Two Other Plays *by Henrik Ibsen* ISBN: *1-59462-112-8* **$19.95**
Henrik Ibsen created this classic when in revolutionary 1848 Rome. Introducing some striking concepts in playwriting for the realist genre, this play has been studied the world over. Fiction/Classics/Plays 308

The Light of Asia *by sir Edwin Arnold* ISBN: *1-59462-204-3* **$13.95**
In this poetic masterpiece, Edwin Arnold describes the life and teachings of Buddha. The man who was to become known as Buddha to the world was born as Prince Gautama of India but he rejected the worldly riches and abandoned the reigns of power when... Religion/History/Biographies Pages 170

The Complete Works of Guy de Maupassant *by Guy de Maupassant* ISBN: *1-59462-157-8* **$16.95**
"For days and days, nights and nights, I had dreamed of that first kiss which was to consecrate our engagement, and I knew not on what spot I should put my lips..." Fiction/Classics Pages 240

The Art of Cross-Examination *by Francis L. Wellman* ISBN: *1-59462-309-0* **$26.95**
Written by a renowned trial lawyer, Wellman imparts his experience and uses case studies to explain how to use psychology to extract desired information through questioning. How-to/Science/Reference Pages 408

Answered or Unanswered? *by Louisa Vaughan* ISBN: *1-59462-248-5* **$10.95**
Miracles of Faith in China Religion Pages 112

The Edinburgh Lectures on Mental Science (1909) *by Thomas* ISBN: *1-59462-008-3* **$11.95**
This book contains the substance of a course of lectures recently given by the writer in the Queen Street Hail, Edinburgh. Its purpose is to indicate the Natural Principles governing the relation between Mental Action and Material Conditions... New Age/Psychology Pages 148

Ayesha *by H. Rider Haggard* ISBN: *1-59462-301-5* **$24.95**
Verily and indeed it is the unexpected that happens! Probably if there was one person upon the earth from whom the Editor of this, and of a certain previous history, did not expect to hear again... Classics Pages 380

Ayala's Angel *by Anthony Trollope* ISBN: *1-59462-352-X* **$29.95**
The two girls were both pretty, but Lucy who was twenty-one who supposed to be simple and comparatively unattractive, whereas Ayala was credited, as her Bombwhat romantic name might show, with poetic charm and a taste for romance. Ayala when her father died was nineteen... Fiction Pages 484

The American Commonwealth *by James Bryce* ISBN: *1-59462-286-8* **$34.45**
An interpretation of American democratic political theory. It examines political mechanics and society from the perspective of Scotsman James Bryce Politics Pages 572

Stories of the Pilgrims *by Margaret P. Pumphrey* ISBN: *1-59462-116-0* **$17.95**
This book explores pilgrims religious oppression in England as well as their escape to Holland and eventual crossing to America on the Mayflower, and their early days in New England... History Pages 268

QTY

The Fasting Cure *by Sinclair Upton*   **ISBN:** *1-59462-222-1*   **$13.95**

In the Cosmopolitan Magazine for May, 1910, and in the Contemporary Review (London) for April, 1910, I published an article dealing with my experiences in fasting. I have written a great many magazine articles, but never one which attracted so much attention... New Age/Self Help/Health Pages 164

Hebrew Astrology *by Sepharial*   **ISBN:** *1-59462-308-2*   **$13.45**

In these days of advanced thinking it is a matter of common observation that we have left many of the old landmarks behind and that we are now pressing forward to greater heights and to a wider horizon than that which represented the mind-content of our progenitors...   Astrology Pages 144

Thought Vibration or The Law of Attraction in the Thought World   **ISBN:** *1-59462-127-6*   **$12.95**

by William Walker Atkinson   *Psychology/Religion Pages 144*

Optimism *by Helen Keller*   **ISBN:** *1-59462-108-X*   **$15.95**

Helen Keller was blind, deaf, and mute since 19 months old, yet famously learned how to overcome these handicaps, communicate with the world, and spread her lectures promoting optimism. An inspiring read for everyone...   Biographies/Inspirational Pages 84

Sara Crewe *by Frances Burnett*   **ISBN:** *1-59462-360-0*   **$9.45**

In the first place, Miss Minchin lived in London. Her home was a large, dull, tall one, in a large, dull square, where all the houses were alike, and all the sparrows were alike, and where all the door-knockers made the same heavy sound...   Childrens/Classic Pages 88

The Autobiography of Benjamin Franklin *by Benjamin Franklin*   **ISBN:** *1-59462-135-7*   **$24.95**

The Autobiography of Benjamin Franklin has probably been more extensively read than any other American historical work, and no other book of its kind has had such ups and downs of fortune. Franklin lived for many years in England, where he was agent...   Biographies/History Pages 332

Name	
Email	
Telephone	
Address	
City, State ZIP	

☐ **Credit Card**   ☐ **Check / Money Order**

Credit Card Number	
Expiration Date	
Signature	

Please Mail to: Book Jungle
PO Box 2226
Champaign, IL 61825
or Fax to: 630-214-0564

ORDERING INFORMATION

web: *www.bookjungle.com*
email: *sales@bookjungle.com*
fax: *630-214-0564*
mail: *Book Jungle PO Box 2226 Champaign, IL 61825*
or PayPal *to sales@bookjungle.com*

Please contact us for bulk discounts

DIRECT-ORDER TERMS

**20% Discount if You Order
Two or More Books**
Free Domestic Shipping!
Accepted: Master Card, Visa,
Discover, American Express

www.ingramcontent.com/pod-product-compliance
Lightning Source LLC
Chambersburg PA
CBHW081140020726
47504CB00009B/1938